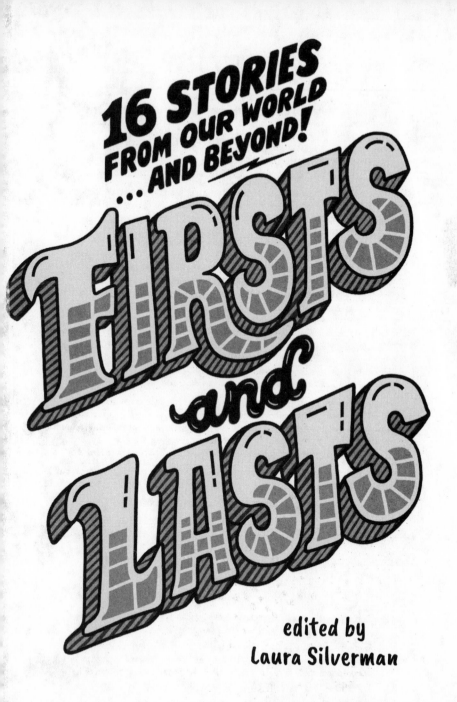

16 STORIES FROM OUR WORLD ...AND BEYOND!

FIRSTS and LASTS

edited by
Laura Silverman

PENGUIN WORKSHOP

PENGUIN WORKSHOP
An imprint of Penguin Random House LLC, New York

First published in the United States of America by Penguin Workshop,
an imprint of Penguin Random House LLC, New York, 2023

Visit us online at penguinrandomhouse.com.

Library of Congress Cataloging-in-Publication Data is available.

Printed in the United States of America

ISBN 9780593523087

1st Printing

LSCH

Edited by Anuoluwapo Ohioma
Design by Mary Claire Cruz

To everyone who has a nostalgic heart and big feelings—LS

Contents

LASTS

The First Time
I Dated a Vampire

BY JULIAN WINTERS

I'm certain of two things: I'm ready for this summer trip to end, and one more night in Santa Monica won't change that.

"Tyrell? We're here."

I blink out of a daze. It happens a lot lately. Moments where I'm anywhere but the present. I jerk to face my mom, the seat belt strap digging into my neck at the sudden movement.

"What?"

Through the windshield, ribbons of gold from fairy lights hung outside glow across Mom's face. We look alike. Warm brown skin with reddish undertones. Smallish noses and long necks. But my curls—kept short with the sides of my head faded—aren't hers. Neither is my bow-shaped mouth or awkward limbs.

Those are all Dad.

Are? Were? How do you describe something you inherited from a parent who's now dead?

These days, I'd prefer *not* to discuss him. Mom hasn't gotten the message yet.

She smiles wearily. "Do you really want to spend your last night watching a movie?"

"Yes."

"We've been here a month. You've barely seen the city. Only the walls of the house we're renting and . . ." Mom gestures to the building across the street.

Reagan's Cinema is a movie theater with old-school vibes: red-velvet-upholstered bucket seats. A giant marquee lit up in neon green and red. Big block letters advertising

FRIDAY NIGHT CLASSICS PRESENTS . . . TWILIGHT!

"Is that really a *classic*?" Mom whines. "I'm so old."

I don't comment.

"I'm surprised you haven't seen it yet," she continues. "You're so obsessed with supernatural things. Your dad loved vampires, too."

"I don't want to see the city," I tell her, quickly avoiding the topic of Dad. "This is fine."

"Ty," she says, cupping my cheek, "there's so much to experience here."

She talks like she hasn't lived in Decatur, Georgia, where we're from, her whole life. As if this isn't the first time for both of us in Santa Monica, where my dad grew up. She's clinging to the brittle memories of who Dad was. Ever since they lowered his body into the ground 182 days ago, I've been pretending none of this is happening.

"Rumor has it"—Mom wiggles her eyebrows—"there are tons of cute guys around your age. Maybe you can—"

"Ugh." I scramble to unbuckle the seat belt strangling my flushed neck. "No, thanks. Just the movie."

Before I can leap out into oncoming traffic, Mom's coral pink nails, which match her sundress, dig into my forearm. She's truly embracing the California aesthetic. Me? Scuffed Vans, black joggers, and a *Rick and Morty* graphic tee. Fitting in feels pointless.

"No curfew tonight." Mom's lips gentle into a grin. "Stay out after the movie."

When I blink, she quickly corrects: "Within reason. You're seventeen. College is around the corner, and—" She pauses, clearing her throat. "Give yourself the chance to fall in love with this place."

I ignore the urge to roll my eyes. "*Mom—*"

"Do you have the list?"

The one she AirDropped to my phone the second we landed. A checklist of all the city sights Dad wanted to show me. The three of us were supposed to be here together. Dad planned the trip early last year. Then he got sick and, well . . .

I nod stiffly.

"Go do things," she insists. "Maybe it'll feel like . . . he's here with you."

It won't, I want to tell her. Nothing does. Being in his hometown without him feels wrong. I don't want to give it a chance. Problem is, I don't want to go home either.

"Okay," I lie through the thickness in my throat. "I'll text you when I'm ready."

Her smile widens. I wonder if she knows I'll never be ready.

Friday nights at Reagan's are like any other—a butter-scented ghost town. It's three blocks from Third Street Promenade, where there are two AMCs less than half a mile from each other. But Reagan's is my favorite spot to watch movies.

I check my phone. Ten minutes before start time. I ignore the pain needling behind my ribs at no new messages from my best friend, Kellan. His last text was days ago. An *lol* to a meme I sent, the extent of our communication now.

It's another reason I don't want to go home. I'm not the "Ty" Kellan's known since middle school.

While I'm at the snack bar, contemplating my options, a throat clears. I lift my eyes and—

Come on, universe, why now?

A boy in a black Reagan's T-shirt leans his elbows on the glass counter. His fair tawny complexion drinks in the bright overhead lights. We're both scrawny, except he looks way more confident in his skin. Black fringe slices into his narrowed dark eyes.

If thunderclouds could take human form, they'd be Sean Kam.

His lips tilt up. "Why am I not surprised to see you?"

"I'm still deciding," I say through my teeth.

"You didn't answer my question."

"Because you should've asked, 'How can I help you?'" I snap. "Like a model employee."

"You get the same thing every Friday."

"What if I got Twizzlers?" I try. "And a Coke?"

More hair falls across his eyes. He scoops it away to say, flatly, "Are you?"

No. My nose wrinkles. "Nachos. Extra cheese." A wicked smirk pulls at his lips. He's waiting. "And a small blue raspberry slush," I whisper.

"Now that we've established you're basic and predictable," he says, moving around the snack bar like there's air under his soles, "Tell me you're not here for . . . *that movie*."

Here we go again. "I heard it's good," I say.

"From who?"

I don't answer. Mom's right. Supernatural stories are my favorite. Dad's too. Secretly, we both believed in the unreal. That underneath this cruel and sometimes unexplainable world, things like monsters and myths must exist.

Not that I've ever seen one.

"The whole thing's tragic." Sean plonks a box of nachos and a large cup of slush on the counter, startling me. I raise an eyebrow when he doesn't charge me for the bigger size. "It's so . . . corny. Also, inaccurate."

"It's a *movie*," I say while paying.

"Your point?"

His features are sharp, almost beautiful when he squints. Unexpected heat blooms under my cheeks. "My point is," I say, "every Friday you give me your hot film takes, even though I never ask. You hate everything, like the last Transformers movie."

"Everyone hated that shitshow."

True. I say, "What about the remake of—"

"Let me stop you right there," he interrupts. "Remakes are inherently awful. The world deserves more original content."

Right, again.

"Fine." I lean on the counter, smiling. "Name one Christopher Nolan movie you like."

"I can't. He's the devil," Sean replies without blinking. His longest rants are always about Nolan. But when did I start caring enough to *save* that information?

Our faces hover inches apart. His eyes are obsidian pools trying to drown me. I quickly straighten. A group of noisy boys charges into the theater I'm supposed to be in.

After a beat, I say, "Vampire movies are never bad."

"Enjoy your suckfest!" Sean calls after I gather my nachos and drink. My hands are too full to flip him off. I disappear into the cinema without another word.

✦ ⧖ ✦

I sit on the curb outside Reagan's after the movie. It's barely 8:00 p.m. The sky's a hypnotic swirl of golds, oranges, and reds. Dipping sunlight glitters off nearby buildings. Santa Monica's nothing like home.

Then again, home isn't a place I know anymore either.

I hug my legs to my chest. It's too early to text Mom. She'll find a way for us to visit every destination on that list, forcing me to love a city I don't want to be in without Dad.

A screaming ache shifts through my blood. I keep trying not to miss him.

The double doors behind me bang open.

Heavy feet thump on the sidewalk. Voices climb the air like stairs. I attempt to make myself smaller. It's hard to do when you're almost six feet tall. Even harder when you're a Black boy sitting alone in a place where no one knows you.

"Yo, that movie blows!"

"Man, I don't care if I was a vampire—there's no way I'm gonna stop making out with some chick I'm thirsting for. Hell no!"

A cacophony of echoing laughter rings in my ears before large shadows surround me.

"Hey, weren't you in the movie with us?"

"Obvi, Reece. You threw popcorn at him."

Another ugly chuckle.

My fingers dig into my forearms. I habitually bite my nails to the quick, so there's no pain. Only pressure.

"Wait . . . are you *crying*?"

Am I? The grief ebbs and flows until I barely notice its aftermath. Sometimes, I'm staring into space for five minutes. Sometimes, there's a throb in my knuckles from absently punching a wall. Sometimes, tears fall without any warning.

"Bro, you're crying over a *movie*?"

"Yeah," I lie monotonously. I finally look up through half-bleary eyes. Five guys, mostly white, stand over me. "Crying over a movie and your face."

"Ooh," the one I suspect is Reece says. "He's got sass!"

His eyes are a muddy brown. Nothing like Sean's. *Why am I thinking about Sean?* I'm distracted enough to miss Reece's hand raise. He shoves my shoulder.

"Don't be rude, prick."

His friends coo. My hands ball into fists. I've never been in a fight. It's five-to-one. They're bigger too, like college athletes. Chances are, if I punch just one of them, the police will find an excuse to point the finger at me.

Another angry Black boy.

My heart is a ten-piece drumline in my ears. I could run. Hide in Reagan's lobby until Mom arrives.

I could—

Another shadow appears. Someone slides between me and the boys. A voice I almost don't recognize snarls, "Leave. Him. Alone."

It's Sean.

Where did he come from?

He's hunched forward, shoulders high. A lion uncaged. His features are blade sharp. The streetlamp's luster twists around his irises, which are . . . crimson?

I blink. *Is it the light or—?*

I manage to stand on shaky legs. Of all the people in this city, Sean Kam is the last one I imagined ready to fight for me. The least I can do is make it two-on-five. The other boys shift on their heels, looking at one another, then at Sean. White-knuckled fists tremble at their sides. They're . . . *scared.*

"Whoa, we were just—"

Sean's upper lip curls. A mouthful of razors. "I said leave him alone," he repeats.

"No prob," Reece says, arms extended to usher his friends back. He gazes past Sean to me, stammering, "S-sorry. We loved the movie! K-Stew for prez—"

"*Now.*"

Sean's voice is like storms colliding. Mountains crumbling. It echoes in my head.

Reece and his goons scramble in the opposite direction, vanishing into a crowd crossing the street.

Seconds pass. Sean keeps his back to me. Our ephemeral silence is interrupted by cars humming down the road. Strangers drifting by. No one bats an eye.

Eventually, Sean's shoulders lower. He whirls around. "Were you really crying over that sobfest?"

I blink again, shocked. "Excuse me?"

"You loved it, didn't you?"

"*Twilight*?"

"Yes!" His posture relaxes. He's still a thundercloud, but the angles of his face aren't as deadly. "You probably gave it five stars on FlixPicks. What's your username? I'm reporting your account for inappropriate content."

His lips lift slyly. He's teasing me.

I've never seen Sean anything but grumpy and cynical and, frankly, dickish.

"Why do you hate *Twilight* so much?"

He sniffs, dismissing my question. Normal-shaped teeth pinch his lower lip. I must've imagined the dagger-sharp canines. Like I imagine waking up to Dad standing over a stack of burnt French toast every morning, smiling through the smoke. It's the grief constantly warping my brain.

Sean studies me. "Are you . . . okay?"

I scrub my cheeks clean. "I will be once I get away from this city."

Surprise widens Sean's midnight-brown eyes. They were always that color, right? Did I really believe he was something else? Something . . . supernatural?

"You don't live around here?"

"I live outside Atlanta. In Georgia."

He scoffs. "I know where Atlanta is. I passed the fourth grade."

Somehow, his petulant pout startles a laugh out of me.

Sean's slipped a gray zip hoodie on over his T-shirt. Random buttons are scattered on it. His mouth opens, then shuts. He pivots on his heels to leave. My stomach sinks to my feet, and I half shout, "You never answered my question," before he's gone.

He twists around, a glint in his eyes.

"Why do you hate *Twilight*?"

Two girls scooter by. Warm August wind pirouettes between us. He pushes swaying threads of inky hair off his forehead before replying, "It glamorizes vampire life."

I tilt my head, a *go on* in my eyes that he reads like a script.

"It's all about how great vampirism is. You can run fast, climb trees, play baseball in a thunderstorm. Shine like diamonds! Bella's a *disaster*, and if she becomes a vampire"—he scowls, a sadness hanging in his voice—"all her problems are solved."

"It's about other things, too," I counter. "Choices. Finding where you belong. Love."

He rolls his eyes.

I cross my arms. "Being heavily invested in a vampire love story doesn't seem like your thing."

"You're right. It's not."

He starts to leave again. Headlights pass over one of his buttons: three stripes—magenta, yellow, cyan. The pan flag.

A feeling so recognizable takes root in my blood. It's what I felt during the QSA meetings I attended back home. Whenever I'm in a crowd of more than five BIPOC.

Safety.

I don't want him to walk away.

My fingers reach out, skimming the back of his hand. It's cold like he's been trapped under ice. Sean works the snack bar, which means he handles dozens of slushes an hour, so of course his fingers are cold. Except Reagan's doesn't see that many customers in a *day*. Maybe I was right earlier?

He glares at our hands.

"My dad died six months ago," I admit, voice wobbly. "He grew up here. My mom wants me to fall in love with Santa Monica, but I don't know how to. Or if I *want* to. It feels like . . ."

I run out of breath.

The words that keep haunting my nightmares dissolve in my throat:

It feels like the second I accept this vacation's happening without him, I'll have to accept he's truly gone.

For weeks, I've wanted to tell someone. Kellan's stopped listening to me. Mom's living in a let's-celebrate-who-he-was world I can't occupy. But Sean watches me without pity or sympathy. His endlessly dark gaze is the one thing keeping me upright.

"I can't face my mom right now," I add. "I just need . . ."

Honestly, I have no idea *what* I need.

Sean's nostrils flare. His annoyance is palpable. "Come on," he grumbles.

"Where?"

"Does it matter?"

When he turns away, I hesitate. Should I go with him? I did just word vomit all my insecurities at him. But we don't know each other. He stood up to those losers, though. And he's openly wearing a pan flag button on his hoodie, so . . .

"I'm not waiting," he grunts.

I sprint to catch up to him. For someone at least three inches shorter than me, he has long strides.

We follow the flood of bodies away from Reagan's.

"Why are we . . ." I drag out the last letter for two beats, eyes dancing around. "Here?"

I wasn't sure what to expect while trailing Sean toward Ocean Avenue. It was hard enough keeping up with how he zigzagged through crowds and recklessly cut across traffic like he gave zero shits about what happened to himself. At first, I thought we were going to the pier. It's the first stop Mom dragged me to after we arrived.

"Don't you kids love hashtag-views?" she asked, laughing at her own joke.

I let out a deep, relieved sigh when Sean guided us down the wooden steps. Away from the noise, closer to the sand and waves.

We're standing on a paved path that winds along the beach. It swirls so far in either direction, I lose sight of it.

"The Strand." Sean stretches his arms out like he's presenting me a gift and not a cardio workout. "You said you didn't know how to fall in love with this place. This is how. Time for you to see the real city."

I squint at him. "By walking?"

"Are you always this difficult?"

I beam. "Only with you."

There's a mild twitch to his sneer. "Let's go." He turns before I can get a glimpse of a real Sean Kam smile.

Our walk is quiet. The day's fading. All the fiery colors of the sky turn deep blue and purple.

Unlike before, Sean's strides are slow and patient. Thin dustings of sand crunch under our sneakers as we follow the snaking pavement. Every few steps, the back of his knuckles brush mine. His skin's icy, mine's volcanic. I find myself drifting nearer to him.

It's a strange comfort.

To our right, the beach is nearly empty. Bikes abandoned in the sand. Vacant volleyball courts. Waves crash onto lonely shores. I try not to think about how my life mirrors those waves—something building only for no one to be around when it finally falls.

"Hey." Sean elbows me. "You're not looking."

I follow his gaze.

Ahead of us, the Strand is endless. A stone river dividing parking lots and buildings from the shore. Palm trees sprout up like crooked fingers trying to scrape the stars from the sky.

"What am I looking at?" I ask, confused.

A raspy laugh vibrates from his throat. "This city is anything you want, at any moment. But only if you see it that way."

"You sound like a tour brochure."

Sean doesn't respond to my joke. His steps thump against the pavement. I know he's only doing what Mom's done all month: introducing me to what makes Santa Monica special.

Thing is, I'm scared.

The weeks before Dad died were unbearable. There were times when he'd laugh, squeeze my hand with whatever strength he had left, then smile like I had nothing to worry about. But he was wrong.

Now I'm terrified any new, happy memories I create will begin to outnumber the ones I have with him.

I'll *never* be able to make a new memory with my dad again.

My hand skims against Sean's. "What do you love about here?"

His dark eyes dart away from my face to the beach. Every hundred yards, an abandoned lifeguard tower appears. A pop of pastel blue against the raven sea.

"Everything," he whispers.

Sean names landmarks. Places he's been with his parents and older sister, June. He points in various directions. All the bite and annoyance in his voice is replaced by appreciation and longing.

I cling to it.

Sean notes the technologies shop his father lingered in for hours. The performing arts center where his mom introduced him to the enchantment of the stage. A cozy restaurant where he'd get pho with June on the weekends. Story after story.

We pass surfers rinsing off at outdoor shower stations. Leftover energy from long-gone crowds soaks the air. It pairs with Sean's melodic voice in my ears.

He talks in past tense. *We had* and *we used to* and *when I was younger.* As if things happened in a time so far from reach.

Sean says, "June and I used to go to Reagan's all the time," like this is the most he's spoken in forever. I let him continue. "Our favorite thing was grading the movies afterward. Once, we saw this movie where, at the end, the boy finally meets his crush on a Ferris wheel. Then, they kiss." His lips gently inch into a grin. It's so genuine, my chest loosens.

"I know that movie!" I tell him. "Isn't it a rom-com?"

His chin lifts, defiantly. "Possibly."

"Hold on." I shake my head. "Mr. '*Twilight* Is Trash' likes rom-coms? Damn. Didn't see that coming."

"Are you done being condescending?"

I snort, whispering, "Mr. Anti-Nolan . . ."

Sean glares. Behind him, the sky's oily black, a silver moon poured into the center, ivory stars flicked all around. None of it compares to the stubborn pout of Sean's almost ruby lips.

"I'm done," I concede.

He snatches my hand to drag me farther along the path. I focus on his wintery skin. On the fact that I've never held a boy's hand before, and suddenly, I'm doing it with my movie nemesis.

After minutes of silence, I force us to pause. Sitting like a beacon on the beach is another lifeguard tower. This one's rainbow-striped. I've seen it all over social media before, but it's right here.

The Venice Pride Flag Lifeguard Tower.

I snap several photos on my phone.

"I love that scene from the movie," I say while swiping through my pictures. "Except, um, I've never kissed anyone before." The words tumble out my mouth like a snowball building to an avalanche.

I wait for Sean to pierce this moment with another one of his sharp-tongued comments. But it never happens. Instead, his hand wraps around my wrist, his thumb pressed to my erratic pulse until my heart calms.

He flashes an arrogant smirk. "Hi, I'm Sean Kam. I hate Nolan. I love rom-coms. Boys kissing on Ferris wheels. Also, I'm a vampire, and you've got popcorn in your hair."

I snatch my hand from his to quickly brush the kernels from my curls. *Reece and those assholes.* When I raise my chin, Sean flexes an expectant eyebrow at me. "What? Is there more?"

"Did you hear what I said?"

"That you're anti-Nolan? Shocker," I deadpan.

The grim line of his mouth doesn't flinch.

"Or was it the part about boys kissing on Ferris wheels?" I ask. "I saw your pan button. I'm gay, so—"

"*Tyrell,*" Sean hisses like a viper, a warning etched deep into his brow.

His eyes flit around. There's no one else in this spot but us. "I'm. A. Vampire."

"Yeah. I heard that."

A cool breeze sweeps through Sean's fringe. He looks so young. Boyish cheeks, unfiltered glow across his skin. He's *beautiful*, even while scowling.

"Do you meet vampires all the time? Are they just strolling around Atlanta?"

I chuckle. "No. You're my first." My casualness startles him.

"Aren't you . . . scared?"

"My dad—" Tears instantly blur my vision. I hold them in. "He loved all things paranormal or mythological. He'd tell me about everything he's read and, I dunno." I shrug. "I've always believed there's more to this world than dicks like Reece and the things we don't see every day."

Sean chews the inside of his cheek.

"Besides," I say, scuffing my sneaker on the grainy pavement, "you haven't proven you're a real vampire. You could be lying."

"What should I do?" Sean's mouth twitches. "*Sparkle?*"

"Do the teeth and eyes thing," I challenge. "Like back at Reagan's."

"Only happens when I'm hungry," Sean mumbles. "Or angry."

I smirk. "*Tenet* was the best movie ever made."

It's sudden. The tension in Sean's jaw. Fists at his side. Crimson expanding across his eyes like blood on a midnight sky. His mouth puckers before he exposes sharpened, perfectly white canines.

"*Shit,*" I hiss, almost giddy.

"Believe me now?"

I nod. He quickly hides his face behind his hands, breathing deeply.

Seconds tick by before he shudders, hands dropping. His face returns to the scowly, irritated one I've seen all month.

"So," I start, noticing his uneasiness at sharing this with me, "do you also stalk pretty, white, queer girls in small towns?"

Sean snorts. No, it's a full, doubled-over, hands on his knees, wild laugh.

I made Sean Kam laugh. Miracles are real.

Somehow, we end up in the Venice Beach Boardwalk. Rows of shops advertise tattoos, souvenirs, and herbal relaxation. Restaurants buzz with noisy patrons. Street vendors sell artwork. A woman with a beat-up guitar sings Florence and the Machine.

"How'd it happen?" I ask. "The—" I wave a hand around my neck, as if it means anything.

"How'd your dad die?"

I flinch hard, steps faltering.

Sean pauses with an apologetic air to his expression. "June and I used to come here a lot. She'd go to the beach with her friends. I'd spend my time skating, thinking I was the next Ryan Sheckler."

His dazed eyes stare past me to a darkened structure. It's huge, all railings and platforms, two hollowed-out pools. Venice Skatepark.

"One day, she got tired of waiting and left me," he continues. "The sun was down. I tried to perfect one last trick, but ate pavement instead. Shredded my whole knee."

My gaze lowers. He's wearing ripped black jeans. The glimpses of tawny skin are blemish-free.

"You can't see it," he notes. "Perks of being an immortal."

Blush stings my cheeks.

"Anyway. This girl came along. I'd seen her before," he says. "She really wanted to help. But she was still . . . *new*. My blood was everywhere and, well."

He licks his canines.

"It's not a thirst in the beginning," Sean explains. "More of a hunger. But if you drink too much, it turns into an unbearable urge. She didn't mean for it to happen. The bite. Eventually, she regained control, but it was too late."

Silence catches us like a spider's web. The air tastes of salt and sea. I can't bring myself to look away when I ask, "Does your family know?"

"Only June." His eyes stare upward. "After two days, I went home to tell her, but I was still . . ."

"New?" I offer.

"I couldn't control it," he says. "She was terrified when she saw me. Told me to leave." He tugs anxiously at his hoodie's sleeves. "I wanted to be with my family, but I didn't want them to think I'd hurt them." He clears his throat. "I never went back home after that. June got accepted to UT in Austin. She convinced my parents to move with her to Texas. To stop waiting for me."

Now that Dad's gone, I wonder if Mom will move with me when I go to college or stay in Georgia, alone.

When I notice Sean clocking the way I'm lost in my thoughts again, he half smiles. "Anyway, *Twilight* is a lie. I'm fast. Kind of strong. But if I tried climbing a palm tree, I'd fall and break my neck."

"But you'd heal quickly," I point out.

We walk back toward the pier.

"Immortality has its benefits, but it doesn't prevent trauma." He pats his chest. "I'll live centuries with my grief. Loss. *All* of it."

I ask, "How old are you?"

"Sixteen."

"For how long now?"

"Two years."

I hide my surprise. The loss is still fresh for him, like me. I tell him, "I don't want to live centuries with *this*," while rubbing at my damp eyes.

"You have to hurt to heal, Tyrell."

Sean doesn't say my name like Mom. Or the grief counselor I saw in the beginning. Not like Kellan, who's grown tired of my withdrawing. Or my teachers, whose patience for me skipping classes or forgetting assignments ran thin after the first month.

He says it like he *knows*.

"Cancer." The word sticks to my throat like bile-flavored gum. "It happened quickly. My dad's diagnosis was late. One day, he's burning French toast in the kitchen. Weeks later, he's gone."

Between us, Sean's hand finds mine. My body swiftly adjusts to his temperature. I tangle our fingers just to know I'm still here.

"So, how do you heal?" I ask.

He tips his head back, thinking. I steal glances at his neck like I'll find the marks that other vampire left behind. He shrugs listlessly. "I don't know."

The walk back is shorter. Soon, Pacific Park is looming over us like a twinkling titan. Sean's expression morphs back into a thundercloud as he rocks on his heels.

"I won't tell anyone," I blurt. "If you were wondering."

"I wasn't worried. I trust you."

"Oh." *Why's my heart trying to smash through my rib cage?* "Thanks?"

An awkward hush drops on us like a downpour.

"So. Just gonna." Sean's head jerks toward the steep hill leading up to

Ocean Avenue. Far from me. "I hope tonight wasn't all bad, Tyrell. Santa Monica is . . . magical. If you get to know it."

He's barely two steps away when I yell, "I have a list of places I was supposed to visit with my dad!"

Once the words are out, I shrink. Who the hell shouts *that* at a striking, irresistible vampire? Also, when did Sean become irresistible?

He smiles, all teeth. Neon lights glint off his sharp, long canines.

"Where do you want to start?"

✧ ⋈ ✧

Santa Monica unfolds around us like a flower blooming. There's something pulsing beyond the petals. It's in the details. The way Sean talks about the places he's been and things he's seen. Life he's experienced.

It's the way he never shies away from my questions.

As we wind around palm trees in Palisades Park, I ask, "Where do you get blood from?"

"Not humans," he replies firmly. "Coyotes. Deer. Cougars. I once drained a racoon—eleven out of ten, do not recommend."

"Do you have any friends?" I ask while trekking up Observation Hill in Tongva Park.

"Smile!"

Begrudgingly, a grin kisses my lips when Sean makes a grumpy face from behind my phone. He's insisted on taking photos at every stop from Dad's list. "For those days you miss him the most. You'll remember you were here."

I hate how right he is.

Even while I'm standing inside a steel cocoon structure that overlooks Ocean Avenue, I think of how Dad said that the middle of this very park is where he decided to go to USC.

The flash goes off.

"Cute," Sean comments, winking. I swear he knows I'm blushing even though it's not visible against my skin. "No friends. People know my face. I know theirs. The end."

"To keep the vampire thing a secret?"

"No. I don't want to add anyone else to the list of people I'll mourn when they die."

The loneliness in his words snags me like barbed wire.

"Next stop: Third Street Promenade," he announces before a follow-up question—or an apology—brushes my mouth.

I pose in front of Dad's favorite thinking spot: the triceratops plant sculpture.

We follow the diminishing night crowd. Sean pulls me into the Coffee Bean & Tea Leaf just before they close for a photo of me holding Dad's go-to order: a caramel iced blended drink.

"That's my fav too," Sean says.

After suffering through a brain freeze chugging the frozen drink, I inquire, "What's next?"

Outside, I request Tom Petty's "Free Fallin'" from a street performer under a tree wrapped in glowing bulbs. On weekends, Dad would sing it around the house in his scratchy voice. When the singer gets to the lyric about vampires, I grab Sean's hand. He squeezes back.

We stroll down Arizona Avenue. I learn so much about Sean:

Food isn't required, but he eats random things occasionally. "To remind myself what it's like."

No sleep either. "Sometimes, it's like I'm dreaming while wide awake."

His roommate is the girl who bit him. "I work at Reagan's to pay rent. Also, it's how I keep June with me. Through movies."

Sean's halfway through a story about spending every Saturday with his parents at the farmers' market when I blurt, "Have you ever tried to reach her? June?"

We pause on a corner. "I emailed her after I . . . got control of the hunger." His fingers flex against mine. "She wants me to visit, but I'm scared. To see my parents. To see her after that last time."

"That's not fair to them."

His eyebrows lower.

Frustration leaves my neck and cheeks flushed. "You said people have to hurt to heal. But you're not giving your family a chance to heal. Just hurt. They know you're not gone, and you won't even visit."

The skin around Sean's eyes tightens. "You have no idea." He releases my hand.

"I have no idea about what? Pain? Fear?" I scowl.

His next words come with a flash of teeth, sharp and pointy. "You'll never have to mourn someone who's still *alive*, Tyrell!"

"You don't have to, either!" A fresh wave of tears prickles my eyes. "I wouldn't give up a second of my last moments with my dad. Not for anything. I *lost* him, Sean."

"And now you can heal," he rasps.

"No." I shake my phone in front of his face. "I'm in a city without him. Trying to make memories from a list. He should be here. I'm not healing. Every second feels closer to me having to accept—"

My voice catches. Sean stays quiet.

"He's gone. He's . . . gone," I repeat to my feet.

To myself.

They're the two words everyone's been trying to help me hear, but I've been too afraid to listen.

"You can't spare people from pain," I croak. "Ignoring your family isn't protecting them. It's bullshit." I turn away. The trembling is almost like breathing now.

"Ty." Sean steps around me. Bends until we're eye level. "Death is bullshit. Grief is, too. It all sucks."

I laugh wetly. "This coming from a vampire."

"I'm . . . adjusting." Moonlight paints across his pinched brow, his poked-out lower lip. His eyes soften as he thinks. "Maybe I'm doing it wrong."

"Maybe."

I glance at the unchecked box on the list in my phone.

"I think," I start, swallowing the thick lump in my throat, "we can't force people to accept things until they're ready. Pain. Death. Loneliness. At least, that's what I got from *Twilight*."

"You and I saw two very different movies."

I laugh again. He slides his fingers between mine again.

"Come on. We're not done yet."

✧ ☒ ✧

The last stop on Dad's list is the Next Page, a bookstore off Santa Monica Boulevard.

When we arrive, the interior's darker than the sky above. I thump the back of my skull against the glass door. "They're closed."

It's after 11:00 p.m. Mom says "no curfew," but what she really means is "Be home before midnight, Cinderella!"

"He spent all his time here." I show Sean a photo from Dad's Facebook. He's seventeen years old, sitting on the bookstore floor with a castle made of paperbacks surrounding him. All the joy in his grin is unsettling the glasses on his nose.

This is where Dad found happiness. I just want five minutes inside to create one final memory.

One with my dad. One with Sean, too.

He must read it on my face. "I can't believe I'm doing this," he grumbles while digging out his phone to send a text.

Twenty minutes later, a college-age girl with bronze skin, wavy black hair falling like water down her back, shoves a key in the bookstore's lock. She hisses, "You owe me so hard."

"Another podcast appearance?" Sean offers.

"A three-part series." She shoulders the door open.

"Rae, Tyrell," Sean introduces. "Tyrell, Rae."

Rae stands in the doorway, arm extending dramatically into the bookstore. "Welcome to the Next Page! Half hour, vampy. My boss'll kill me if she finds out."

"She knows?" I whisper as Sean guides me in.

"Don't worry. I'll mindwipe her after we leave."

I whip around, mouth agape. The lethal corners of Sean's mouth pull up into intense angles. "You can't do that, can you?" I accuse.

"Wouldn't you like to know."

He disappears into the deep shadows of the store while Rae flips on a couple overhead lights near the front. She flops behind the counter, earbuds already in.

The bookstore's magic instantly clings to my skin. Endless rows of stuffed shelves. Paperbacks line the walls like tiles. I browse the stacks. Dad's love for fantasy and sci-fi is in my bones. My fingers skim spines. When they catch on *The Hundred Thousand Kingdoms* by N. K. Jemisin, a smile ghosts over my lips.

Maybe vampires aren't the only ones thriving in the night.

I sit with my back braced against a bookcase. A paperback trail starts at my feet, surrounding me like a protective circle built from words.

Sean settles next to me. Warmth melting into cold. "You look alike." He swipes to Dad's Facebook photo, then the one he just took of me.

"Tonight's been weird," I say softly. "He's not here, but it's like—"

"He is?"

I nod.

Sean exhales quietly. "It's like that for me too sometimes."

"My dad's gone," I say, this time without tears, "but I guess he'll always be here. In Santa Monica." I press my index finger to the center of my chest. "And here, too."

A slow grin curls his mouth.

"And your family will always be here." I tap his chest. "Even when they're gone."

He doesn't comment. Instead, he lets me quiz him about his favorite vampire movies while I flip through pages. *Blade* is number one, followed by the Underworld series. *Twilight*, of course, is last.

"What about *Van Helsing*?" I ask.

"Sweet Bella Swan, your taste is gross."

A broken laugh escapes my throat. The light falls against Sean's face in a way that, I swear, he's blushing. *Do vampires blush?* I don't ask.

"Can vampires take selfies?" I say. "Will you be invisible if we—"

"Tyrell, please, shut up."

He angles my phone until we're both in the frame. His tawny skin, hair like a crow's feathers falling near his eyes, a crooked grin exposing one fang. My awkward smile, blush hidden behind my raised cheeks. He whispers, "One, two . . ."

I rest my head on his shoulder.

And there we are—a smirky, thundercloud of a vampire and me, grinning like I never want to leave his side.

But I have to.

It's 11:54 p.m. when Rae relocks the bookstore. I've already sent Mom my location.

"I mean it, Mr. Pointy." Rae glares at Sean. "Three-part series. We're talking coffins, blood rituals, urban legends, origins—"

"I've only been this way for two years!"

She ignores Sean's grumbling to pass me a bag of used paperbacks. "Start with Octavia Butler," she commands before strutting away like she's not acquaintances—*friends?*—with an immortal being.

We stand quietly. The city's still an open vessel, pouring out light and noise and comfort I couldn't feel four weeks ago.

Sean speaks first.

"Will you visit—" He pauses, eyes lowering. His feet shuffle. Slim fingers flex and curl at his sides. "Santa Monica again?"

"Santa Monica?"

His nostrils flare. I can see the hesitation, but I won't rush him. One fang scrapes over his lip before his gaze lifts, uncertainty pooling around the brown.

"I know this is hard," I tell him. "You don't like people. You keep your distance. You don't want to lose anyone else and—"

"Ty," he interrupts, huffing, "will you visit *me*?"

I suck in a breath.

Mom texts: *stuck in traffic.*

The extra time ignites the endorphins in my blood. I edge closer to Sean. His eyebrows disappear behind fringe.

"Thanks for tonight. I didn't think I'd like it here because it's my dad's city, and . . ." I exhale slowly. "I was scared making new memories without him would mean I'd lose the ones I have with him." Sean's eyes don't leave my face as I say, "But I want to make my own memories. Here."

A toothy smile appears. "I'm gonna call June," Sean says. "Maybe it's time to let my family decide what happens next."

I grin, nodding.

Shyly, he asks again, "Will you visit me?"

My eyes trace his expression. Something like hope circles his dark eyes. It beats fiercely beneath my ribs.

I answer his question with a kiss, embedding a memory I hope he clings to until I come back.

The First Day of College

BY MONICA GOMEZ-HIRA

The sign on the dorm room door said "Isabella Morales." Unmistakably, swirled in glitter letters, like a wedding invitation. Reminding me that everyone here was expected to shine.

"Gold," Mami said, touching her finger to it. A bit of the glitter stuck there, and she smiled at it.

My older brother, Edgar, snorted. "Glitter glue? Really, Isa? Is this college or is this kindergarten?" He grunted and shifted the piles of my moving boxes in his arms.

I'd been wondering the same thing, but I wasn't going to let him get away with that.

"Maybe you'd know the difference between the two if you hadn't dropped out in your second semester?" I said sweetly.

I knew he'd had a good reason to quit, a full-time job that paid more than many college graduates make years out of school. But that didn't mean he could make fun of me. Especially not when my nerves were as jangly as they were right now.

He narrowed his eyes. The words came fast enough that I knew that I'd struck a chord.

"Oh, yeah? Maybe I shouldn't have bothered to take two days off just to haul your ass—"

Mami held up a hand. She knew where this was going, where this always went. "Ya. Basta."

She only came up to Edgar's shoulder, but she could do damage. We shut up.

"Should we . . . should we knock or something?" Marta touched the door like she was looking for the hidden lock. Because the doorknob . . . was too obvious somehow? She hoisted my niece, Brenda, on her hip, angling her away from the sign even as Brenda reached out for it, as entranced by the glitter as her abuela had been.

"It has Isa's name on it," Papi muttered, pushing his Mets cap off his forehead a little and leaning forward, squinting at the glitter, now a little smudged from where Mami had marred it. Two more boxes were in his arms.

I put the key in the lock, and it opened with barely a nudge. The door, the key—they knew I belonged here. Now to convince the rest of my family. Now to convince myself.

Edgar gave a low whistle when we walked in. It wasn't a big room, but it was bigger than the bedroom I shared with Marta and Brenda in the apartment. Everything smelled new—no lingering onion and garlic smells. No in-your-face aromas of Mami's body wash and Marta's coconut shampoo and Brenda's Agua de Colonia and my own stress-baked brownies. It smelled the way a showroom did. Understated. Expensive.

There were two windows, one bare of anything but a shade and another with a white fluttering drape. The sun made the honey wood of the furniture glow—two desks, two dressers, two beds with the extra-long mattresses that had given Mami and me fits while shopping for the sheets on the recommended list sent by the school. No differences between my roommate, the other golden name on the door, and me.

But that was only true of the official school-supplied furniture. Everywhere, I could see signs that my roommate had beaten me here. The plush rug next to her bed, which was covered with three extra over-stuffed pillows and a plush antique quilt. Antique, not old. A few candles artfully placed on her dresser. Above her bed was a framed print of Monet's *Water Lilies*. I knew *that* wasn't authentic.

Right?

Tucked into her corner of the room were a few pieces of luggage. "Looks like yours, Isa . . . ," Marta said, then smirked. "Except these look real." She sat down on my roommate's bed (seriously?) and let Brenda crawl around on top of it (I ask again . . . *seriously?*). At least she slipped Brenda's little Mary Janes off first.

"Jeez, who cares?" Edgar said, plopping my boxes down on my side of the room. The barren side.

Mami shook her head. "Everybody cares, Edgar. And those are definitely real. I would know."

I'm not sure how exactly she would know. She worked where I used to—Noelle Fashions—me part-time in accounts receivable and her as a foreman—forewoman—on the shop floor. We specialized in stuff that LOOKED like that luggage, if you didn't look too closely.

Still. It wasn't like my luggage was *bad*. It was new, no tears and all matching. And I'd saved for a month to buy something nice for school. Even with my employee discount, it hadn't been cheap for me.

Now I kind of wished I'd chosen a different pattern, though. My *L*s and *V*s were definitely missing a patina of *something*.

But then I remembered that I knew the word *patina* and could use it in a sentence. And stuff like that is what got me here, not my faux luggage (and the word *faux* too, even if I did pronounce the *x* for way too long).

God, if I had to spend the next four years defending my *vocabulary*, I was going to end up like . . . like . . . Okay, see? I couldn't even find the words.

Was that fancy luggage *laughing* at me?

No, it was just Papi, readjusting his baseball cap again and then shaking his head. "If you go by what this school costs, it's *for sure* real."

Now, don't get it twisted. We might have seen the true cost on the forms the school sent along, but that's not what we were paying. I'd hustled for four years of high school, eight years of elementary before that, two years of preschool before that (look, I was a toddler with a plan, okay?), and between that and the fact that we were a family of six renting a three-bedroom apartment—my financial aid package was pretty sweet. Not a full ride. But almost.

Still, we were responsible for some of it. And even those numbers were scary. At least to me.

Marta was nosing around in my roommate's closet now that Brenda was occupied on the bed. Mami peered past Marta, also staring into the closet. Then she glared at me. "Isabella de la Fe Morales, I *told* you to bring some more formal clothes. Mira eso!" She gestured at the outfits, neat on their hangers. "I'll bet you didn't even bring up that sixty-four-piece makeup case I bought you!"

Someday Mami was going to realize that was about, oh, sixty pieces of makeup too many for me.

Marta ignored us, fingering a sequined dress sheathed in a dry cleaner bag. "Wow . . . think she would lend you this? Because this is HOT."

I yanked her away. "Don't touch anything!" I folded my arms. "And like I would ask."

"You'll have to," she argued. She pointed to a crisp pair of black slacks. "You could cuff them if they're too long, but they would be perfect for a fancy meeting with your professor or something. Or . . ." She pointed to the sequined dress and wiggled her eyebrows at me. "A hot date? Like . . . with a Harvard dude or something?"

"She wouldn't need to borrow anything if she'd listened to me and brought her own nice clothes. Plus," Mami said sharply, "she's here to study, not party." Mami sat on my bed and unzipped my bag, sighing at the messy explosion of black sweats and graphic T-shirts. I saw her glancing a bit longingly at my new roommate's closet. Add her to the women my mother approved of, I guess.

"Why not both?" Marta laughed.

"Both is what got you in this mess," Mami muttered. Marta scowled at her. My brother-in-law, Javier, was serving overseas in the army, which was why Marta and Brenda were living with us. But yeah . . . Mami wasn't wrong. Brenda hadn't exactly been part of Marta's short-term goals. Hence why she was on a one-class-a-semester plan at our community college. Four states away from where we were right now.

"You act like I was a child bride, Mami," Marta said.

"No, pero . . . did you *have* to do everything in the wrong order? Late-in-life baby—"

"*Late in life?* I'm only twenty-nine!"

"No degree—"

"I'm CLEARLY working on it—"

This was an old argument, from when Marta first quit college, at my age. You'd think Mami would relate to the whole idea of trying to improve yourself at any age, change for your kids. After all, Mami had moved to the US to improve her own life, improve the chances for her children. And it had worked—look where we were right now.

But maybe she thought that only applied to her. Or she thought Marta was doing it wrong, yet again.

Mami sighed then, deep and dramatic. "Bueno, whatever. Isabella is meant for different things."

It scared me when my family said that. I hated when they made it sound like I was oh so different from them, because it reminded me that, because I was the youngest, I'd missed tons of their history. Our history.

And I also hated it because . . . what exactly were they expecting?

Well, that's not entirely honest. I knew what they were expecting.

I just wasn't sure if I could deliver.

Mami pulled out three tall votive candles—covered in colorful art depicting la Virgen del Carmen, el Corazón Sagrado, and San Judas. Lined them up for roll call on my desk.

Yeah, that wasn't going to work.

I laid San Judas gently in the drawer. "Why don't we wait to see how it goes before we call on the patron saint of lost causes?" I said to Mami.

"You don't need to wait to be lost to call on him," Mami said back. "You need all the protection you can get. All alone here at college." Did I mention that I was the first and only kid in my family to do the uber American thing and go away to school? To say that they were ambivalent about it was an understatement. Their feelings about me rooming at college changed as fast as those roosters on the top of barns, spinning in a tornado.

"I'm impressed you only packed three," I said.

"In *this* bag."

Papi laughed. "Her roommate is going to think she's starting some sort of church here."

"Eh. Maybe it's a good idea. Put the fear of God into her," Edgar said.

"No pun intended," I muttered.

Mami jerked her head toward the other side of the room. "*She* has candles."

"Yeah . . . those aren't even close to the same," I said.

She shrugged. "Candles are candles." Which, c'mon, she didn't believe that. Ours were supposed to be a hotline to the Lord. Hers were clearly a one-way pass to the Diptyque section of Saks.

I glanced at the fancy clock across the room—more roommate swag—and picked up the pace. I didn't want her coming back here and seeing us taking up all the space and breathing up all her air. I wanted to meet her by myself, so she could see me without having to widen the frame to include Papi and Mami and Marta and Brenda and Edgar.

I put my hands on my hips. "Is that everything?"

Mami shifted her eyes away. "I *think* there might be one more box. Una cosa mas."

Oh? A good luck present, perhaps? AirPods to replace the knockoffs I'd got for ten dollars that always died just when the song got good?

"I'll go with you, Mami," I said sweetly, ready to follow her out of the room and collect my goodies.

"Ah . . . why don't you keep unpacking? We can't keep the car there forever . . . It's going to get towed." Before I could argue that the school probably wasn't planning on towing the parents of an incoming first year, Mami, with her long, wavy hair, kitten heels, and pressed linen pants (if Mami wasn't overdressed she didn't feel dressed at all), walked off and shut the door behind her.

"That was weird," Marta said, echoing what we were all thinking.

"Be nice to your mother," Papi said while he untangled the power cord for my laptop. "This isn't exactly easy for her. You're gonna be all by yourself, Isa. And you know that moving brings back bad memories."

There wasn't much to say after that. Mami, Edgar, and Marta were the only ones who had moved to the States from Colombia. Edgar was nine, Marta seven. Mami and Papi had met here, he'd adopted my siblings, and they'd had me. And maybe that last part seemed like it happened faster than I was comfortable sharing.

I might sound like I'm just giving the bullet points of the official story, but that's really all I know myself. Mami doesn't like to talk much about Colombia or why she took my siblings and left. It's as if her hard drive was wiped as soon as she stepped onto American soil. Beyond Edgar and Marta, Mami hadn't brought much from her homeland.

Mami came back, triumphantly bearing another small box. One I recognized.

Oh.

Because I knew what lived in that box. It was something I'd sort of been hoping to never see again.

You see, Mami didn't like to share much about her biography with us, but there was one thing she had done that had made her inordinately proud. When she was a teenager, she had been chosen as la Reina del Carnaval de Sincelejo, her hometown. It had been a very big deal, especially to seventeen-year-old Mami. So much so that something she HAD brought from there to here was her tiara, almost as spangly and shiny as it was back then.

"What—why?" I asked her.

"Because I want you to have it here," she said simply. "A little piece of us. With you."

I didn't hate that idea. I just wanted it to be a *different* piece of them. Because this tiara and I . . . we have history. I was probably around Brenda's age when I first saw it, reaching out my chubby fingers to grab the Shiny.

And Mami would whisk it away. "No lo toques, Isabella."

I heard a variation of that for the rest of my life.

As I got older and my chubby toddler fingers became chubby tween and teen fingers, I figured out I'd never be the kind of girl who deserved to touch something like Mami's Queen of the Carnival tiara. I wasn't willowy like her, had never mastered the art of looking down just so until my lashes fanned out over my cheeks. The crown might be a part of Mami's history, but it didn't belong in mine. Not in any good ways, anyway.

I'd wanted to wear it to my quinceañera three years ago, and she'd actually pretended she was going to let me, and I swear, that was the only coming-of-age ritual I really needed. Forget the fancy party and the oversize dress. Marta could keep those memories—the poofy pink dress and Mami's crown bobby pinned securely to her head. I just needed to be the next one to wear it, to have Mami and Marta put that tiara on my head, so that for one night, I could feel like I was finally about to be inducted into their Circle of Womanhood.

But two days before the quince, she'd pulled me into her bedroom and presented me with . . . TA-DA. Not the Real Tiara. But some random tiara impostor.

"But . . . ?" I'd started, digging my fingers into the edge of the mattress, willing myself to listen before I argued.

"This one is more modern," she'd said as she fitted it on my braid. "Look. Brand-new."

I hadn't wanted brand-new, though. I hadn't wanted another reminder of the separation between me and Mami and Marta. I had wanted to prove that I could be trusted with a physical relic of our history.

Still, she'd bought the fake one, and I would wear it. There wouldn't be an argument. There never really was. Not between Mami and me, anyway.

So I was surprised to see that she was leaving it here in my dorm room. Granted, this was a pretty fancy school, but it wasn't like I was going to wear it to class.

"Pretty!" Brenda cried, and reached out. Just like I had. And was denied. Just like I was.

Mami nestled it on the top level of my desk bookshelf, right in the center of the votive candles.

Papi was right. It did look like I was working on starting my own weird, rhinestone-centered religion.

"Mami—um . . . It's just—"

Marta snorted. "The candles were bad enough, but that's tacky as hell, Mami. C'mon, now."

"Hell! Hell!" Brenda repeated cheerfully. Mami gave Marta a look before swinging her eyes my way. "Tacky? Pero . . . Isabella . . . you always wanted . . ." She looked confused.

Wanted as in past tense. But that didn't mean I wanted to hurt her feelings either.

Instead, I said, "It just . . . belongs with you, that's all. At home. I don't think—"

The rest of the words died in my mouth as just then, the door swung open. My roommate, the other name on the door, had arrived.

First thing I notice is that we all have to look up at her. My new roommate is probably over six feet tall, even in her sandals, with her blond hair sleeked back into a topknot.

She's beautiful.

"Uh, hi. I'm Tamara. Tamara Quinn," she says, her eyes flicking around the room. I know what she's seeing. My brother, arms crossed, deciding if she's going to be friend or foe. Brenda sitting on Tamara's bed, nomming on a corner of Tamara's quilt, with Marta trying to pull it out of Brenda's hands. And failing.

Mami and Papi, standing stock-still by my desk, tentative smiles on their faces, clearly waiting for me to introduce them.

And me, hair pulled back in a very not-sleek topknot. My skin sweaty, flushed, and bare of makeup. The opposite of everything the Tiara represented, in spite of its position in the middle of the patron saints of Maybe I'll Never Belong Here.

"Hi," I started, wiping my hand and walking toward her.

But her gaze had already moved past me, staring in fascination at the tiara and the votive candles. I mean, I couldn't exactly blame her. It was weird.

I cleared my throat. Then cleared it again. Finally, I was deemed more interesting than the tiara and candles.

"You must be Isabella," she said, shaking my hand with a strong grip.

"Isa. And hi, Tamara."

"Got it in one," she said, then blushed. "Okay, I have no idea why I just said that. I'm nervous."

I grinned back. "Me too." Maybe this wouldn't be so bad.

Mami cleared her throat.

"Oh, and . . . This is my mother and father. And my sister and brother—" I rattled off quickly, well aware that most people probably didn't have the whole family with them when they moved into their room. There were almost more Moraleses in the room than furniture.

"Who have NAMES," Marta said. "Hi, Tamara, I'm Marta, this is my daughter, Brenda, and the old guy trying to impress you with his muscles is our brother, Edgar."

Edgar immediately stopped the "subtle" flexing he was doing and held out his own hand. "Hi, pleased to meet you. And I was just stretching."

Marta and I rolled our eyes in unison, and I realized with a pang how seldom I was going to get to do that after today. Somehow, having Tamara here reminded me that this wasn't just about me moving to college. This was about me leaving them.

Mami kept glancing at the door. "So, Tamara . . . where is your family?"

Tamara looked confused. "Uh, home? My boyfriend dropped me off yesterday."

My parents both looked scandalized.

But Tamara's eyes had slid back to the tiara. In a moment, she walked toward it and reached out her fingers to glide them along the top. The sharp, pointy top.

"Ouch!" She pulled her hand back and stuck her index finger in her mouth.

I would have mentioned the possibility of injury. If she had asked.

"What is that, a weapon?" she said, half-laughing.

Of sorts, yeah.

"A family heirloom," Mami said shortly.

Tamara giggled again. "Seriously? From where? Party City?" She opened her eyes, wide and teasing. "Or are you all secretly royalty?"

It took her a second to realize that no one else was laughing. "Oh, shit, um, that came out way meaner than I expected . . . I talk a lot when I'm—I mean . . . I'm really, really sorry . . ."

Mami stood up. "I think I'll go check on the car."

"I'll go with you," I said hastily, rushing toward her. I grabbed the tiara and its box on the way out. She eyed it in my hand but didn't mention it.

"You don't have to come," she muttered instead.

"I *want* to," I said.

We speed walked past a bunch of open dorm rooms, more families straining under the weight of boxes and steamer trunks. Arguing, laughing, voices stacked one on top of the other like Jenga sticks.

But none of the families looked like us.

Walking outside, I was hit again by how cinematic my campus was. I'd seen images like this on the website—it was a huge reason why I'd wanted to apply. But . . . somehow it was different to feel like I was *in* the picture this time, for the first time. Green trees waved their branches over a grassy slope dotted with students, lying on blankets or playing Frisbee or strumming guitars. This is what I'd always thought college should be, not the urban link of buildings that Edgar had gone to for a hot second, or the squat boxes that made up Marta's community college. When you saw college on the screen, when you closed your eyes and gave it some thought, it looked just like the scene in front of me. Edgar's and Marta's schools were real, don't get me wrong, and people learned there too, obviously, but . . . this was what I'd worked so hard to achieve. This wasn't just what I wanted. This was the pinnacle of my parents' expectations for me. And for once, I felt like I'd actually lived up to their dreams. This was something that *I* could give them, that my siblings hadn't.

So, yeah. To me, this was *real* college. Just like Tamara's luggage was *real* Louis Vuitton.

And mine wasn't.

Mami leaned her forehead by the driver window of our Kia for a second. The late August breeze ruffled her hair, carrying the scent of sunscreen from my fellow students. A group of them were playing hacky sack close enough to the car that I could hear the rhythmic slap of the sack against their feet. The whole thing felt like we were at a state park, or a resort, or something.

I put my hand on her shoulder. "You okay, Mami?" The words felt strange in my mouth. Usually, the person comforting her was Marta. They were so much alike—that's probably why they fought so much. They shared so much history that I only knew secondhand. I remembered when I was little and Marta used to tell me stories, born out of her own homesickness. Stories of crispy arepas on the beach, the salty sea air the best seasoning. Or the sticky raspaos, fruit syrup over ice, that Mami bought them on their birthdays. Marta always said food wasn't as good in the States, and I agreed with her, even if I had never tasted the alternative.

When Mami overheard our whispers, she'd get this look on her face that none of us ever wanted to see. Sad eyes and her mouth in a straight line.

Marta learned to stop telling me those stories, and the silences between me and the rest of my family grew.

Just like the silence between Mami and me right now. And soon they'd all be gone. And I'd be here, on my cinematic campus, with just my votive candles for company.

Maybe having the patron saint of lost causes around wouldn't be such a bad idea.

"The tiara isn't from Party City, you know," Mami began in a low voice.

"I know that—it's from Colombia. The last thing you packed." I knew this part of the history as well as I knew myself. This was one of the things from her past she was always happy to talk about. The last link she had to her old life, packed away for the new one. The symbol of the Circle of Womanhood.

She leaned her back against the car, staring blankly at the commons. I looked in the same direction. I'd read that sometimes people find it easier to open up when nobody is looking at them. Although Mami LOVED to have people looking at her.

"It . . . it's not from Colombia either."

"What?" Like I said, I knew the story. And this wasn't a part of it.

Now my eyes were fully on her face. But she still wasn't looking at me.

"I mean . . . I bought it on Bergenline Avenue, at a bridal and quinceañera shop, back when we used to live there. All of us."

"What?" I repeat, my brain struggling to process this new information.

She finally looked over at me, a reluctant smirk on her face. "Here we are at your fancy college, and all you can think to say is 'what?'"

"Yeah . . . because I literally don't understand? All that stuff . . . about la Reina del Carnaval was . . . fake?"

Her eyes blazed at me. "No! That part was absolutely true! But . . ." She stared down at her red manicure for a second, and then, "I didn't get to bring the tiara with me. I wanted to, but . . . it was all so sudden, and it's not like we could bring as much stuff to America as you brought here today. There was only so much luggage allowance, and it had to be enough for all of us. So . . . things had to stay behind."

"But it's not like it's even that big—"

"It just didn't fit, that's all. I had to make a choice, and I made it." Her voice had been edging up, until a few of the hacky sackers started to stare. She stopped and stared back, hard. When they finally looked away, she began again, in a lower voice. "I asked your tías to keep it safe for me, and they promised. And when we went back to visit with your papi, after we got married, I went looking for it. But . . ." Her voice shook now. "But . . . they couldn't find it. Didn't know where it had gone. Like my corona had grown legs and walked!" She sighed. "Either way, I wasn't going to get it back. And I mean . . . it shouldn't have mattered. I had a good life now! We were in America, we were with your papi, we were safe. But . . . la corona was from before. Sabes? Un recuerdo de otros tiempos—tiempos buenos. Un recuerdo de otra Veronica. And it's not like I wasn't happy, but . . . I wasn't that Veronica anymore. And I think I wanted a reminder that I once had been. I'd once been a girl who was beautiful enough to rule over the entire carnival. I'd once been the girl that they'd chosen to represent them."

I mean, I kind of understood that. I'd never been chosen in the same way Mami and Marta had. Never been beautiful like them, never even had a boyfriend. But I was chosen by this school. And I had that welcome screen saved to my camera roll for all time. So I got why she'd needed something, too. Proof.

"For some reason, coming back after that trip was hard," she said.

"It was like . . . it hit me, you know? This was it. We weren't going back, couldn't. Not with your papi—he was an Americano, and this was where he'd always want to be. And I didn't belong there anymore. I wasn't that girl anymore. I was a wife, a mother of two young children and you on the way. But that didn't mean I belonged here either."

We watched the hacky sackers for a second after that. This wasn't the "here" she was talking about, but I knew exactly how she felt.

"So, one Saturday after we got back, I was alone. Well, you were in my stomach, kicking away, but your brother and sister were both at the playground with your dad. The streets were full of people talking, talking, but I could only understand, like, half of what everyone was saying, even though so many people on Bergenline speak Spanish. All I could hear was noise, music with words I couldn't always understand. Conversations that didn't include me. When I walked past that store, I just wanted to remember what it used to feel like to be . . . someone else. The girl, Veronica. La Reina del Carnaval. So I ducked in, told the saleswoman I needed a quince tiara for my sobrina, and gave her half of the grocery money for the week." She chuckled. "When your papi didn't even get mad at me . . . I knew again that I'd made a good choice."

She looked at me, the smile dying on her lips. "But when Marta wore it for her quince, I felt guilty. It was a lie. It was fake. That's why I didn't want you to wear it for your quince, or for Marta to wear it again on her wedding day. You both deserve real things." She took my hands. "Even if I can't always give them to you."

We were silent for a bit, while I searched my supposedly smart brain for something intelligent and meaningful to say. I wanted to say something about how it had felt like she hadn't wanted me to have it because I'd failed at all the things she'd always said were important. I wasn't beautiful. I'd never be chosen as a glamorous queen of anything. I wasn't her.

But it wasn't about any of that at all. All those reasons I'd invented, all that history . . . was fake.

The tiara, though? It wasn't. It was just an incomplete story.

"I mean . . . it's real. It's a real tiara that exists. It just tried to maim my roommate."

That wasn't the wisdom I'd wanted to share, but at least it got my mother to give a sniffly chuckle.

"What I mean is . . . Mami . . . you've given us ALL the real things. I wouldn't be here without you and Papi—"

"You are on a scholarship—"

"Which I couldn't have earned without you and Papi—"

"We could never even help you with your homework—"

"But you encouraged me to find people who could, even when I was so shy to ask them anything. You made me feel like . . . like it didn't mean that I was dumb if I needed help. You made me feel like someone who could do things. Because you did things. All the time. You're so strong."

Strong enough to realize that it was okay, in a low moment, to buy a stand-in prop just because you needed to remind yourself that you had lived through more than a hurried walk down a busy street with music blaring in a language you didn't always understand.

"But you . . . YOU are the someone who can do things," she said, bristling and waving an arm at the scenery like a game show model. "Look at this place! You are a full Americana."

"So are you, Mami," I said. And she was. There's more than one

America, and me going to school in a different type of one didn't invalidate the America I'd grown up in.

"Now I *know* you should take the tiara back with you," I said to her. "I don't want you to have to leave it behind again."

"Oh, Isabella," she said, and took me into her arms. "I know it sounds crazy, but now that you know the truth . . . I don't think I need it anymore. Because I have you, and Edgar, and Marta, and Brenda, and Javier, and your papi. Reina of the Carnaval was a nice thing, but . . . ultimately it was a great part of a story that ended so sadly for me, a story that I wanted to keep from you because I was glad that you hadn't ever had to experience it. I'd wanted you to have the tiara here so that you could remember that, once upon a time, maybe I'd been as beautiful and important as the other parents you are going to meet here. So you shouldn't forget where you came from, or be ashamed of us." She grimaced. "All about me, when it should have been all about you. And maybe that's always been one of my problems . . ."

She paused, as if waiting for me to argue. But . . . no way was I going to interrupt this. Not when I felt like I'd been waiting to hear this my whole life.

Mami put her hand on my cheek, and I leaned into her. "But . . . now that it's here . . . hearing what your roommate said. She didn't know the truth of it, but . . . neither did you. And that . . . that wasn't fair. I was afraid that you'd distance yourself from us . . . because that's what I'd done with my own history. But that's not you. You've always wanted to know everything about all of us, to belong to us. And I wasn't the best at telling you that. So I'm telling you now, and I want you to remember it. You didn't live with us in Colombia, but you are still as much as Colombiana as you are an Americana. You are a part of everything we are."

She pulled back then, holding me by the forearms. I could feel tears stinging in my eyes and see the same in hers.

After a second, she grinned. "Come to think of it, maybe I should buy tiaras for your brother and sister. Reminders of the family historia for them, too." She ruffled my hair, without the usual commentary on how it was too messy. "But you'll have the original. Well, the new original. So don't forget to pack it when you come back to us."

"I would never. I mean, it's a family heirloom," I reminded her in a teary voice. She might think I hadn't needed to hear all that. But I did. I did so much. And now every time I looked at the tiara, I'd remember.

We held hands as we walked back to my dorm room; the sun was setting into a pink cloud as the mosquitoes awoke and drove the hacky sackers away.

My family needed to get on the road soon, a fact that felt like it was rising up from my guts to choke me. I'd never lived away from them before. But at least, unlike Mami, I knew I'd be going back home. To them.

Tamara had discreetly left the room, and we were alone. Our good-byes at the door were rushed, teary, Brenda clutching at me now instead of at anything else. How big would she be the next time I went home?

Before they left, I made sure to put the tiara on each of their heads—yes, even Edgar and Papi—and I took pictures. Because regardless of what it had once meant to me, the story had changed. Maybe it *had* been a fake, an impostor. But it wasn't anymore. Maybe my luggage and Tamara's meant different things to each of us. Maybe they were different kinds of real.

I put my head down on my desk a long time after they left, still hearing their waterlogged voices promising to call. Or was that my own? Our voices overlapped, after all. Just like Jenga sticks.

I felt a cool hand on the back of my neck. "Hey, I just wanted to say that I'm really, really sorry about before. When I'm nervous, it's like my mouth doesn't connect to my brain. I promise, I'm not an asshole. There's a party tonight. Want to come with? We can, you know, start over. Or officially. Or whatever."

My first instinct would have been to say no. But then I looked at the tiara, winking at me in the fluorescent overhead light. It was time to start the next chapter of the tiara's story. Isa at College.

"Sure." I stood up and wiped my eyes. "Just let me get changed."

"You gonna wear the weapon?" she teased. And I liked that she did.

"Nah," I said. "But it's actually tied to a really cool story. In fact . . . I'll tell you all about it on the way . . ."

The First Kiss

BY NINA MORENO

Every year on my birthday I shuffled my tarot cards and asked the universe about my upcoming year. Because when the stars granted you the dark and gothic greatness of being born on Halloween, what better way to start a new year than with a little magic? I turned seventeen today, and by the light of three flickering candles and the Hello Kitty night-light in my closet I saw that the universe had given me the Lovers.

"Holy shit," my best friend, Dani, excitedly murmured.

I stared at the card in my hand. The Lovers may not have been such a huge revelation to someone else. But to me? The horniest virgin who'd never been kissed? It was a declaration of war. Well, not war. But it was definitely a sign that it was high time to get out of this closet and make something happen.

"I should do a love spell," I said, feeling breathless. "The energy for one is on fire right now."

"Do you know any love spells?"

My magic was a patchwork of rituals and practices I'd learned from books, online witches, and the enigmatic shopkeeper who worked at the botanica. I jumped to my feet, my mind spinning with ideas. Ten minutes later, we dashed back into my closet. I dropped the bottle I'd just stolen from the kitchen cabinet between us. Dani picked it up as I set up the rest of the ritual. "Why do you need sazón?"

"Because it has coriander, garlic, salt, and oregano." It was my mom's homemade version.

She sniffed it. "What kind of spell is this?"

I set a ceramic bowl between us and lit the tiny piece of coal inside, pleased by the way it crackled and sparked like a little black rock that held lightning. "Coriander for love. Oregano for joy. Garlic for protection. Salt for cleansing." Sazón had it all. But I had to be careful. My witchy interests had gotten me into trouble before. Back in the sixth grade I talked everyone at Maya Ramirez's birthday party into performing a séance. Her parents had stormed into her room when they realized a bunch of rambunctious preteens had suddenly gone quiet and were now huddling together, holding hands in the dark. Instead of a spinning bottle, they found me leading their impressionable daughter and friends to communicate with the dead. To avoid getting in trouble, the girls immediately blamed me. That was my last party invite. Because middle school was the worst, I'd been labeled the weirdo witch ever since.

I dug into the other herbs and added them to the smoking coal. "Rosemary to clear out all of our bad luck. Dried rose petals for new romance. Cinnamon for love. *Sensual* love." I waved the fragrant smoke toward both of us.

"Please don't say *sensual*," Dani complained.

I shook more cinnamon onto the coal just to be sure. "Now we write a name of someone we like on a bay leaf." I handed her one, then grabbed three for myself.

"Why do you get three?"

"I always do things in threes," I explained. "Do you have three crushes?"

We both knew she only had one. Amira Hassan, the captain of the girls' varsity basketball team. Dani had been in love with her ever since ninth grade. That was also the year when she and I became best friends after she found the only empty seat in biology next to the goth girl. She was a short, freckled lesbian who dressed in baggy flannel, while I was a tall, brown bisexual who liked fishnets and black dresses. We were an odd set to some of our classmates.

I carefully wrote the name *Dylan* on my first bay leaf. I *really* wanted him to be my first kiss. He had perfectly disheveled blond hair that fell in a swoop over his eye like a mysterious anime character. He borrowed my favorite pen in chemistry last year and then never gave it back. While I was upset about the loss of a pen that wrote so smoothly, it was a thrill to watch him use it every day. But a kiss would probably never happen, because he was leaving Florida for California soon because his stupid dad got some stupid job on the other side of the stupid country.

On the next leaf I wrote down Dylan's best friend, Luke. He once used me to cheat on his math test, but he had a swimmer's body and smelled a little like chlorine and weed. In a good way.

I stalled over my third leaf. While I liked doing things in threes, I didn't have another name. One popped into my head uninvited, but I immediately dismissed it and instead scribbled a heart and question mark next to it, leaving this one up to the universe. I tossed all three leaves onto the small burning coal just as my closet door flew open. Dani screamed, and I nearly knocked over the lit cauldron in my haste to hide it, sure that my parents had caught me.

But it was just my cousin, Cecilia. Better known as Cece, a ninth-grade nightmare.

"Are you doing drugs in here?" she asked, sounding excited as she smacked her gum. "Let me have some."

"Get. Out," I hissed at her, trying to hide the cauldron.

She did not get out. She instead made herself comfortable and dropped down to sit beside us in my now-cramped closet. "You never invite me to do witchy shit with you." She sniffed the air. "Are you sure this isn't drugs?"

"What are you doing here? Aren't you grounded right now?"

"Mom and Dad brought me along for your birthday cake and to drop off my heathen siblings. I can't believe it's your birthday and you're just going to walk them around the neighborhood again."

"I like taking them trick-or-treating." I *loved* Halloween. Unfortunately, by the time you get to high school, everyone's outgrown the holiday. So I didn't mind the chance to keep playing and pretending with my little cousins.

Cece popped her gum. "Well, thanks to being *sort of* grounded, I'm stuck here huffing cinnamon with you instead of being at an actual party tonight."

"We're not huffing it," Dani explained. "We're burning it for love."

Cece grinned. "How scandalous of you."

"*That* is why I don't invite you to do witchy shit with me." With a glower, because I couldn't help my curiosity, I asked, "What party?"

"A Halloween one." She shrugged like it wasn't a big deal to be invited. "Some guy's throwing it. Luis, I think."

It was ridiculous that my fifteen-year-old cousin knew more people than I did. "Luis? Which Luis?"

Her brows scrunched up in thought. "I don't know. The one on the swim team?"

"Swim team?" I gasped. "Do you mean *Luke* Sheridan?"

She snapped her finger. "Yeah, that's it. Luke. Supposed to be some big send-off for his friend who's moving tomorrow."

"Dylan's moving *tomorrow*?" I hadn't realized it would be so soon. I clutched my chest as a pained exhale escaped me.

Cece slid me a doubtful look. "Do you know them?"

Dani choked on a disbelieving laugh from my side. "Dylan stole Mabel's pencil once."

"Pen," I clarified.

"Outrageous." Cece smacked her gum and got to her feet. "Well, I'll leave y'all to your herbs and spices."

I stumbled out of my closet and dashed down the hall after her. But ran into two of my younger cousins, wrestling over a PlayStation controller in the narrow hallway. An elbow caught me in the stomach.

"*Move* it, Ricky." To Cece, I called, "I need to go to that party."

"You want to go to Luis's party?" she asked with a disinterested air as she deftly slipped past her fighting siblings.

"*Luke's!*" Dani and I both shrieked.

"Right, right." Cece stopped and turned back to consider me. "But you're not really the party type."

There was *lots* of stuff I wanted to do that no one considered me the type for. Like parties and dancing and kissing with some under-the-shirt action. Maybe school would have been different for me if I'd been bolder. If I hadn't been so earnest about that damned séance. If I was one of those badass witches who glowered and didn't care about anyone else's opinion. Unfortunately, I was a soft touch with a penchant for shyness. But I'd just tossed a ton of cinnamon into a magical fire, and the universe had given me the Lovers. On Dylan's last night in Florida. Anything could happen on someone's last night in their hometown.

"Because it's my birthday."

But Cece looked even more confused. "Why would you want to go to someone else's party on *your* birthday?"

"Because I'm seventeen now. A senior and whole ass woman. I am powerful. I am confident. I *am* sensual."

Dani raised a staying hand. "Okay, stop."

"Sensual, huh?"

My mouth snapped shut at the sound of that familiar teasing voice right behind me. Elías Santiago. Former bad boy next door and onetime friend. Well, sort of friend. He was a year older but had hung out with me during that lonely summer after my fifth-grade debacle. But Elías fell in with a rowdy older crowd soon after. His single mom was an overworked ER nurse, so my dad brought him into his auto shop to keep him out of trouble. It mostly worked.

I turned to face Elías.

"Nice dress," he said with a flash of a cocky smile. In honor of the special day, I was wearing a black thigh-length dress with long, lacy sleeves. It did the double duty of flattering my small chest and wide hips. It was an *amazing* dress. Elías was chewing on a toothpick while wearing the same dark blue uniform shirt and pants my dad wore for work. They looked way better on Elias, but that was neither here nor there.

"Hey, Eli," Cece said in a singsong voice.

"Cecilia." Elías nodded at her. "Heard you're on a first-name basis with Principal Vazquez these days."

"Yeah? Well, she says hello." Cece rolled her eyes. "You mechanics gossip worse than old ladies." Her dad—my uncle—was also a mechanic at Dad's shop. "If you're looking for chisme, the hot goss of the day is that our dear Mabel here wants to let loose and attend a wild party tonight."

His left eyebrow arched as his gaze returned to me. My stomach did a flip that I ignored. He had a scar that split that brow, thanks to racing a bike with no brakes. I'd been on the back pegs and had a matching scar on my knee from that fall. "Whose party?" he asked me. "Any ghosts I know going to be there?"

I slammed my fists onto my hips and cackled at the joke.

Elías shook like he'd just gotten the chills and murmured, "Witch." The way he said it didn't sound like a bad thing though.

Cece leaned closer to me. "Listen, if you want to go to Luis's party—"

"*Luke!*" I hissed.

"Whoever." Cece rolled her eyes.

"Whomever," Dani corrected.

Cece jabbed a finger in my chest. "If you want to go, you have to get your parents to convince mine to let us go."

"What?" Panic set in as I realized I had to ask my parents. To go to a party. At nighttime. "Why do they have to convince yours? You go out all the time!"

"Because I'm still grounded," she reminded me. "Sort of. But I'm also your ticket in, Miss Sensual Seventeen. So, work some magic."

I sat in front of my cake as my family, Dani, and Elías gathered around me at the kitchen table. I'd wanted a chance to talk to Mom first, but this could work, too. This was actually perfect. Candle magic. No one could argue with candle magic on your birthday.

Once they were done with the song, I leaned forward and blew out the candle in a quick whoosh of an exhale. Then—before I could lose my nerve—announced, "I can't take the kids trick-or-treating, because I want to go to a party."

Smiles turned into frowns. *"What?"* my aunt and uncle blurted. "But you always take the kids!" They were in some seriously slinky, shiny Miami party clothes and practically already had a foot out the door, ready for their Friday night with a guaranteed babysitter.

I turned to my parents. "There's a party tonight."

Dad, still in his work clothes, slid a confused look at Mom. "Did you know about this?"

"No," Mom said. A caterer with a rare Friday off, she looked fresh out of the shower and ready for a night in. "Where is this party?"

I needed to go for broke here. It's not that my parents were unreasonably strict, but unlike Cece, I'd kept to myself throughout high school, so I hadn't really asked to do anything beyond going to the movies with Dani. They'd been out of the parental permission game as long as me.

Dani piped up from my side. "Luke Sheridan's house."

"Luke Sheridan?" Dad's gruff voice got all high. "Who is that? I don't know any Luke." He looked at Mom. "Do you know a Luke?"

Mom nervously drummed her fingers on the table. "I don't."

"She can't just go to some random guy's house for a party. We don't even know his people. You always said we have to know the parents first. That was the rule . . . before."

Before I got stamped with the weird girl label by my fellow middle-school brethren. When I was still invited to birthday parties and sleepovers. When I had friends other than Dani. Asking to go out *was* out of character for me.

Dad glanced back at the living room before leaning closer. "But you always walk the kids around the neighborhood on Halloween."

Tío Emilio and Tía Isa—the middle-aged duo in the provocative party clothes—looked worried about getting stuck with their kids for the night.

Cece sat up, her eyes bright. "I know Lui—Luke! I know him! I can go with her. She won't be alone."

Tío Emilio frowned at Cece. "Nice try, but you're still grounded."

"I'll be with Mabel! She's a saint."

The kids' screams were reaching a higher register. Tía Isa side-eyed her daughter. "Why don't *you* walk your little brothers and sister?"

"Because it's Mabel's birthday, and she needs me, Mom. It's her first party, and *I* know Luke's people." Cece's eyes went wide with innocence. "And I did get that A on my last algebra test."

I mumbled, "It's not my *first* party."

Cece spared me an amused glance. "Your first without a Ouija board."

Mom was okay with candles and me tracking the moon, but anything to do with spirits and opening doors to the "other side"—as she said—worried her. She made a pained sound as Dad rubbed his brow like a headache was looming. It was not the time to remind them of my bruja antics.

The doorbell rang, echoing through the house, signaling the start of trick-or-treating. My cousins screamed about sunset. Tío Emilio looked grouchy in his tight, shimmery shirt and layers of gold chains. But after sliding a look between Dad and Mom, he smiled smugly. "Sure, Cecilia. You can go. But only if Mabel can."

It was the moment of truth. I held my breath as something passed between my parents. I was seventeen now. A senior. Powerful. But I was also the teenage daughter of immigrants, and I was asking to go to a stranger's party after dark.

Dad sucked his teeth and gave a short nod. Mom smiled at me. Tío Emilio mumbled a curse. My chest crackled with heat and anticipation like the lightning in the coal.

Until Dad added, "Elías will take you."

✧ ⛤ ✧

"You can just drop us off when we get there, okay?"

"Sure," Elías agreed as he shifted gears. "As soon as I check to make sure the parents are actually home like your dad asked."

"You are *so* old." Cece sat forward, between our seats. "Can we get some music? I'm dying back here."

"Put your seat belt back on," Elías told her. And then to me, "Which house is it?"

According to a text from a friend of a friend of Cece's, the brick house in front of me was Luke's. There was a big inflatable black cat with glowing green eyes, jack-o'-lanterns along the front porch, and an ominously flickering porch light. But there were no cars. No loud music or anything to tell me that an actual party was taking place here.

"That one." I did a quick check of my makeup in the mirror, then cleared my throat and strove for confidence when I added, "My parents have the address. You can just drop us off here."

Elías laughed as he parked the car and climbed out with us.

"You are not invited!" I told him as I rounded the car.

He pocketed his keys as he walked up the driveway. "Neither were you, Mabel."

Dani skipped up to my side. "Are we sure this is Luke's house?"

"No, we are not," I whispered back.

Elías went right to the door and knocked three times. "I'm not leaving you in some rich kid's neighborhood."

The door opened. Two boys stood there. They looked like middle schoolers. "Yeah?" one of them asked.

I stepped forward. "Hi. Is this Luke Sheridan's house?"

They nodded but offered nothing more.

"Is there a party here?" Elías asked, impatient.

One of the boys rolled his eyes. The other sighed impatiently like we were wasting his time. "Did you bring the stuff?"

"What stuff?" Cece asked.

Another eye roll. Another long-suffering sigh. "If you want to know where the party is, you have to pay the toll."

I noticed several bowls of candy inside the house on a table. Not fun-size candy either, but huge, king-size candy bars.

"This *is* a rich kid's neighborhood," Dani muttered.

The bouncer twins gave us a bored look. "You want to know where the party is? You come back with candy. The good stuff." They slammed the door in our faces.

"Well, hope you had fun." Elías pulled his keys back out of his pocket and marched down the driveway. "Because I'm taking you home now."

"No!" I hurried forward and grabbed his arm to stop him. "This party is even better now!"

"This isn't a party, Mabel. It's a scheme."

"Or a kidnapping plot," Dani offered.

Stars glittered in the clear night sky above us as streetlights created orbs of light along the sidewalk. Families and various groups of kids were still walking from house to house in search of sweets. The night had gone sideways, so heading home made sense. But I'd sent magic out into the universe tonight and things were *happening*. On Halloween. The night for weirdos like me.

I squeezed Elías's arm. "Listen, we'll run over to the corner store, get the mafioso middle schoolers their candy, and find out where the party is. You can stay with us and make sure we don't get kidnapped."

Elías was already shaking his head. "I told your dad I would take you to a party. Not all over town."

"And you're still taking me," I said. "It's just taking a few extra steps to get there."

When he stepped closer to me, I noticed he smelled like diesel and that orange soap mechanics used. And that I still had a death grip on his forearm. I quickly let it go and put my hands together in a pleading gesture. "I can't go home yet. Let's see what happens?"

"Famous last words," Dani said.

Elías blew out a sharp, frustrated breath.

"He's such a dad," Cece teased, still chewing that wad of gum as she nodded at Elías. "A hot dadd—"

"No," he said to her. My mouth fell open, but just as I was about to argue, he turned to me and said, "If there's *any* sign of something weird, we're out. Got it?"

"The quest continues!" Cece sang out as we raced back to the car.

✧ ⌧ ✧

I studied all of the options in the candy aisle at 7-Eleven. The store was mostly empty, the fluorescent lights outrageously bright after being out in the night. "Do you think it matters which one we get?"

"It definitely has to be chocolate," Dani said, then exchanged a candy bar for a bag of gummies. "Or maybe something sour?"

"Is it one for each kid? Or one from each of us? They didn't offer enough details."

"Because they're con artists." Elías stepped between us and grabbed a handful of candy bars. "Let's go get this over with." He led us to the register.

Cece stepped up next to us with a jumbo Slurpee. She set it on the counter with a smile. "Thanks, Dad."

I tried to elbow Elías aside. "You don't have to buy the candy. You're already driving us."

He didn't budge. "Consider it a birthday present. Just the candy," he said to the cashier. "Not the Slurpee."

The cashier was an older woman with bright red hair and a raspy voice. Her name tag said "Ethel (she/her)." She had a small radio beside her and was listening to an old, strange song about a guy named Butcher Pete. She scanned the candy and studied me for a moment. "You a witch?" she asked me in that smoker's voice.

My eyes widened. Awed, I asked her, "How did you know?"

"Been trying to figure out everyone's costumes tonight." She glanced at the others. "We got a mechanic and . . ." She studied Dani and guessed, "A lesbian from the nineties?"

Dani beamed with pleasure. "Perfect."

"And I am the wizard making sure my witchy cousin catches herself a prince." Cece slid her Slurpee forward to be scanned along with the candy.

"Teenagers have been in here all night buying up candy bars. Figured the point of Halloween was to get *free* candy."

I elbowed Dani excitedly. "Did they say anything about where they were going after this?"

She took Elías's cash and counted out his change. "Only that they had to be in costume." Ethel sucked her teeth as her gaze went over Cece and me. "The little lesbian and mechanic look all right, but you two might need something more." She pointed at the nearly empty shelf where only a few cheap-looking costumes in plastic sleeves were left.

"But I'm a witch," I told her. "You said so yourself."

"You're just trying to sell us what you couldn't get rid of," Elías argued.

Ethel ignored Elías. "Every witch needs a hat."

She was right. I absolutely needed a hat. Cece grabbed two packs. Elías muttered a curse, then told Ethel to ring them up.

We returned to Luke Sheridan's house with a big bag of candy. I now also had my purple witch hat, while Cece ended up with a blue cape and matching mask around her eyes. We were guessing superhero or wrestler. When the boys opened the door, Cece, Dani, and I happily sang out, "Trick or treat!"

"Here's the ransom," Elías grunted, then tossed over the bag of nine king-size candy bars. Three sets of three. We got another sigh and eye roll for our trouble, but we also got a flyer that had a map to the party.

"Don't touch any of the dead people's stuff." They slammed the door closed before any of us could react to the grim warning.

The directions led us off the main road and down a dirt one with only rusty signage. Elías turned off the radio. "Is this the right road?"

"Yes," I told him again. Then double-checked. "We took the third left, though, right?" I looked at Elías—but he was focused on the road—and then spun around in my seat for confirmation from Dani and Cece. *"Right?"*

"Left or right, Mabel?" Elías demanded.

"We took the left, right?" I shot back.

"Jesus, I hope so." Elías had a death grip on the steering wheel as we bounced along the bumpy road. "I wonder if we'll be murdered before this road tears up my suspension."

The night sank into darkness as the last of the streetlights gave way to oak trees that became denser, blocking out the moonlight we'd had to guide us. Left only with headlights and a map given to us by questionable middle schoolers, my burgeoning confidence started to whimper.

"You guys think there are animals out there?" Cece asked, leaning out the backseat window.

"Gators, I bet," Dani said from the other window. "Black bears, too."

The creepy murder swamp road finally opened into a clearing, revealing all the revelry lit by a full moon. It wasn't a prank. My relief was quickly drowned out by anxiety, though. Because it also was *not* a house party like I'd initially thought.

"Whoa. Creepy," Cece said.

The cars were parked in front of an old, weathered church bearing some serious abandoned-after-a-long-ago-hurricane vibes. You'd think that was the part I found chilling. You'd be wrong. I loved the Spanish moss spilling from ancient live oaks and cool night breeze sweeping across my skin like a whisper. The rusted wrought-iron fence around the graveyard dotted with tombstones and offerings. None of that had my heart racing. Instead it was speakers that rattled with bass-heavy songs. The headlights and lanterns illuminating all the dancing and debauchery. The couple making out against the angel monument.

I took a hesitant step back. And moved right into Elías. "Sorry, sorry."

"Gotta watch those combat boots." He chuckled near my ear. When I didn't say anything back, he cleared his throat. "This party looks right up your alley."

I laughed dryly. "Because of all the dead people?"

"Nah," he said, his voice low. "Because it's your vibe. Mysterious and fun."

My gaze jumped to his. He wore his usual smirk, but there was something soft in his dark brown eyes.

"Look, there's Luis." Cece grabbed my arm, yanking me away from Elías.

"Luke," Dani corrected her.

"Whatever, let's *go*."

I stumbled forward as my superhero wrestler cousin pulled my best friend and me along. I looked back at Elías and called out to him, "Are you coming?"

The party was too loud to catch what he said. Unexpected regret felt like ice in my chest as he shook his head and stayed near his car.

Cece pulled me forward into the fray. We boldly crossed the line between the living and dead as we marched past the wrought-iron fence and into the graveyard where we flew past ghosts, vampires, and fellow witches. I'd been so impatient to get here, but now it was all happening too quickly. We stopped suddenly right in front of Luke. He was wearing a toga with a crown. And holding a rake for some reason.

"Zeus?" I guessed aloud before I could even catch my breath.

The swim team captain pounded the ground with his rake. "Poseidon."

Sweat prickled my skin despite the cooler air. "This is a really . . . epic party." Epic? *Really, Mabel?* I tried not to physically cringe.

"Thanks," Luke said, sounding bored despite the atmosphere. He twirled the rake in his hand. "My parents own this land."

"Can anyone really own stolen land, though?"

"What?" he called over the music.

"You own the church and graveyard too?" I asked, louder.

He looked at me funny, then laughed like he had suddenly remembered something hilarious. "Don't try to raise the dead or anything."

I started to laugh, too. And then the joke landed like a punch. Or a bucket of pig's blood at prom. My nervous laughter was swallowed whole by an unblinking scowl.

"It was so weird how you took it *so* seriously."

"You're literally having a party in a graveyard."

He raised a red plastic cup. "This is actually fun and not, like . . . devil worshipping."

Dani stepped forward. "Hey, now."

"I wasn't worship—you know what? You were a waste of a wish."

His nose wrinkled. "A what?"

"A curse," Cece nearly bellowed. Then in a quieter, ominous tone, "She cursed you."

Luke blinked, then crushed the empty plastic cup in his hand. "Still weird," he muttered as he walked away.

Cece turned to me. "*That's* who you spent all that cinnamon on?"

"He was technically second. The first was—"

"*Dylan!*" Dani squeaked, then subtly gestured to our left, where Dylan was laughing with a mermaid. He wasn't wearing an obvious costume. Only a guitar on his back. Was he a musician? Had he written lyrics with the pen he'd stolen?

"So, *that* is the cinnamon prince," Cece murmured, then immediately yanked us forward just as the mermaid walked off. "Hi!" she greeted Dylan, who smiled in return. "Can you please tell my cousin that she looks amazing in this dress?" Cece's charm and ease with people were the real witchcraft.

He flipped his hair out of his eye and offered a heartbreaking smile. "Mabel, hey. Your dress does look amazing."

I touched my forehead, almost knocking my hat off. I managed a laugh. "Thanks."

"Keep an eye on her, will you?" Cece asked Dylan. "I'll be right back. Come on, Dani, show me where you sprinkled your cinnamon."

Dylan was still smiling as he watched them go. I was pretty sure I had a fever as I swayed toward him. This was it. I was out of the house. Making magic. I hadn't crumbled beneath Luke's joke. And I wasn't waiting for a sign from the universe. Only for the boy who just told me I looked amazing to look at me again.

I swallowed hard. "So, you're moving tomorrow?"

"Yup," he said. I couldn't tell if he was disappointed or not. His tone offered no clues. If anything, he sounded distracted.

I stood in place, waiting for some kind of spark. A breathless feeling of anticipation. Lightning.

Dylan turned those beautiful blue eyes on me. "Can I ask you a question?"

I nodded quickly, and he leaned closer. Boy soap and sweat. Definitely weed. His cheek touched mine.

It was happening.

I pressed my painted lips together and leaned up on my toes a little. I started to slowly turn my face toward his. No lightning yet, but soon.

My first kiss. Dylan's warm mouth went to my ear and whispered, "Is your cousin single?"

"Yes," I breathed, and then froze. "*Wait*, what?"

"Your cousin," he repeated. "She got a boyfriend?"

My head whipped back. "Cece?"

"I guess. The superhero girl."

"No, but—" I paused and said the next part very emphatically. "She's fifteen."

But that didn't seem to bother him as he waited for my answer. All my fluttery anticipation boiled into anger. "Aren't you moving tomorrow?"

He shrugged. "Still wanted to hook up tonight."

I gasped. The absolute nerve. "I can't believe I wasted both of my wishes."

"You did what?"

I jabbed my finger in his chest and sank venom into my voice. "Stay away from my cousin, or else."

His eyes widened. Maybe I'd thought myself a soft touch, but it turned out I could be plenty scary when it came to my family.

"Also, you owe me a pen, asshole." I marched away, pushing past the rowdy crowd. They were dancing and making out in a graveyard, yet I'd been a pariah for enjoying the macabre. What a joke. I found Cece and Dani. They were with Dani's crush, Amira, who was dressed up as Coraline.

"Did you get your kiss?" Cece asked me.

Just as I was about to bemoan my awful luck, Dani laughed at something Amira said, each of them looking utterly charmed by the other. Dani's freckled skin was blushing wildly. Our wizard/superhero/wrestler was a total matchmaker.

"The prince was a dud," I quietly admitted to Cece as Dani continued flirting.

Cece shrugged, her shoulder bumping into mine. "It happens."

Neither of my wishes had worked out, but the night was still beyond all expectation. We'd gone on an actual *quest* to get here. My best friend was giggling with her crush. Maybe I wouldn't get my first kiss tonight, but I could still dance on Halloween, beneath a full moon. I was seventeen and queen of the underworld tonight, wearing my best dress in a graveyard, beside an abandoned church. So strange, so perfectly me.

I turned to Cece. "Want to dance?"

"You weirdo," she said affectionately. "Of course I do!"

This time I pulled Cece into the madness, where we spun and stomped and laughed. And I finally stopped caring about sixth grade or whatever reputation everyone else had cobbled together for me.

After four songs and one plastic cup of mysteriously green punch worryingly labeled as swamp water, Cece's phone rang. "It's my dad, hold on." She plugged a finger in her ear and answered. "Hey, Dad . . . I'm at the party with Mabel, why?" Cece's eyes widened, and she silently mouthed a curse. "We're on our way."

"What happened?" I asked her when she clicked off.

"Your parents know that you're not at Luke's house."

"*What?*"

"And that you're actually in the middle of the woods."

This had now become my *last* party ever.

I raced back to the parking lot, shouting for Dani, who didn't need to be asked twice before hurrying behind us. Elías was leaning against his car, talking to some guy.

"We gotta go!" I shouted at him.

He straightened. "What's wrong?"

I jumped into the passenger seat. Breathless, I told him, "My parents think I lied to them about where I am tonight."

He checked his phone. "Shit, I have no reception out here." He cranked the car and smoothly zipped out of the parking spot. "What happened?"

"My parents track my phone's GPS, and unfortunately, my reception is impeccable," Cece admitted. "My bad, y'all." An unbothered Cece elbowed Dani and playfully asked, "Coraline, huh?"

Dani pressed her hands against her blushing cheeks. "I think I'm in love."

Cece laughed. "You witches and lesbians are intense."

I was possibly on my way to getting majorly grounded for not telling my parents that I'd changed locations, but the car windows were open and cool night air whooshed inside as we raced home. My hair flew around me as Elías glanced at me with those unexpectedly soft brown eyes. He slowed the car into first gear and looked pleased as he said, "You look like you had fun."

I thought of the whole entire night. The quest and dancing. And him. "I did."

Whatever happened, this had been the best night ever.

"And then the boys gave us a map to the actual party. But we didn't know it was going to be in a graveyard."

I was back at the kitchen table with my family sitting around us. The kids were passed out from sugar on the couch. Cece was beside me in the hot seat. Elías was dropping Dani off at her house.

"You followed some weird kid's map down a dirt road?" Tío Emilio asked us, aghast over our irresponsibility.

"Yeah, but we were outside," Cece said like a calm and collected defense lawyer.

"*So?*" her dad shot back. "How is that any better?"

"You always say that kids are too soft nowadays. Staring at our phones instead of playing outside like you did?" Cece wore an innocent expression, but there was a calculating gleam in her eyes. "Mom once told me you used to drive a lowered Honda Civic with an illegal sound system when you were in high school and drove out to field parties when your parents thought you were at your friend's house."

Her mom pressed her lips together. Dad smiled into his fist.

Tío Emilio shot to his feet. "You need to go home and clean your room." He rounded on Dad. "Don't act like you weren't the one who showed me those parties." He dropped a kiss on my head as he passed me. "Happy birthday, kid."

Cece winked at me on her way out.

Once they were gone, Dad laid into me. It was a ten-minute speech filled with dramatic reenactments of everything that could have happened to me. His hands flew in front of him as he told me about missing girls and all the terrible things that could happen to them. I meekly nodded, because he was right. But I also knew that terrible things happened to careful girls.

Mom stayed quiet beside me. Dad ended with a prayer and then squeezed my hand before he disappeared down the hall.

When he was gone, I looked at Mom. "How grounded am I?"

With her chin in hand, she studied me. "Did you have fun?"

The question was so unexpected, it took me a moment. I nodded quickly. But the longer she looked at me, the harder it became to hold back my outrageous smile.

"Good," she said, and squeezed my hand. "Just please tell me when your plans change next time, okay?"

My brows shot up. "Seriously? That's it?"

"Seriously," she said, and got to her feet with a tired grunt. She squeezed me against her. "We trust you, Mabel. We always have. You've always been so honest and yourself."

"Strange, you mean."

"No," she said. "True. Real. You just have to trust yourself." She cut me a slice of my birthday cake and set it down in front of me. "But please, do your mother a favor . . . no field parties."

"Or Honda Civics."

She laughed on her way to their room.

I was almost done with the cake when the sliding door opened. Elías ducked inside. I jumped forward and asked, "Dani get home okay?"

"Yeah," he said. "What about you? In trouble?"

"Surprisingly not." I ate the last bite and pulled the spoon out of my mouth after a breathy groan. Lemon cake was the best. I got up to take my plate to the sink, asking Elías, over my shoulder, "You want a piece?"

When he didn't say anything, I turned and found him almost right behind me. I backed up a step into the counter. His hands came to my shoulders.

"Did you get your kiss?" he asked, his voice low. Like a secret.

"No," I whispered.

His eyes fell to my mouth. "Can I kiss you?"

I nodded immediately, then whispered back, "Yes."

He ducked his head and pressed his mouth against mine. His hands slid from my shoulders, up my neck before slipping into my hair. They were rough from the work he did, but still so gentle and sure with me. My lips parted, and I breathed him in as he deepened the kiss. It tasted of lemon cake and surprise. His body held mine against the kitchen counter as my arms wrapped around his waist, wanting him closer.

When he suddenly broke the kiss and stepped back, my hands flew out across the counter to catch me as my knees gave a little, my feet feeling like they were on roller skates. I knew I looked shaken. But so did he. There was a frantic look in his eyes just before he closed the space and kissed me again, quick and hard. He dropped his forehead against mine.

"You're not weird, Mabel," he whispered against my heated skin. "You're perfectly you."

I looked up and immediately wanted to kiss him again. "Mysterious and cool." Ruby red marked his mouth. I'd done that. Power sang through me. "You have lipstick on you."

His eyes stayed on mine as he slid his thumb across his lip and took a step back. "Happy birthday."

"Thank you for getting me there and back safely."

"Always," he said. He tapped his eyebrow scar and left.

My smile felt like a spark that kicked off a storm of lightning in my chest. I let out a happy, muffled shriek, and it took me another minute to gather myself. As I straightened away from the counter, my hand knocked over a jar. It was the sazón seasoning.

Like I said. Powerful stuff.

The First Time We Buried a Body

BY TESS SHARPE

I didn't really plan on killing Jayden Thomas in the Blackberry Diner parking lot. If I had planned on it, I would've chosen a better locale. But he was the one who chose to get all rapey by the dumpsters, so here we are.

Here being by the dumpsters, Monday's chicken and dumplings ripe in the air, cast-iron skillet clattering to the ground . . . and a very dead Jayden at my feet.

We being me and Evie Taylor. Jayden's girlfriend—well, ex-girlfriend now. Jayden is not included in our little *we* because, again: cast-iron skillet to the head. Twice.

My mother told me, *You ever hit a man, you better make sure he stays down. They're meaner getting up.*

The bottom of Evie's shirt is ripped. I don't know why I'm so focused on that instead of Jayden's dead body, but I did kind of crack his skull open, and it's not pretty, and looking at Evie is better.

Is she okay? I need her to be okay.

"Meredith." It's the first thing she's said. I haven't uttered a word.

I just came out here to try to scrape off the burnt bits on the skillet;

then I saw him and she was yelling *no* and he wasn't stopping and I just—

I didn't even think.

I clocked him, and when he didn't drop, I hit him a second time and then he went down like a sack of flour.

I really put my arm into it. All those years of softball have paid off.

"*Meredith.*"

I'm staring at Jayden instead of Evie now. Her voice jerks me out of it.

"That's me."

"Look at me," Evie orders.

"I can do that."

Her hands are on my arms before I actually do it. Her eyes and mine. Have we ever actually stared this long at each other before? I know we haven't.

I'd remember.

"You killed him," she squeaks out, like she has to whisper it.

"I did," I say. I look down again. Shit. "I really, really did."

Her fingers shake, wrapped around my wrists.

"Are you okay?" I ask her.

There is a lot of blood on the ground. I shouldn't think about that. But I kind of *need* to think about it.

Focus, Mer.

Evie's eyes are huge in the flicker of the Blackberry's neon sign. Purple and green washes over her in blinks, a metronome of light.

"Evie, are you okay?"

"You killed him," she says again. "He—he wouldn't *stop*." Her breath quickens at the memory. My hands grip hers back tight.

"It's okay," I tell her. "He can't hurt you anymore."

The wonder that passes over her face makes me feel sick. And then, when she repeats my words—"He can't hurt me anymore"—like she's just realizing it, like she didn't think there'd ever be a day . . .

"Evie, what's he been doing to you?" Maybe I shouldn't ask, but I have to. Has he been hitting her? If this isn't the first time he forced himself—

My stomach swoops like I've fallen off a cliff. A sickening lurch of a free fall. I suck in air through my nose, trying to calm down.

Evie's staring down at him, almost curiously. "It doesn't matter anymore," she says, but I think it really, really does, if he was abusing her. "We need . . . we need to call the sheriff."

She doesn't say it like it's a fact. She says it like a question.

She says it like she wants me to disagree with her.

My mind shuffles through the facts like music on a playlist. I was defending Evie. But there are no cameras in the parking lot. No proof (no evidence). Jayden's family has money. Connections. And I live in a trailer in the woods with my mom, who's been in and out of NA since I was a toddler. She's clean now. Five whole years. She's put her life together, but this town . . .

It never forgets.

If it's me and Evie against Jayden's family . . . we're fucked. Evie's dad makes good money—he's a pharmacist. But he's got no power. Jayden's dad's on town council. I'm pretty sure one of his uncles is a deputy. And I *know* his grandpa is one of the county's oldest judges. He's the one who put my mom in jail for three years when I was six and gave her boyfriend, Vick, a more lenient sentence for turning on her. And Vick was the one with the meth lab in his spare bedroom.

This town is too small for a girl to get justice in the courts. Hell, let's be real: This *world* is too small and run by dudes to get justice most of the time.

"We need to call the sheriff. Right?" Evie asks. She's still shaking in my grip.

"You didn't do anything," I insist. "I did it. I hit him. I'll tell them he was—"

"Meredith." It's just my name but oh, shit, she's right. She's completely right before she even says it.

"He was my boyfriend. I said yes other times."

"Just because you said yes before doesn't give him the right—"

"I know," she interrupts me. Her pupils are blown wide. Terror does that to you. "But they don't ever believe the girl . . . even when the guy's alive after."

Anger flares. Hot and heavy, just like when I heard her say *no* and he didn't even pause as she pushed at him . . . that absolute *asshole*. I'm so glad he's dead.

"Okay," I say, even though I'm not even sure what I'm agreeing to. "What . . . what do you want to do?"

"I dunno," she blurts out. "If they don't believe us . . ."

We're screwed.

"We could just . . . leave him?" But before I can answer, she shakes her head. "No. No, that wouldn't work. They'd question you. You work here. Um." She rubs at her arms like she's cold, shuffling her feet, trying to think it through.

"We could . . . we could get rid of him?" Her voice lilts up at the end, almost a question, but mostly just plain panic.

I swallow. All around us is forest. Salt Creek is a gold rush town turned lumber town turned nothing town. A little slice of dusty, dated civilization carved out of the red dirt cliffs and pine tree sprawl.

Jayden could go missing. They'd look for him. But people go missing out here all the time. There are hundreds of acres of woods. If he was never found . . .

This much forest, all you'd need to do was pick the right spot, dig a deep enough hole, and make sure to clean up the crime scene. I've watched enough Law & Order to know how to *not* get caught.

"Okay," I say again. I nod to follow it through. Grit my teeth. This is going to get messy. I've field-dressed deer before. I know blood trails and how it pools.

"We need to wrap his head. If we don't—" I take a deep breath. "If we don't, the blood trail to the car . . ." She nods shakily. And that's it. We're doing this.

We're getting rid of him and saving ourselves.

"Do you have your car?" I ask. "Because I've got my truck, and—"

"I have my car."

"Okay." I look back to the diner. I just finished closing up, but I haven't turned off the lights. "I'll go get the garbage bags. You back up the car to the dumpsters."

"What are we gonna do with him?"

"Bury him. Somewhere no one can find him. We'll figure out where." She nods.

My feet are proving hard to move. My body buzzes like I've touched an electric fence. But I force myself forward, toward the diner, away from the mess I've made.

"Meredith?"

I turn back to her. The keys clutched in her fist shine silver against her pale skin.

"Why did you save me? We barely ever talk at school."

There's two answers to this.

Neither of them are easy.

The first being: *I've watched you all my life, but hopefully not in a creepy way. But you've always been there, and you always smile at me, and it's never those pity smiles I get from other people. And I think I've never had anything steady, but when you smile, I feel something like steady.*

"You needed help," I say.

The second answer is a lot less sweet.

When I was the girl saying *no*, I was too little to lift a skillet, let alone swing it.

I'm not too little anymore.

✧ ⊠ ✧

I walk into the diner, and I don't make a beeline for the storage room where the garbage bags are. No, I walk right to the kitchen, fling open the walk-in, step inside, and as soon as the door closes, I grab a package of spinach and scream into it. Spinach is not the most sound-muffling of vegetables, but it's better than using the chub of ground beef.

I need to breathe. I need to think.

I need to get rid of Jayden's body. Because I killed him.

I really didn't mean to. Thus the screaming and the vomiting that's imminent if I don't get my act together and *breathe*.

Setting the spinach back on the shelf, I swallow the spit in my mouth and breathe out, shaky and slow. Once. Twice. *Think*, Mer.

I stare at the walk-in door. My eyes snag on the laminated prep to-do list. The neat row of check marks on the ingredients and dishes.

I could make a list. A how-to-get-rid-of-Jayden list. Take it step by step. Focus.

1. *Get the garbage bags.*

I shut the lights off as I go. The light on my phone is all that's left by the time I get to the supply closet.

One good thing about working in a diner? The garbage bags are huge. I take eight of them, just to be sure. I toss a box of gloves and a roll of duct tape in my bag, and I'm ready to go.

The last thing I do before locking up is switch off the sign. I tug the door handle to make sure it's secure before I turn to the parking lot. Evie's brake lights shine red across the asphalt.

2. *Wrap him up.*

Evie sits in her car, door open, staring at her phone, but it's not on. In the dim light, I can see the bruises on her wrist. She'll need to wear long sleeves. It'll be suspicious otherwise when they start looking for him.

We have to make sure they never find him.

"Evie, are you okay?"

She nods, jerky. "My dad texted me to remind me my curfew's at midnight," she says, the words fast and jumbled. Is she panicking? She lets out a laugh. Oh yeah, she's definitely panicking. I can't blame her. She didn't get to scream into the spinach like I did. "How is real life going on right now?"

I crouch down next to the car. "Evie, we can go to the police. It was justified—"

"It'll never be fair. Not with Jayden's grandpa knowing every judge in Northern California. Are you seventeen?"

"I turned eighteen last month."

She shakes her head again. She just keeps shaking it like she's fallen into a loop. "They'll try you as an adult. Your mom—Meredith, your mom makes *soap*."

She doesn't say what she's probably thinking.

Meredith, your mom's a recovered addict.

Meredith, you live in a trailer on a plot of land.

Meredith, you're white trash.

Meredith, you couldn't even afford a bad lawyer, let alone a good one.

She wouldn't be wrong if she said any of that, but she's much too nice to ever do it.

"They will not believe us," Evie says. "You know it."

She pushes herself out of the car, rising to her feet. Her chin tilts up and trembles. "You saved me. Now we save each other."

I've survived enough to know a lifeline when I see it. So I grab on to her—metaphorically—and hold on.

"Then tie up your hair and take these gloves," I say. "We need to check his pockets. Where's his phone?"

"It's at home," Evie says.

"Seriously?"

"He was doing a tech cleanse. Which actually means he just kept stealing my phone to use it."

"Well, that's good for us, I guess." I snap on my gloves. "Ready?"

She nods.

It's disgusting. I'm not going to sugarcoat it. There are bits of I don't even know what on the ground I scrape up with the paper towels before we wrap his head in three trash bags just to be safe. But it turns out, when you have enough fifty-gallon trash bags and duct tape, you can do a lot in the body disposal scheme of things. Who knew.

I wipe the outside of the dumpster down with the bleach spray, because I've seen enough TV to know about blood splatter, and it's dark out here.

3. Jayden → Trunk.

When Evie opens the trunk, we both kind of stare into it. It's empty, which is good. Convenient. Since it's about to be kind of full.

"Last chance to back out."

Evie's expression hardens. "You're not going to go to jail for this. I'll get his shoulders. You get his feet."

And that's exactly what we do. Between unloading freight at the diner and softball, I'm strong. Evie's smaller than me, but she's a swimmer, so she holds her own as we hoist him into the trunk. He barely fits, but we manage to get it closed.

"Now what?" she pants.

There's a stain where Jayden's head was, so I dump the rest of the bottle of bleach on it. "Help me," I say, walking over to one side of the dumpster. She goes over to the other side and we push the stinking metal forward, covering up the stain. I grab the skillet from beneath the dumpster and wrap it in the final trash bag, along with our gloves. "I'll come back and clean before morning shift."

"Let's go," Evie says.

She gets in the car, and I hop in the other side, tucking the skillet under my seat. Getting out of the parking lot and leaving behind the cavorting statues of bears and their giant blackberries is over in a blink, and we're halfway down the street before I even realize we're moving.

4. Deal with Evie's curfew.

"We need to get you home," I say, staring at the clock on the dash. It's eleven. "Your curfew."

"I can't bring you *and* him home with me," Evie says. Her fingers drum on the steering wheel as she makes a right, heading away from the main drag of town toward the highway instead. "My dad will notice the smell by morning."

The highway leads to the woods. Away from her dad's house on Spruce Street, where the people who get paid in salaries instead of by the hour live.

"Evie . . . ," I warn as she slows to a stop in front of the on-ramp to the Five. "You need to turn around and go home. I'll deal with it and then bring your car back. Tell your dad my truck broke down and you loaned me yours—"

"You may be all tall and strong, but you can't drag a corpse through the woods and then dig a properly deep hole on your own. I am not leaving you. He was about to—" She stops, losing the rest of the words in a shudder. "I am *not* leaving you," she says again. "What about your place?"

"What about it?"

"Is it just your mom there?"

"My mom's in Scott Valley with my grandma right now. There's a craft fair this weekend."

"So there's no one at the trailer?"

I shake my head.

Evie flips on the turn signal and takes the on-ramp.

"Get out my phone. Text my dad: *'Spending the night at Meredith's. She needs my help with Spanish.'*"

Evie merges behind a semi hauling lumber. "You've got to use whole sentences and proper punctuation," she adds quickly. "It took me forever to get him to accept texting at all, and god forbid if I use *u* instead of *you*."

"Got it." I tap out the text just as she said and press send. "Is he going to buy it?"

"He can never keep track of my friends' names. He still calls Hannah Anna, and we've been best friends since kindergarten."

Her fingers keep tapping against the steering wheel. She's driving just under the sixty-five speed limit as we head north. Where are we going to go?

"We can't bury him at my place," I say.

"Of course not," Evie replies. "We need to take him somewhere hard to reach. Do you have tools at your place?"

I nod.

"It's up near Pollard Flat, right?"

"How do you—"

"We've been at the same school since the second grade. Just because we don't hang out with the same people at school doesn't mean I haven't noticed you, Mer," she says. "Sometimes I look for you, and you're always *just* looking away. Like you don't want to get caught."

My cheeks burn. "I—" I can't gaslight her and deny it. Not right now. Not when I've literally *killed* a guy for her. That kind of says it all, doesn't it?

"Am I right?"

"What?" I'm staring at her now.

"I should take the Pollard Flat exit?"

"Yes. Right at the stop sign."

My phone buzzes against my leg. I pull it out and swear when I see the text from Harris: *where r u*

"Shit."

"What?" Evie asks.

"I totally forgot. Harris is having a party. I was supposed to go after work. I'll just tell him I'm too tired or something."

Her brows draw together as we pass a sign that says "Pollard Flat Exit, 10 miles."

"What are you thinking?" I ask her.

"Jayden probably told some of his friends that he was hanging out with me. That way if they needed him, they'd call my phone."

"Because of his tech cleanse."

She nods. Her fingers tap out a nervous beat against the steering wheel. "When they realize he's missing, I'm the first person they're going to come to."

"You're the last person who saw him. We need to come up with a story," I say.

5. Establish an alibi.

"We can go to the party, and if your friends wonder why we came together," Evie says slowly, "you can say I got dumped and you felt sorry for me, so you dragged me along to the party."

"We'll tell anyone who asks that he broke up with you in the diner parking lot," I say. "I was out there on my break around ten and saw him walk away. I offered to take you to Harris's party, so you waited until I was off. Simple. Easy. We don't deviate from it. If we both say he walked away, then they can't pin it on us."

"What if the police check cameras—"

"There aren't any cameras on that street."

Her dark brows scrunch up. "How are you so sure?"

I have to stop myself from laughing. "You're such a townie sometimes. The Blackberry is owned by criminals."

"What? It is not."

I don't say anything. Because it totally is.

Her mouth twists, eyes narrowing. "Okay, we're going to talk about how you're working for a crime front that makes delicious jam later. But that means we'll be fine if we stick to the story. I think?"

"As long as we put him somewhere no one's going to find and tell the same story, we'll be fine."

"Okay. What do I say?"

"About what?"

"The breakup. I'm gonna get asked why we broke up."

She has a point. "Well, he's a year older. Maybe he broke up with you because he wanted to be single in college?"

"Okay. Okay. He wanted to be single. Yes. That works."

"Can you act heartbroken?" I ask.

"I feel like I'm about to have a nervous breakdown, so I'm pretty sure if I just pinch myself a little, I'll start crying. That's good enough, I think."

"Evie . . ." I look over at her worriedly. "I can do this on my own."

She shakes her head. "We've covered this: You save me. I save you. We save each other."

"That is very *Titanic* of you."

"That was about *jumping*, not saving. Plus, both of them didn't survive that movie."

"But we're going to survive ours? You're gonna let me on the wooden door or plank or whatever it was Rose was floating on at the end?"

She lets out a breath that's almost a laugh, and then her face crumples like she just realized she could still laugh.

There's a body in the trunk.

  6. Get to Harris's party.

"Where's Harris's house?" she asks.

"Just a few more miles."

✧ ⊠ ✧

I'm not going to say I'm in love with Evie Taylor.

It's just that she's kind of hard to get out of your mind once she's in it. And she's been on my mind for a while.

Sometimes it feels like forever.

Everyone loves Evie, you know? She never treats anyone badly. She spent all of junior high feeding the feral cats behind our school. She even tamed some of them and got them homes. That's the kind of patient she is. The kind of person who can love feral cats into learning trust.

She doesn't deserve any of this.

We weave along the single-lane road in the dark, shadows of pine trees splashing against asphalt as the headlights hit them. We are mountain girls, both of us, but like I said: There's a difference between town and out here.

"It's the next turn," I tell her as we pass the gully, the car dipping down. If I let my hand trail out the window, the air will be cooler as we near the creek. Nature's air conditioner.

She pulls onto the gravel road when I point. As the beat-up mobile home comes into view, I can hear the music from here, and the Christmas lights strung up outside shine bright in the special kind of dark that falls in the forest. People mill on the deck Harris and his brother built around the house, drinking and dancing.

Evie parks behind the crowd of cars and trucks, but she doesn't turn off the ignition.

Someone's gonna pull up behind us soon and notice we're just sitting here. No one can come near this car.

Her fingers drum against the steering wheel.

"I'm not gonna let anything happen to you, Evie," I promise.

"Ditto," she says.

"Now we're getting into *Ghost* territory," I tell her, and the trembling smile she gives me hits me like a fist to the boob. A memorable kind of pain, if you ask me.

"If I knew you liked all these old movies, I would've asked you to hang out a long time ago," she says, and then without another word, she gets out of the car, and I've got no choice but to follow.

"No one's gonna know, right?" she asks as we crunch up the gravel road.

"That he's in the trunk? No."

"He's not going to start smelling or—"

"I dunno—it's my first time killing someone, Evie," I hiss as we get closer and closer to the crowd on the deck.

"You say that like there's going to be another time!"

"Well, I don't know! I didn't expect this night to start like it did. Now, keep your voice down: Remember to act normal."

"Right. You're right. Oh my god," she mutters to herself as Harris catches sight of us. Harris is . . . *Harris*. 530 tatted on the back of his neck and a pot leaf on his calf—too big to escape notice—both the tattoos and Harris.

He smiles and waves when he sees me, and then his face kind of freezes in surprise when he spots Evie next to me.

"Hi," he says, walking toward us, arms wide, a beer in each hand. He hugs me, brushing a kiss on my cheek. "What the hell are you doing with Evie Taylor?" he mutters in my ear.

"Long story. Tell you later. Evie needs a beer."

Harris shoots me a curious look as he hands the beer to Evie. She takes it and downs it—so fast that it has Harris laughing, impressed.

"Lou brought marshmallows, and Jackie keeps burning them," Harris informs us as we walk toward the house. The group around the firepit is—sure enough—waving around burnt marshmallows on sticks and fighting drunkenly with them, wielding the sticks like swords.

"You're gonna set the forest on fire," I tell Harris.

"I've got an extinguisher," he says, gesturing for us to sit down on one of the benches. "You need a beer, Mer?"

"I'm good. I'm gonna drive."

"You are *not* driving my car," Evie says, cheeks flushed from chugging that entire beer in thirty seconds. Has she even eaten today? Was that on an empty stomach? The last thing I need is to try to get rid of a dead body with a drunk Evie.

But I also kind of can't deny her any way she wants to numb herself, because I'm not the victim here.

I'm the murderer.

Is it murder when it's kind of an accident and self-defense? I don't even know. Maybe not legally.

Depends on what judge you get marched in front of, I guess.

". . . You okay?"

I snap out of my thoughts. Shit. Harris is looking at me weird.

"I'm fine," I tell him. "Long day at work."

Next to me, Evie's practically vibrating. Harris keeps stealing side glances at her, confusion spreading over his face.

Evie Taylor does not come to parties like this. Evie is class treasurer. She always did the extra credit in math class even when she didn't need it. She goes to youth group and actually enjoys it, which is a whole thing I don't understand.

"Can I use your bathroom?" Evie asks Harris as the music switches from thumping to slow.

"Yeah, just go straight in; it's the door to the left."

"Be right back," Evie says.

I turn around to watch her leave, worried she's going to stumble, but she's steady. She disappears into the mobile home, and only then do I breathe a little.

When I turn back, Harris is staring at me.

"What the fuck, dude?" he asks.

"I hate it when you call me dude," I remind him.

"Okay, what the fuck, Mer?"

"I told you: It was a long day."

"Elaborate," he says, pulling out a pipe and a baggie. "You want?"

"I'm driving, remember?" I tuck my hair behind my ears. "So I'm on break at work, smoking outside, and I look over and Jayden Thomas is dumping Evie in the parking lot. She's crying, and he's being all hangdog *I need to do this for myself* and *college is coming up* before he walks off like he's Bender at the end of *The Breakfast Club*."

"He has nowhere near the attitude for that," Harris says. "I thought for sure she'd be the one to dump him. Once she found out about all the other girls."

My stomach sinks. Shit. I forgot what a cheater Jayden was.

Did Jayden hurt other girls? Did I just free North County of a serial rapist? Do you get a medal from the mayor for that? Maybe a key to the city?

Maybe in a just world.

It's never only once with guys like that. Especially when they're so damn bold they're trying to force themselves on someone in a parking lot.

They never think there are consequences.

But this time, there were.

"Just be nice to her," I say, glancing back over my shoulder. How long has it been? "She looked so pitiful, I couldn't just leave her there."

"Since when do you do good deeds?"

"You don't leave another girl crying in a parking lot. It's a rule. You have brothers—you wouldn't get it."

"This has nothing to do with the fact that you always look like you've been hit by a bus when she walks by?"

"Oh, shut up." I shove him with my shoulder, and he laughs.

"Now you can make your move."

"You don't need to take another hit off that." I nod to the pipe. "You're already high enough." I get up. She's been gone too long. "I'm gonna go check on her."

"Make a mooooove," he catcalls behind me, and I flip him off.

I push through the crowd and into the house. But Evie's not freaking out in the bathroom like I expected—she's standing in the living room next to the couch that has a spring that hits you wrong if you put any weight on it. She's not alone. A tall blond boy looms over her, and she's practically shrinking in his shadow.

What is this—Intimidate Evie Day? Screw it. Where's a skillet when a girl needs one?

Tad—yes, that's his name—looks up at the rush of sound when I open the door. I should've remembered: Jayden's best friend buys weed from Harris and his brother. Of course he's around.

"Did you bring her here?" he demands.

"Excuse me?" I shut the door with enough force to make the walls shake a little.

"She doesn't belong here," Tad says. "Jayden will freak—"

Jayden already had his freak-out. Now he's not gonna be doing much of anything.

"Evie," I say, holding out my hand.

She *rushes* toward me, grabbing my hand like it's a lifeline. I squeeze it, trying to be reassuring . . . trying to ignore the flip of my stomach.

"I told you, Jayden dumped me," she says to Tad. "I can go wherever I want, with anyone I want."

"You're not implying she can't, are you, Tad?" I ask him. "Because that would be weird and controlling."

"I—" His mouth snaps shut, his expression scrunching like thinking hurts.

"Come on," I say, grabbing the door handle. I don't even have to tug lightly; she just comes with me.

I am so done with this day . . . and there's still so much to do.

"Hey, I'm talking to you!" Tad calls, but we just keep walking, pushing through the crowd until we're in the middle of the crush.

"He kept asking me where Jayden was," Evie says. "I don't know if he believed me—"

"Breathe," I tell her, lifting her hand to drape it around the back of my neck. Tad's craning to watch us, his expression stormy like he's the Evie Police. "Just move."

"Move?" Her hand tightens around my neck, and it's like she's just realized what everyone's doing around us. "Oh," she says, stepping closer, her other hand around my neck.

"I'm gonna put my hands on your shoulders, okay?"

She nods, and I do, and just like that, we're dancing.

I wish I could say everything fades away and it is just her and me, but when you've got a dead body to get rid of, it's just *there*. Like the biggest mood killer in the world.

"We've gotta get out of here," Evie says.

Tad's eyeing us from the edge of the crowd, like he's waiting for a moment to cut in. I will stomp his foot if he does. Hard.

"Lean against me. Pretend you're crying," I say.

She blinks up at me, her eyebrows scrunching up. Her fingers trace my neck, and I feel it all the way to my goddamn toes.

Evie sniffs, sinking into my shoulder and burying her face. The brush of her eyelashes against my collarbone is whispery-wet, like she *is* on the edge of tears. I don't blame her: I've been about five seconds away from sobbing or screaming ever since the pan made contact with Jayden's head.

"It's okay, Evie," I say, too loud, so it carries over the music.

She wails a little, and I pat her on the back.

"It was a terrible idea to go out," she sobs, and we're really drawing attention now.

"I know. Come on."

I tug her off the deck, still pressed against my side, face hidden in my neck. We walk right past Tad, who's glaring.

"I'm gonna have her crash at my place," I tell Harris as we pass him on the bench. "I'll text you tomorrow."

"You want some bud for her?" he asks, but I shake my head, even though it'd probably be way easier to do this stoned.

"Hurry, hurry," I say under my breath as we walk away from the party, eyes on us.

"I think it's working," Evie whispers.

I glance over my shoulder, and relief plops inside me like a water balloon breaking. Tad's not following us.

"Oh, I was not kidding about driving," I say when she reaches for the driver's seat. "Give me your keys."

"Mer, I only drank one—"

"My grandma's paralyzed from the waist down because of a drunk driver. I don't care who's in the trunk, Evie—I will *not* get in this car with you."

Her eyes go huge because, yeah, my voice got way too intense there.

"Crap—okay, sorry," she says. "I didn't know."

"Well, now you do." I hate talking about it.

She tosses me the keys, and I catch them.

"Let's go," she says.

We're completely silent on the drive to my house. Then I pull up into the driveway—we don't have gravel like Harris, just dirt that turns to mud in the winter and a fire-starter of dry grass in the summer.

   7. Get shovels and a tarp.

"Everything's in the shed," I say as I park next to the prefab shed Mom installed on cinder blocks across from the trailer.

"Where are we going to dig?" she asks. "If we google—"

"We're not googling. We're going to leave our phones in the trailer. We'll tell anyone who asks we watched *Titanic* and *Ghost* and then we went to bed. You'll drop me off for my shift in the morning, and we'll be fine. It'll be fine."

I unbuckle my seat, open the car door, and throw up all over. It's awful, because vomiting is always awful. But it's extra awful because Evie gets out of the car and rushes to help, and you don't want the girl you're in like/love/whatever with seeing you spew.

I want to scream. But there's no spinach around to muffle it, so I focus on what I can control. I need to get the shovels.

"We need to hurry," I say when we get inside the shed. "Evie?"

She's across the shed, next to Mom's shelf of soapmaking supplies, frowning at a bucket on the bottom shelf.

"What's wrong?"

"Nothing," she says. "Your mom has lye."

"Yeah, she makes soap," I remind her gently.

Evie bends down and grabs the bucket of lye.

My eyes widen, and the shed spins for a second. "Evie, you don't want to . . . like . . . dissolve him?"

"I think we need more stuff than just lye for that. But if we bury him with a bunch of lye scattered over him, it'll destroy him a lot faster."

"And it'll destroy any evidence."

Evie nods.

"Grab the lye."

    8. *Use the lye.*

Evie packs up the car while I go inside our trailer. I need to think ahead. If we're going to dig, we're going to get dirty. That means we'll need to get rid of our clothes.

I grab two shirts and two pairs of shorts out of the little hanging bag I keep my clothes in. Evie will be swimming in them, but it's better than nothing.

For a second, I just stand there in the trailer, wondering.

Not *how* or *why*.

But *where*. Where do we go? Where do we put him?

Where will he not be found?

There are hundreds of acres of forest around us. He might never be found if we bury him a few miles into the forest anywhere around here.

But things happen. Hikers go off trail. Forest fires put firefighters in places most don't go. People buy land and build their dream houses.

We need somewhere that doesn't get touched.

It hits me all at once, so fast that I sag against the wall in relief.

I know exactly where to go.

9. *Bury Jayden in the woods.*

"Where we are we going?" Evie asks again as I pull off the highway, thirty miles north of my house. Another fifty miles, and we'd be out of the mountains and in the stretch of ranchland that separates the last bit of California from Oregon.

"There's this old silver mine," I explain. "My grandpa brought me up there once when I was little. The land can't be disturbed. Some sort of historical thing. No one's going to find him up there."

When I pull off the highway and onto the main road, then onto a fork that winds down, down, down the mountain, the world gets darker and cooler. Like we're descending into the belly of the beast.

It's so deep in the forest that the stars are brilliant in the sky as we get out and begin to walk, our headlamps bobbing.

It doesn't take long to find a spot. But it takes hours to dig it deep enough. Sweaty, backbreaking work that's possible only because what the hell else are we going to do? Every time I want to stop, every time I want to scream, I think, *He can't win* . . . and I push the shovel even deeper.

Getting him to the hole is harder than I thought. He's gotten heavier—stiffer, I guess. But we do it. We layer the lye over him, and then the dirt, and then pine needles and leaves and branches, until it looks like just another spot of forest floor.

Just like that, he's gone.

And just as fast, so are we.

✦ ⧓ ✦

We burn our clothes and wash in the creek. It takes a long time to scrub everything from my skin, but I manage. I shiver in my bra and underwear, keeping my back to Evie to give her privacy. But when I turn to grab my spare set of clothes, I catch a glimpse of her standing waist-deep in the water, and before I look away just as fast, I see the bruises on her rib cage. The kind that are old enough to have turned green.

My fingers clench, and the sick rush of anger is almost blotted out by the relief.

He'll never hurt her again.

He'll never hurt *anyone* again.

If I never do anything else in my sad little life, I can die knowing that.

✦ ⧓ ✦

Evie gets out of the water as I kneel on the bank, concentrating on the water.

As she pulls on her clothes, I wash the skillet in the creek. The blue-purple sky begins to lighten into a fuzzy gray color.

We both watch as the rusty colored water trickles away, and by the time anyone thinks to look for it, the skillet will be back in the Blackberry kitchen . . . and as soon as it's set on a burner, any chance at leftover evidence will be burned away.

I set the skillet down on the bank as Evie dips her toes back in the water.

"Do you really have to take it back?" she asks, looking at it squeamishly.

"It'll be missed. And it's not like I hit him with the inside of the pan."

"I guess so," Evie says. "It doesn't seem food-safe."

I laugh, and then suddenly, I can't stop. It's like I'm the lightest cloth, gossamer thin and fraying at every edge. My laugh echoes across the water, twisting into a sound that's more panic than mirth.

Evie takes my hand, and that's it: I just stop. Like the moment needs the silence. When I look down at her, she's looking at me, searching.

I know we have to do the final thing on my list:

    10. *Get home before dawn.*

But I don't move. I just let her seek whatever answers in my face she's looking for.

My muscles tremble under the force of letting myself be seen.

I don't know what she finds in me. But it's something, because the next thing I know, she's laying her head on my shoulder.

The weight of her . . . it's like it's been missing.

The First Breakup

BY ANNA MERIANO

I cry in the shower after I dump Justin, because it seems like the thing to do.

I didn't cry during our breakup. I was too surprised by the words coming out of my mouth. And besides, we were in the campus coffee shop, and I didn't want to make more of a scene than I had to, and it had taken so much effort to get Justin to agree to do something I wanted to do in the first place that my main emotion at that point was just *tired*.

Justin cried when I dumped him. In stoic silence, of course, looking angry about it the whole time, like he did the first month we were dating, when I finally convinced him to watch *Up* with me. He refused to look away from his phone after the first scene gave him Emotions.

I mostly let him pick our movies after that. Or at the very least, I tried to choose less emotional things to watch for our date nights after that, movies and shows that would never open with scenes of a character crying in the shower. Justin would hate this.

I'm standing here, in the shower, letting the tears and scalding water run down, not even bothering to reach for the soap, like I'm some grungy white influencer who's a little too into my body's natural oils. I'm not a white influencer, and my mom and abuela wouldn't let me grow up to be grungy, but I wasn't someone who broke up with people either, not until today, so who knows what I might become next?

I had never dated anyone before Justin, but I've asked people out plenty of times, so it's fair to say that I'm comfortable with rejection. Maybe too comfortable—I probably could've let myself feel a bit more embarrassed when I asked Wyatt Wright out while he was telling me about his crush on our other dance team member. Or when I slipped that detailed pencil portrait of Samantha Raptis into her locker on Valentine's Day. Or when I made fifteen Spotify playlists for Riley Sanchez over the course of the one semester we had Business and Communication Skills together. But unfortunately for my dignity, Mom and Abuela raised me with a deep-seated belief that I was inherently lovable, and that someday, somewhere, someone would recognize that.

For the entirety of high school, though, no one did. And it definitely wasn't because I was some introverted Jane Bennet type, scaring potential suitors away with my unreadable heart. All my friends passed milestones like first date, first kiss, first awkward birth control discussion, and I was still scaring away people of all genders like *pan* was short for "induce-panic-sexual."

And then I got to college, barely stepped into freshman orientation, and there was Justin. He wasn't scared away. Quite the opposite: He asked me out almost before I knew what was happening. I guess part of me, a big part of me, thought that was going to be it. Cue the violins, run the credits. I finally got my love story. But now, almost six months later, I've got this jarring sequel to deal with.

"Julyssa!" A knock on the door interrupts my sad, soapless shower. "Code Pee! Come on!"

I scramble for my towel and grope for the bathroom door handle to let my roommate, Angel, in. She was in class when I got into the shower, so I didn't get a chance to call for a pee check before locking her out. Also, that means I've been in here for at least forty minutes, and while I know my individual consumption habits can't add up to the environmental damage caused by corporate greed, that's still a waste of water. So, I towel off and get dressed while Angel takes care of her Code Pee.

"Okay," Angel says when she gets out of the bathroom and joins me on our flimsy Bed Bath & Beyond couch. As a force of habit, we both clutch the frame as it shakes until she settles in. "What's wrong?"

I make a half-hearted attempt at deception before sighing. "Justin and I broke up . . . I broke up with him."

Angel's little sympathy hiss quickly turns into a comforting "shh-shh" as I start to cry again. "It's okay," she says. "The dining hall just opened, and I will bring you the entire ice cream cooler. We can watch as many rom-coms as you want, and I won't even complain about them, or I can show you the best horror movies without a hint of romance to get your mind off it. You're going to be okay."

I let Angel's soft voice and her hand on my shoulder calm me enough to speak. "But we have the party tonight." The visual arts and theater department hosts a big themed party every couple of months to raise money and to recycle their sets and costumes and decorations. This semester is Y2K themed, inspired by their *High School Musical: The Musical* performance last year. Angel and I have been looking forward to it, planning our themed outfits and everything, all week.

Angel eyes me carefully. "Do you still want to go? Maybe we should—"

"I want to go."

I broke up with Justin after I brought up the party. He didn't want to go (as expected), and he didn't particularly want me to go, and I didn't particularly want to have that discussion again, and I definitely didn't want to give in, spend the night sitting in his dimly lit dorm rewatching TV shows that we both have memorized, scrolling through my phone and feeling resentful while everyone I *wanted* to be hanging out with dressed up and had fun without me. So I just said that it wasn't working, and then he said, "What do you mean?" and he tried to backpedal because, of course, he never meant to make me feel bad or stop me from spending time with my friends. And I knew that was true, but it was too late. I couldn't un–break up with him.

So no matter how wobbly my emotions feel right now, I still refuse to miss the party.

"Okay." Angel nods, a tiny crease between her eyebrows. "If you're sure. Do you want to grab some dinner before I get started on your hair?"

✧ ⌧ ✧

Justin was—is—a really, truly relentlessly nice person. There was a niceness to the way he stood at my side and smiled, the way he always wanted to be around me, no question. I never had an elaborate scheme to capture his attention or steal his heart. I didn't need one. He just liked me, and it was so nice, and it had never happened to me before.

When people are nice like that, what could be wrong? When nice things end, you're supposed to want them back, aren't you?

But I don't regret breaking up with Justin. And I think that's why I'm still crying (into an ice cream sandwich) while Angel pulls out the treasures her mom provided us for a perfect Y2K transformation—a flat iron and a crimping iron. I finally got the relationship I always wanted. What do I do now that I've thrown it away?

Angel's fingers on my scalp are an instant comfort, breaking my spiral of confusion with soft, familiar sensation. She's been helping part-time at her mom's salon for years now, and I've been offering my head up for styling experiments even longer, from our first bleaching catastrophe in seventh grade to my current burgundy long layers that she cut and dyed just a few weeks ago.

Justin was weird about that whole hair journey, I suddenly remember, latching on to the negative more now than I did at the time. He was nice to me, of course, said I looked cute as a redhead and everything, but he was totally weird about Angel. He got all moody when she was showing off her handiwork and saying how hot the new look was, and then later he was annoyed because I said that Angel was the only person I would trust to touch my hair and I didn't include him as a second option. Which makes no sense, since he can't even braid, much less detangle, style, or cut my thick curls. But obviously it wasn't about that.

Now that I'm not making excuses for him, or trying to convince myself that it's no big deal, it kind of reads like maybe he was jealous of Angel.

Which is silly, because Angel and I have been best friends for a million years, and we talk about crushes and stuff all the time, so if something were going to happen it definitely would have by now.

Right?

Angel's a little less than halfway through my hair, and she starts humming softly as she goes, totally in her element. It's not like I don't like Angel—I love Angel. She's my person. People warned us that rooming together could ruin a friendship, but, I don't know, that's just not how it is. I like living with Angel, learning her schedule, starting the electric kettle five minutes before her three-hour evening seminar ends so she can come home to a warm cup of tea. I don't know if I could do the whole out-of-town college life thing without her, someone who code-switches between Spanglish and Academia with me and who gets why I'm on the phone with Mom and Abuela all the time, someone who'll carpool down with me a couple times each month for this cousin's birthday or that uncle's wedding.

I did kind of dump Justin so that I could be here with her. Maybe his jealousy wasn't entirely unfounded.

"Done!" Angel pats the top of my head and sends me to check myself out in the mirror, taking a few extra moments to crimp her own barely chin-length black bob. "I guess I could've done extensions for the true Y2K vibe, but I lack the commitment to sparkle motion."

"You look great already," I tell her, and even though the words come instinctively, they're also true. Sitting sideways on the couch with her knees at odd angles, half her hair crimped and the other half straight, round face scrunched in concentration, she looks perfect.

She catches me watching, smiles with extra softness. "You know, Justin didn't deserve you."

Which is the kind of thing best friends are supposed to say. Angel has made this claim before. Before, I always had a list handy, a carefully constructed defense of my boyfriend. Justin has nice arms. He has good grades. He likes to rewatch old sitcoms as much as I do. He has an interesting sense of humor that grows on you. He's dependable and constant.

Now the list rises in my mind unbidden, but everything is flipped and ugly. Justin spent more time at the gym and the library than he did with me. Justin never took me on a real date, just takeout and reruns in his dark dorm. Justin's dry cynicism was less of a joke and more of a tiresome personality trait. Justin was boring.

I feel guilty thinking it. "Maybe I didn't deserve him, did you ever think of that?"

Angel doesn't turn away or laugh. "No, that's definitely not it. I would know. Anyone would be lucky—"

There's a knock at the door.

Since Angel's hands are full of fire hazards, I hop to open it and suppress an eye roll at the massive figure in the doorway. Jackson raises his hands and takes a step back like I'm going to bite, which is both annoyingly unfair and even more annoyingly justified. The last time he was over here while I was, I did sort of chew him out.

"Hi, Julyssa," he says, overly polite and pleasant. Like he's some paragon of reason and virtue, which he is not. He's one of the Guys at the End of the Hall, a group of slightly obnoxious, hot, bro-y dudes who room together on our floor. They all play one of those weird sports you only hear about in college, lacrosse or ultimate rugby or whatever, and they all think they're cooler than they really are.

I tried to give Jackson the benefit of the doubt because he joined the Service Committee with Angel and took teacher ed classes with me, but his true obnoxious nature soon revealed itself. He spends an annoying amount of time in our room, for one thing, spreading his body spray scent everywhere. Just because he's Angel's friend doesn't mean I want him there. It's rude and distracting. And he always interrupts me in our Psychology of Education class, repeating my own points back to me and totally stealing credit from Dr. Wiles. Plus he's unpredictable, swinging between acting like I'm one of his buddies (I'm not) and acting like I'm some sharp-tongued demon that he has to handle with care (I'm not!).

I mean I do sometimes yell at him, but how else are you supposed to react when you come out of the shower to find an obnoxiously cool hot guy on your couch inspecting your old ratty towel? Does he not realize that some people have boundaries and boyfriends?

Used to have boyfriends, I guess.

"Jackson!" Angel waves him in, and he flashes me a grin and flips his surfer-dude black hair as he steps past me. "What's the plan for tonight?"

Because she is saintly and nonjudgmental, Angel is friends with all of the Guys at the End of the Hall. I tolerate them for Angel's sake and because their oversize six-person suite is almost always open for small parties.

"Pregame is in our room at nineish," Jackson says. "The public party won't be good until at least eleven, so that's plenty of time."

Oh, that's another thing. It annoys me that Jackson, a freshman like all of us, always acts so plugged in to campus life. It's like he's trying to remind me how much I don't know about how everything works.

"You're welcome to join, too, Julyssa."

I scoff at the formal invitation. If Jackson thinks he's accomplishing something with this attitude, he's sadly mistaken.

Except that after I scoff at his olive branch, Angel frowns at me and mouths, "Be nice!" So maybe his mission—to make me seem irrational and unfair—was accomplished after all.

I retreat to my room and dig through my closet, refusing to let Jackson make me look bad anymore. He does that enough in class.

"Bye, Julyssa," Jackson singsongs as I leave, which sounds innocent, but he's only doing it to annoy me. Up until our first big fight, he used to call me Jules.

There were a few days last semester, after Angel found out that Justin liked me but before I knew, when she was dropping hints that someone was crushing on me to try to gauge how I would react. And one of her not-very-subtle hints was something about how we'd be one of those families where everyone's name starts with the same letter and our kids would go through every J name, and for like a minute—a split second—my brain was like, *Oh it's probably Jackson.*

I'm obviously extremely glad it didn't turn out to be true, but for those couple of days, I kind of considered not being so super annoyed by him because I was flattered that one of the hot Guys at the End of the Hall was interested in me, and so for those couple of days I convinced myself that the way he called me Jules was flirty.

But then Justin asked me out, and I asked Jackson to use my full name, which he thought was a weird request. He kept asking me why it bothered me, and eventually I got annoyed and told him to stop being such a dick and leave me alone, and since then he's been extra annoyingly careful to use my name. Which I know is what I asked him to do, but the way he says it still feels like a teasing reminder of our fight. Angel said I was out of line, but she thinks Jackson can do no wrong just because he puts together a mean toy drive or whatever.

Angel and Jackson are talking pregame playlists on the other side of the door while I put together my most iconic Y2K outfit by wearing several outfits on top of one another—colorful leggings, jean skirt, lace-lined tank top, crop top, and vest. I add some lip gloss, give my hair an extra scrunch even though Angel's work is flawless, and take a couple of mirror selfies.

And then I remember that I have no one to text my mirror selfies to, because I broke up with Justin, and the wave of loneliness hits with a heaping side of anxiety. Justin hates parties, but he was always on the other side of the phone screen, always sending smileys and hearts when

I needed a confidence boost. He was my proof that I was doing college right, that I was moving forward and checking boxes and making it all work here. And then, for some unfathomable reason, I decided to torpedo all of that.

I shove my phone into the pocket of my jean skirt (not very satisfying since only two-thirds of the phone fits). If I hadn't broken up with Justin, he would be telling me how good I looked but also how much he wished I would hang out with him instead. I would be feeling guilty, or torn, or suffocated.

I return to the common space, slamming my door louder than necessary. Jackson, his large frame sprawled across our too-small couch with his head hanging upside down, startles. "Whoa . . . nice, uh, look." He waves his hand to indicate my whole situation, which is admittedly a lot, but he doesn't have to look so gobsmacked about it.

He's such a dick.

"I'll be right out!" Angel has her door cracked for better acoustics while she gets dressed. "Don't snark each other to death before I'm ready!"

I huff and consider going back to my room, but then I decide it would be too sad. Instead, I lean awkwardly on my door. For Angel's sake (and definitely not for my own), I can be civil.

There's a long pause where I guess we're both trying not to do or say anything that will make Angel mad. "So," Jackson finally says. "Did you pick a topic for your midterm reflection yet?" He shifts so he's sitting on one side of the couch instead of taking up the whole thing.

"Why?" I ask, feeling my temper rise as soon as he mentions our Psychology of Ed class. "Planning to steal my idea?" I don't add "again," which is proof that I am trying.

But instead of rising to the bait, Jackson laughs and shakes his head. "I don't think I could if I tried. You always know what's going on in class, while I'm like, 'Did I miss a prereq at some point?' I have no idea what's happening half the time."

Huh? Is this part of his fake polite act? "You seem like you keep up," I say. "Dr. Wiles loves you." *Especially when you interrupt me to say the same thing I was saying,* I think.

"Heh, yeah, I'm very charming." Jackson winks and tosses his hair. He's not in costume for the party yet—or maybe he is? I guess basketball shorts and T-shirts haven't changed that much since the turn of the millennium—but he's oozing charismatic boy band vibes to rival any Y2K celebrity.

Ugh. This is exactly the kind of thing obnoxiously hot bros do. And everyone just falls for it because they're hot and obnoxious and hot and . . . What was I saying?

"But no, really." He continues, which I guess means he was joking, which I guess means he isn't really that full of himself. "I never know what Dr. Wiles is talking about, or half the students. You're the only one who talks like a real person, so I actually have a chance to get what you're saying. That's why I always go after you in class discussions—I don't know if you noticed."

"Oh . . ." There doesn't seem to be any kind of trick here, just a compliment. "Uh, well, I haven't picked my topic yet, but, you know, if you want to talk about ideas, I'm . . . happy to help."

Jackson's face lights up. "Thanks, Jules! Uh, sorry, sorry. I mean Julyssa." Huh.

Maybe he isn't using my full name to annoy me. Maybe he's using it because I asked him to.

Maybe what I took for fake politeness was just Jackson being genuinely polite. But that would mean I've been . . . the opposite of polite back to him.

Angel opens her door dramatically. "What do you think?"

She's wearing a white tank top with thin straps and has added rhinestones along the pockets of her jeans. She has a weird trucker hat and a skinny scarf. Her smile is wide and dimpled. She looks flawless.

"Great," Jackson says. "Now that you're ready, you can come down to our room and help set up! Matt got some of those LED laser projectors, and we have to move the furniture."

Angel nods, grabbing her purse and reaching a hand to haul Jackson off the couch even though he's nearly two feet taller than she is. They head to the door, and I watch them both, feeling loneliness creep up again.

"Have fun."

"Julyssa, I already told you that you're invited," Jackson says, rolling his eyes.

"Yeah, come on." Angel holds her hand out to me. "I'm not leaving you here in your vulnerable emotional state."

✧ ⚙ ✧

It feels weirdly not weird to pregame in the Guys at the End of the Hall's suite. Most people don't even ask about Justin, which makes sense because I usually do big social gatherings without him. Everything is pretty much exactly how it would have been if I was still in a relationship, except for the lack of texts on my phone and the sinking feeling I have whenever I remember the reason why.

In honor of the public party, the music in the suite is about half early 2000s pop music and half modern chill vibes. Billie Eilish comes on after "Hollaback Girl" by Gwen Stefani, and I take a seat on one of the armchairs, piled with blankets and pillows, making up the couch jumble lining the walls.

Or try to. The cushion I attempted to sit on *oomphs* and squirms, and I leap up, apologizing to the skinny goth figure disentangling from the camouflage of the dark blanket and upholstery.

"Don't worry," the not-cushion person mutters. "Happens all the time."

Which only makes me feel worse.

I settle onto a nearby love seat. I haven't seen this person at any of the hall bonding events, and between the rainbow nail polish and the curly undercut and the high cheekbones, I definitely would have remembered. "I'm Julyssa," I say. "Sorry I sat on you." Exactly how you want to meet a mysterious and attractive new person, right?

"Ha, cool, I'm Alyssa. Uh, but just Ally is fine."

I don't want to assume that a feminine name means feminine pronouns, but I also don't want to assume that being hot and looking queer automatically means neutral pronouns, so I decide Ally is pronounless in my head until further information can be gathered.

Example sentences: Ally is wearing the hell out of Ally's ripped black skinny jeans. Ally, in addition to looking goth, is also wearing enough eyeliner and metal to look perfectly on-theme for Y2K, which is very cool because a lot of people don't bother with the theme, which totally defeats the purpose of a themed party, so that makes me like Ally even more. I would like to get to know Ally better, if Ally is down for that.

At this point my brain stops being starstruck and kicks back into function, first remembering that I'm in a relationship and therefore not supposed to want to get to know new people just because they're attractive, and then whiplash-quick remembering that's not true any-more because I broke up with Justin, and what kind of person tries to hit on (and sit on) someone the same day they ended their first-ever relationship?

Besides, Ally doesn't normally come to this hall to party, which most likely means that Ally came here with someone.

Right?

"Do you know any of the Guys?" I ask.

Ally nods and points to Heberto, one of the chillest of the Guys at the End of the Hall. Maybe second to Jackson. I'm still deciding about that.

"We were in high school together," Ally says of Heberto, "and he's been guilting me about ditching him now that we live on opposite sides of campus."

"Oh, so you're from one of those crappy, ancient dorms," I tease.

"Yeah, but I spend more time holed up in the media lab than any-where else. Uh, wait, no, what I meant to say is that I am very cool and popular and have many friends, as evidenced by how good I am at par-ticipating in parties." Ally grimaces and pulls the blanket closer. "God, I'm bad at this."

I laugh. "What's in the media lab?"

And Ally tells me about vlogging and film classes and editing soft-ware that the university has available. "But, like, I promise I do other, cooler, less lonely things, too. I don't always hide under pillows during social situations. I just got cold."

"That will happen when you visit a newly constructed dorm from one that was built pre–central A/C," I say. "But, also, you don't have to con-vince me. You're here. And all that stuff sounds cool."

Rainbow-painted nails run through tight curls on the long side of Ally's hair. "Heh, thanks, that's . . ."

The music bursts into high violin riffs, and the whole room takes a collective breath before whooping and charging back to the makeshift dance floor. Angel waves from across the room and holds out a hand, screaming, "Britney! She's free, bitches!"

I glance back at Ally as I stand, and we share a moment of silent communication, quirked eyebrows, and a rueful smile. The result is that Ally stands too, and follows me toward Angel's beckoning, swaying form. My stomach flips pleasantly because, somehow, I went from "Sorry I sat on you" to "Join me on the dance floor?" and that's never happened to me before.

Lots of firsts today.

"I guess this is a good way to stay warm," Ally shouts over the music. "And I'm less likely to be crushed here. Slightly." A few kids are rowdy in their pregame dancing, but we dodge them without too much of a problem. Ally leans against me sometimes as we navigate, which makes me warm and flustered.

We join Angel, whose dancing is joyful and loose and infectious. She twirls around Jackson, who bobs his head with a lot of enthusiasm but not a lot of grace. They both welcome us as we approach with dramatic lip syncing that I happily join in with. Angel and Jackson seem to know Ally already, or at least they accept a fellow dancer without question. Angel spins me around, and I feel dizzy and bubbly with her hand in mine. Jackson challenges me to a dance-off, and instead of annoyed, I feel the thrill of friendly competition surge between us.

Now that I'm not dating Justin, everything has an undercurrent, a spark of possibility, a whisper of romance. I close my eyes and take a deep breath and realize I missed this.

"Julyssa."

Justin's voice cuts through the music like a stone through a stained-glass window. I open my eyes and find him standing next to me, incongruously fixed and solid in the middle of the dance floor, wearing his usual joggers and gray T-shirt. What is he doing here?

"You didn't pick up." He answers the question I didn't ask. He's always been good at guessing what I'm thinking, or reading my too-expressive face. "And I needed to talk to you."

I put my arm out to stop Angel, who's already trying to put herself between us, because of course she is. "It's okay," I tell her. "Give us a sec."

Ally takes in the scene and then tactfully pivots the dance circle to one side. Angel and Jackson share a look before following suit. The air conditioning feels colder without them surrounding me. I want to shift with them. Instead, I make myself face my ex.

"What's up?" I ask Justin.

"I think you made a mistake," he says. "We're good together, and I understand that I need to be more . . . open to things, but that's part of it. We make each other better. And I'm here to prove it. Plus, maybe I shouldn't have let you leave without saying this in the first place. Maybe you think I didn't fight for you enough. I'm sorry. I don't want to break up. I want to be with you."

It's as surprising and intoxicating now as it was six months ago. It's everything I imagined I was missing, everything I dreamed I would someday get.

And I'm not tempted by it at all.

I'm not a fan of rejection. I don't love throwing my heart at the wall and watching it slide down, waiting for the day it will finally stick. But I can't avoid that sharp pain by accepting a duller version. I waited so long to be chosen, for someone to want me, that when it happened, I temporarily forgot the part where I have to choose, too. I thought Justin was saving me from the angst and drama of unrequited crushes. But the truth is, I never even had a crush on him. I was settling.

I never felt excited about Justin; I only liked that he liked me. I didn't throw away something great on a whim, or sabotage a solid foundation. I broke up with Justin because I wanted more.

Maybe trying to date someone I choose will take longer. Maybe I'll face a lot more rejection; maybe I'll screw things up and be lonely and cry in the shower more.

But I'm excited to rejoin my sweet best friend, my good-hearted rival, and my mysterious new acquaintance in the dance. I'm excited to try.

"Come on," Justin says, reading my expression drastically, hopelessly wrong this time. He holds out a hand. "Let's get out of here."

"I'm sorry," I tell him. And this is the part where I should probably tell him that he's very sweet and he'll find someone better suited, but instead I just say, "I don't want to."

I'll tell him all that stuff another time. But right now, I turn and make my way back to the dancing. And Justin—because he *is* sweet, and he isn't dramatic, and he never wanted to come to this party in the first place—nods slowly and heads out, back to his comfortable dorm and his comfortable life.

My circle welcomes me back without questions. I'm grateful for that as I sway slowly, slightly out of sync, shaking off the last sadness like shower droplets. It doesn't take long. I like where I am, and soon I'm smiling again.

"Toxic" turns into "Get Low" and then some pop punk I don't recognize but dance to anyway. Angel checks her phone and says we should finish up soon and head to the public party, but then stays when Avril Lavigne comes on. Jackson's dancing intensifies until his whole body is head-banging, shaking the sticky linoleum floor. The contrast between Angel's fluid moves and Jackson's pogo-stick style makes for a funny routine. Ally copies both of their moves, and I'm laughing along with everyone, bathed in colorful lights and loud music and opportunity. Part of the dance. Ready to follow wherever it takes me, ready for the ups and downs and the unknowns and the pounding of my heart through it all.

The First Time I Saw the Stars

BY SHAUN DAVID HUTCHINSON

There were three kinds of people at St. Benedict's: those who'd never seen the stars, liars, and Devin Doucette.

"I don't know the name of the planet I'm from. I got lost here when I was little." Devin Doucette was awkward. He was taller than the rest of us in the group, but he moved like a colt still trying to figure out how limbs worked. His eyes were too big, his nose too small, and I didn't know if he couldn't shut his mouth or just never did. I think he was sixteen, like me.

Joss rolled his eyes, but Joss rolled his eyes at everything. "That's convenient, don't you think?"

Dr. Ronald Burrows sat on his throne in the center of the circle, his legs crossed at the ankles and his fingers laced together. He looked unamused. "We've talked about this, Joss."

"But it's ridiculous!" Joss threw his hands in the air. He was a little dramatic. He was also the youngest of us at thirteen, so I cut him some slack. "Devin gets to claim he's seen the stars because he's an alien, but he can't even tell us where he's from? It's bullshit!"

Devin maintained an eerie calm. He sat in his chair in the circle with his hands in his lap and his mouth hanging open and waited for Joss to shut up before responding. "Me getting lost on Earth is like an Earth kid getting lost in the grocery store. How many little kids don't know their addresses? How many don't even know their parents have names other than Mom or Dad?"

He had a point. "He's got a point," I said.

"Welcome to the conversation, Keen." Dr. Ronald Burrows smiled like I was his favorite dog and had finally learned to sit on command. I didn't even get a treat. "Do you have something to add?"

I thought I'd said it. I did say it, right?

"Uh . . . I got lost at the fair when I was eight. My sister was supposed to be watching me, but she got distracted and then I wandered off. I was scared when I realized I was alone. But then my parents called me and told me to stay where I was and came and found me. My sister got grounded for a week. She never lets me forget I'm the cause of every problem she's ever had and that the entire universe would definitely be better off without me. I'm done talking now."

The other boys in the group began shouting all at once. Joss went off about how Devin's story was ridiculous, Bryon was laughing, Ramon began listing the names of birds and insects we'd lost since the haze obscured the sky, Eric asked Devin for details about the day he got lost on Earth, and Harry was calmly describing the different ways he'd like to kill us if he had the chance. Even Dr. Ronald Burrows was busy trying to rein the others in and bring the group back under control.

The only person other than me who wasn't adding to the noise was Devin Doucette. He was just sitting there, wearing a cute smile like this had been his plan all along.

I leaned toward Devin, keeping my voice low. "You think your parents will ever find you?"

Devin's smile slipped. I wouldn't have noticed it if I hadn't been watching him so closely. "Maybe," he said, but he didn't sound too sure.

✧ ⊠ ✧

My parents came to visit on Tuesdays. Those were my least favorite days. Sometimes they brought Juno, sometimes they brought me some fresh clothes that had been picked over by the nurses to make sure there was nothing in them I could use to harm myself or anyone else. We didn't talk much. They didn't know what news might agitate me, and we hadn't had a lot in common to begin with. Inevitably, they asked the same question they asked each time their visit neared its end.

"When are you coming home, Keen?"

Sometimes my dad asked, sometimes my mom. Did they play rock paper scissors in the car in the parking lot to decide who had to ask? Was the question a habit, or did they genuinely want to know? What answer were they hoping to hear? It probably changed like the weather. Even if they did want me to come home, I doubted they weren't grateful for the tranquility left in the wake of my absence.

"I dunno."

It was my standard answer.

Why didn't you turn in your homework, Keen? I dunno. Why were you walking along I-95 in the middle of the night in your underwear? I dunno. Why didn't you vacuum the living room like I asked you to? I dunno. Why did you drink a cocktail of cleaning supplies? I dunno. Because I was thirsty?

It was also a truthful answer. Dr. Ronald Burrows liked to tell us that we were the only ones who could decide when we were ready to go home, but we weren't allowed to leave unless he signed off on it, so it was a very confusing question.

"Your doctor says you've been participating in group," my mom said. I hated the hope in her voice. It was too full of expectation. Join group, talk to people, get better, leave St. Benedict's, return to school, be a normal son, hang out with friends, graduate, go to college, get a job, get married, have kids, bitch about the cost of health insurance, drown slowly under the weight of college tuition loans and a mortgage, die alone of cancer or lung rot or terminal boredom.

"You've been here three months," Dad said. "Don't you *want* to come home?"

"I dun . . . no."

◇ ☒ ◇

The rhythm of life at St. Benedict's was like jazz. It seemed random unless you understood the basic principles underpinning the system. I didn't like jazz, but music was one of the few things in the world that made sense to me. It made following the patterns at St. Benedict's a breeze.

For example, we were allowed to spend thirty minutes in the garden after breakfast. Nurse Kelly usually accompanied us, except on days Eric refused to eat because she was the only one who could convince him the food wasn't poisoned. Nurse James would volunteer to chaperone us in Nurse Kelly's place unless Joss was acting up because he'd had a bad night. Joss suffered from frequent nightmares, and the lack of sleep made him more difficult to handle than usual. Nurse Franklin didn't mind Joss's moods, though. Devin, however, couldn't stand Nurse Franklin because she'd once asked him if he was from Uranus. As a result, if Nurse Franklin accompanied the group to the garden, Devin would refuse to go and remain inside.

So, before bed, where I was sure Joss could hear us, I told Ramon a scary story my sister had told me when I was little that had terrified me so badly I'd slept in my parents' room for a week. And then before breakfast, I asked Eric if dinner the night before had tasted weird to him and complained I'd had stomach cramps all night.

I might not have liked jazz, but I knew how to play it.

Devin was alone in the common room watching TV. He'd been at St. Benedict's since I'd arrived, but we hadn't talked much. He gave off easygoing vibes, like he was the kind of person at school who would've invited the new kid to sit at his table at lunch. I hated high school. And being the new kid. *And* lunch.

I sat on the love seat catty-cornered to the sofa Devin was lounging on. He hadn't taken his eyes off the TV since I'd arrived. "Have you really seen the stars?" I asked.

"Yes."

"How? The haze has been clogging up the sky since my grandparents were younger than me. Anyone alive who's seen the stars is probably too old to actually remember them."

"If you don't believe me, why'd you ask?" Devin had a smooth, deep voice that gave me tingles. Tingles were against regulations at St. Benedict's.

Anyway, Devin had asked a fair question. "So then tell me what the stars are like. How'd you see them?"

Devin muted the TV and curled his legs under his butt as he turned toward me. It made me nervous and a little excited to be the sole recipient of his attention. Excitement was also against regs. "I saw them out the window of the ship that brought me here. They were amazing. They were everywhere. It was like some enormous Titan had tossed a handful of glittery sand into the void."

I couldn't imagine it. The sky was just the sky. It was a hazy yellow-ish dome that hung over our heads. A constant in our miserable lives. Sometimes we could see the glow of the sun through the haze, but it was more of a suggestion than a star.

"Haven't you ever seen the stars in movies?"

"It's not the same," I said.

Devin bobbed his head like a parrot. "Yeah."

There were a lot of things I'd only seen in movies. Stars, blue skies, the moon. When my parents were my age, scientists told people they were on the verge of a breakthrough that would enable them to clear the haze. Every week, it seemed, there was a new announcement. A new program. A new promise. By the time I was born, the haze was a fact of life. And we accepted it because what else could we do? Water was scarce, the sky was yellow, and if a global pandemic didn't kill us, there was a good chance we'd die of starvation before we learned to efficiently farm bugs for food.

"Are you really an alien?"

"Did you really try to kill yourself by drinking a bunch of cleaning supplies?"

The nurses had big mouths, but it wasn't like I'd tried to hide why I was at St. Benedict's. "I spent three weeks in the hospital puking up the lining of my stomach."

Devin's bulging eyes made him look like he was always on the receiving end of an unpleasant surprise, so I could never tell what he was thinking. "Seems like an inefficient way to end your life."

"The alternatives were worse."

Devin was quiet a moment. "Yes. I'm really an alien. Are you going to try to end your life again?"

Most people wanted to know *why* I'd tried to kill myself. The only other person who'd asked me if I intended to try again was Dr. Ronald Burrows. I told Devin the same thing I told him. "My life's already over. All that's left is to convince my body of it."

✧ ⌗ ✧

I didn't get out of bed except to eat and use the bathroom for the next four days.

This wasn't new. The first time it happened, I was thirteen. I thought I had that disease where a person's bones calcify and they can't move. My limbs were dense and heavy. Breathing felt like too much effort. The doctor told me I didn't have fibrodysplasia ossificans progressiva after all. Instead, I had depression. He prescribed pills and referred me to a therapist. I stopped taking the pills because they gave me headaches, a runny nose, and spontaneous ejaculations. Being thirteen and depressed was difficult enough without randomly blowing my load in my pants during class. The therapy helped until it didn't. Dr. Ronald Burrows put me on a medication with fewer spontaneous side effects when I checked into St. Benedict's, but it didn't seem to be working.

I just wanted to stay in bed where it was warm and soft and no one pretended to be an alien claiming to see impossible things.

On the first day, Ramon came by to rat out Joss for playing the piano in the rec room without washing his hands first. He always had food on his hands. Peanut butter, ranch dressing, pudding, marinara sauce. Sometimes he'd lick his fingers before he played, which was gross enough, but when he didn't, he'd transfer whatever crap was on his hands to the keys. It was disgusting, and usually, I'd drop whatever I was doing to prevent him from crudding up my piano.

That day, I couldn't be bothered.

Juno dropped by the second day. It was a Tuesday. My parents were in the visiting area, and they'd sent my sister to fetch me.

"I'm sleeping."

"You suck, you know that?" I didn't have to see Juno to feel her disapproving glare.

"You never let me forget it."

"Boo-hoo, your life's so bad. Why don't you just—" Juno stopped.

"Go on, finish what you were gonna say." I rolled over to look at her.

Juno had her hand over her mouth. She was effortlessly stylish. The kind of person who created trends rather than followed them. Today, she was wearing an outfit that looked like she was trying to answer the question *What if intestinal parasites were fashion?* Her makeup was cute, though. "I didn't mean . . ."

"Sure."

Juno's shame morphed into familiar anger. "Why was that the *one* time you did what I told you to do? How many times have I told you to stop leaving your wet towels on our bathroom floor? You never do *that*."

I turned my back to her again. "You're a terrible big sister."

"You're not much of a little brother." Her footsteps thunked on the linoleum as she walked toward the door. "I would've rather found a hundred wet towels on the floor than you. I still love you, though, Keen. We all do."

Dr. Ronald Burrows dropped by my room on day three to ask me nicely to attend group. I asked him nicely to go orally pleasure a goat and leave me alone. He upped the dosage on my medication.

Devin appeared on day four. Technically, it was night: 1:04 a.m. by the bedside clock. I opened my eyes in the dark, and I could feel someone in the room. When I flipped on the lamp, Devin was sitting cross-legged at the end of my bed with a book open in his lap. I didn't know how he was reading in the dark, and I was too exhausted to ask.

"I don't care if Joss is rubbing his balls on the keys, I'm not getting out of bed."

I had just reached over to switch off the lamp again when Devin said, "Wanna see the stars?"

I learned about the stars the same way I learned about everything my parents were too scared to discuss with me: from the internet. Adults wanted to act like the universe ended with the haze, but I found a video of footage recorded from a space station that used to orbit Earth, and there was no haze. Just a blue sphere and a seemingly infinite number of glimmering lights in the darkness. After that, I was hooked. I became determined to learn as much about the stars as possible. I never dreamed I'd get to see them.

I sat up in bed and fixed Devin with a frigid stare. "Don't bullshit me."

Devin had a crooked smile. Everything about him was slightly off. "Have I ever?"

"Maybe. How should I know?"

"Fair enough," Devin said. "I haven't, though. I'm unable to lie. If I could, I wouldn't have ended up here."

None of us at St. Benedict's knew for certain why Devin was there. We assumed it was because of the alien thing, but Devin refused to answer when we asked.

"So, how are we going to get to wherever this place is where we can see the stars?" I asked. "Is your ship gonna beam us up like in those old movies?"

Devin shook his head and pointed to the window over my bed.

"We're going to walk, so you should probably change into something more appropriate."

While I decided what to wear on our adventure, Devin stood on my bed messing with the window.

"You'll never get through the bars."

Devin didn't respond, but less than a minute later, the bars popped off, and he dropped them to the grass under my window.

I stared open-mouthed at him. "How'd you . . . ?"

"I used my enhanced alien strength."

"Are you serious?" I asked.

Devin laughed. I think it was the first time I'd seen him actually laugh out loud. It softened the sharp lines of his face in a way that made him almost beautiful. "No."

"I thought you couldn't lie."

"That wasn't a lie. It was a joke."

"So, you can't lie unless you think the lie is funny?" I shook my head. "You're the weirdest alien ever."

Devin smiled and held out his hand. "Come on or we'll be late."

I broke out of St. Benedict's once before. It was a week after I'd checked in, and it wasn't difficult. The nurses expected we'd try to run off during our time outside in the garden, so they made sure to keep a close eye on us. But who was going to try to run away on sundae Sunday? They assumed the promise of sugary dairy products and hot fudge would ensure we stayed on our best behavior while the nurses hid in the office watching football.

What they didn't account for was my lactose intolerance. I loved sundaes as much as anyone, but they didn't love me back. While the other boys were busy stuffing their faces and the nurses were busy cheering on their chosen team, I walked out the doors to freedom. The police found me two hours later at McDonald's. After three weeks of puking up my stomach lining, two weeks of bland hospital meals, and a week of St. Benedict's awful food, I just wanted a Double McGrub with Cheez, and fries.

Escaping with Devin was even easier. Granted, he did the hard work of removing the bars from my window, but all we had to do after was climb outside and walk away. It took me a few minutes to shake the lethargy from my limbs. My head felt full of wet concrete. I needed a soda or a coffee or a quick jump in the ocean. Something to wake my brain. But Devin was focused on our destination, and I doubted he'd be willing to stop to get me a caffeine fix.

Even in the dark, I could feel the haze. It was like a wet wool blanket I couldn't escape from under. Sometimes I imagined I could reach up and touch it. Everything felt muted and gray. The air tasted like ash. It was probably similar to being trapped in a burning house, except the house was the planet and we'd started the fire.

I ran into Devin's back when he stopped suddenly. We were at the edge of the St. Benedict's parking lot. Devin turned around and pressed his finger to his lips.

"Quiet," I said. "Got it." I followed Devin as he wound through the parked cars. Finally, he stopped at an older model electric vehicle and opened the door. "How'd you—"

Devin looked at me and arched his eyebrow.

"Right. Quiet."

"Go unplug it from the charging station," Devin whispered.

If Devin's big plan was to steal a car, we weren't going anywhere. A coder with a decent rig could probably hack an older model EV given enough time, but Devin didn't have a laptop. He didn't have the key or the owner's biometric data either. But I went around front and disconnected the car anyway. When I finished, Devin was in the driver's seat and the nearly silent engine was running.

"Is this your car?" I asked when I slid into the passenger seat. "It's got to be your car, right?"

"This car belongs to Nurse Phillips."

"Then explain how you started it without a key or a laptop." I stopped as a thought occurred to me. "You don't have Nurse Phillips's finger in your pocket, do you?"

"I don't have any fingers in any of my pockets at the moment."

"'At the moment' implies you've had fingers in your pockets at some point," I said.

"It does." Devin put the car in drive, turned to me, and smiled. "Seat belt, please."

✧ ☒ ✧

Devin had an interesting singing voice. It might've been more interesting if he'd known the words to the songs he sang along with. We'd gotten on I-95 going north, and I still had no idea where Devin was taking me.

"So . . ." I turned down the music. "Where are you taking me?"

"To see the stars." Devin glanced at me out of the corner of his eye. "Didn't we establish that already?"

"Okay, yeah, but I meant more specifically. Will we be driving for an hour? Five hours?"

"I don't know."

"How can you not know? You're taking us there?" I was calmer than I expected. Devin could have been a serial killer who was planning to dismember me in the woods where no one would hear me scream, but I wasn't too concerned. It was probably the medication. As side effects went, I was on the fence whether a subdued fear response was better than the alternative, but since I didn't have a change of clothes, I supposed I shouldn't complain.

"It's difficult to explain," Devin said.

"Try?"

Devin scrunched his lips and nose in the cutest way. I tingled again, but since St. Benedict's regulations didn't extend to the car, I didn't feel guilty about it.

"Do you know how some birds have magnetite in their beaks and specialized cells in their eyes that might make it possible for them to sense magnetic fields?"

"No?"

"Okay," Devin said. "Well, some birds have magnetite—"

"I get it. Magnetic fields. Like a compass."

"Exactly!" Devin served up a smile with a side of dimples. He was way too excited about birds. "Well, I have something similar that helps me find my way to where *we're* going."

It wasn't the most ludicrous thing Devin had ever said. I once walked in on him eating a frozen burrito still frozen. He told me he'd stored up microwave radiation while he was in space and was using it to heat up his burrito while it traveled to his primary stomach.

"So, what you're saying is you'll know it when you get there?"

Devin seemed to weigh my question before nodding. "Is that okay? Have you changed your mind? I can let you out."

"No, I was just thinking if we're going to be on the road awhile, I'd really love a slushie."

"Oh. That's easy." Devin took the next exit and drove around until we found a convenience store. It was too far from the interstate to actually be all that convenient, but there wasn't much else around either.

I bought a cherry slushie and a bag of Twizzlers and then waited for Devin at the car. I'd been scared when I'd thumbed the pay pad that it would be rejected, but it had gone through. The downside was that now my parents would find out I'd escaped and would soon be phoning St. Benedict's to let them know. Devin came out of the store carrying a paper sack filled with chips, candy, and soda. I had no idea how he'd paid.

"Hungry?"

"No," Devin said. I waited for him to elaborate, but he seemed satisfied with his non-answer, so I let it drop.

When we were back on the interstate driving north and I was happily full of sugar, I turned down the music again and asked, "Are you really an alien?"

"Yes."

"What kind? What's your species? What planet are you from?"

"None of the answers would make sense to you," Devin said. "And I don't have the time to teach you the math you'd need for them to make sense."

It was kind of a dodge, but also plausible. Aliens in books and movies were always so humanoid, so relatable. Also, pretty murdery. It made sense that real aliens would be, well, alien.

"Wait," I said. "Didn't you tell Joss during group that you couldn't remember what planet you're from? Was that a lie?"

"It was a joke."

"I'm not sure you actually know what that word means." On the other hand, it *was* kind of fun winding Joss up. "Can you tell me why, if you're an alien, you look human?"

Devin drummed his fingers on the steering wheel. "Let's play a game. A question for a question."

I assumed I was being hustled because no one proposed playing a game unless they thought they had the upper hand. But I was bored, so I said, "Sure, why not?"

"Good. You already got the first question, which makes it my turn."

I opened my mouth to protest, but I'd walked right into Devin's diabolical trap. "Fine. Ask your stupid question."

"Why did you stay in bed for ninety-one hours?"

It wasn't the question I thought he'd ask, and I struggled with how to answer. "Have you ever been hiking?"

"Oh yes!" Devin said. "There's a planet with mountains made of spongy rocks that scream when you walk on them. They're not really screaming. The gases released from the compression of being stepped on only *sounds* like screaming."

All I could do was stare at him for a minute. "Right. Anyway, I assume you had a pack? Well, most days, being out of bed is like hiking with a thirty-pound pack strapped to my back. Some days, it's a little lighter; others, a little heavier. Then there are days it feels like it's filled with five hundred pounds of lead, and on those days, it's impossible to get out of bed."

I'd tried to explain this to Dr. Ronald Burrows, but he'd responded with a story about these hikers who'd gotten lost in the woods and resorted to cannibalism. I'm still not sure how it was supposed to help me.

"You should take off the backpack when it gets too heavy," Devin said.

"What?"

"Take it off. If it's full of lead, then it's not particularly useful. So get rid of it."

Was he serious? He looked serious. There was nothing in his expression to make me think he was anything other than serious. I'm not sure whether that made his suggestion better or worse. Either way, it annoyed me that he thought it was just that easy. Besides, wasn't trying to take off the pack how I'd wound up in the hospital in the first place?

"Why are you still at St. Benedict's?" Devin asked while I was lost in thought.

"Whoa. It's my turn to ask a question."

Devin shook his head. "You asked if I'd ever been hiking. Technically, I shouldn't have answered because you asked your question out of turn, but regardless, that makes it my turn."

"You're terrible at this game."

The corners of Devin's mouth twitched. "Or very good."

"I hate you." Because he was right. He was very good at the game. "Fine. Um, I guess because I'm embarrassed."

"Elaborate."

I liked how he'd phrased it as a command rather than a question so I couldn't turn his own rules back on him. I didn't have to say more, but I couldn't see any reason not to.

"Everyone at school knows what I did. If I go back, they'll either treat me like a freak or like a glass figurine. I just want them to forget about it. Especially my friends. Dina tried to come by the hospital, but I refused to see her. She's my best friend. Kind of my only friend. I know she's gonna be pissed at me, and I don't blame her. My family's no better. My sister thinks I've done all this for attention, and my parents treat me like I'm broken, but I'm not broken. I'm just tired."

Devin nodded along. When I finished, he said, "It sounds like you don't want to leave St. Benedict's because you've got lead in your backpack."

I saw what he was trying to do, and I didn't appreciate it. I already had a therapist. I didn't need another. Especially not one who was either pretending he was an alien or actually believed he was. "That wasn't a question."

"No."

"Then it's my turn."

"Yes."

I wanted an answer from Devin, a real answer, so I considered my question carefully, making sure I constructed it in such a way that he couldn't shimmy out of it with a joke or a vague reply.

"What is your primary reason for driving to wherever our final destination winds up being?"

"Good question," he said.

"Then answer."

Devin let out a soft sigh. "I'm going home."

"Like, Orlando?" We'd been driving north since we left St. Benedict's, so it seemed like a good guess.

"My real home."

I waited for him to laugh. The alien thing was just a quirk. A harmless bit of magical thinking to help him deal with the complexities of the world. When I was ten, I told people I was adopted because it was easier than accepting I was stuck with the family I'd been born into. It was an obvious lie. I looked way too much like both my parents. But Devin didn't laugh.

"So, your parents found you?" I asked, even though it wasn't my turn.

"Kind of."

"Kind of?"

"I let them find me."

"Now I'm confused," I said. "I thought you got lost."

Devin bit his bottom lip and furrowed his brow. "I got lost by accident. I stayed lost on purpose."

This was making my head hurt. "So, you ran away?"

"I suppose you could look at it that way."

"For someone who can't lie, you say an awful lot of things that aren't true."

Devin was perplexing. Did I believe he was an alien? No. But I also couldn't explain how he'd busted the bars off my window or started the car without any of Nurse Phillips's fingers.

"Why did you run away?"

Since I'd asked, like, ten questions since his last one, I didn't expect him to answer. I was surprised when he did.

"We have a tradition where I'm from. When we reach a certain age, we make a series of choices that shape the rest of our lives."

"Sounds like college," I muttered.

"The choices scared me. I was terrified of making the wrong ones. Earth was the last stop on my parents' mission before we returned home. When I got lost, I figured if I stayed lost long enough, I wouldn't have to choose and I couldn't mess up the rest of my life."

The world passed by as we flew down the interstate. "That really sucks, Devin. It's kind of the same here. If I don't do the things my parents expect me to do, I know they'll be disappointed."

"And you don't want to do those things?"

"What's the point?" I said. "The future's a shit sandwich, and everyone I know is lining up to stuff their faces. I just can't. Everything is awful and everything hurts, and it's not worth it. You never get to take off your pack. You have to keep carrying it no matter how heavy it gets. At least at St. Benedict's, I don't have to carry it very far."

Devin nodded. "I see, I was wrong to suggest you could remove your pack. Maybe, instead, what you need is someone to help you carry it." He cranked up the music and started singing again. He still didn't know the words, but he looked like he was having fun.

After an hour, Devin pulled off the interstate and drove down a series of roads until we reached a park. It was still the middle of the night, so we had to leave the car and hop the fence. I couldn't have said why I continued following Devin. I could have hitchhiked back to St. Benedict's, but I'd already come this far. Besides, what if he really could show me the stars? That had to be worth the risk, right?

"What's with the snacks?" I asked as we hit the trail. I couldn't see much in the dark, but Devin seemed confident, so I kept close to him.

Devin held up the paper sack. "We don't have these back home."

"Oh."

"Humans take so much for granted. Potato chips, dreams, music—"

"You don't have music?"

Devin sighed. "We do, but it's nothing like what you have. Remember the screaming mountains I told you about? They're more melodic than the music my people create."

"Then why don't you take some music with you?"

"I am." Devin tapped the side of his head and grinned. "It's all up here."

That was a scary thought. "Can I ask you a question?"

"You've asked me many questions, Keen. I've been keeping track. I think I won the game."

I couldn't help laughing. "Right. Fine. You won. This isn't for the game."

"Okay."

"You said you let your alien parents find you, which means you could've stayed lost. Why didn't you?"

Devin stopped and looked at me. He was a little taller. Under the canopy of trees and the yellow of the haze, he actually *looked* a little alien.

"Because I realized that not making a choice is still making a choice."

"So you're going to go home and make some choices? I still don't get why that scares you."

"I could make the wrong choices."

"Right," I said. "But so what? You can change your mind. As long as you don't hurt someone else, your choices aren't permanent. Nothing's permanent, really."

Devin rested his hand on my shoulder. "Except death."

"Touché." Our faces were so close, and he was looking at me with those soulful eyes. He was a handsome maybe-alien who'd escaped from a psychiatric hospital, and it was kind of doing it for me in that moment. I wondered what it would be like to kiss him. Devin had given me tingles before, but this was like a constant thrum from a low-level electrical shock. I made a choice of my own, leaned forward, and kissed him.

The moment I pressed my lips to Devin's, I realized I'd made a mistake. He flinched and backed away.

"Sorry!" I said. "Sorry. I just thought . . . I mean, you're cute, and I figured if you're lying about being an alien and really are planning to murder me, I didn't want the last person I kissed to be Alex Mayer with his awful rotten-egg breath."

Devin coughed and cleared his throat. "You surprised me is all. It's not a big deal."

"I should've asked before I attacked you with my tongue. You probably don't even like guys, do you?"

"Humans," Devin said.

"What?"

"Your gender is irrelevant. I'm not attracted to your entire species."

"Oh! Oh. Okay."

"Yes," Devin said. "Your people are repellent. And your mating rituals are the most disgusting I've ever witnessed. The places you put your mouths—"

"Got it! You can stop now!"

"But hugging is nice. May I hug you now?"

"I'd . . ." I tried to think of the last time someone had hugged me. The last time I'd let them. "I think I'd like that."

Devin crashed into me, throwing his arms around me and burying his face in my neck.

The tears began, and I didn't know where they'd come from, but my eyes were full and I shook, and Devin squeezed me like he was trying to wring me out.

When the wave of tears passed, I apologized.

"This is nice," Devin said. "Hugging is another thing your people take for granted."

"Yeah."

"Would you like me to touch your butt?"

I laughed. A giggle at first, but then I couldn't stop. I couldn't catch my breath. And then Devin laughed, and it was the most ridiculous sound I'd ever heard in my life, and that's saying something, seeing as I spent a couple hours trapped in a car listening to him sing.

"I knew I was funny," Devin said. And that started me laughing all over again.

When we were done, he grabbed my hand and pulled me into the dark. "Come on. They're almost here."

✧ ✠ ✧

The clearing was empty. Devin found a log to sit on and set down his bag of snacks. "Thank you for coming with me. This journey would've been boring without you."

I considered sitting beside him, but I'd spent so long in bed and then in a car that I couldn't bear to sit still. "So that's why you brought me along? For entertainment?"

"And so you could see the stars."

The sky was still empty, the stars hidden behind the haze. "You know it's okay if you've never seen them."

"But I have! And you will too!" There was an urgency in his voice I'd never heard from him before.

"Why is it so important to you? You don't even know me."

Devin was up and across the clearing quicker than I thought possible. He grabbed my shoulders and shook me. "The stars are the promise that there's more to the universe than you can know. That you're alive even when you feel like you shouldn't be."

His intensity caught me off guard. "I know!"

"You don't," he said. "Because if you did, then you never would've tried to end your life. So you don't know, but I want you to. I want you to know the stars are out there waiting for you even if you can't see them!"

"But why do you care what happens to me?"

Devin relaxed. He smiled. "Why shouldn't I care, Keen? Just because we don't know each other doesn't mean you don't matter."

I didn't know what to say. There were days I didn't feel like I mattered to the people closest to me, yet here was this weird stranger telling me I was important. And the thing that blew my mind most was that I believed him.

A breeze tore through the clearing, whipping up dirt and leaves. I pressed my arm to my eyes.

"They're here!" Devin shouted over the noise. He kicked off his shoes and began unbuttoning his shirt.

"What the hell are you doing?"

"I can't go to my ship wearing clothes." Devin said it like it was completely logical. Then he yanked off his pants.

Thankfully, it was still dark. Until it wasn't. Lights from above illuminated the clearing, centered on Devin. He was definitely an alien.

"Eyes up here, Keen," Devin said. "Humanity's obsession with your floppy bits is the second strangest thing I've encountered on this planet."

"What's the first?"

"Mayonnaise."

I ran to him and threw my arms around his neck. "Don't go."

"I have to," he said. "But maybe one day I'll come back. I hope you'll be here."

The lights pulsed and grew brighter. I handed Devin his bag of snacks.

"Goodbye, Keen. Thank Nurse Phillips for the use of his car when you return it."

"Wait! I can't drive!" The light grew blindingly bright, and I had to shut my eyes. When I opened them again, Devin was gone, and I was alone in the dark.

Except it wasn't totally dark.

I looked up. There was a hole in the haze, a portal to the rest of the universe filled with twinkling lights. Stars. They were so far away but close enough to touch. They were wishes and dreams. The promise that there was always more out there to explore. And Devin had given them to me. It was a gift I could never repay.

I fell to my knees and watched the stars until the haze had knit back together. But even though I couldn't see them anymore, I carried the stars in my heart. I was lost, but that didn't mean I had to stay lost forever. My pack was heavy, but I didn't have to carry it alone.

When I was ready, I stood and hiked back to the parking lot. I used the phone in Nurse Phillips's car to make a call.

"Hey, Mom," I said when she answered. "I think I'm ready to come home now."

The First Crush

BY KEAH BROWN

"Gina Newman is throwing an anti–Valentine's Day party tomorrow night. You two coming?" Kristen Andrews asked Jackie and Lila from where they stood at Jackie's locker.

"No, we don't even like Gina. She's rude, self-centered, and honestly, exhausting to be around. Right, Jackie?" Lila asked. Jackie was too busy watching the harsh hallway lights reflect a sparkle in Kristen's green eyes. She was a goner. A slight breeze ran through the hall from the open door nearby, pulling free one of Kristen's tight brown curls before it fell against her right eye and touched her glowing brown skin. Jackie could have written sonnets about that singular curl, and she might, later. Kristen's Paramore merch T-shirt was rolled at the sleeves. A couple of students walked past them, saying a pointed hello to Kristen and Lila only, but Jackie remained unaware.

"Earth to Jackie," Lila teased, waving her hand in front of Jackie's face, knocking her out of her stupor. Jackie shook her head and cleared her throat, wiping the sweat from her hands onto her jeans. She pulled a braid out of her face and back into her ponytail, tightening it once more. That motion made the temporary sunflower tattoo on her arm even more noticeable. Her best friends were watching her curiously. She knew she couldn't come out and say she was in love with Kristen, but she couldn't remain quiet either; they were both beginning to look at her funny. She had to think of an excuse quickly.

"Uh, yeah, we don't," Jackie managed, making quick eye contact with her shoes. She felt Lila's eyes on her, so she looked at her and smiled faintly. It worked, for now.

"No one likes Gina, but her parents are out of town, and JKL need to let off some steam," Kristen exclaimed, her curly brown hair bouncing as she rocked back and forth on her heels. Kristen ran a hand through her hair, pulling her eyes back into view again. Jackie was starting to find everything Kristen did cute. Her JKL (Jackie, Kristen, Lila) nickname, her contagious excitement, the way she smelled like lilies and hope, the way she said Jackie's name when she was fondly exasperated. Jackie hadn't noticed it until a month ago when they were in her room studying and Lila went to the bathroom, leaving Jackie and Kristen alone. Kristen kept excitedly high-fiving Jackie every time she got an answer right while they quizzed each other on math equations. Jackie found herself wanting to hold Kristen's hand in place before flipping it over to map out the lines on her palm. The realization hit Jackie like a semitruck. Lila interrupted them shortly after. Pulling herself from the memory, Jackie couldn't stop the smile spreading across her face.

"What about tradition?" Lila asked, crossing her arms. Every Valentine's Day weekend since middle school, Kristen, Jackie, and Lila spent that time watching romantic comedies and eating pizza while Jackie's parents went out to dinner. Jackie was even planning to throw in a few cheesy friendship films because platonic love was just as important as romantic love, and she was lucky to have it with Kristen and Lila. Though now she was hoping for the latter with Kristen.

"We can do tradition after the party. You know I love you two best, but this is our junior year of high school, and we won't have too many more moments like this. So, what do you say? Come on, Lils! Jackie, don't leave me hanging," Kristen pleaded, grabbing Jackie's hand and spinning her around like they did when they were kids. All Jackie could do was yelp in surprise at their closeness. As she spun, she watched a smirk make its way onto Lila's face. When Kristen dipped her, Jackie held her breath, inches from Kristen's face, trying to count the freckles just above her best friend's lips. There were at least ten freckles that danced across the span of Kristen's lips as she gave a wide smile and returned them both upright. "I have to run to my locker really quick. I'll meet y'all there."

Jackie let out a breath, and Lila came to stand beside her. "So, when are you going to tell her?" Lila asked, the smirk likely permanent on her face now. Jackie rolled her eyes, taking her jean jacket out of her locker and pulling it on slowly; her left arm locking in place made it take a few extra minutes. She waited impatiently for her body to cooperate, eager to hide the goose bumps on her black skin.

"What are you talking about?" Jackie asked, her heart racing. Was she that obvious? God, she hoped not.

"I've known you since we were in the third grade. Please," Lila said, shutting Jackie's locker door. "If it makes you feel any better, I don't think she has a clue."

Honestly, it did make Jackie feel better, because she had no plans of ever telling Kristen how she felt and risking what was sure to be inevitable rejection. Jackie was certain that she was too shy, awkward, and quiet for someone as vibrant, bold, and exciting as Kristen. She looked at Lila and let out a breath. Jackie knew she'd have to go into detail later, and it was kind of a relief that someone knew, especially someone who would take it to her grave if Jackie asked her to.

"Can we change the subject? I'm not ready to talk about it yet, especially not here," Jackie said. Lila nodded her head once and pressed on.

"Well, in other related news, I'm in love," Lila exclaimed. She stood next to Jackie in a blue jean jacket and a sunflower dress. Jackie rolled her eyes but happily took the arm held out to her. "Come on, we are going to be late for yearbook," Jackie said as they walked down the hallway arm in arm. She nodded politely at the teachers they passed and tried her best to pay attention to the words coming out of her lovesick friend's mouth.

"He's probably the one," Lila started, stopping to twirl them both in a circle. "We'd have two kids and a house with a porch swing—"

"Naturally," Jackie cut in, laughing when her friend looked at her with a serious expression.

"You'll still buy the house next door, like you promised, right?" Lila asked, pressing her free hand to her chest.

"Yes, Lee," Jackie reassured her. Lila did this a lot, falling in love every two weeks with someone new and convincing herself that they were her soulmate. Jackie and Kristen had to live to the right and the left of her respectively. First there had been Theo Saldana, Lila and Theo were going to travel the world together, starting in Spain; next was Pete Rose, Lila planned for them to be professors at the same university; Henry Whitman followed Pete; and Bradley Fine followed him. The only issue with these crushes for Jackie was that she had to be there to pick up Lila's broken heart each time. Lila was chronically in love, something Jackie was decidedly never going to let herself be. She planned to squash her crush on her other best friend as quickly as possible to avoid making anyone feel uncomfortable. "Who is the lucky guy this week?"

"Lucas Reid," Lila announced as though the answer were obvious. Jackie tried her hardest to hide a giggle behind her hand.

"The new kid who sits in front of us in homeroom? Have you ever even spoken to him?" Jackie asked, pulling a piece of gum out of her pocket and popping it in her mouth.

"Not exactly, because he's new, but he's perfect. He is funny, smart, kind, and beautiful," Lila promised. Steps away from the yearbook meeting, Lila leaned into Jackie conspiratorially. "And, he just joined yearbook."

"Oh, my goodness, well then, it's fate. I better start planning your wedding now," Jackie said, laughing as Lila punched her arm before they both walked inside. The other yearbook committee members were all talking and laughing around the huge circular table that Mr. Sanchez, the yearbook advisor and social studies teacher, said fostered team morale. Jackie and Lila sat in the two open seats and made small talk with the people nearest them before Mr. Sanchez started the meeting.

"First order of business is for us to welcome Lucas Reid to yearbook. You like photography, don't you, Lucas?" Mr. Sanchez led. Lucas's floppy red hair fell into his eyes quickly before he brushed it aside. He wore a white T-shirt, black jeans, and green Converses. Jackie looked over quickly to find Lila swooning. Lila's favorite color was green, so Jackie was already mentally preparing for that hour-long debrief at her house later.

"Yeah, I do. I fell in love with it at my old school. Portraits are my favorite. Anyway, I'm excited to be here, so, uh, that's it," Lucas said. He sat down in the free seat across from Lila, who was currently hitting

Jackie's sneaker-covered toe repeatedly to get her attention. Jackie squeezed her best friend's hand under the table in encouragement.

"Hi, Lucas, I'm Lila, managing editor. To the left of me is Jackie, our photo editor, though she should be writing for the school paper. She slums it with us instead," Lila said. Jackie perked up and smiled politely when she heard her name. "I like yearbook better," Jackie said. She used to work on the paper too, but the advisor, Mr. Fedder, kept trying to write her articles for her because he claimed her chronic pain made her work a little slower than the rest of the staff, and he didn't want to accommodate her disability. Jackie did quit last semester, but she still wrote in her free time.

Lila began introducing Lucas to everyone, but Jackie tuned her out when she caught sight of who was at the door. Kristen walked in and winked at Jackie before taking the seat directly across from her. Then Kristen pulled out her phone.

Kristen: Forgot to save me a seat right next to yours, Jacks?

Jackie: Sorry, it was already taken when we got here

Kristen: That's okay, I like the view from here anyway:)

Jackie watched as Kristen quickly put her phone away and pulled her glasses up off the bridge of her nose and apologized for being late. Jackie was still unsure what Kristen meant by enjoying the view from where she sat. There wasn't much to see in the classroom as it was. Jackie didn't want to feel this way, like her heart would hammer out of her chest if she didn't press her hand over it.

She knew she wasn't supposed to give anyone this much power over her. She knew it was ridiculous that a look her way, a small smile, or a playful dip from Kristen could determine how she felt about herself that day, but here she was, dependent upon them. Crushes were Lila's thing, not hers. Jackie hated the way her own brain betrayed her by creating fake scenarios that might never become reality. Like dancing with Kristen under the harsh fluorescent lights at prom next year, making out in between classes at the staircase on the west end of the school that the popular kids hung out at, Kristen realizing she was in love after asking what Jackie was listening to. For that last fantasy, they would share headphones; Jackie would take the left, and Kristen would take the right, locking eyes quickly before leaning in for a kiss.

Jackie found the whole thing to be cliché even as she continued to daydream while the meeting wore on and Lila sent her knowing glances. When Jackie's fingers brushed Kristen's as they were going over design ideas for the placement of the club photos, Jackie wanted to jump out of her own skin. She was being ridiculous, and her only saving grace was the fact that Kristen was none the wiser. When the meeting was dismissed, Jackie was the first one out of the room before realizing she needed to double back and grab her backpack.

Once they were safely inside Jackie's car, Lila let out a fit of giggles. Jackie shot her a glare, but it did nothing to stop her blond-haired, blue-eyed best friend and current tormentor.

"I thought you didn't do crushes, Jacks," Lila teased, turning up the radio as Jackie pulled out of the school's parking lot and moved carefully onto the street.

"I don't know what you're talking about," Jackie tried. She sang along to the songs on the radio before she got to her street. Jackie stopped singing and started avoiding direct eye contact as she pulled into her driveway. Her dad, James, was outside mowing the lawn—he loved that machine a little too much. Jackie waved to him as she and Lila got out of the car, and he cut the lawn mower off.

"Hi, ladies. How was school, and where is Kristen?" he called out, pulling his sunglasses off.

"Good. She's with her dad today," Jackie and Lila said in unison, walking toward the front door.

"Mom's inside. Say hi before you go shut yourselves away in that room," Dad said before turning on the mower and getting back to his quality time with his favorite kid. Lila nudged Jackie's shoulder and winked.

"Besides, Kristen is cute! She's got great freckles and the prettiest brown eye—" Lila began.

"Green," Jackie cut in. "Her eyes are green."

"Is that so?" Lila teased.

"Shut up," Jackie whined before pushing past Lila and walking into her house. Inside, they found Jackie's mom, a short Black woman with a black pixie cut, arranging cheesecake bars on a plate. Lila bounced over excitedly while Jackie gave her mom a "hi!" and took her time walking. The thing about Angela Harris was that she always knew when something was up with one of her kids, and since Jackie's brother, Sam, was away at college, Jackie knew her mother's senses were heightened. By the time Jackie reached the kitchen island and grabbed a cheesecake bar for herself, Lila had already eaten two and told Jackie's mom she loved her most. Jackie pulled out her phone and began scrolling mindlessly as her mom asked about school and yearbook, and if they wanted to go shopping to help her pick out her Valentine's Day outfit.

"Mom, you know Valentine's Day is just a fake holiday made up to get people to buy gifts, right?" Jackie asked, anticipating the matching groans that came out of Lila's and her mother's mouths.

"So is your birthday, sweetie. You still accept the gifts you get," her mother retorted, and Lila patted Jackie's hand sympathetically before laughing. Jackie went back to scrolling, liking posts here and there, commenting on the pictures that Sam posted, because she missed him, though she would never say it aloud. "Where is Kristen?" Angela asked. Jackie looked up from her phone to answer.

"She's with her dad today. Also, can I go to Gina Newman's anti–Valentine's Day party tomorrow?" Jackie asked. She held her breath, still scrolling in an effort to appear calm and disinterested while her mother looked at Lila.

"I thought we didn't like Gina after she spent a few months making your life hell because your brother wouldn't go out with her. Lila, are Trish and Valerie letting you go?" Angela asked, and Lila nodded enthusiastically.

"Correct, we still don't like Gina. I texted my moms during lunch. As we all know, I'm very pro-love, but somebody has to keep an eye on Kristen, and Jackie, the number one Valentine's Day hater."

"Thank you for your service." Angela bowed playfully, turning to wink at Lila.

Jackie rolled her eyes and continued scrolling. She had just passed a meme with a bunny when a selfie of Kristen popped up. She had paint all over her face and clothes, and she was smiling to the camera, looking so happy and carefree that Jackie couldn't have stopped her own smile from spreading if she'd tried. A text alert let her know that she was getting a new message.

Kristen: Hi! Please tell me Momma H said yes to the party?

Jackie: She said yes. Lee said she's going to keep an eye on us.

Kristen: typical Lee haha. I'll meet you guys there. Give everyone a hug from me. They're calling our name for a table bye!

Jackie: bye!

Kristen: Oh, and Jacks?

Jackie: Yeah?

Kristen: I hope you'll save a dance for me tomorrow:)

Jackie studied the text intently before hearting it and closing out the message. She couldn't let herself think too much of it. Kristen just liked to dance, and Jackie was painfully shy. Kristen was just trying to help her get out of her shell. Jackie turned back to the picture instead, intently deducing that Kristen was with a girl she didn't recognize. Lila would probably know—she knew everyone. There was a risk in asking her, though. She'd tease Jackie mercilessly, which, fine, she kind of deserved it. The other risk was having her mother start asking questions Jackie wasn't really sure how to answer herself.

"Well, Jackie pretends she doesn't believe in love and crushes, but I'm not buying it. In fact, when the right girl comes along, she'll be more lovesick than the rest of us," Lila teased, bumping into Jackie, who silently scoffed without malice behind it.

"I believe it. There's got to be a reason she's smiling at her phone like that," Jackie's mom prompted, laughing at the way Jackie's eyes jumped up from the screen to her.

"What? I wasn't smiling," Jackie responded. She liked Kristen's picture and put her phone in her pocket.

By the time Jackie and Lila pulled up to Gina Newman's house, the party was in full swing. The sign on the front lawn that read LOVE SUCKS was blowing in the wind. As they made their way up the front steps, they could hear "Since U Been Gone" by Kelly Clarkson blasting from the speakers. Lila rang the doorbell, then began singing along. A few moments later, Gina answered the door and pulled Lila into a big hug.

"Hey, girl! I'm so glad you made it!" Gina exclaimed. Lila looked at Jackie, but Jackie just shrugged. Jackie made eye contact with Gina and was surprised when Gina leveled a smile her way. "I'm even happy to see you, Julie," Gina urged. "Come in, come in." She stepped aside for Lila and Jackie to walk through the door, leaving behind the smell of cheap vodka in her wake.

"That explains it," Lila whispered to Jackie. That was the last time Jackie was going to be able to hear anything, she thought as they stepped further inside. Directly ahead of her, Jackie could see Austin Fleming, who was losing a game of beer pong against his lacrosse teammates while some of the nicer cheerleaders, Felicia Barton, Jenny Wise, and Maria Santarini, made conversation with one another as they watched the game. It wasn't long before they waved Jackie and Lila over. At first they made small talk about the classes they shared with Jackie: gym, financial literacy, math, and government. Jackie kept her answers brief until Maria offered to get Jackie a rum and Coke. Surprising even herself, Jackie agreed—drinking wasn't her thing. She was normally the designated driver, having decided that most alcohol tasted like cough medicine anyway. However, in this moment, Jackie felt so awkward that she hoped nursing a drink would give her something to do with her hands. After two drinks, though, Jackie found she couldn't stop talking. She felt like she blinked and the game was over, but her conversations were not. There she stood, holding court with the most popular kids in school, one of her best friends included, and everyone seemed to be having a good time.

"We became best friends when Lee spilled red paint all over the very cute white pants I was wearing in Mrs. Johnson's art class," Jackie started.

"In my defense, we were eight and my hands were clammy," Lila cut in, rolling her eyes fondly. Jackie bumped her shoulder playfully before continuing.

"Anyway, I'm obviously trying not to cry at this point. I mean, these are the jeans I saved up three weeks of allowance for, right? So at this point, I'm hyperventilating. It feels like hours have passed. Our teacher is, for some odd reason, doing absolutely nothing to help." Jackie paused, her captive audience leaning in. So, this was what momentary power felt like? Nice.

"I'm dabbing her pants with a wet paper towel, very much making it worse," Lila said. "We're both crying at this point, we couldn't hold it in any longer. And then this really adorable girl with brown curly hair—"

"Kristen," Jackie clarified.

"Kristen comes over to help me with more wet paper towels. I'm crying, Jacks is crying, and the teacher is still doing very little to help." Lila laughed at the memory.

"It never gets any better of course. My pants are effectively ruined, but—"

"Kristen put red paint on her own pants so Jacks wouldn't be alone, and then I did too," Lila cut in.

"Exactly," Jackie finished, to a round of applause. She and Lila bowed playfully before Jackie polished off her drink.

"You two should go on the road," Gina interrupted sarcastically. Lila arched an eyebrow at her, ready to verbally spar if need be. Gina laughed dismissively, waving a hand at Lila as she walked to Jackie's free side and looped Jackie's arm in hers. "Where is Kristen? I'm surprised she's not with you two. I heard she's seeing someone. That would surely break your heart, wouldn't it, Jacks?" Gina stage-whispered, satisfied when everyone gasped.

"If she was seeing someone, we would know," Jackie stated, but she felt a little unsure after seeing Kristen's earlier post. Lila stepped up, putting space between Jackie and Gina. Jackie was grateful; so much about Gina made Jackie feel uncomfortable and insecure.

"You know everything, don't you, Miss Photo Editor?" Gina asked, her words beginning to slur.

"Yep, that's why Mr. Sanchez chose her over you," Lila shot back.

"Is it? Rumor has it, there were *other* factors at play," Gina sneered.

"What did you just say?" Lila asked, pushing into Gina's space. It was Jackie's turn to interfere. Gina wasn't worth the trouble. Jackie grabbed Lila's arm and calmed her down. The doorbell rang, and everyone turned toward the sound.

"That's my cue," Gina said, walking through the now-parted crowd to the door. Someone turned the music back up, and the party was in full swing again.

"Kristen! Just the girl we've been waiting for, and who is this?" Gina purred from her perch at the front door. Jackie's eyes snapped to attention, and Kristen waved at her. Standing next to her was the girl from the Instagram photo. Jackie tried her best to smile, but she felt nauseous. She agreed to another drink that Maria went to get them—a drink Jackie couldn't pronounce the name of, but one she knew would take the edge off and make standing in a spinning room with her unrequited crush more bearable. (*When did the room start spinning? And why is it so hot all of a sudden?*) Lila squeezed Jackie's hand quickly. Jackie closed her eyes and took a breath, and when she opened them again, Maria was handing her a cup with blue liquid in it. Jackie took a large gulp as Kristen and her mystery guest made their way to the group. Gina wasn't far behind, a permanent smirk on her lips.

"Hey, everyone, sorry we are late. I couldn't find my glasses," Kristen said, her hand nervously stroking the back of her neck. Jackie tried and failed not to follow the movement. "Ilana, this is Lee and Jacks, and everyone," Kristen said while Jackie finished off the last of her drink. She was feeling it now, drunk and nauseous, though she was certain the nausea came from seeing the gorgeous girl at her best friend's side. The kind of girl Jackie was sure she could never be. A leggy brunette who looked like she'd just stepped off of a runway, she commanded attention in the room without even trying. Jackie was pretty sure she heard some of the guys gasp as Ilana walked in—she did, too. Her hair was in a perfect dark brown bob, and she had perfect skin, unlike Jackie's, which was littered with scars from surgeries she couldn't avoid. She held her head high as she walked; Jackie, on the other hand, was always watching her feet as she moved, trying not to fall. Jackie had to worry about taking breaks after long stretches of walking and had to constantly apologize for the ways in which her body gave out on her at the worst possible times. With all of her body complications, Jackie didn't think Kristen would ever want to date her. However, Photo Girl seemed perfectly datable.

"I've heard so much about all of you. Especially you two. It's very nice to meet you," Ilana said. She stuck her hand out to Lila first, who shook it enthusiastically, giving Jackie enough time to find a smile that felt genuine. Ilana turned to Jackie and winked. "This one wouldn't shut up about you," Ilana teased, and Jackie watched as Kristen punched Ilana's arm, refusing to make eye contact with Jackie. What did that even mean? Jackie's head was swimming. She wanted to ask Ilana what she meant, but she just laughed awkwardly and waited for Jackie to shake her hand. That was when things took a turn for the worst.

"Your girlfriend is really pretty," Jackie slurred as she tried and failed to grab Ilana's outstretched hand.

"What?" Kristen asked.

Jackie opened her mouth to apologize before vomiting all over Ilana's and Kristen's shoes.

"EW, Julie, get out," Gina yelled. Jackie let Lila and Maria help her to her car and place her in the passenger seat. She watched Lila mouth an apology to Kristen and Ilana, and Jackie realized she'd ruined this for Lila, too. She shut her eyes and could taste the vomit in her mouth. Lila climbed into the driver seat and put the windows down.

"I'm glad we already agreed that I'd be the DD. Let's get you home." Lila started the engine and pulled the car out of the driveway.

"I really messed this up, huh?" Jackie groaned. She pulled out her phone and texted.

Jackie: I'm really sorry.

She watched as three dots danced across her screen and disappeared before reappearing and disappearing once more. It took Jackie a moment to realize she'd started crying.

✧ ⊠ ✧

When they got to Jackie's house, Kristen still had not texted back. And when Jackie's parents saw how drunk she was, they grounded her and took her phone. The following Monday at school, Jackie was admittedly avoiding Kristen. She wasn't even sure what she was supposed to say exactly. "Sorry for getting drunk and throwing up on your and your girlfriend's shoes"? That would have gone over as well as a giraffe in a tiny house. Besides, Jackie figured that if she ignored Kristen, she could avoid having the let's-stop-being-friends conversation she was sure was coming. By the next Wednesday, the universe had decided to cut Jackie's plan short and punish Jackie further. Mr. Turner, the biology teacher, partnered her up with Kristen for their yearlong set of science experiments. Kristen had never responded to her texts, and Jackie's parents had taken her phone as soon as she got home, so she couldn't try again. Jackie got the hint, though, because Kristen was avoiding her at all costs, too, in school hallways and at yearbook.

Now, if she'd been Lila, a hopeless romantic who loved a redemption story, Jackie would have found this development exciting, worn her cutest clothes on lab days, and tried her best to flirt and bat her eyelashes. And by the end of the second or third lab, Kristen would have been accepting her apology. The problem was, Jackie was not Lila, and although she did try to look extra cute on the first lab day at the encouragement of her other best friend, Jackie was immensely nervous. She didn't know what to say, despite the fact that they never used to have a problem filling silences before. So she sat there next to Kristen, croaking out yeses and nos like she was recovering from tonsil surgery.

"If we pour too much of this clear liquid into that beaker, it will explode, right?" Kristen asked. Jackie nodded. Kristen let out a huff and placed the beaker back on the table. Jackie picked up a beaker of green liquid next to it and added it slowly. The green liquid became clear, and Jackie set it back down. Even though she couldn't speak, her body still managed to betray her. Every time Kristen spoke to her, Jackie felt like her eyes were seconds away from turning into those hearts from old cartoons. Her hands were sweaty, and not in the cute movie way—in the is-she-pouring-water-directly-onto-her-palm? way.

"What do we do next, Jackie?" Kristen said. The frustration in her voice was evident. Jackie understood, really. Kristen already struggled in science, and Jackie wasn't making it easy. "You giving me the silent treatment is rich, considering you're the one who—"

"You have been the one ignoring me, too. Plus, I have no idea how to talk to you now," Jackie interrupted.

"You've never had any problems speaking to me," Kristen muttered back.

"Well, that was before," Jackie said.

"Before what?" Kristen asked. "Before you threw up on my and my soon-to-be stepsister's shoes before calling her my girlfriend?"

"What? Your what?" Jackie stammered.

"My future stepsister—my dad proposed to Vivian at dinner. I told you and Lee that Viv has a daughter who lives in California." Jackie ran through her memory bank. Kristen had mentioned her a few times before, but never by name. "They had some random week off, so she was visiting. And you threw up on her shoes."

"I'm—"

"Don't say sorry, Jacks. I know that you're sorry for that, but what about the rest of it? The way you have barely said more than a sentence to me this past week, you've avoided me in yearbook, you avoid my locker. Are you shutting me out because Ilana said I wouldn't stop talking about you?" Kristen asked, and she began to back away from where Jackie stood. Jackie tried to reach for Kristen, to do what, she wasn't sure. In the process, she almost broke three test beakers, and by that point, Mr. Turner was walking toward their lab station.

"What happened here?" Mr. Turner asked as the rest of the class turned to look at them. Jackie's eyes never left Kristen's face, but Kristen refused to look at her.

"Can I be excused?" Kristen asked before leaving the classroom.

By the time Jackie saw Lila for sixth period study hall, Lila told Jackie that Kristen had texted her about what happened. Lila and Jackie were asked to deliver papers to the main office, which was perfect, because it gave Jackie the chance to walk past Mr. Gabriel's math class, where Kristen always sat in the front row. Jackie sounded like a creep even to herself, but she was now even more afraid to lose Kristen. Jackie had just finished explaining the disaster that was biology class to Lila. Lila blew out a pitying breath and smiled.

"I don't think this means the end of your friendship. I just think you need to tell her how you feel."

"I can't," Jackie said.

"Well, then, years from now, when you look back at this defining moment, all you'll be able to say is at least you looked cute during lab," Lila said. Though it didn't make her feel better, Jackie smiled at her friend in thanks. The whole getting drunk and throwing up on her best friend and her best friend's almost stepsister's shoes at the house of the most popular girl in school was definitely not what she wanted as a defining moment. Not to mention, the blatant snickering, even from the classmates who weren't there but had heard about it, was mortifying.

"That'll be my only consolation," Jackie cried, stopping to adjust some of the papers in her hand.

"Not if you tell her," Lila singsonged. Jackie ignored her and pretended to look at a stack of papers in the main office to the left of her.

"I hate feeling like this," Jackie moaned. They said goodbye to the secretary on their way out.

"What is wrong with having a crush? And while we are at it, let me ask you the same question you always ask me: What is it that you like most about her?" Lila retorted.

"I don't know," Jackie said, skirting around Lila's second question. "I feel like it's just too much. I don't know how you don't get overwhelmed with how much you end up thinking about and caring about someone."

"That's half the fun," Lila said.

"I like the way she looks at life, okay! She's endlessly hopeful, super smart, she always smells great, and she is very, very hot. And she never makes me feel like she is embarrassed by me. Neither of you do. Also, she makes it easier to believe that needing help with carrying my books, and retying my shoes after gym class, and needing to rest my body doesn't make me a burden," Jackie said. One of the perks of having parents who were ready and willing to fight to get you the accommodations you needed was that they lobbied the school to give you extra time to get your books and your choice of a helper. Kristen always volunteered.

"You'll never be a burden," Lila promised. "So, let's say Kristen were into you, too. What do you think dating her would be like?" Lila asked as they made their way to Jackie's locker to grab her next set of books and folders for class. Jackie made sure that her face looked pained, but she was secretly excited to play along. Most days, she felt like singing "I Can Hear the Bells" from the *Hairspray* soundtrack whenever Kristen was near or brought up.

She closed her locker and began walking down the hallway toward study hall.

"She'd meet me at my locker every morning, and we'd talk about what work we have to do, or she'd tell me about a song that reminded her of me," Jackie said. "We'd make plans for the weekend—"

"Double dates?" Lila asked.

"Double dates. Every morning before she'd leave my locker, she'd kiss my cheek and say, 'See you in bio, gorgeous.' And then next year, when we can start leaving campus for lunch, I'd drive the four of us to Starbucks at least once a week just because I could," Jackie finished, unlooping her arm from Lila's so she could walk into class.

"That sounds nice," Lila said dreamily as they sat at the desks in the back of the classroom. It did sound nice, perfect even . . . The more she thought about it, the more she couldn't find a reason to keep her secret any longer.

By the time the first Friday bell rang, Jackie was relieved. She hadn't spoken to Kristen since Wednesday, giving her the space she asked for. And the space gave her time to think as well. If she couldn't tell Kristen how she felt, she was going to write it. Jackie started with how she felt like she could fly when she was with her, how her breath caught when she looked at her, and how she wanted so badly to be the kind of girl Kristen would be proud to have on her arm. She shared all the things she hoped for with Kristen, the double dates, dances, trips to the movie theater, concerts, and Starbucks runs. When she finished, she folded the note and placed it carefully in her front pocket. She had just enough time before the next class to find Kristen and tell her everything.

Jackie walked to the west side of campus, hoping to catch Kristen on her way out of math, and the trek there left her breathless. She wasn't sure if that was because she needed to stretch more or because she was nervous. Probably both. When she got to the classroom door, Jackie's heart rate sped up as she looked around for her friend's curly brown hair. She wasn't there. But Denise Feldstein was looking at her curiously.

"Need help with something?" she asked.

"No, but have you seen Kristen?" Jackie asked, taking the time to catch her breath.

"Last I saw her, she was near the art wing," Denise said.

"Thank you," Jackie called, moving as quickly as she could toward the end of the hallway. She was willing to be late for her next class because she didn't know if she'd have the nerve to do this again.

The art wing was empty, but she could hear piano notes coming from the music hall nearby. Maybe the person playing might have seen Kristen. When Jackie walked in the room, though, she was surprised to find Kristen sitting at the piano playing a song Jackie had never heard. She listened for a few moments, letting herself get lost in it. Jackie reached for the note in her pocket and held the folded piece of paper like she was afraid it might slip through her fingers. Jackie took a deep breath in self-assurance before stepping toward the piano.

"Hey, can we talk?" Jackie asked. Kristen stopped playing and turned around like she already knew Jackie was there. Kristen nodded her head and folded her hands on her lap in front of her. God, Jackie thought she looked so beautiful even in the low light of the music room; she could count her freckles here, too. The way Kristen was looking at her, though, she gathered that now wasn't the time to try. "I know that I'm probably the last person you want to see, but I just need to say this and then if you want me to leave, I'll go."

"Jackie—"

"Please, let me just get this out. I wrote you this note and you can read it if you want but the truth is that I can't breathe when you look at me, and my heart races when I make you laugh. You make me want to dance down these hallways with you, be bold and brave. I didn't shut you out because of anything Ilana said. For the life of me, I can't remember letting her get to say much at all. I really am sorry about that. Kristen, being one of your best friends is one of the greatest honors of my life, but I want more of you, I want more with you. I'm aware how selfish that sounds, and I'm not the one that's good with words—you and Lila are—but I think I love you. Okay, that's it, that's all." Jackie blew out a breath. She watched Kristen's face soften, and then Jackie found an interesting spot on her boots to stare at. She'd done it, she'd said the words she needed to. And yet she couldn't get her feet to move, unsure of what Kristen would say but expecting the worst.

"I think I love you, too," Kristen said. Jackie's head snapped up to find that Kristen was standing in front of her now. She could smell the lilies. She could pull the curl that fell out of her ponytail and into her line of sight back behind her ear; God, she wanted to.

"What?" Jackie asked instead. She couldn't believe her ears.

"I love you too, Jackie Harris. I told Lila a couple of months ago and swore her to secrecy."

"What? Lila knew?" Jackie asked, her mind running a mile a minute. She owed Lila a fruit basket or a spa day, something to show her appreciation for keeping both of their secrets.

"I planned to tell you at the party, but—"

"I threw up on your shoes." They both laughed.

"Are you going to throw up now?" Kristen asked, cupping Jackie's face and leaning in.

"No." Jackie smiled, her eyes fluttering closed.

"There's so much to like about you too, Jacks. Your infectious smile, your very dry but hilarious sense of humor, the way you're always there when Lila and I need you the most. Impromptu dancing with you is my favorite thing to do. And, Jacks, this one is important too: Your butt always looks amazing in jeans."

Jackie opened her eyes once more, laughing loudly at the last of Kristen's words.

"You've been checking me out?" Jackie asked.

"Blatantly." Kristen shrugged.

"Then kiss me already," Jackie demanded.

They kissed and kissed. Long after the bell rang for the last period of the day, long after Jackie dipped her with a giggle, and long after the music teacher cleared her throat and they ran out of the room hand in hand.

The First Job

BY YAMILE SAIED MÉNDEZ

If Chloe didn't run out of the smoothie store, she was going to commit a crime. Another one. But who could really blame her? She hurried to the exit and ran out, almost hitting two middle-school girls with the door. She imagined that the judge that lived inside her mind would be like, "Tell me, Ms. Brown, what made you do it?"

She'd be wearing a black dress that reached from her chin to her toes to show her regret as she explained, "I'm sorry, Your Honor. But the girls were innocent casualties. You see? It's actually Carmen's fault. If she, my best friend since we were in day care, hadn't stolen my boyfriend of two years, then this wouldn't have happened."

She shook her head to erase the imaginary court trial that would declare her guilty on all counts and got into her car.

She knew she was being irrational. As a staunch feminist, she knew it wasn't Carmen's fault. Well, not all of it. After all, Victor deserved some of her anger, didn't he? He was the one telling her he loved her and wanted to move in with her once they went off to college and were far from their controlling, conservative parents' reach. He said that and then turned to make out—and who knew what else—with Chloe's best friend behind her back.

Hot tears blurred her vision, but she managed to get out of the roundabout safe and sound, before heading toward the countryside, away from their small town of Grayson, Utah, population one thousand, where everyone knew everyone else's business.

School had started a couple of weeks ago. Homecoming had been a success. Chloe, obsessed with the vintage look of film and the surprise of not knowing what the camera would catch until the film got developed, had bought a disposable camera to memorialize the occasion. In the middle of her favorite Bad Bunny song, one of the boys had taken the camera from her, and after he snapped a picture, he passed it on to the next person.

"Give it back!" Victor had yelled, but Chloe kissed him and said, "It's okay, babe! It'll be fun to see random shots from the party."

She got it back at the end of the night when she was waiting to meet up with Victor and Carmen to get their coats.

On Monday, Chloe took the camera to be developed at the photo place in Provo. A couple of hours later, she picked up the prints. She couldn't help herself and checked them in the car. She smiled like a dork at the shot of beautiful Victor in his suit, his eyes full of love for her. She placed this print on the dashboard and quickly flipped through the rest until she saw something that solidified the air in her lungs.

"Motherfu—" she managed to gasp.

One of the shots was of a group making funny faces at the camera. And in the background were Victor and Carmen kissing, his hand cupping her perfect peach butt.

Chloe knew how that hand felt against hers because she and Victor had dated since sophomore year, and now into their senior year, they had been a lot more intimate than anyone had imagined. Chloe hadn't told Carmen that she and Victor had started sleeping together during the summer. Their last summer of high school. But even if Carmen hadn't known this, she knew Chloe and Victor had been an item for years.

There was no excuse.

A couple of times Victor had joked that the two friends were basically the same person.

It was true, in a way.

Chloe and Carmen had many things in common. Besides the initials of their first names, both girls were second-generation Latinas. They both had decent grades. The same taste in movies, music, and books.

Obviously, they also had the same taste in boys.

Athletic, attractive, assholes.

Victor was all of the above. But he had been Chloe's asshole.

Or maybe he'd never been?

The memory of her discovery still had her gasping for air. She studied the snapshots of that night against the background of her memory to understand how she could have been so oblivious.

The worst was that Carmen and Victor looked hot together. No, they looked *right*.

Or maybe Chloe was just now seeing clearly for the first time.

All the times Victor offered to drive Carmen home? The looks Carmen sent him when she thought Chloe didn't notice? The way Carmen blushed when Victor entered a room? It was all so clear now.

She'd mentioned this to them once, pretending like she was joking, and Victor got all offended, accusing her of *seeing things*.

The signs had been there. Chloe had just ignored them. She'd ignored what her instinct was telling her. She'd learned to ignore her inner voice. She was so mad at herself.

She rolled the window down. Immediately, the wind tangled her long, curly hair, and untangled the knots in her shoulders and her thoughts. Sooner or later, she'd have to turn her car around. It would get dark soon, and she still hadn't fixed the busted taillight from after she'd hit Victor's car when she'd seen them whispering frantically in the school parking lot.

He and his parents had promised they wouldn't press charges, but she still had to pay for the body and paint job. The worst part of Chloe losing her mind was that Carmen and Victor had become the victims. No one sided with Chloe, not even her family.

Her dad had insisted she get a job to pay for what she'd done.

That was why she'd gone to the smoothie place. To apply for a job. Little had she known that Carmen and Victor had beaten her to it, again, and been working there already.

Jobs for high schoolers were few in their small town. She could drive to Provo, but she didn't want to spend her paycheck in gas—she'd never earn enough to pay off her debt. She wanted to leave Grayson and never look back.

But look back at the rearview mirror was what she did.

She passed a sign that said "Help Wanted," and then "Rotten Hill Grove." At first she shivered, thinking of getting a job at the one Halloween attraction in the area. Other than sheep and fruit trees, there wasn't much in their town for other people to come see. But the haunted forest brought people from miles and miles around.

People signed up to work months in advance, and they usually had a long waiting list for the few open positions they had.

Was this another sign from the universe?

She wasn't going to ignore it.

She turned and drove back to the haunted place sign. She got out of the car and walked to the wooden sign. It was real. It was there.

She glanced at the long, graveled road that led to a beat-up trailer with an Office sign written with red spray paint. The writing looked rusty, like old blood. She started walking, kicking up dust.

She imagined what her parents would say when she told them she was working at the haunted place. It would confirm their opinion that she'd lost her mind. That her anger was unwarranted. That she was going through a crisis because she didn't know how to let go of a grudge.

But they couldn't expect her to work alongside the people who had destroyed her. She didn't have any other close friends besides Carmen and Victor. What they'd done to her was so wrong and twisted. Why was she required to forgive them?

She was so angry she thought her blood was boiling. She hesitated. If she walked to the trailer and interviewed, she might come across as unhinged. Exactly what she wanted to avoid. But she needed a job.

As she walked closer to the trailer, she could hear soft piano music, and the scent of coffee wafted from under the door. She knocked.

A woman's shriek rang from inside, draining the air from Chloe's lungs as if she'd been the one who'd screamed.

Frightened, Chloe looked around, but she might as well have been the only human in the world. The hair on the back of her neck stood up painfully.

When she was about to turn around to leave, the sound of approaching footsteps stopped her. She should've driven on the gravel road. Now even if she ran, she was, like, half a mile away from the car, and a sprinter she was not. She'd be killed, and nobody would know what had happened to her. Would anyone even care?

Although they were mad at her now, her parents and her sister, Oriana, might, right? But what about the rest of the world?

She imagined Carmen and Victor at the school assembly, crying, pretending they were sad for her although secretly they had to be so relieved that Chloe was dead and nothing stood in the way of their love.

The image was enough to give her a different kind of determination. She wouldn't go down without a fight.

She wouldn't give them the satisfaction.

As she scrambled to trace her steps back, she saw a branch and grabbed it. It was a pathetic excuse for a weapon to defend herself, but it was better than nothing. If worse came to worse, she could use it to gouge the eye out of whoever was coming in her direction.

The door opened with a creak, and Chloe stumbled over a coil of rope she hadn't seen and fell on the dusty ground.

"Uy!" A man's voice came from behind her. "Are you okay?"

He sounded kind. Chloe couldn't tell for sure, but something inside her relaxed when he spoke. She got back on her feet and was shaking the dust off her clothes when the man walked up to her, and she turned.

He looked nothing like she'd imagined. He was about her dad's age, but tall and pale, like he spent a lot of time inside or only came out in the dark. His expression, though, was soft and tired-looking. It was his clear blue eyes that had a youthful spark.

"Are you here for the sign?" He pointed at the road and smiled shyly. "You must have gotten scared with the sounds. It's a recording to add to the crazy scientist's station." He shrugged.

"That makes sense." She chuckled.

There was a moment of awkward silence.

"You're here for the job, then?" he asked again, snapping Chloe out of her shyness.

She looked down at her clothes, covered in dust. Her tennis shoes were muddy. She dropped the branch she was still holding and tried to smooth her hair down to make herself presentable. She gave up. "I guess I don't look very professional, do I?"

"That depends on what job you're applying for." The man chuckled. "You could make a very convincing specter."

She grimaced. He must have felt the bitterness of her broken heart, because he brushed a hand over his head and said, "No need to worry about looks now. The pay is good. The job is just until Halloween, but most of my employees really like it and keep coming back."

"So why is there an opening?"

He rolled his eyes and shook his head. "One of my regulars couldn't take time off from her office job. It's the first station we ever opened, and Rotten Hill Grove wouldn't be the same without the Ghost Bride from the Well."

The Ghost Bride from the Well?

Chloe bit her lip to hide her smile. Like the man said, the Ghost Bride was an iconic feature of the haunted forest. Chloe had been equal parts obsessed with and terrified of it since the first time she'd seen the ad in the mail-in coupon when she was twelve.

"What does the person have to do for that job?" she asked, her heart beating so fast it hurt. She wanted that position more than she had known. Now that the man had mentioned it, Chloe thought she'd never be happy again in this life if she didn't get to play this role during Halloween.

"Every five minutes, you'll crawl out of the well and cry your lungs out. When people approach to comfort you—"

"When, not if?" She couldn't imagine trying to comfort a ghost even if it was brokenhearted.

The man laughed. "Yes, when. You'd be surprised at how weird human beings are. Some will do anything to avoid witnessing another's suffering, but others can't stop themselves and try to help in any way they can. Even if they know it's just a game, a show. But when these people approach you, you lunge at them, baring your teeth."

Chloe imagined the scenario. This time, she couldn't hide the thrill. It was a welcome change to the anger burning so hot inside her that for the last few days since *that day*, she'd been having acid reflux.

"Are you interested, then?" the man asked.

"I am."

"I'm Vaughn. What's your name?"

"Chloe," she said, shaking the hand he offered.

From the corner of her eye, she saw the distinct image of a boy dressed from head to toe in black clothes. She had never seen him at school, although he looked about her age. Maybe he was an out-of-towner? There was something different about him that was impossible to ignore. She couldn't explain what.

She stared at the boy as he stood underneath a gnarled tree, holding a plastic hose. He was pale and slim, and his hair was so black it looked wet under the sunshine.

"Chloe, let me introduce you to Wendy, my makeup and costume director," Vaughn said.

"Sure," she said. When she glanced back at the tree, the boy was gone.

Vaughn followed her gaze, and then shrugged. "We start next week." He looked at her with piercing eyes. "Are you in?"

For the first time, Chloe hesitated.

Just then, a blond woman with a friendly smile waved at her from the door, a makeup brush in hand. "Welcome, new Ghost Bride!"

Ghost Bride.

Chloe imagined the look on Victor's and Carmen's faces when they heard Chloe was the most popular attraction at the most popular hangout of the season.

"I'm in," she said, and followed Vaughn inside the trailer.

"You what?" Oriana asked.

Chloe had pulled out all her warmest underclothes and gloves and had laid them on her bed, trying to figure out what could match with her costume, a flimsy bridal dress, and keep her warm. In early October, the days were still warmish, but as soon as the sun set, the temperature drop would make her miserable.

Vaughn and Wendy had explained that there would be heaters inside the well and hanging from the ceiling of the house porch that she'd be haunting to keep her warm (and dry in case it rained), but that her hands and feet would feel the brunt of the inclemency of weather. That was why the job paid so well. It wasn't for the faint of heart.

Chloe had no intention of still being a ghost bride next year, but she was going to give this role her whole effort. She imagined that after graduation, she'd head to LA and start auditioning for movies and TV shows. She was a light-skinned Latina of medium height, tottering on the edge of thicc and pudgy. The drama teacher had said she was *ethnically ambiguous*, whatever that was. There had to be something she could do, and then she'd never look back.

"I could've found you a position at the call center, you know?" Oriana said, looking at her with pity. She was a manager in the customer service department of an essential oils company.

Chloe would rather have been dead than have her sister as either a workmate or, yuck, her boss. "You think you're punishing Mom and Dad with this, but you're hurting yourself, Chlo. People are going to say you're crazy for real."

Prickly heat rose up Chloe's neck.

"Let them talk and say whatever they want," she said. "It's a good job. I don't want to hear complaints all day long. Is it so bad that I want to make people laugh?"

Oriana grimaced. "Making people laugh? You want to scare people. Is that funny to you? Is that why you keep hurting *us*?"

"What do you mean, hurting you?"

Oriana crossed her arms as if to protect herself. "The way you crashed into Victor's car was scary. Mom is devastated. Papi is beside himself with worry. I'm just so embarrassed."

"Embarrassed?"

"Yes! Your boyfriend cheated on you with your best friend. Guess what? You're not the first person this has happened to, and you won't be the last. Friends are overrated, anyway, so stop freaking out and get your emotions in check! You're ruining my reputation, too."

How was Oriana, the family's spokesperson, making it about her?

Not even one of them had comforted her. No one expressed even a drop of sympathy. And she couldn't believe her family was telling her not to freak out over this. When her dad got angry, he shouted at everyone. Then their mom turned around and screamed at them.

And her sister? When she was angry, she shut the world out by building a wall around her. Wasn't that as destructive as crashing a car? Plus, it had been an accident. The flight response had kicked in, and she had to flee that place before she said something stupid. She just stepped on the wrong pedal.

One mistake—no, one accident, and now her whole life was ruined?

But Oriana or their parents wouldn't understand it.

Chloe smiled at her perfect older sister and said, "There's a family discount. You and your friends are welcome to use it through the whole month. Oh, I forgot you have no friends."

Oriana scoffed. "You don't either," she said, and turned around and left the room.

Her words were like a slap.

That was the only attempt from her family to stop her from taking the job. Since they didn't know how to deal with emotional stuff, they didn't deal at all. That was a choice, too. They ignored her as if she was doing something illegal. But her dad worked as a car salesman, and everyone knew that his methods left much to be desired. And Oriana was selling oils to desperate people with the promise that they healed anything from depression to heart disease to issues no medicine would even make a dent on . . . Wasn't that dishonest?

Like it was dishonest of them to treat her like she wasn't even there, like she was a ghost, so this was the perfect job for her. It wasn't what she imagined she'd do as her first job. All her friends had flipped burgers, mowed lawns, babysat, or made slushies at the ice cone shack by the elementary school. But at least at Rotten Hill Grove, people would see her and be scared and, yes, have fun and laugh.

Chloe was excited.

✧ ⬨ ✧

This time of the year, the sun set not long after school was over. Chloe had always hated the darkness. Sunset dread, Victor called it. Now she was grateful for the darkness because it was time for work. Sunset glee.

Chloe was giddy by the time she arrived at Rotten Hill Grove.

A line of cars headed toward the haunted forest. Opening night was still a few days away, but the place was already crowded for the employee orientation.

Some of the people were her age, but most looked way older. They parked in the employee parking lot, about a mile away from the attraction, and waited for a shuttle to drive them to their posts. Chloe's face was impassive, but now that her glee had fizzled away, she was nervous. She shivered. The air was chilly, but she was sweating under her woolen leggings and long-sleeve undershirt.

All around her, people exclaimed in surprise and joy at meeting one another. A couple of long-haired boys who looked like they were college age shared a vape pen as easily as they swapped stories from the previous year with a group of older girls. Three grandmotherly looking women cackled like witches as they hugged one another. It was like a joyous reunion, and Chloe seemed to be the only newcomer. But people were friendly and smiled at her. Perhaps sensing that she wasn't here to make friends, they respected her silent request to be left alone.

Chloe's nerves eased a little.

The main building through which customers entered the premises was decorated like a haunted manor. But the upstairs was reserved as the changing areas for the cast and a break room.

In the manor house, people went straight to their costumes, and Wendy and her assistants went around helping people finish their makeup.

"Yours isn't that hard to do because you're supposed to be a beautiful bride, only sad," Wendy explained as she put foundation on—three shades lighter than what Chloe normally wore—to make her look pale and drawn. She smudged eyeliner under Chloe's eyes and painted her lips in bright red. "There's nothing worse for people to see than another person's suffering. It's a horror. No one will be looking at you and thinking you're ugly. They'll just be scared for the possibility that one day what they see—a heartbroken, abandoned person—is them." She looked at Chloe for a second, and then added, "You look perfect. You can do the makeup yourself if you want to from now on, but I'm always here to help in any way I can, okay?"

"Okay," Chloe said. Wendy's words were slowly sinking in.

Wendy rose from the chair and headed to the next person: a zombie with a zipper from the chin up. It was terrifying.

Chloe had never imagined she'd be learning such deep lessons in a haunted house of all places.

When Chloe looked at herself in the mirror, she looked just like a girl with a broken heart who'd cried her eyes out. The Llorona of her abuela's stories, the ultimate horror.

She smiled.

✦ ⬨ ✦

Tonight was the soft opening, and select people from the community and the area had been invited to go through the forest. It was kind of like a test to see that all the attractions were working okay and everyone was convincing. And most importantly, that the guests were safe. Theirs wasn't a haunted house that had different levels of scariness. No one could be touched. It made things easier to have a uniform rule.

Chloe's glee grew into joy through the evening, even if she was lonely.

Skeletons verified the tickets in two booths. A tall Frankenstein greeted the guests, and a pair of Mexican Catrinas ushered them and led them inside the house. There was only one path to follow, but cast members were stationed at the ends of hallways, entrances, exits, and crossroads to make sure people didn't venture off the path.

The forest, a natural cluster of trees, was charming during the day. But at night, the machine-created fog and the yellow light from light posts strategically positioned to cast shadows conjured an eerie landscape. Speakers broadcast magnified sounds of nature—crickets, frogs, and night birds—mixed with shrieks, crying, and sinister laughter. Under regular circumstances, Chloe would never have ventured into the forest on her own, even if she knew it was just a set like in a play. Now she wandered around like this was her home.

The stations were standard for this kind of amusement park. An iconic haunted house with trick mirrors and slanted floors and walls. Then a walk through a pumpkin patch and corn maze, complete with specters jumping out at people. There was an abandoned school bus. It looked like it had been the scene of a crime and then burned. The college-aged kids Chloe had seen in the shuttle worked there together, pretending they were dead, and when people walked by them, they twitched and opened their eyes. Sometimes they sat up as the horrified customers ran toward the exit. A recorded voice repeating "mind your step" blared from a speaker at the back exit.

Beyond the trees, there were a derelict church and a cemetery where a middle-aged man that looked like a respectable banker turned into a werewolf even without a full moon and howled at the passersby. Zombies chased the people that lingered, afraid to venture into an abandoned circus tent where a mad scientist cut people in half and made terrible experiments with them. The three grandmotherly women worked in this station, crying and begging people to save them from the frenzied doctor, their bodies half-sawn-off inside a box, or their heads on a table under which they sat comfortably.

The three of them would switch roles through the night to keep things interesting.

Chloe's was the second-to-last station. Next to a small, abandoned house with a white picket fence, there was a water well. The legend about her character said that when she'd discovered her brand-new husband had a mistress, she had confronted him as they walked into their house. He'd thrown her down the well, where she'd never been found. As a ghost, she came out from the well when she heard footsteps and asked for help, but people kept walking.

From the very first moment, Chloe loved playing her role. The well wasn't deep at all and had a platform where she could stand comfortably before she climbed the sturdy ladder to the top and emerged, crying like her heart was torn into pieces. She varied the things she cried about. When the first group of guests arrived, she kept to the script, but by the time the fourth group strolled over, she cried for real over what Carmen and Victor had done to her. These were the first tears she had allowed herself.

In the lulls between groups, she sat in the rocking chair on the porch and laughed at the shrieks of the people who were being chased by a few teen boys with chainsaws. They worked at the station next to her. On her first night, she caught a peek of one chainsaw wielder. She hadn't seen him during the orientation or in the shuttle, but he seemed familiar.

He laughed merrily as another boy with a chainsaw chased people toward the exit. She laughed too, and when he turned in her direction, she realized he was the boy she'd seen the day she'd come in to apply for the job.

His laughter was contagious.

She waved at him. He seemed taken aback but smiled at her.

Footsteps and laughter approached her station, and she hurried into the well.

This time, the reaction of a man, how he hid behind his wife in fear, made her cackle hysterically.

If only she had a friend to share these moments with! Yes, the cast members usually passed around snacks and told anecdotes of their favorite moments from the night, but she didn't click with anyone in particular and always drove back home as soon as she changed out of her costume. Despite Oriana's mantra that friendship was overrated, Chloe still yearned for someone.

One night near the end of her first week at work, everything changed. It was raining, and the wind threatened to turn the rain into the first snow of the season. There had been almost no customers. Chloe's stomach growled, and the cold had numbed her feet. The thought of quitting flitted through her mind. She'd already earned about a third of what she owed Victor, and she was sure she could find another, warmer job.

She was in the rocking chair, eating a granola bar, when she felt someone beside her. She didn't know if she wasn't supposed to eat on the clock. Should she try to hide the food? Play it cool?

She went for the latter.

She turned. The boy she'd seen on the first night stared at her.

"Hey," she said, chewing the corner of the bar. "Do you want some?" She offered him an extra bar she had in the pocket of her bride dress.

He seemed like he'd forgotten how to speak. Usually, his voice was loud as he laughed, chasing people away from the forest. She interpreted his silence as a no and put the granola bar back in her pocket.

He was still looking at her like he'd never seen a girl.

"I'm Chloe, by the way," she said after she'd swallowed. When he didn't say anything, she made a motion with her hand and said, "It's okay if you don't want to tell me your name, but we'll be working side by side until the end of the month, and we might as well exchange information in case a real monster comes in and kills us or something."

The corner of his mouth twitched. "I'm Toby," he said, his voice a tremulous thread.

His voice gave her goose bumps, but she wasn't scared.

"Nice to meet you, Toby."

There was a pause, but it wasn't awkward. The sound of the rain soothed her, like it was nourishing her soul, parched with anger and heartbreak.

"How long have you worked here?" she asked.

He swallowed. His Adam's apple bobbed up and down, as if he didn't know what to say. Maybe it was true that this place was full of weirdos, like her sister had said. But then, Chloe was now part of the weirdo club—no one should be this dehydrated from crying—and she wasn't going to give up her card because the boy was shy.

"This is my first year," she said. "It's peaceful. I kind of get why some people like cemeteries—"

A shriek pierced the night and then laughter from an approaching group.

Toby smiled. There was some color in his face. Was he blushing?

"You better get ready for this group. Need help climbing down the well?" he asked.

"I got it," she said. "Now, head back to your station before they see us and start a rumor that the Ghost Bride and the Chainsaw Guy are having a fling."

She didn't know why she said that. Only that being out in the dark, safe—in a place that would terrify any girl Chloe knew—made her feel like a badass.

She watched him walk back to his friends for a little longer than necessary.

The group of customers was almost on her. She wouldn't have time to hop inside the well, so she decided to improvise and go rogue.

She stood in the middle of the path, placing her hands in prayer, looking directly at the approaching group of boys and girls.

"It was about time you came to see me, sweetheart," she said in a syrupy voice that sent a chill up her own spine. "I've missed you."

The same girl who'd screamed in the previous station shrieked again, while the boy who looked like her boyfriend tried to comfort her. It was such a tender gesture.

A part of Chloe wondered if he was just pretending to care.

She moved closer to the well and beckoned the couple with a curling finger. "I dropped something here," she said, pointing toward the well. "Can you help me look for it? It's my cheating fiancé," she added in a guttural, loud voice. "Want to join him?"

As she'd expected, the girl screamed, horrified. But instead of going frozen, the girl jumped as if the ground was lava and ran toward Toby.

"Shit," Chloe muttered under her breath. She'd ruined the choreography, and now Toby was unprepared. The sound of the chainsaw was the clue for the vampires to usher the customers out.

But she shouldn't have worried. One moment Toby was in the middle of the path, and the next, he was on top of the hill, next to his friends, the chainsaws coming to life in their hands.

The boyfriend was the one who ran first. In his defense, though, he never let go of his girl's hand and dragged her behind him urging her to "run!" in a high-pitched voice that made Chloe laugh.

Quietly, Toby walked through the hedges back to her side.

She was inwardly happy to see him, to finally have someone to talk to, but she hadn't gotten this job to make friends. Friends (and boyfriends) hurt you and broke your heart.

"No one's gonna come by for a while. I just heard on the walkie in my station. Wanna hang out with me and my friends?" he asked, motioning toward the hill.

Dread made Chloe's stomach clench.

"No," she said, and went into the well.

✦ ⊠ ✦

Chloe peeked over the rim of the well five minutes later.

Toby was still standing by the rocking chair as if Chloe's rudeness had turned him into a statue. She bit her lip to stop herself from laughing while the rain pelted her. The urge to laugh was nonsensical. Was she actually losing control of her emotions like Oriana said?

Finally, she shook her head and climbed out of the well.

"Here," Toby said, and handed her a blanket that had been tucked behind the chair.

"I'd never seen that there," she said, wrapping it around her like a cape. "Thanks."

"You're welcome. There's a thermos of hot chocolate, too. It gets replaced every day."

Her jaw fell. "I never knew!"

She hadn't seen it, and it had been in plain sight.

"You never talk to anyone."

It didn't sound like an accusation.

She sat down on the rocking chair, and he leaned against the wall of the cabin. "There's a bathroom inside your cabin, too."

"There's a what?" She pretty much spat the words out.

"Yep. We've had to either hold it or trek back to the manor when things got urgent." He laughed.

It was impossible not to laugh with him.

"Why didn't anyone tell me about the bathroom?"

Toby shrugged. "You looked like you needed space."

It was the nicest thing anyone had done for her in a long time.

They stood side by side through the rest of her shift. Chloe wanted to poke him to make sure he wasn't a figment of her imagination, but she knew that would be too weird. No one had been this nice to her since homecoming. But if Toby actually wanted to hurt her, he'd had plenty of chances.

"I saw you the day I applied for the job. I thought you were a ghost," she said, feeling out of breath like she'd run laps around the forest. Accepting his company was the bravest thing she'd done since taking this job. Every time Chloe walked through the halls at school, her anger festered into hatred, and she wanted to scream at everyone who may have known about Victor and Carmen. *Had they been laughing at her behind her back the entire time?* She shook the thought from her head. "Do you miss the previous Ghost Bride?"

Toby laughed. "Patricia treated us like lackeys! She was in her thirties and thought she was our mom." He sighed. "Yes, we miss her. I mean, me and the boys. Reese and Lalo. They're cool. Weird but cool, you know?"

"Like you?" she said.

He looked into her eyes for a few seconds, and then his mouth twitched again. "And you too."

Chloe wasn't even offended.

"Why did you decide to work at a place like this?" he asked.

Chloe opened up, and her heartbreak spilled like over-risen dough.

She told him the whole story of Carmen and Victor, and how she'd been noticing things between them for a few months but hadn't wanted to accept the truth until she had no choice. Now she couldn't let go of how foolish she'd been to believe her so-called friends.

Toby listened, then said, "First, always trust your gut. And second, screw them! They aren't worth the stress." Then he told her about his family (his mom was Korean) and how he and the boys lived up in Orem, north of Provo.

The rain continued falling, and the wind joined it, relentless. Chloe and Toby talked and talked. No one interrupted them.

Until Vaughn came by.

"There you both are!" he exclaimed. His face lit up, and his shoulders fell like he'd dropped a heavy weight.

"Why? What did we do?" she asked, getting defensive.

"Nothing, really. But neither of you came to the shuttle area, and we got worried."

Chloe and Toby exchanged a look. How long had they been talking?

"What time is it?" she asked.

"It's one in the morning. We closed an hour ago because of the weather. Didn't you hear us calling for you? We sent Lalo and Reese, but they said they checked this area and couldn't find you."

Toby didn't look shocked; he knew Reese and Lalo probably didn't even walk past the hill.

"We've been here the whole time. Some friends you have," she said, playfully slapping Toby's arm.

Toby shrugged. "They're the best . . . And I'll introduce you to them tomorrow, if you're up for socializing."

After another quiet ride on the shuttle and a lonely drive home, Chloe couldn't stop wondering if she had imagined the whole thing. Since Carmen had always been by her side, Chloe had never learned how to make other friends. She didn't think she'd need to. Talking to Toby felt normal. Would it be that easy to talk to Lalo and Reese?

The next day, Chloe was the first one to arrive at Rotten Hill Grove, bracing herself for everything to go back to normal—her, alone in the well, crying about the past.

But her fears were unfounded.

"Hey!" Toby said, his face all lit up at seeing her. "Do you want space, or are you still up for meeting the boys today?"

"Lead the way," she replied.

✧ ⊠ ✧

Reese, a tall Black boy with the softest eyes she'd seen in the world, was incredibly sweet. And she was able to connect with Lalo through their shared culture, except unlike her, he'd moved to the States when he was seven.

When the guests began to arrive, Reese passed Chloe a walkie-talkie before walking to his post. "Let's keep in touch, Ghost Bride."

✧ ⊠ ✧

During the following weeks, Chloe and the boys grew closer. She liked all of them, but Toby had a special place in her heart. Maybe because he'd stuck around those first few days when she'd been at her rudest. They didn't look similar or share the same taste in music, movies, or books, but Toby was always honest. He even offered to beat up Victor if he ever ran into him. But then changed his mind after seeing pictures of Victor at homecoming. She didn't blame him.

By the time Halloween night approached, Chloe realized Toby was the best friend she's had in a long time. Maybe ever.

That night, as closing time ticked closer and closer, Chloe confessed, "I want to come back and work here next year. I hope Patricia won't mind." She glanced up at his face, and he gave her one of those smiles that told her she'd be okay.

But then he looked over her shoulder and his face went stony.

"Don't be nervous," he said in a voice she didn't recognize. It wasn't the soft, sweet Toby. There was a fierceness that gave her goose bumps. "We got you."

She turned, afraid of what she'd see, and her body clenched in terror.

Carmen and Victor walked toward her station, hand in hand.

Chloe's first impulse was to hide behind Toby.

"It's them, right?" His eyes glinted in a strange way.

All she could think about was the picture of them kissing. A part of Chloe woke up. The part that had tried to run Victor and Carmen over. The one that wanted to destroy them. The part she'd been scared of unleashing, because who knew if she could rein it back in?

She nodded.

"What do you want to do?" Toby asked, his eyes still on Victor and Carmen, like a predator fixated on his prey.

She considered for a few minutes. The vicious, vindictive part of her deflated.

It wasn't worth it. They weren't worth it.

She didn't want to spend the last night at the place she'd been the happiest on them.

When the initial shock of seeing them subsided, Chloe realized the betrayal didn't hurt that much anymore. The scar in her heart would always be there, but unlike the Ghost Bride from the Well, Chloe would have a life, a happy life with her new friends.

She didn't need to tell Toby any of this. He read it on her face. He'd let her rant and cry and be weird all she needed. And he'd asked for nothing in return.

From the corner of her eye, she saw Lalo and Reese exchange a look with Toby, and they headed back up to the hill with their fake chainsaws.

Carmen and Victor walked past her but didn't even glance in her direction.

Chloe fought the urge to trip them as they went by. She refused to let them control how her life unfolded.

The sound of two chainsaws broke the emotional moment. A piercing shriek rang through the forest, and another one echoed it.

Victor and Carmen.

Reese and Lalo.

Toby winked at Chloe, and they laughed. They laughed so much, tears ran down their faces.

✧ ☒ ✧

Later, on the way back to the shuttles, Reese asked, "Are you applying for the Holiday Light Carnival, Chlo? It's only twenty minutes from here. We'll talk to the manager, and he'll hire you right away."

"What do you do there?" she asked, leaning on Toby's bony shoulder.

"We're angels," Lalo said.

"Angels of doom," Toby said in a guttural tone that made the whole shuttle laugh.

Chloe closed her eyes, contented.

She didn't need a picture of this moment to remember it for the rest of her life.

The Last Dinosaur

BY LAURA SILVERMAN

We found Abraham on my ninth birthday.

On what should have been *our* ninth birthday.

It had been six months since Sarah had died. Six months alone after having a sister at my side for my entire life.

Abraham approached us cautiously from a crested hill, a branch of green leaves in his mouth. He was young and barely bigger than a black Lab puppy. Thick skin, mottled green and purple, with small horns all the way down his spine from neck to tailbone. His sweet yellow eyes looked like drops of honey in black tea. A fanned-out ridge of translucent skin circled his head like one of those Victorian collars.

He walked toward us, and while my parents were busy picking their jaws up off the ground, I leaned over and scratched his leathery ear. Abraham mewled like a kitten and didn't leave my side for the rest of our trek through a beginner's section of the Appalachian Trail. Later, we rode home together in the backseat, his blunt teeth munching carrots out of my palm while *Frozen* played on the SUV screen.

When we got home, there was a circus.

Of course there was.

After all, we had discovered a dinosaur in the twenty-first century.

✦ ⧖ ✦

The scientists and paleontologists were enthralled and obsessive. They explained to us how Abraham came to exist. I still don't understand the details. Something about frozen embryos and hibernation and mononuclear fertilization. It doesn't really matter how he came to exist. What matters is that he was born alone, millions of years after his ancestors, and we found him, and we took him home with us, and now he's family. That's why we named him Abraham, after my great-grandfather. We thought it was a fitting designation for an old soul.

The government tried to take Abraham away from us. But there are no laws forbidding dinosaurs as pets. Why would there be? They're *dinosaurs*. They're extinct. Abraham's entire existence was one giant loophole. He was happy and safe with us. We weren't going to hand him over to be poked and prodded at for the rest of his life.

There was media, too. News crews camped outside of our house twenty-four seven. Requests from all of the daily shows. Magazines and television and movies. Everyone wanted a glimpse of Abraham. A piece of him.

But my parents protected him like stalwart knights outside castle walls.

✧ ⌧ ✧

Thank goodness we had a big backyard. He grew faster than we could have imagined. He was ten feet long by my bat mitzvah.

Abraham was an herbivore, and we fed him by the truckload. Pallets of cabbage and sweet potatoes donated by local farms and grocery stores. Anything that would have gone to waste went right to Abraham's stomach. His favorite was watermelon. He'd smash them with his feet and then scarf down the pink pulp in glee. He liked broccoli as well, snapping up the heads in quick Pac-Man bites.

Abraham quickly became my best friend. My confidant.

He couldn't replace my sister, Sarah, but he came close, pasting up the gaping hole she left behind.

I spent all of my time with him, running home from school each day to play in the backyard, kicking an oversize soccer ball back and forth, creating his likeness with finger paints on cheap canvas, singing to each other, my pop ballads pairing with his roars. On the weekends, we would doze together on sunny afternoons and once even went on an excursion to a pumpkin patch, where a kind farmer allowed him to have free rein.

Abraham was my best friend.

Safe and warm and familiar.

✧ ⌧ ✧

Abraham is even larger now. He surpassed twenty-five feet last month on my eighteenth birthday. His head easily reaches my second-floor window, which he'll tap in the mornings when he's hungry.

But lately, his appetite has waned, pallets of vegetables shoved to the side. His trough of water barely touched. I offer him berries, a rare treat, tumbling out of their cartons like expensive jewels. He eats those, but I worry he does it for me more than for himself.

Sometimes I catch him staring at our dogs, a trio of golden Labrador siblings. He doesn't stare out of hunger. It's something else. Sadness, I think. Loneliness.

I know the feeling all too well. The pain in his eyes ties my stomach in knots.

✧ ⌧ ✧

As young children, Sarah and I used to play a game called "Pick Up Potions." Whenever one of us felt sad, the other had to mix them a potion to make them happy again. We'd combine chocolate milk with food coloring and Pop Rocks. One sip, and one very messy kitchen later, we'd always feel better.

Of course, the magic wasn't real. It wasn't about the potions. It was about taking care of each other.

Sarah was always there when I needed her. Until one day she was gone.

⋄ ⌧ ⋄

Abraham's only family lived and died millions of years before he was born. He has us, but it's not the same. Just like I have my parents, but it's not the same.

On the days when his eyes grow soft and sad, I skip school and stay with him in the backyard, curled up against the soft side of his belly, reading collections of poetry by wise women. Abraham doesn't understand English any better than our dogs, but I know he's comforted by my voice, by my presence. He lets out pleasant hums, his warm breath whistling through the grass like wind.

There have been more sad days than happy days recently, Abraham's head growing heavy, like his decorative collar has become a weighted chain. My parents say I can't miss any more class. The school is calling. I'm going to get in trouble. Fall behind. Have to repeat my senior year. But I won't leave Abraham when he looks at me like that, like he's the loneliest creature in the world.

Instead, I nestle further into his belly.

The poetry isn't working today. Neither is the overpriced, out-of-season watermelon. His eyes follow our three dogs as they run across the yard, playing and barking. They include him whenever he wants, running circles around him, using his tail like a jump rope. But he hasn't been interested in any of that lately.

Our veterinarian, Dr. Ortiz, is a woman with so many degrees I can hardly keep track—veterinarian, paleontologist, geneticist. She's one of the only people we let near Abraham. She took care of his broken foot and his case of dermathrush, which turned his green skin yellow and pockmarked for three weeks straight. We've had her check on him, but she can't find the root of what's wrong. He's deteriorating every day, the life slowly fading from him.

It's an illness in his heart that we cannot see.

✧ ⌧ ✧

I didn't understand at first, that Sarah would never be back.

I would wake up in the mornings and expect to see her in the bed next to mine, already awake and reading her favorite book. I would come home from school and expect to find her on the couch, piled up with blankets and slurping down a bowl of matzo ball soup, happy to have watched Disney Channel all day and eager for me to fill her in on school gossip.

At eight, I knew what death was. I'd lost a grandparent. A dog. A classmate's mother.

I knew what it was, but I didn't understand it, not really.

I didn't understand that someone could be gone forever, even if you loved them more than you loved yourself.

I didn't understand the grief could carve me in half like a band saw. Make my heart ache with no potion to cure it.

✧ ⌧ ✧

The news is all over our TV. All over our phones. People won't stop calling. The camera crews are already lining up outside like they did at the beginning. My palms grow clammy as I peek at it all through the blinds.

Everyone wants to interview us. Wants to hear our reactions. Wants footage of Abraham. Wants. Wants. *Wants.*

I can't believe this is happening. I thought it was impossible.

But the thing is, everything about Abraham's existence has always been impossible.

And yet he's still here.

And apparently, a sibling is here, too.

✧ ⋈ ✧

Violet was discovered yesterday, sixty miles south of where we found Abraham almost a decade ago. She's larger than Abraham was at his discovery. Already five feet long and weighing two hundred pounds. It's shocking she escaped notice for so long, but she was in a more remote portion of the Appalachian Mountains, and her dark green and brown skin camouflaged perfectly into the tree trunks and spring foliage.

A backpacker found her and called in the discovery immediately. By the next day, Violet belonged to the government, and the backpacker was being interviewed on *Good Morning America*. By that evening, we had a phone call from Dr. Ortiz.

"We'd like her and Abraham to meet. If you'll allow it."

✧ ⋈ ✧

A week has passed since we agreed to the meeting. I've barely slept. Tossing and turning every night, my room too warm and still, like the wind has forgotten how to blow through my cracked window.

Abraham knows something is happening. He's been acting differently since we agreed to let Violet visit, as if he can feel an electric charge in the air. He's begun to play with the dogs again, and he's eating more than ever, joyfully munching through whole crates of sweet potatoes and every last melon rind we can find. The color has returned to his cheeks, and he lets out trumpeting sounds of excitement whenever I walk into the yard.

This should make me happy.

Mom and Dad are thrilled.

But I'm sick to my stomach.

In the morning, I try to force down Mom's famous eggs Benedict. That's a mistake that sends me to the toilet, knees tender on the hardwood floor, palms clammy and ears ringing.

Abraham is my best friend. We're meant for each other. We belong together. Two lonely creatures, roaming the earth with only each other to lean on.

But now Abraham has a sister.

He has a sister, and I don't.

A dark current rises up within me as I pray for the meeting to go horribly wrong.

✦ ◌ ✦

We allow one camera crew to film. Not the news. Nancy Beauchamp, a critically lauded nature documentarian. The crew stays at a distance, promising not to interfere with or touch the animals. Nancy is a soft-spoken woman dressed in khaki shorts and a jean button-up. She has pink cheeks and warm eyes, and her breath catches when her sight lands on Abraham for the first time.

Even with the small group, it feels claustrophobic in our yard. The extra six people set my nerves on edge. I walk toward Abraham, who seems more excited than nervous about all of the new visitors. He's peering at them through the leaves of our maple tree, his golden eyes wide with curiosity.

"Hi, sweet boy," I murmur, petting his leathery knee.

Abraham looks down at me with an appreciative mewl, then lifts his foot a few inches off of the ground to signal me. I slip onto the foot and hold tight as he agilely lifts me toward his head, nuzzling his giant cheek against mine.

My nervous pulse calms its rhythm.

✧ ⌧ ✧

When I was ten, I'd hold tea parties for us in the backyard. I'd cut crusts off of PB&J sandwiches and mix myself a pot of fruit punch. I'd serve Abraham a kiddie pool of water and a lineup of fruit in ascending size from raspberries to pumpkins. I'd tell him all about my day—my mean math teacher, my new project in art class, my crush on the sweet and shy soccer star Simon Montclair. Abraham always ate like a gentleman at our tea parties. Instead of wolfing his food down like usual, he'd nibble his fruit in small bites and daintily lap at his pool of water.

I loved spending Saturdays in the backyard with Abraham. My parents would try and persuade me to also spend time with kids from school. Birthday parties at roller skating rinks and pottery studios. Movies with sticky floors and pizza parties at neighborhood pools.

But spending time with my peers made my chest constrict, my breath shallow.

I didn't know how to be normal without Sarah. I didn't know how to navigate crowds without her securely at my side. I didn't know how to exist when she didn't.

It was easier with Abraham. Safer. Just the two of us.

✧ ⌧ ✧

They're pulling up the driveway now, a giant military caravan to bring Violet to us. My parents and I stand in front of our house to greet them.

There's a sour taste in the back of my throat, and I worry I'll have to run for the bathroom again.

I easily recognize the backpacker, Paul Rutgers. His image has been plastered all over the internet. He's wearing head-to-toe REI. Sponsored, obviously. His haircut looks more expensive than my parents' car payments.

Annoyance rattles through me as he strides toward us with a Crest-whitened smile. He extends a hand to my dad first. "It's a pleasure to meet you, sir," Paul says.

Instead of shaking his hand, Dad nods at me. "Let me introduce you to my daughter, Talia. She's the one who discovered Abraham and has taken such good care of him."

With a quick pivot, Paul turns and shakes my hand instead. His skin is cool and calloused. "Great to meet you," he says, eyes sparkling. "How exciting is this? The entire world watching history happen."

Not history, I want to bite back.

Not an exhibition.

Not an event.

They're animals.

They're *souls*.

Mom and Dad haven't earned a single penny off of Abraham's existence. We accept donations to keep him fed and watered and healthy, and that's it. Any proceeds from this documentary will go to a nature preservation nonprofit.

"So exciting," I mumble back, a bite to my soft voice.

There's a noise from the truck, a sweet guttural whinny so recognizable it makes my throat catch. From our backyard, the sound is echoed.

They hear each other.

Connected in a way I'll never be able to access. An intangible link, like the one I had with Sarah.

✧ ⊠ ✧

I was popular again the year we discovered Abraham. No longer the weird, grief-ridden loner but now the proud owner of an honest-to-god dinosaur. It was like I had won the lottery. Become a celebrity.

Everyone wanted to be my friend so they could meet him. So they could have a piece of him. Of the magic.

But I pushed them all away, over and over again, month after month, year after year. Until finally, they stopped asking.

Until they stopped talking to me altogether.

✧ ⊠ ✧

Time stops when Abraham sees Violet. His honey eyes well with emotion. Everyone holds still as Violet quietly moves further into the yard.

She's a beautiful animal. Younger than Abraham and half his size. The purples in her skin are a deep plum color, and her eyes are profound amber. The collar around her neck is opaline and practically transparent. She would make a beautiful painting, and for a moment, I itch to run inside for my oil set.

She walks with the grace of an animal a fraction of her size, footsteps silent on our packed dirt. My throat tightens as she nears Abraham.

They bend their heads toward each other, touching skull to skull, breathing deeply as one. Beside me, there are tears on Dad's cheeks. Mom grips his hand tightly. My head feels so light I might faint.

"Incredible." Nancy breathes out the word.

"History before our very eyes!" Paul says.

His abrasive tone rubs like sandpaper.

✧ ⊠ ✧

Losing Sarah happened so quickly. Diagnosis, treatment, and organ failure all within six short months. Even when I was eight, when I'd lived less than a hundred months all together, when a long summer weekend could feel like an infinity of pool days and melting ice cream and movie marathons, even then, six months felt like no time at all, shorter than a school year. She was diagnosed right after Passover and gone by the time we put on the fall play.

It didn't make sense how my entire world could change so quickly.

You would think it would take more time to knock the planet off its axis.

✧ ⧖ ✧

Within seconds, I know I've lost him.

Abraham is no longer just mine.

He belongs to Violet now too, their connection as thick as the blood that runs through their oversize veins.

Nancy narrates their union: "Two old souls at last finding a counterpart."

My heart aches at her words, my hand trembling. When I glance back at my house, my eyes are wet with tears, and for a moment I swear I see Sarah in our window, her doe brown eyes and full lashes. She waves, wondering why I'm not up there playing with her.

I blink, and my vision clears, and she's gone.

She's still gone.

✧ ⧖ ✧

We host Violet for the full weekend so the two can get to know each other.

During the day, they play, kicking our oversize soccer ball back and forth, trumpeting blasts of sound that vibrate the air, exciting the dogs as they run circles between their thick legs.

In the evenings, they snore together under the canopy of stars, their rumbles soft and content, Violet's head in my spot on Abraham's expansive stomach.

In the kitchen, my parents whisper late into the night about what to do.

After Violet's visit, she'll be moved to a nature preserve in the North Carolina woods. Fifty acres of sanctuary land. She'll live out the rest of her days there. No experiments by the scientists, only observations.

Abraham has an open invitation to visit or to live there, too.

With his sister. Where he belongs.

I curl up against my window, the glass cold against my bare skin, and try to find the shadows of my best friend in the darkness.

✧ ☒ ✧

Abraham lets out a mournful sigh when Violet is taken away by the caravan.

My parents exchange worried looks as he lies down in the grass, his head as heavy as his eyes. My throat clogs as I make my way toward him, offering him a rare delicacy of peeled kiwis, green ovals juicy and ripe.

Abraham doesn't even sniff them, just stares at the gate, as if incapable of movement until Violet walks back through it.

✧ ☒ ✧

"You want to go see her, don't you?" I ask Abraham three days later.

He's barely eaten and has only taken a few tepid laps from his water trough. I don't think he understands where she's gone and if he'll ever be with her again. It makes me ill thinking he might be mourning her like I mourned Sarah.

I curl against his stomach, his breath a gentle hum that vibrates my body.

"We'll go see her," I tell him, my throat clogged with fear. "We'll go right away."

✧ ⧖ ✧

A week later, we're in North Carolina. We had to wait until the weekend because I can't miss any more school, and it takes time to transport a two-ton animal across state borders.

The National Guard stepped in to help out, setting up an entire caravan to get Abraham safely moved. They make it clear that this visitation is a one-time offer. If Abraham wants to visit Violet a second time, it'll be on our dime.

I'm not allowed to ride with him, so I pack him a container of all of his favorite snacks, including a fresh basket of tomatoes that he munches on like Gushers and twenty pounds of yams to satisfy his sweet tooth.

My parents and I ride in the truck right in front of him, and I keep my eyes on the rearview mirror for half the trip, only pulling them away to look down at my sketchpad. I keep scratching out my designs, unsatisfied with what's in front of me.

✧ ⧖ ✧

The reserve is better than I would have ever expected. Tall green trees and dense black soil. Natural wildlife all around, far more abundant than in our backyard. A cleared pasture on one side of the reserve that leads up to a crystalline lake and acres upon acres of trees to roam through. Fruits that can be eaten straight from the branches or dug up from the ground, plus an ever-abundant buffet of choices put out by the workers each morning.

But by far more important than all of that, there's Violet.

She makes her way through the tree line as we step out of the truck. Her anticipatory whinny sticks in her throat, her legs trembling.

I can hear Abraham stomping in his transport, eager to be released. The National Guard are shouting at one another, chaos erupting. My spine tightens in fear, and I sprint toward the back of the transport and shoo them all aside, throwing my arms out wide. "It's me, Abraham!" I call out to my best friend. "I'm here. I'm letting you out now to see Violet. Just calm down a bit for us, okay? For me?"

His stomping ceases, and they open up the truck doors. I expect him to race toward Violet, leaving us all in a cloud of dust. But he moves toward me first, gently nuzzling his leathery cheek against my entire torso.

Thank you. I can hear his unspoken words. *I love you.*

My eyes brim with tears.

"I love you too," I tell him, the words sticking in my throat.

✦ ⧖ ✦

You would think the worst day of my life would have been the day Sarah died.

But it wasn't.

The worst day of my life was my first day at school without her.

I sat in a hardbacked chair, overwhelmed by the dissonance of my chattering classmates and the pocket of silence right at my side. All day I turned to her to say something funny or to share my snack, and she wasn't there. All day the ache of her absence bruised my ribs.

I skipped the whole next week of school until my parents bribed me to go back, promising a trip to the Appalachian Mountains on my birthday, on *our* birthday. We'd sketch the landscapes and collect rocks and tumble them at home, then carefully sort them into Sarah's prized collection.

The next few months at school were a blur. I didn't learn a thing. I was lost.

But then we went to the mountains.

And when we found Abraham, it was like I was found, too.

"It's a family decision," my parents tell me two days later.

It's Sunday morning, and we're eating oatmeal and fresh fruit on the porch of a cabin that overlooks the reserve. In the distance, the treetops sway and the ground rumbles as Abraham and Violet scour through the woods for their own breakfast. He's taken a particular liking to the banana trees, eating a whole bunch in one bite.

"Everyone has to agree," Dad says. "We won't do anything you're uncomfortable with."

They've treated me with silk gloves ever since Sarah passed away. I know it's out of love. But it's out of fear as well. Fear that if they say no, they'll push me away. Lose me too.

They would keep Abraham if I asked. We could take him back home and live out the rest of our years together. I could go to college remotely or skip it altogether. Pursue my art from my childhood bedroom. We could spend our afternoons reading poetry in the backyard, and in the evenings, I could listen to his snores through my open window. I would be happy. Or, if not happy, at least safe.

It would be easy to say no. To say I want to keep him all to myself. It would be easy to be selfish.

But I love Abraham so deeply that it's even easier to say, "Yes."

I look up at my parents. "I agree. He belongs here."

"Abraham," I call out to him as I approach the tree line. There's silence, and for a moment my heart drops in fear that he won't answer me.

But then there's movement, the rumbles of the ground growing deeper. "Abraham!" I shout again so he can trace my voice. "Over here!"

He breaks through the forest at a stride, bucktoothed smile wide as he runs up to me. "Easy, there." I laugh, dust clouds coming up around us.

He offers his leg, and I take it, allowing him to lift me until I'm level with his cheek.

"Hi, sweet boy," I say, breathing in his familiar scent and pressing against his rough skin.

He's my child, my sibling, and my best friend, all wrapped up in one. He's my everything.

But I need to let him go now. For him, for myself. We're two separate beings, capable of growing and thriving without each other. It's time for me to stand up on my own and not let him continue to lift me.

Something wet presses against my cheek. Giant tears, sliding from the corners of his eyes. "I know," I tell him. "I'll miss you, too. But I'll visit. And you'll be so happy here with Violet. That's what you want, isn't it?"

We both know the answer is yes.

We sit there for a long time, enjoying the mingling of the warm sun and the cool breeze. I slide my phone from my pocket and recite his favorite poem until we're both so drowsy that we doze off.

When I wake up, the sun has fallen from the horizon, and it's time to go home. My parents say their goodbyes and then wait for me by the car. I hug Abraham's leg so hard I hope it leaves my impression.

I'm terrified to say goodbye.

But it's not like last time. It's not like with Sarah. Because Abraham will still be here, and I can visit whenever I want.

"I'll see you soon," I promise him, pressing a kiss against his leathery skin.

He kisses me back, his dry snout nosing into the whole of my back.

In the fall, I struggle through my first semester at Brosch Community Arts. All of the students are so talkative, so extroverted, have something to say about everything. I can't wait to get home at the end of each day, curling up alone in my room with my paints and a comfort TV show. I live for the weekends I can get away to see Abraham, soaking up his presence as he shows me around his new home.

But slowly, things improve. In the spring, I make a friend, Hazel. And another friend, Anthony. And one more named Laurence. In class, we sit together and quietly laugh at inside jokes. Because we have those, inside jokes. On the weekends, we go to museums together and sketch famous pieces of art and attend poetry readings. And in the evenings, we drink flat beer in the backyards of older students. Hazel and I talk about moving into an apartment together next year, and how we'll hang paintings on the walls and plant a garden of lavender and basil and a blueberry patch. My final art project is hung in a local gallery, and my parents take pictures of me beside it.

And then it's summer again, and we have so much free time. And I find myself asking my friends if they want to meet Abraham. And of course, they all say yes.

We bring him kiwis and strawberries and pounds of watermelon.

And when he blasts out of the woods to greet us, trumpeting a happy tune, I turn to them and say, "Everyone, meet Abraham. My best friend."

The Last Purity Ball

BY JOY MCCULLOUGH

May your thoughts always be pure, your appearance reflect the purity within, and your nails always shine with the glory of God's love.

THE BOOK OF KAT, CHAPTER 2, VERSE 11

"Hellfire?" Renata waves a bottle of shocking red nail polish with a hopeful waggle of her eyebrows.

"No, thank you. French, please."

She sighs and pulls out the bottles of Snow White and Palest Petal. Yes, it's what I've gotten every time she's done my nails since sixth-grade graduation, but a classic is a classic for a reason.

Renata's cat, Diablo, winds around my legs, mrowling pitifully.

"Don't mind him," she says as she swipes the base coat across the tip of my pointer finger. "Sofi feeds him when she gets home, and she's late."

My mind snaps out of its to-do list. If Renata's daughter might return while I'm still getting my manicure, I can invite her to the ball again. She said no the first eleven times I asked. But I'm pretty sure it's an opportunity to develop perseverance. And anyway, there are twelve disciples, so that's a holy number.

"How's she doing? Has she made her college decision yet?"

I applied early decision to Dobson and got in with a full ride. All the years of worship team, Purity Ball Committee, and finally, this year, chairing Purity Ball paid off.

Not that I wouldn't have done all those things for the joy of serving. But still.

Anyway, my decision has been made since the fall. I have so much compassion for my classmates like Sofi, who must make such life changing decisions in the next few weeks. One wrong move could change the course of their entire lives.

"Decision?" Renata sticks my right hand under the fan to dry while she takes my left hand. "She's going to the community college."

I frown. Not that there's anything wrong with the community college. But Sofi's the editor of our high school's award-winning paper. She's aced every class we've been in together. Sure, I don't think she has the same community service résumé I have, but she's also on the softball team, and secular colleges like things like that.

She must have gotten in to lots of great schools. Why would she choose the community college?

Not that I'm judging.

"Ah, here she is," Renata says as the door opens behind me and the cat goes sprinting out from under my chair. "Buenas, mija linda," she says to Sofi.

Sofi comes over and kisses her mom on the cheek, barely glancing at me. "Hey. Sorry I'm late. Crisis at the paper."

"Hi, Sofi!" My voice is too bright, too cheery. I attempt to wrestle it into a casual register. "Have you given any more thought—"

"Nope."

"You didn't even let me finish!"

Sofi's gaze narrows as she pulls a can of cat food from the cupboard. "Were you about to invite me yet again to your virginity ball?"

Renata chokes on the sip of coffee she just took.

"Purity Ball," I correct. But she knows that. Sofi doesn't misspeak. It's one of the few things we have in common. "You know, it's not a requirement to be . . . pure. You can always rededicate yourself."

Renata's now having a coughing fit.

"Dude," Sofi says as she comes over to pound her mom on the back.

"Sorry. I don't mean to be pushy. I just want you to know you're welcome."

"Sure."

"Don't be rude, Sofita," Renata says as she begins applying careful swipes of white across the tips of my fingers. "It sounds interesting to me."

"You're welcome to rededicate your virginity, Mami."

Renata laughs long and loud. "Oh, mija, I don't think even Kat here can work a spell that powerful!"

I shift in the hard plastic chair. Purity is not about magic spells. It's commitment and self-control and holding fast to one's beliefs. But it's always a fine line, demonstrating a good example of how God wants us to live without appearing to judge alternate lifestyles.

"Still," Renata says, their hilarity finally dying out. "I'd kill for a view inside this Purity Party Kat's been telling me so much about."

"Purity Ball," I correct again. It doesn't matter. It shouldn't matter. But it matters to me. It's all I've been thinking about for six months. I mean, aside from my relationship with God, which is obviously first. And Finn, who's going to be my husband eventually. But the Purity Ball has been number three in my mind ever since I was named chair at the beginning of the school year.

"If you change your mind," I say.

"I won't," Sofi says with a shudder.

All right, then. She's a challenge. She's been a challenge for four years. But there's a month left until the ball itself, and I'm going to keep trying. It's what Jesus would do.

Be mindful of not only your own purity, but also that of your boyfriend, who may need your help to avoid temptation in the world. For this reason, intimacy is permissible as long as one avoids PIV.

THE BOOK OF KAT, CHAPTER 5, VERSE 19

Finn's awkward boy fingers fumble with my bra closure. "Babe? A little help?"

"Oh, sorry." I unclasp it for him, then return to my mental checklist. "Do you think I made the right choice about the band?"

"Yeah," he says, his voice muffled in my neck as he lays a trail of hot kisses from below my ear to points south.

"I just keep thinking—they've never done an event like this. On the one hand, I want to give them the opportunity, but—"

He pulls back, withdrawing his hands from beneath my sweater. "Kat, seriously. It's under control. Are you going to second-guess every little thing for the next three weeks? Can we just forget about it for a few minutes? And be together?"

He's not wrong. But also, he is.

The Purity Ball isn't only the event of the year for the youth of our denomination. In the West Orange County region, at least. It's our chance to rededicate ourselves, to strengthen our commitment to placing our love of Jesus above our earthly bodies—Finn bumps my shoulder with his elbow as he pulls his shirt off—and for us seniors, it's our last chance to do so before going off to college, where the sins of the world are going to be laid before us like buffets before starving prisoners of war.

And for me, it's everything I've worked toward not only this year, but for six years, serving on planning committees all through junior high and high school and finally being awarded my due as chair this year.

With humility.

Finn pushes my sweater and bra up and places gentle kisses on the underside of one breast.

Then again, I do deserve a break. Especially considering Finn's father, Pastor Mark, is in staff meetings from four to six on Thursdays. I run my hands down Finn's arms, the muscles strong from baseball season, and sigh. He feels me letting the to-do list go and kisses me while letting his hands take over where his lips were a moment before.

"I love you," he murmurs as he pulls my sweater over my head.

I disentangle myself from the unhooked bra and toss it across the room, then pull him down with me onto the bed. I love the weight of him on top of me, the feeling that nothing else can get to me, that nothing else matters except him and me, here and now, our connection. We're the only two people in the world.

Until Finn's door flies open with a crash that knocks his baseball trophies off his shelf.

"Finnegan Joseph O'Connor!"

Finn leaps off me, and cold air hits where a moment before I felt only his skin. He grabs for his shirt as I clutch my arms over my chest in horror.

"Father," Finn gasps.

"Pastor Mark." I don't know where my sweater is. I grab the quilt Finn's mom made from all his old baseball jerseys and wrap myself in it. I have never identified so much with Adam and Eve suddenly realizing they were naked and covering themselves with fig leaves.

"My office, now," he says, glaring at Finn. "Young lady, recover your decency and wait in the living room for me to drive you home."

Finn throws me an agonized look, but follows his father out of the room. Of course he does. What other choice does he have?

I want to stay wrapped in this quilt forever. The second I drop it, the bite of air on my bare skin will make this nightmare real. There'll be no way to pretend I wasn't just half-naked in front of my boyfriend's father, my pastor. But also I have to get out of here, and that means getting dressed. I move on autopilot, the only thing in my mind a sort of buzzing white noise, with a thrum of dread underneath.

When we first started dating, we only made out downstairs, where we could hear the garage door open and leap into our positions on opposite sides of the coffee table before Pastor Mark came inside.

As we got more serious, we migrated upstairs. Some things can't happen without a door that closes. But with the upside of that bedroom door comes the downside of no longer being able to hear the garage door opening. Which is why we only give in to our desires on a strictly determined schedule of Pastor Mark's weekly meetings.

But something changed today and brought him home early.

This is no ordinary parent-walks-in-on-teenagers mortification. This is my pastor!

Will I have to confess my sin to the congregation? Will he call Dobson and get my scholarship rescinded? There's no question he'll bar me from attending the ball I've thrown myself into for a year.

Young lady, recover your decency.

There's no way to recover my decency. Not after he saw me topless, covered only by his son. I stop at the mirror, which is lined with pictures of us—at the Trunk or Treat as freshmen, at the leadership retreat as sophomores, at the awards banquet as juniors. I smooth my hair. I will my lips to look less swollen.

I take one last look at the room, since I'm certain I'll never step foot in it again, and head down to await my doom.

✧ ⬦ ✧

Pastor Mark is silent as confessional prayer for the entire ride to my house. I keep expecting Finn to text, but my phone doesn't vibrate once.

"Um, Pastor?"

His eyes flick toward me, but bounce off like he can't stand to even look at my impurity. Still, there are things he needs to know if the Purity Ball is going to go on without me.

"There's a lot that needs to happen in the next few weeks. Cameron is vice chair, but Grace is best equipped to take over my role—"

"No one is taking over." He releases his grip on the steering wheel and turns to me, eyes blazing. "We say nothing about this. How would it look to the congregation if it gets out what the chair of the Purity Ball has been doing with my son? We'll get through the ball, then you'll quietly break up. Is that clear?"

My heart stutters. I'm not even sure I heard him right. Break up? But only after pretending nothing happened? Surely that can't be what he meant. But we sit in frigid silence for the rest of the drive. He doesn't backtrack, or rephrase.

Not until we pull up in front of my apartment building and he says, "Not a word until after the ball. You've done enough harm already."

I'm supposed to keep up appearances for three weeks, while orchestrating every detail of the Purity Ball, and then stand next to Pastor Mark as he leads us in prayer for our sexual purity. Finn and I are supposed to play the happy couple when we know our relationship is doomed? There are so many things wrong with this, starting with the fact that Finn and I love each other.

But all I say is, "Yes, sir."

✦ ⌧ ✦

Finn doesn't reply to my texts. He doesn't pick up when I call. Pastor Mark might have taken his phone. But I can't help wondering if Finn blames me, if this is somehow my fault. Boys are weak, after all. I should have been firmer about our physical boundaries.

Mom's working late, so at least I don't have to pretend I'm fine for her.

I text Grace, checking on tasks I know she's already completed. She replies immediately to each one with a checkmark emoji. She doesn't indicate she's heard anything about my disastrous afternoon. But she wouldn't have. Pastor Mark is keeping this as locked down as he wants my chastity.

Bex, though. Bex's mom is Pastor Mark's personal secretary. I text her, asking if she's finalized the contract with the caterer. Her only response: "Everything's under control. Take a bath, Kat."

I let out a deranged laugh that startles our ancient dog, Guster. Take a bath? I am never getting naked again.

✦ ⌧ ✦

Let your yes be yes and your no be no, except when the truth might cause
someone else to stumble.

THE BOOK OF KAT, CHAPTER 2, VERSE 19

The next couple weeks pass in a blur. Finn and I continue to sit stiffly next to each other in our regular spots during school lunch and church events. But he's not responding to my texts.

"Did your dad take your phone?" I ask quietly at the lunch table so no one can hear.

But Finn just joins in on laughter about some joke he probably didn't even hear.

After worship band practice on Thursday, I'm surprised when Finn follows Grace and me to her car. She always drives us to Finn's house, since Thursdays after worship band Pastor Mark is guaranteed to be in his Ecumenical Council meeting.

Finn doesn't look at me, though. He just ducks into the backseat without a word. I want to sit back there with him and try to make him talk to me. But Grace isn't an Uber driver, and that would just make everything even weirder. I sit up front.

Sunlight glints off Grace's purity ring, and I squeeze my eyes shut.

"Are you all right?" she asks.

I nod. Because what am I supposed to say? Grace is a year younger than us, and ever since I shepherded her away from the field hockey team and into the New Hope circle, I've felt responsible for her. Like she looks up to me. I mean, I think she seriously believes Finn and I do a couples Bible study together on Thursday afternoons.

"Okay, seriously, what is up with you guys?" Grace asks when Finn gets out at his house and I don't go with him. Grace never knew how far Finn and I went. None of our friends did. But she knows how important this time is to us.

I could tell her everything. But it would crumble the entire foundation of our friendship. Her faith. Her own commitment to purity!

"I just have to finish that English paper," I say with a bright smile.

The only person who knows what's going on is Renata, who hasn't questioned why I've been getting so many manicures. It helps that we live in the same building. There's something about sitting in her living room, letting her peel dead skin off my cuticles that makes me feel like I can tell her anything. And I do.

"Pendejo," she mutters, and I don't know if she's talking about Pastor Mark or Finn.

"It isn't Finn's fault," I insist. "I just wish he'd talk to me. But his dad took his phone."

"He still has his phone."

I jump at the sound of Sofi's voice, and one of Renata's sharp tools jabs me, drawing blood on my pinkie cuticle.

"Ay, Dios, I'm so sorry, Kat!"

"We're in a group project for European history," Sofi says, coming into view from wherever she was skulking. (All right, granted, it is her apartment, but she really should announce herself, shouldn't she? A manicure is basically a therapy appointment with hand massage.) "He's still active on the text chain."

Forget the spot of blood Renata's dabbing at. I feel like Sofi just punched me.

"Ay, linda," Renata coos.

Sofi is less sympathetic. "I don't know why you'd want to talk to that asshole. But I can make it happen, if you want."

✧ ⬦ ✧

During math the next day, Sofi pops her head in. "Hey, Mr. Barker? Can I grab Kat Taylor? It's for the paper." I freeze. Sofi said she'd help me, but I can't fathom how she'd do that by pulling me out of class.

But Mr. Barker, who's the organist at my church, doesn't bat an eye. "Of course, dear."

"You should grab your stuff," Sofi says.

I shrug at Grace, whose eyes are boring into me. She's the head of PR for the ball, so if Sofi was interviewing me for the paper, Grace would have been the one to set it up.

I sling my backpack onto my shoulder and follow Sofi out the door.

"What is this?" I ask. "If you want to talk to someone about the ball—"

"I don't care about your ball, dumbass," Sofi says, striding quickly a few doors down. She opens the journalism door and shoves me into an empty classroom. Except for one seat, where Finn sits. "Hey, Finn, quick change of plans," Sofi says. "No history group meeting after all. Okay, byeeee!"

Then she's gone, and I'm finally alone with Finn, who looks every bit as panicked as he did the moment Pastor Mark walked in on us.

"Finn." I rush over, feeling as pulled to him as always, but I stop short when he doesn't get up to hug me, or comfort me, or anything. Instead, I sit on the desk in front of him. "What's going on? Why haven't you answered any of my texts? Are you okay?"

"Yeah." He doesn't meet my eyes. "Yeah, whatever, I'm fine."

That's it? He's fine? Our lives have exploded, and he's fine? He's obviously not fine, and I don't know why he won't open up to me. After all, I'm the only one who understands exactly how he's feeling right now.

"Finn, I know how awful this feels, but we're going to get through it. We both are. It's not what I imagined for our senior year Purity Ball, but—"

"You think I care about your stupid Purity Ball?"

I can't hold in the yelp of indignation, but I slap a hand over my mouth so a teacher doesn't come running. I gather enough composure to let out a strangled "What?"

"It's like your whole world or something," he says, choosing now to meet my eyes. "Like you think if you can prove to the world how pure you are, you'll finally be loved enough."

"I'm not trying to prove anything," I say, my voice wobbling.

"Of course you are! You're always trying to prove everything! To everyone!"

After the first tear falls, I don't bother trying to hold the rest back. "Why are you so mad at me?"

Finn jostles his seat as he unfolds himself from the desk. "Because without you, I wouldn't be in this situation!"

He's striding for the door.

"Finn, wait!" He stops. After three years together, he gives me that much. "I'm so sorry."

He turns to face me, and I rush to him.

"You're right. I'm sorry." Finn and his dad have been on their own as long as Mom and I have. Their relationship is the most important thing in the world to him, and if my sin has done anything to jeopardize that, I'll never forgive myself. "I never should have let things go so far between us."

His face softens, and he brushes a lock of hair behind my ear. I lean into his hand like a cat.

"You'll always be my first love," Finn says.

My heart breaks open. "We don't have to end things! I know what your dad said, but after we're at Dobson—"

"I'm not going to Dobson."

I stumble back. Now I'm the wild-eyed one. What is he talking about? We've been planning the rest of our lives forever, starting with going to the same college. We visited the campus together, wrote our applications together.

"I'm going to take a gap year and go work with my uncle in Thailand. Then I'll see. Maybe I'll go to Liberty instead. The only thing I know for sure is that this?" He motions between us. "Is over. I can't be with someone who would lead me so far astray."

He's gone and I'm frozen and I don't even realize until much later that while I fell all over myself, he never made any apologies to me.

Every new day is a chance to shine your light on those less fortunate than you, and to be an empty vessel, ready to be filled with the love of your church family.
THE BOOK OF KAT, CHAPTER 6, VERSE 3

Saturday morning I wake from a night full of wrestling with visions of Pastor Mark announcing my impurity and hypocrisy and yanking away everything I've worked for while Finn points and cackles with everyone else.

But there's only one week until the Purity Ball, and even if this ocean liner has hit an iceberg, there are deck chairs to arrange. I reach for my phone, planning to send reminder emails to each committee member about what I need from them, but instead I see seventeen messages. None of them about the Purity Ball.

GRACE:
Call me

GRACE:
CALL ME

BEX:
Are you okay?

GINNY:
This is so messed up.

GRACE:
This looks bad but it's going to be okay.

BEX:
We all fall short. You'll be forgiven

GINNY:
Did you know he was going to do that?

JACOB:
I can't believe you did that. You're a disgusting hypocrite

GRACE:
Do you want me to come over? Is your mom home?

BEX:
This won't change anything with Dobson. I don't think. Unless they find out.

GRACE:
K, I'm getting worried.

Heart pounding, hands shaking, I open up the Purity Ball planning committee Slack and then I can't breathe. Hundreds of messages I've missed, all discussing me. And Finn, but mostly me. Everyone knows, apparently, that we broke up. But not only that.

They know why. At least, Finn's version. They know every detail of how far we've gone. Finn's spilled his guts, his guilt, his concern for my walk with the Lord. My stomach turns.

He only wanted to do Bible study with me, but I couldn't keep my hands off him. He kept trying to walk things back, but I was too tempting. A dull ache where I'm clenching my jaw.

And then, there they are. Photos. Photos I sent Finn on his birthday. Because he asked! And I wanted to please him. I wanted to give him what he wanted, so he wouldn't be tempted to turn elsewhere.

And now they're there for everyone to see. Everyone who looks up to me, who elected me Purity Ball chair. People who've come to me with their struggles and listened to my advice, and now they can't get enough of my downfall.

I'm going to throw up. I haven't eaten anything since lunch yesterday, but I barely make it to the bathroom before I'm dry heaving. I should be crying, or screaming, but I'm weirdly numb.

I stumble out to the kitchen, where there's a note from Mom on the table. *Early shift! Have a good meeting today! Hope you have fun!*

She's never gotten it. The Purity Ball was never supposed to be fun. When a president goes to their inauguration ball, their mom doesn't say, "Have tons of fun!"

It's a culmination, a massive achievement. A monumental humiliation. No matter what Pastor Mark says, I can't go now!

My phone's buzzing again, but I don't even look at it. I'm dizzy, lurching sideways and smashing my thumb against the doorway. My nail rips, jagged and brutal, deep into my nail bed. That pain, sharp and bright, cuts through everything, and finally, I cry.

Somehow, I end up on Sofi and Renata's doorstep, no memory of getting in the elevator and descending three floors. Sofi opens the door, wearing flannel pants and a raggedy T-shirt that says "I am inimitable, I am an original." I stare at it, like if I figure out what *inimitable* means, everything else will make sense, too.

"Dude," Sofi says after I've stared at her chest too long, apparently. "My eyes are up here."

I hold the hand with the jagged nail up. "I broke my nail!"

Renata isn't home, but Sofi leads me inside because it's that or leave me sobbing on her doorstep, and she probably doesn't want to do that to the neighbors.

"Can you fix it?" I wail, sinking into the familiar chair at her mom's manicure station, which takes up half the living room.

Sofi looks at me like I have two heads, but she sits in her mom's chair, across the table from me, and examines the nail. "That looks like it hurt," she says.

"It did! The worst part is I didn't see it coming. Like, getting caught was one thing, and being ordered to break up was another thing, but to have those pictures out there?!"

I'm still sobbing and shaking, but a new feeling is rising in me. It might be . . . anger? Which is sinful. Unless it's righteous. Which this totally is.

Sofi sets my hand down. "I guess things didn't go so well in the journalism room yesterday?"

Which is when I realize that even though it feels like the entire world knows what happened during my four-year relationship with Finn, it's really only the New Hope community. Which is eight thousand people.

So I tell Sofi everything. Some of it she's heard from listening in on my manicures. Some of it I've never told anyone. But the things I never would have told my friends don't faze Sofi. She's not scandalized or about to hop on a group chat to fret over my soul, not because she's not in the group, but because she truly doesn't seem to think anything I'm saying is a big deal.

"So is the problem that you were topless?" she asks at one point.

"No! I mean, yes, but not just that—"

"Well, I mean, you weren't having sex. I'm trying to figure out what you were doing wrong. Like, it's embarrassing that he walked in on you, but are you not allowed to make out?"

"No! I mean . . . I don't know. What even is making out? How's that defined?"

"You tell me," she says.

But I can't. Because the lines aren't defined, but we're still not supposed to cross them.

The part that bothers Sofi most, though, is how everyone else is reacting.

"That's messed up," she says about twelve times when I tell her about the Slack implosion. She commandeers my phone and scrolls through my texts and the Slack, which I haven't been able to bring myself to look at since that first glance.

"Okay," she says, letting a long, controlled breath out. "Let's move to more comfortable seats. Do you want coffee? Or hot chocolate?"

I stare absently at the photos lining the mantel while she makes hot chocolate. Sofi and her mom at various ages, always together, always beaming the same huge smiles. They look so happy.

"Okay." Sofi sets two steaming mugs onto the chipped coffee table and settles herself onto the couch. "Do you want to know what I figured out?"

I perch on the edge of the couch and cradle the mug in my hands. "I don't know, do I?" Then something hits me. I turn on Sofi in horror. "Wait, you're not going to report about this, are you? Off the record! This is all off the record!"

"Oh my God, of course," she says, and my relief is so strong I barely even notice that she's taken the Lord's name in vain. "What kind of monster do you think I am?"

"Sorry."

"No, it's fine. To be fair, all your friends are monsters, so."

My friends aren't monsters. Are they? A sick realization dawns on me that I have been on the other side of this. When Maddy got pregnant . . . when Byron got caught with porn . . . when Leah got wasted at that party . . . I was right there with everyone else, group chatting about how we couldn't let their sin drag us down. If they're monsters, then so am I.

"Tell me." I have to know what everyone else thinks they know, no matter how much it might make me want to crawl into a hole and never emerge.

Sofi sighs. "Okay. So. As far as I can tell, yesterday after dumping you in the journalism room, your dirtbag boyfriend was consumed by guilt and decided to brag—I'm sorry, 'confess his sins'—to his prayer group."

I groan and flop over to bury my face in a pillow.

"And once he got going on sharing his sins, he had to share the photos you sent him on his birthday, because they had been such a 'stumbling block.' What does that even mean?"

As Sofi stares in puzzlement at this church language she's not fluent in, my phone lights up with a call. "Oh, hell no," she says, holding it up so I can see the caller. Pastor Mark.

Before I can decide what to do, Sofi declines the call.

"Wait, no, you can't do that!"

"Why?"

"Because he's my pastor! He's my spiritual authority!" Sofi rolls her eyes. More quietly, I say, "He could get my college scholarship rescinded."

That gives her pause. "Look," she finally says. "I'm trying to be respectful of your actual faith, because that's none of my business. But these are awful people! This 'spiritual authority' ordering you to lie for him, demanding you break up on his say-so? Finn's weak-ass self spilling your intimate details, your personal photos to your supposed friends? And then they spread it all around in the name of 'accountability' and 'concern'?"

Even after everything, my strongest instinct is to defend them all. But there's another part of me that's starting to wonder if Sofi has a point. How much does the purity of our bodies even matter if we're not showing basic kindness to one another?

"Look, Mami and I only go to Mass on Christmas Eve, but isn't Jesus supposed to be all about love? None of this is loving."

My phone buzzes with a text. I can't look.

Sofi sighs again. "This asshole."

I peek through my fingers. "Finn?"

"No, his dad. Your 'spiritual authority' has decided that since he can't get away with lying anymore, you're no longer welcome at the Purity Ball."

✧ ⧓ ✧

There exists no obstacle that can't be overcome with a positive attitude,
an organized to-do list, and a fresh coat of lip gloss. Also Jesus.
THE BOOK OF KAT, CHAPTER 11, VERSE 9

Sofi says I can stay, but I need some space. I need to think.

Pastor Mark didn't have to tell me not to go to the ball. Now that everyone's seen me at my most vulnerable, I never want to face any of them again. The texts full of faux concern keep coming, but they're posting a whirlwind on the Slack like I didn't create the group and can't see what they're saying about me. I guess I'm not in a great position to call them hypocrites, but pot, kettle, etc.

After a while I cut myself off from opening Slack, but each time I see my home screen, the number of new messages is exponentially higher than it was before.

When I don't go to church on Sunday morning, Mom finally clues in that something is up. "Oh, Kitty-Kat," she says, pampering me like she's so sympathetic, even though she's been saying for years that Finn and I were too serious.

But her sympathy stretches far enough to buy the "stomach bug" that keeps me home all week. I'm a senior with only a few weeks of school left. No one will care. My friends certainly don't. Grace has the audacity to text me multiple questions about Purity Ball things only I know, but she never asks how I am. No one does. I don't respond to Grace's questions.

It's a tiny rebellion, knowing answers that would help the event go better and not sharing them. And I don't know if I'm rebelling, so much as I just don't see the point of anything anymore.

Either way, she stops texting. And when I crack and check the Slack, I find out I've been removed from the group.

✦ ⊠ ✦

Sofi gives me space until Friday afternoon. The day of the ball. I don't answer her knock until she shouts, "Let me in, Kat! I'm not leaving!"

She marches past me when I open the door and heads straight for the kitchen, where she browses cupboards, finding what she needs to heat up whatever containers of food she brought.

"What is that?" I ask as the rich, savory smell reminds me I haven't eaten all day.

"Paches," she says. "They're like tamales, but made with potato, not corn. And jocón—basically chicken in a salsa verde."

They smell amazing, but I'm not one hundred percent convinced I can keep food down.

"Eat," she insists, shoving a plate of food in front of me. "You need your strength for tonight."

It takes me a second to process what she said. "Tonight? I'm not going tonight."

"Of course you are. We both are."

"What are you talking about?"

She shrugs. "I told Grace I want to write a story for the paper. And I will. It's my last chance to write a feature. But don't worry, I'll leave your drama out of it."

"Your last chance at the high school paper. You'll write plenty more in college."

She lets out a sad laugh. "The community college paper is pathetic."

"But after that. You'll transfer to a university."

"Maybe? Probably not? Not everyone has a full-ride scholarship. And anyway, if I do make it to a four-year college, I'm studying something that'll guarantee me an income. That won't be journalism."

I frown. This makes no sense. Sofi is a fantastic reporter. The world needs people like her digging for truth and making sure people know when things are messed up.

"But the point is," she says, "we're going."

"Nope. Not me."

"What do you think will happen? Is Pastor Mark going to call the police because you showed your boobies to his eighteen-year-old son?"

"No! But he will humiliate me in front of everyone when all I've done for four years is work so hard to earn their respect!"

"What about your own?"

"What?"

"What about some self-respect? From where I stand, you're this incredible, driven, smart, organized person who's managed to plan a massive event, which takes serious skills, but you're about to let some gossip take it away from you."

"It's not just gossip! It's true!"

"What part of it is true?"

I stare at my nails, all ripped down below the quick over the last week. "All of it."

"Say it out loud. What did you do wrong?"

So many things, I can't even begin to name them all. When everything first came out, I would have said I let things go too far, too fast with Finn. I gave in to my earthly desires. My shame was entirely wrapped up in the impurity of it all.

But as the days have gone on, and the very community that taught me how much those things matter has thrown me out like so much trash, I'm realizing my failures go even deeper.

I put my trust in a boy who spread my private pictures around to his friends and dumped me the second things got uncomfortable. I put my entire high school life into a church group that was supposed to be my family but dumped me just as quickly. I let myself believe I could be pure enough to be worthy of not just God's love, but their love, too.

Because God loves me no matter what. No matter how warped things have gotten, I've understood that. Really, I've been chasing something else.

But I can't tell Sofi all of this. I don't even understand it fully myself. So I stick to the basics: "I'm a hypocrite spouting purity while going way too far with my boyfriend."

"Excuse me," Sofi says. "I just need to translate that out of Christian-ese: You're a normal, healthy teen exploring sexuality in a consensual relationship. It was consensual, right?"

"Yes!" My face flushes.

"Pleasurable even?"

"Stop."

"But that's good, Kat. It means that somehow you've managed to not let your church's repressive teachings get in the way of your own pleasure, which you deserve.

"The hypocrisy I'll give you, but we all talk a big game and then act completely differently, depending on our self-interests."

"Okay, but even if that's true—"

"It is."

"There's no way I'm walking in there in a white ball gown when everyone will know how impure I am."

"Ooh! How about I spray-paint a big scarlet *S* on your dress?"

I pluck a silk flower from the arrangement on the counter between us and throw it at Sofi. She catches it with the agility of a softball player and grins. "But we might be able to do better than that."

If all else fails: fake it till you make it.
THE BOOK OF KAT, CHAPTER 12, VERSE 17

"Okay," Sofi says, squeezing my hand in the back of Renata's car as we make our way to the event space. "I know I pretty much pressured you into this, but I don't want to take any more choices away from you. We can go in there and show everyone how kick-ass you are. Or we can keep driving and go eat burgers in ball gowns."

"You're not wearing a ball gown."

"We'll stop at Goodwill."

"You'd wear a ball gown for me?"

"You're wearing one for me."

"No. I'm not." My fingers play with the petals of a purple silk flower on my skirt. "I'm wearing it for me."

"Careful," Sofi says, batting my hand away from the flowers. "I'm not sure I'm the best seamstress."

But it won't matter if this one flower falls off. There are about a hundred more. Starting from the right shoulder of my (formerly) pure white dress, the rainbow of brightly colored flowers cascades across the bodice to the opposite hip and then trails down the length of the full skirt.

It's absolutely gorgeous, so much more interesting than the plain white dress I thought I loved so much. So much more me.

I thought I wanted to be pure. But pure means untouched, inexperienced, childlike. I'm not a child anymore. I still love Jesus, but I love Him in the world, in a body He made for pleasure, and why would He design it that way and then command me to ignore its design?

These ideas terrify me. I'm still figuring it out. All I know for sure right now is that I'm wearing a beautiful gown, standing next to someone who sees me for who I am, outside an event I've been working on for a year. And now it's time to go inside and show them what I'm made of.

Show myself what I'm made of.

I squeeze Sofi's hand and make a choice. My choice. "Let's go."

The Last Bout

BY AMANDA JOY

I: KAMARA

I sink low in my chair and tug down the brim of my hat, affecting my usual air of nonchalance. Normally this requires little effort on my part, considering I am always bored without my fire or a weapon in hand. The single exception to that rule dances across the golden sands below, and regrettably, it's become impossible to look away from her.

Sweat gathers on my nape; despite the light fabric of my uniform—silk from Xoshi and good Sumitrian cotton—I'm boiling. I shift again, seeking a more comfortable position, and a cold line of sweat drips half-way down my spine. For the first time, I'm seated in the royal boxes of the open-air stadium a short ride from the Sapphire Palace. A small reward for my successes in the tournament so far, offering a perfect view of the match that will decide my final adversary in the tournament.

A few rows below me, Queen Enokia perches on a miniature throne, which is about five times larger than the one my ass is barely fitting in. A wind-worker in a uniform exactly like mine, but white to match her element, stands just behind her, guiding cool air toward the fans of a servingman. The wind-worker looks small for her age at fifteen, and I can't help but wonder exactly how many of the Gifted do queens need at their beck and call?

As soon as I think it, I feel a stab of guilt. I'm the last person who should be ungrateful. The stipend the Queen gives us all to attend the Academy helps keep the debt collectors at bay. When my gift made itself known, I burned down the small home my mother and I shared. Though I emerged unscathed, my mother's burns very nearly killed her. Over the years, I've amassed debts paying dozens of healers I couldn't afford, but I have a plan. When I win this tournament and become the Queen's Champion, I'll have access to royal healers and a high salary. I'll finally be able to dig myself out of the pit that opened beneath my feet when I discovered my gift.

Above us, canopies coated with wax and fragrant black iris oil provide meager protection from the glaring sun. Days like this, we Sutri like to say someone has caught the attention of Solari. Considering I handily won three bouts already and will soon clinch the final match to become Queen Enokia's champion, I'd like to think the sun goddess's eye is on me. I'm a fire-breather, gifted with the ability to do so by Solari herself. But I suspect if the goddess was bound in flesh and trapped in one of the too-small seats beside me, she would be just as captivated.

Sanaa lets out a hiss, and by some feat of Sumitrian engineering, the sound carries up to the royal boxes, making gooseflesh sprout up my arms. I lean forward unwittingly and, like the rest of the thousands of Sumitri packed into the narrow rows of the arena, I gasp as Sanaa throws herself into a back handspring. Her opponent's sword sweeps past, narrowly missing Sanaa's torso. I can barely recall the name of her opponent—*Is it Itra? Vinta?*—even though it was announced at the start of the match and I know her face from the Academy.

Whoever she is, she loses her match right then. Still mid-flip, Sanaa's toe connects with the other girl's sword hand, launching the slightly curved blade all the way out of the ring. If she steps outside the ring to retrieve it, the match will be forfeit. If she attacks now using only her gift, the match will be over.

The rules of the tournament are simple—opponents face off in a fifteen-foot ring marked by bright red rope. The objective is to force your opponent out of the ring, using the method determined by a coin toss at the start of the match. To avoid any deadly injuries, we are only allowed to fight with weapons *or* our gifts. We spent our childhoods at the Academy training to use both steel and our elements in tandem, to devastating effect, but this tournament is only for the Queen and the island's entertainment. There's no need to show off the deadly abilities our instructors stoked in us.

Itra (or is it Vinta?) swears and backs away from Sanaa, who is already back bouncing on the balls of her feet, having retrieved the twin scythes she dropped while flipping. A thin chain of ice connects the two, though the bulk of the chain is wound around Sanaa's waist. Despite that chain, the referees decided that Sanaa's weapon didn't break the rules of the tournament, because even though she uses the chain to swing those scythes about, she doesn't require the use of her gift to maintain it. The scythes, like all of our weapons, are made from sacred ore and designed to work with our gifts, never against them. Even though we are all near melting, Sanaa's chain doesn't budge.

Itra won the coin toss and she must have thought she'd chosen wisely, making Sanaa, the Academy's pet prodigy water-weaver, fight without her gift. And to be fair, the other girl is an earth-shaker—and water versus earth is a notoriously bad matchup—but I knew immediately it was a mistake.

Sanaa's my longtime rival; during the handful of years we've spent together at the Academy, she's the only one who has ever matched my power. Not many people intimidate me, but I spied on Sanaa many nights while she was alone in the practice rings. She whipped those half-moon blades around her body with a frenzy that made my mouth dry up. She became a tornado of ice and water and steel. It was wonderful and terrifying—and, annoyingly enough, kind of hot. Not that I'll ever tell Sanaa that. Everyone is always in her face, making moon eyes at her and calling her a genius. I've no interest in piling on more adoration.

Though I suppose telling Sanaa that I dislike her just as fervently as I want to kiss her isn't exactly adoration. Still the wanting itself has always been embarrassing enough for me to keep my mouth shut.

The crowd roars as Sanaa swings one of the scythes in an arc overhead. Her unbound curls sway with the rising wind, and Itra (I've decided it's Itra) scuttles backward in the sand until her foot touches red rope. She sags with relief when Sanaa lets the scythes drop to the earth. Victorious, Sanaa beams at the islanders already rising from their seats to cheer her name.

I stand, but don't clap, and start making my way down to the fighting sands. I wasn't surprised when at the start of the tournament, Sanaa instantly became the favorite to win. Despite my annoyance at Sanaa's name being chanted like a prayer, I get it. Sanaa *is* deadly and brilliant . . . and *beautiful*, but must they say it? Do they need to stand up and cry for her and throw blue lilies from the stands? If only they knew as I do that Sanaa is also insufferable, joyless, and yes, talented, but I'm better. And I cannot wait to be the first one to knock her out of that ring.

II: SANAA

Sumitri girls usually learn whether they've been blessed by one of the four cardinal gods of the island between ages five and ten. One day they fall asleep with the brown eyes all Sumitri share and wake the next with a bright rim of color between brown iris and black pupil.

Red for the fire-breathers, blessed by Solari, goddess of the sun and all the world's fires. Green for the earth-shakers, favored by Ord, the restless god of the heaving earth. White for the wind-workers, dearest to Loatma, goddess of the wind which touches all things. And blue for the water-weavers, beloved by Niahm, god of the boundless sea.

Wealthy families mark the time with celebrations and pilgrimages across the island to all four of the High Temples, to beg for the gods' attention. But for poor Sumitri, with little means or education, a girl child with elemental gifts isn't just a symbol of piety; she represents one of the few sure paths out of poverty on the island. Our queens pay for every child with a ring of color in their eyes to be educated and trained at the Academy, along with awarding a generous stipend to the family. Considering the Gifted are Sumitri's most profitable export, we're a worthy investment. Our island is small, with only one great city and a handful of coastal villages. Only seven-melons, named so for the seven seasons they spend ripening and prized for their healing properties, bring as much money to the island. The Gifted are also shipped off to countries all over the world, for the exact opposite purpose, to kill.

There had been no such wondering and worrying for me, because I was born with blue in my eyes. I have never known a day without a keen awareness of water—in the air, in the bodies of my mother and my siblings, and the drumming rhythms of Niahm's sea, battering the island.

Not that my mother would have been able to afford celebrations or the time off of work for a pilgrimage. When I was born and bundled off to the Sapphire Palace not a week later, she and my four older brothers were living at the edge of a slum in the tanning district. I used to dream about what the first years of my life would have been like without my gift. Half-starved in the slums with a family who loved me because we were blood, not because of what I could *provide*. I always felt ungrateful, imagining that version of my life, but I still sometimes daydream about that girl, and what her life could have been.

The tall girl leaning on a staff a few feet across from me is my exact opposite. Kamara is what our instructors call a *deathpetal*. Named after the crimson night-blooming flowers that only appear at the very end of summer. Kamara came to the Academy five years ago; she'd been placed in our year with the rest of the thirteen-year-olds. The color in her eyes had just appeared days before her arrival, and the worst gossips said the shock had caused her to burn down her family's home—with them inside. That's part of the reason for the name—crushed deathpetals make a deadly poison, and late bloomers are similarly lethal. I doubt the rumors are true, because if Kamara killed her family, who did she spend the last five years visiting every weekend? However, I never bring this up in conversations, because it might lead those same gossipmongers to wonder why I even know what Kamara does on the weekends.

Kamara's deathpetal reputation doesn't usually scare me. She may have more power than I do, but what she has in sheer force, I more than make up for in skill. But today isn't just a sparring match at the Academy. I have to win. Failing to become champion, being shipped off to the highest bidder . . . it is not an option.

However, as I give Kamara a quick scan, the smirk on her lips gives me pause.

It shouldn't. Not when I've fought Kamara for years, matches with weapons, with our elements, and even with just our bare hands—and most of the time, I win. I can conjure an image of her look of pre-fight anticipation with my eyes closed. I know she favors her left side but rarely leaves the right unprotected. I know her tell when she's gathering magic and when she's feinting. The difficulty is, she knows all the same about me.

I don't know why I didn't let myself think about this moment before now—I sat through Kamara's first match only yesterday, but I didn't need to watch to know she would win. I just knew when this all began, our paths would lead right to each other. Kamara and I lose to only each other. Maybe also because I know instinctively that thinking too long on Kamara leads me to spiral like this. Gods, I can't stand her.

Her smirk widens as if she knows what I'm thinking. I let my annoyance show on my face. Must she lean so insolently on that staff when almost the whole island is watching? Why can't she take this seriously? Kamara scratches at the back of her shaved head and then has the nerve to wink at me! At least she's seen fit to remove that ridiculous hat of hers.

"For our final match between Sanaa Uma and Kamara Lagasi," the Gifted crier in the royal box announces. I know little of working the winds, but with a series of elegant hand gestures, as though she's gathering air in her chest, her voice echoes around the arena, clear as a bell. "These two rival students are in their final year at the Academy. I'm told they are two of the most promising warriors of their generation. We are in for a treat! Now for the coin toss!"

The referee, a first-year instructor at the Academy, stands beside us holding up a gleaming gold coin. Newly minted for our newly crowned Queen Enokia, the cause for this tournament. The Queen has to have a champion, and she must be chosen among the best. The referee turns to me, but before I can call heads, Kamara lifts a hand. "Why do the coin toss? We both know we're not fighting with"—she pounds the staff into the dirt for emphasis—"these."

The referee sputters, and I roll my eyes at Kamara. "You sure about that? Water douses fire, you remember?" As the words leave my mouth, I have this weird sense of memories layered on top of one another, like I've said this to Kamara a hundred times. I probably have.

Kamara winks *again*, and white smoke billows from her full lips when she fires back, "Fire kills all, remember? The sun need not fear the sea."

"The sea fears nothing at all," I say, more a reminder to myself than to Kamara. We've had this argument so many times. Water versus fire.

Sun versus the sea.

Kamara versus me.

I lift my nose into the air and arch an eyebrow. Once I overheard Kamara telling a friend, *I don't know how someone so small manages to look down their nose at every single person they encounter.* I had smiled at the heat in her voice, gratified to have finally gotten a rise out of her for once instead of the other way around. She didn't know, and probably still doesn't, that I know her secret. However much she complains about me, Kamara enjoys fighting me. More than anything, she likes a challenge—even so, I've always suspected she held back in our matches. Waiting, probably, for a moment like this, when she can defeat me in front of everyone. Now she has the perfect opportunity to truly test her power against mine, and I'll let her until I find my opening. Then I'm kicking her out of this ring and becoming champion.

The Queen's Champion earns more gold even than the island's generals. It would finally be enough to not only keep my brothers fed, but also buy them a house and get them tutors so they may one day find apprenticeships and leave behind poverty entirely. Winning this bout means I can stop hearing my mother's spiraling fears about life near the slum whenever I'm alone.

I will win.

Then I'll move right into the Sapphire Palace, cutting short my last few months at the Academy—and with Kamara.

Which, I remind myself, is a relief. Though right now it makes my chest tight with panic. I've only known life at the Academy. I push the feeling away and nod at the referee. "You can call it. We'll be wielding elements."

The woman does a hand gesture, and the crier announces our decision to the crowd before she steps out of the ring. A brief hush settles over the arena, followed by a roar of anticipation that leaves both of us grinning.

Kamara bows and I return it. No matter what, at the end of this, we'll have our answer. We'll know who's best. I stretch out a hand and Kamara takes it.

III: KAMARA

A chill ripples up my arm. Sanaa's skin is several degrees cooler than mine. The shock nearly distracts me from her other hand reaching for the pouch at her waist. The water-weavers' uniforms draw moisture from the wearers' sweat and the environment, giving them a constant source of their element.

My laugh comes out as a plume of smoke. Clever, sneaky Sanaa. Her fingers slip from mine, and the other fist, coated in thick ice, strikes at my middle. I barely dodge the blow. I take two steps back and suck in a deep breath. I exhale a wall of flame, in defense against the ice Sanaa is already calling forth. She flicks her fingers, shooting ice spears as long as my arm. They melt instantly in the fire. My next exhalation goes into my palms; blue flames wreath my fingers.

I crouch as steam, from my fire meeting her ice, turns Sanaa into a murky silhouette. I send a prayer to Solari to burn it away quick. I risk a glance behind me. The edge of the ring is close—too close. And yet I find myself smiling as I creep closer.

A pang of some unknowable feeling hits me, almost like both longing and grief, and yet neither of those fit. I will miss this—miss her.

After today, whoever wins, their time will be exclusively dedicated to protecting the queen. And the loser will likely be sent off the island, to whichever country bid highest for her contract.

This isn't just the last fight of the tournament; it's the final match of hundreds during our five years at the Academy together. Five years of never really knowing which of us was strongest. At some point, the other girls in our year started keeping a tally.

With a sharp gesture of her fingers, Sanaa draws the water from the steam back to her. The steam coalesces into wavering globes of iridescence swirling around her body. Our eyes meet for an instant before hers flutter closed, and her hands come together as if in prayer.

"Rocks," I curse. I extend to my full height, and with a flex of my will, the flames on my hands grow to envelop my body.

When Sanaa's eyes open again, they are entirely blue. No whites, no pupil, no warm brown, just a deep, ever-shifting cerulean, exactly the same as the Unquiet Sea. I've been told my eyes turn crimson when I bring forth my hottest flames, which is not at all comforting.

It sets the alarm bells in my head clanging—and is the only warning I get before water, salt water by the smell of it, gushes from the sand behind Sanaa. She raises her hands, and a wave of it crests behind her, casting us both in shadow.

"Give me a chance to warm up at least," I call. My heart throws itself against my ribs like a tiger on a leash—and I can't tell if it's fury or wonder or fear.

"Give you a chance?" Sanaa snorts. "I thought you'd be impressed."

"I'd be impressed if I expected any less from you," I yell. "You're mad, you know that? Calling up a spring in the middle of the arena, Sanaa, of all the ways to show off—"

With a flex of Sanaa's hands, the wave comes barreling toward me.

IV: SANAA

Kamara *erupts*.

The wave cuts around me. Before it reaches Kamara, the flames around her go from just a shield for her body to a massive, blindingly bright nimbus of flame. Gouts of blue-white blast from her hands and feet, launching her a few feet into the air. She lands even closer to me, where the water is high enough that I thought it would engulf her and snuff out all that fire. But no, it isn't enough. I'll need the whole sea at my disposal to snuff out her flame.

The already terrible heat of the day becomes unbearable, with Kamara like a tiny version of the sun. Where the water hits Kamara, it instantly evaporates. She's become so hot that even the scant bit of water in the air is being burned off. For a moment, Kamara's heat is all I can feel—it's disorienting.

I draw again on the water I called up from a pocket within the island's crust. I wrap it around me like a blanket, ducking my head beneath. The second the water washes over my skin, I feel more settled.

I call up wave after wave, swaying with the effort. When Kamara flies again, I turn the next wave into ice, more a flex of my mind than my hands.

Kamara lands in a crouch, already sinking as the ice melts beneath her. She grins and opens her mouth, sending flames rippling across the ice toward me. My shield of ice melts on contact. I throw up another and another as I back away.

I need to plan my next move, but Kamara isn't giving me a chance. She takes one more of those flaming leaps.

Thank Niahm, I have the foresight to glance over my shoulder. The rope isn't even six inches behind me. I root myself to the ground by freezing the water around my ankles and gather the rest of it to slam into Kamara.

I'm too slow, though, because Kamara is right there, smiling at me from a bare hand width away, grinning like a jackal. Instead of forcing me back with more flames, she claps her hands, and the fire shielding her drops. Kamara snaps, and it roars back to life, only with me inside.

"What are you doing?" I growl. "You could've just beaten me—stop playing games."

"Aw, don't be put out, Sanaa. You know I can't resist that look on your face." Kamara pouts. "This is the last chance we get to play before I beat you."

"Before I beat you," I correct her. "The way you're dragging this out, you must realize everyone will see through you now. All the hate you pretended to have is just an obsession."

Kamara shrugs. "What do I care? After *my* win, you'll be leaving. Soon enough no one on this island will remember your name."

Something in me goes still at the regret in her voice. It echoes what I felt earlier, when I realized this was our last bout.

"You will. You'll still be wondering if I was better all this time," I say. I feel certain we're no longer talking about the match, but what we were talking about exactly, I can't say.

"Won't I always be proving myself to you?" Kamara asks. The fire engulfing us grows even hotter. "Prodigy versus deathpetal?"

I cringe as her words continue to echo my earlier musings. "I was under the impression you don't care what anyone thinks of you. Especially not me."

"Yes and no. I wish I didn't care what you think," Kamara says. Though sweat beads my face, I can't even see the effects of the heat on Kamara. Our bodies are resistant to the damage our elements cause as long as we are wielding them. But a red flush spreads across her cheeks.

This must be some new trick of hers.

"Liar," I snap.

"Why would I lie now?"

"I don't know! To confuse me so you can win." I clench my fists and step into her personal space, hissing, "Stop playing games!"

The flames around us grow higher and higher, blocking us off from the audience.

For the briefest of moments, Kamara's lips press against mine. I grab her collar, intending to shove her away. Instead I find myself deepening the kiss. Kamara's lips part, and I expect her to taste like smoke, but she's sweet as cloudberries.

The roar of the crowd pierces the crackling flames around us and panic makes me reach for the well I created earlier. But my grasping is too wild, too panicked, and the wave crashes over us both.

V: KAMARA

"May I speak, Your Majesty?" one of the advisors sitting beside the young Queen asks. "It seems the candidates to become your champion are not taking this match as seriously as they should. I say we forget the ring and let them fight to first blood. So they understand the deadly serious nature of this position."

After Sanaa essentially flushed us both out of the ring, the referee could not decide a victor, because we both left at the same time. Five minutes ago, the referee dragged us up to the royal box and began conferring heatedly with the Queen's advisors. The moment we ascended the stairs of the arena, I knew something worse was coming. The people in the royal box watch us with silent, disapproving eyes. Yet I'm sure no one saw me kiss Sanaa through the flames.

I still don't know what came over me. I can barely pay attention to the advisor. I only catch the words *first blood,* which can't be right. I can't get the memory of the kiss to stop replaying.

"Please, my lord," Sanaa protests. "Is that truly necessary? Believe me, we take our duties very seriously."

The man sniffs. "I'm sure you do, Sanaa Uma, but your opponent doesn't seem to share your reverence."

I open my mouth to protest—because I do take it all quite seriously—but Sanaa cuts me a look. I can almost hear her voice in my head, prim and sharp, *Leave this to me, Lagasi.* I want to point out that she is the one who caused all this mess, because I never intended to kiss her. However, Sanaa may disagree, so I remain silent. My hands curl into fists, already slick with nervous sweat.

First blood.

Why should we have to wound each other when this tournament

is only for the Queen's vanity? And why does the thought of actually wounding Sanaa nauseate me?

The advisor turns back to the Queen, who inclines her head, watching us both. "Well, I for one would like to get out of this heat. I warn you both, if we should need a third bout, I'm sure my advisors can suggest another way to raise the stakes."

My mouth goes dry. My mind, the traitor, conjures an image of Sanaa, her mouth dripping blood. I swallow back a retch and bow alongside Sanaa.

We follow the referee back down to the heart of the arena. I try to think back on all of my matches against Sanaa—have I ever drawn blood? The few times I remember a choice between beating her and hurting her, I always found excuses to let Sanaa win. She was the golden child of our cohort—and I was the thorn in seemingly all of my instructors' sides. Hurting her would only make me more enemies—or so I told myself. In my first few years at the Academy, I was punished for losing control in matches. I was so full of rage at myself for burning down our home and nearly killing the only parent I have. Self-loathing wasn't enough of an outlet for that anger, so it spilled into my fights— and yet Sanaa isn't in a single one of those memories.

Because even though Sanaa has always infuriated me, with her perfect manners and effortless skill, I have never been able to convince myself to hate her. She never uses her status to intimidate others, and she constantly fields requests for help from other water-weavers, from the younglings to those near or past graduation. I can barely make it through our required hours babysitting the younglings during their practice sessions. I liked throwing my power up against hers because it seemed to be the only time when she wasn't doing something for someone else's benefit. Just for herself. And the Sanaa that was revealed during our matches, she wasn't proper and well-mannered—she was passionate and joyful and often scary.

I feel numb as we trudge toward the fighting pit. Nothing has changed—I still have to win, for my mother and my debts. But now it's the last thing I want. I have never—not since that terrible day five years ago, when my hands caught fire in my sleep—hurt anyone I cared about with my gift. I swore to my mother and to the sun goddess, I will never use my flames on someone who doesn't deserve to burn—yet another reason why leaving our island to become a glorified sell-sword cannot be my fate.

Protecting our Queen from all of the outside powers who covet our island and our Gifted? That is a noble cause. But hurting Sanaa for no reason but the whims of a young Queen cannot be why I have this gift.

Fire doesn't limit itself—it consumes. It devours. How can I turn my fire on the only significant relationship in my life besides my mother? Even if our relationship is a rivalry, it's more than I have with any other classmate or instructor at the Academy.

Before we step back out into the sun, Sanaa elbows my side. "What's wrong with you? This is all your fault, you know."

"Yeah." I cut her off, my frustration shifting toward her for a second before it settles back on me. "Well aware. I'm sorry, if that counts for something."

"Sorry for what?" Sanaa whispers.

The kiss . . . and what I must do next. I say nothing and push past her, following the referee onto the sands.

We stand across from each other, no ring to hold us back. Sanaa gives me a long, piercing look. I drop my eyes from hers and bow.

Sanaa swings a whip of water toward me. I push it away with a shield of flame. The strike is tentative compared to what she can do, and that stirs me to at least pretend I'm not spiraling. I shield myself and begin launching a few fireballs in her direction, only allowing them near Sanaa so she'll think I'm back in this fight. So she will end it, not me.

I close in, throwing out fire faster and faster, until Sanaa throws up a thick wall of ice. It falls easily beneath my onslaught, revealing Sanaa, her fingers bound in threads of water. I've never seen Sanaa wield this particular attack against anyone living—only the practice dummies she sliced to pieces during our first lesson. I'd been so annoyed at her instant mastery that I skipped out on the rest of the class and took a nap beneath my favorite tree.

I ought to feel fear at the sight, but relief leaves room for little else as Sanaa casts out with the first threads.

I drop my shield and shut my eyes as Sanaa's web of threads falls over me.

VI: SANAA

A scream rings out. It takes me a moment to realize the sound is coming from me, and not Kamara. Her gasp of pain is barely audible over the roaring crowd. They're cheering for me, and yet tears burn my eyes as Kamara crashes to her knees. Blood spills from the dozens of cuts I gave her.

I rush toward Kamara, unable to keep the anger out of my voice.

I drop to my knees, my fingers already in motion, keeping the wounds from weeping more blood. Already the sand beneath me is wet with it. "What in all hells were you thinking?" I hiss. I call over my shoulder, "We need a medic!"

Kamara winces, but her tone is light. "I would say you ought to have been a healer, but I think my body is proof your bloodthirst wouldn't be sated by simple bloodletting."

"Bloodletting? Have you not noticed how I am refusing to *let* your blood spill now? For Gods' sakes, Kamara, why did you let those threads fall?"

Kamara's smile remains in place, though her eyes darken with pain. "I couldn't hurt you."

For a long beat, I say nothing. "Why not?"

Kamara squirms. "You've heard the gossip. Everyone thinks I killed my family in a fire. I didn't, but I did hurt my mother, and she still hasn't fully recovered. She still needs healing, and more help than I can give with just our stipend. But she would hate to see me win like this. I promised her to never burn someone I cared for when I went to the Academy. Don't overthink it, Sanaa. It was a promise kept." She shrugs uncomfortably, then grimaces in pain as blood from a wound on her upper arm wells. In an instant, though, Kamara's expression turns vulpine. "And I figured having another reason to guilt you would be useful."

A long moment passes while I take this in. Not only did she provide an answer to who she spends her weekends with, but she also confirmed the feelings I thought I sensed earlier. My face grows warm, even as my stomach churns with worry at her injuries. Articulating the confused jumble of feelings I have for Kamara is beyond me. Finally I say, "Guilt me into what?"

"Another kiss, I think. Don't worry, I won't make you pay up just yet. Now that you're the Queen's Champion, such public displays will soon be beneath you."

"Is that so?"

"Oh yes, I'm quite sure. And I'm hoping a certain fire-breather might find her way beneath you, you know, before they ship me off and make a mercenary out of me." The humor in her voice doesn't quite hide the panic underneath it.

Ah. The fact of my victory had so quickly flown from my head as soon as Kamara's blood spilled in the sand. "Give me a moment."

Now that I know about Kamara's mother, I can't let this be the end. I didn't win—Kamara let me. I can't just take this from her. If it means I can't be champion, so be it. I can always send money back to the island, though it's far from ideal. My mother and brothers will still have one another. Kamara and her mother don't have that luxury.

I stand and find the stadium all but silent as they watch us. The only furious discussion comes from the Queen's box; the advisors buzz around Enokia like bees in a hive. I wave my arms until they notice me. "Your Majesty, may I speak?" I yell. Somehow the words carry. I bow low, till my forehead is nearly flush with the sand. "Please?"

I straighten as one of the advisors strides forward, but Enokia places a lissome hand upon his arm. She then inclines her head toward me. The sunlight striking the diamonds and opals on her crown blinds me. I shut my eyes and offer a prayer to Niahm. Then I risk everything by meeting the Queen's stern gaze. "Your Majesty, as you and everyone else has witnessed during this match, Kamara Lagasi is my match in strength and talent. Some of you must have seen that I only won our last bout because Kamara let the match end."

"As I said," the advisor pipes up, "she does not take this matter seriously enough. That is reason enough to disqualify the fire-breather from becoming champion."

"Your Majesty, I assure you this is not because Kamara doesn't take this tournament seriously, but because she . . . *we* cannot consent to harming each other with our gifts. As you know, it is anathema for the Gifted to wield our gifts against innocent Sumitri—this is what your advisors have asked of us. That is not why Niahm and Solari have blessed us, Your Majesty."

I bow my head again as the advisors close in around the Queen again. They have little time to confer, though, as Queen Enokia rises from her seat. "I have decided. You have both shown your gifts to their full heights today. I agree there was no clear winner—yet to choose a champion other than you two would not only betray the spirit of this tournament, but may offend Niahm and Solari by rejecting two so blessed by them. You will both serve as champion for the duration of my rule of the Isle of Sumir. Let us all rejoice for the blessings the gods have bestowed!"

My mouth falls open as the arena erupts into thunderous applause.

I turn back to Kamara, relieved, as three healers finally make their way to the sands. "I think I'll have time to fulfill that debt. You know, as soon as you don't run the risk of bleeding all over me."

The healers check every cut to see if it's deep enough to need immediate attention before I allow them to move her. Kamara curses and hisses like a cat doused in water as they hoist her onto the stretcher. "Sanaa," she begins, after she catches her breath. "I ought to have clarified, when I said a kiss, I meant one for each wound you so viciously dealt me. There should be time enough between our royal duties for that."

I sigh, but the guilt churning in my stomach melts at the grin on Kamara's face. My cheeks aflame, I give Sanaa a small smile, this time just for her. "Very well. I shall do my best to oblige and see that you do as well."

The Last Days in the Only Place That Ever Felt Like Home

BY ADI ALSAID

Her whole life, Gwen had been a potted plant. As her parents moved around the world and signed her and her little brother, Aiden, up for international school after international school, Gwen had been able to fit in pretty well. Her roots were self-contained, wrapping around her in a comforting, protective hug, but she was still a plant among others. Many other kids at those schools often moved, their lives a constantly revolving door of new faces. They made friends quickly and said goodbye easily. Even the more permanent students were used to people coming and going. At sixteen, Gwen had never been lonely, had only missed people for a little while before accepting the new ones into her life.

Throughout all these moves, Gwen often found herself wanting to speed time up. She was always looking forward to something in the future, counting down the days until it arrived. At the start of the school year, it was winter break and the beach trips that often came along with it. When winter arrived, she would look forward to spring break, and the basketball tournament that would come right after, during which Gwen would look forward to summer, the brief glimpse of life back in the US: seeing her cousins, who each year cemented themselves in the

American lifestyle. Then a new assignment would come in for her parents, and Gwen would imagine the new life to come.

The new language she would master, the new foods she would taste, the new friends that she knew would be waiting for her, even if they invariably became another group of near-strangers she was eager to leave behind in favor of the next ones. The future was always unwaveringly shiny in Gwen's mind, even if the present was always a little dull and disappointing. And yes, she knew the present had at one point been the future she was excited about, and that, if she were being thoughtful about the cycles of her life, she should expect the future not to live up to her expectations. That wasn't how her brain worked, though.

Not until Taipei, anyway.

Now that she'd lived in Taipei, now that she'd discovered the fountain, her brain knew the future could only be disappointing.

Because her tomorrow wasn't going to be spent in Taiwan. It wasn't going to come with night markets or cafés inhabited by cats (whether they were cat cafés or not). It wasn't going to be replete with warm, welcoming strangers, their smiles wider than anywhere else Gwen had lived. It wouldn't have goofy posters for dozens of mayoral candidates, or hole-in-the-wall lu rou fan spots, whole strips of stationery stores, most of which also boasted a resident cat napping in the sun. It wouldn't have old rickety trains that could take her from city to mountains to beaches.

Whatever tomorrow would bring, it wasn't going to have Jill and Shichen and Raul. It wasn't going to be the same. So she didn't want to look forward like she always did. She wanted to look back.

✧ ⧫ ✧

She'd discovered the fountain about a month into her time in Taiwan. School had been going on for a few weeks, long enough that the sheen of excitement had already begun to fade. She'd made a few acquaintances that she could see turning into friendships, given the right circumstances and enough time. There was a girl in her AP History class named Jill who'd been friendly with her and had even saved her number into Gwen's phone.

But she wouldn't call Jill a friend yet, and there were no other strong prospects in that department, just a few people who asked her if she played volleyball or basketball because she was tall. The quick crushes Gwen had developed—she'd been unable to resist fantasizing about a bright-burning romance—had already soured after finding out the guy was a jerk or boring or couldn't actually hold a conversation. On top of that, she was struggling to learn her first tonal language, and basketball tryouts wouldn't be held for another month, leaving her with a lot of lonely afternoons.

So she did what she always did the first month into a new place: explored, and imagined the future would be better. Gwen started by meandering through the neighborhood she lived in after school, first getting acquainted with the major streets, then the offshoots. After a few days of that, rather than taking the thirty-minute bus ride back home, she stuck around the area near school, in the Beitou District. Using a trick a friend in Brussels had taught her, Gwen would look at the yellow spots on Google maps to find busy areas. And if those didn't interest her, she'd look for restaurants or food stands in the area and visit those.

The food, at least, lived up to even her wildest prearrival expectations. It was impossible to decide at the night markets whether to go back to the dishes she'd already fallen in love with or seek out yet another new experience that might outdo the ones before. There was a beef noodle soup at a spot near Tianshou Park that had quickly become one of her favorite meals of all time.

It was while walking off that delectable dish that she stumbled upon the fountain.

It was a simple drinking fountain, strangely designed to look like a rock, maybe in order to fit in with the nature of the tiny park and the canal it was near. (Or was it a river? Gwen couldn't tell.) She studied it for a moment longer than she would have any other water fountain, then leaned in for a quick drink and continued on her way to the MRT station.

It was a Friday, and though she'd heard people talking about a party, no one had extended her an invite. Instead, she was going to take the subway down to Taipei 101 and explore that side of town, then meet her family for dinner at Din Tai Fung.

She boarded the train confidently, having done it a couple of times now. She'd even been able to do it while being very much in her head, not paying much attention to her surroundings. A silly thing to be proud of, maybe, but as someone who had lived in several cities, it was always a nice milestone to cross: getting on public transportation without having to think much about it.

It had taken her a while to notice anything, that first time. It wasn't until she'd been walking for a while in the area around Taipei 101 after she'd deboarded the train that she realized her movement was quicker than everyone else's. A cultural thing, maybe. She recalled a study about the average walking speeds of people in different countries. Then she'd passed by a man just as he was ashing his cigarette, and noticed the gray flakes sauntering down slower than they had any right to. A full second passed, and they still hadn't hit the ground.

The next hour had been an exercise in wrapping her mind around what had happened. She had to sit on a bench and stare at the stopwatch app on her phone, counting too many *Mississippi*s from one second to the next. She grabbed her water bottle from her backpack and poured out its contents. The water refused to pour in real time. It was going slow enough that she was able to pull her hand away and scoop all the water up again before it hit the ground. She yanked out a single hair from her head and then let it go, watching the dark brown strand dance hypnotically in front of her eyes before being slowly carried away by a slight breeze.

By the time she met her parents and Aiden for dinner, things were back to normal, thankfully, because she didn't know how she would have acted otherwise.

She'd been reasonably distracted during dinner, trying to figure out what had blown up her understanding of the world. Had it been a hallucination caused by something she ate? Her dad was a bit of a hypochondriac, so she'd done her fair share of googling *food poisoning*. If that was the case, though, she probably would have had stomach pains or nausea too, or maybe a fever. None of which she'd experienced.

As she bit the top off another xiao long bao to let the steam out, and listened to Aiden talking about his day at school, she wondered about whether she'd been drugged somehow. She thought back to everything she'd consumed that day, trying to remember if there was a chance anyone had slipped something into her water bottle.

Water bottle.

Water.

The fountain?

Just as that thought led her to the fountain she drank from, her phone buzzed on the table. Everyone paused to look at it. "Friends?" her mom asked.

"Too early for Gwen to have friends," Aiden said, picking at some mustard greens with ginger.

"True," Gwen said, though when she looked down at her phone, she saw it was a text from Jill inviting her to that party.

She was going to ignore it, her mind latching on to the fountain, the possibility that it was somehow the culprit. But her dad nudged the phone toward her. "You can answer it. You know making friends early is key."

"Read it out loud so we can pretend we have friends too," her mom chimed in.

Gwen rolled her eyes but then read the text, albeit without much inflection in her voice. That didn't stop her parents from dancing in their seats. "A party! You have to go," her dad said.

"Can I go?" Aiden asked.

Gwen's dad looked at her mom, eyebrows raised.

"No. Just Gwen. Be back home by midnight."

Once her parents were excited about socializing, it was hard to get them to stop.

When she arrived at the party, instead of leaving her to wander through the rooms hugging the walls and hoping for someone to talk to her, Jill greeted her warmly with a hug almost as soon as she stepped in the door.

She led her straight to her little circle of friends. Or maybe triangle was the appropriate shape, since it was just two of them: Raul, Chilean, tall and quiet, with perpetually crooked and smudged glasses that he kept dropping. And Shichen, Taiwanese, smiley and cute, who Gwen learned was quick to let a joke fly and didn't care so much if it landed all the time.

She forgot about the fountain for a while, joking around with the trio as if they'd been friends for much longer. When they went to get another drink, they made sure she came with them, and though occasionally one of them would turn to speak to another classmate Gwen hadn't met yet, they kept returning to one another, like they'd been a square all this time and had just been waiting for Gwen to arrive.

Which was probably why, later in the night, when it was approaching her curfew and Jill casually asked Gwen what she'd done that day, Gwen found it easy to share the whole truth. She didn't care what it sounded like, didn't care if they'd think she was high or too strange or like someone trying too hard to describe a dream.

They had a lot of questions, reasonably so. What she hadn't expected, though, was for Jill to look at her Apple Watch to check the time and then say, "Why don't we go test out the fountain? See if you're right."

✧ ⌧ ✧

It had only been a year since that first group visit to the fountain. But throughout that year there were hours lived at a tenth of the speed. The four of them huddled together in a coffee shop doing all their homework in fifteen minutes so that the rest of the day was free to spend however they wanted. Another stop by the fountain, then off to one of their houses to run experiments, figure out the rules, even though the rules seemed fluid. Sometimes it would last an hour, sometimes three. Sometimes their voices came out in high-pitched, chipmunk squeaks, other times they could speak normally, not just to themselves but to others around them. There was no discernible way to predict which it would be.

Life felt full to the brim. There was always enough time. Time to sleep, time to do the work expected of them, time to read. Movies and video games sometimes worked under the influence of the fountain (though, when the latter did, it came with accusations of cheating from everyone on the internet who struggled to keep up).

But books. Books bent to their will. Gwen had never just sat somewhere in the sun with friends and read before. Books were their own little time machines, portals to worlds, magic vessels that put her in someone else's head. And maybe all of that was the fountain, or maybe it was the crack in her self-contained pot, maybe it was her roots uncurling and brushing up against the others'. Whatever the reason, Gwen had never been so comfortable in anyone else's silence before.

The four of them would ride the MRT, sitting perfectly still, watching people come and go. Oh, the joy in observing a stranger and knowing that if they sensed you looking, you would have turned your head long before they could catch you in the act.

They started playing games with strangers, taking a man's hat off for ten of their slowed-down seconds and then putting it back on his head, stifling their giggles when he instinctively raised a hand to check for it and was confused to find it still there. At night markets, they would swap two people's dishes and see if they noticed, or they'd hang around and wait until someone was rude to a worker, and then steal morsels from their plate.

If fucking with someone else creates a strong bond (and who were they lying to, it did), then helping others brought them even closer. They realized they could be guardian angels a dozen times a day. They rescued coffee cups from tipping over, held someone upright when they tripped stepping off a curb, and brought back a distracted woman's forgotten purse and hung it on her shoulder as she walked off the train car.

It got to the point where Gwen wanted to go to the fountain at all times. Before school, right after, Fridays when it was the four of them, she'd lead them straight there, as if there was no question about it.

On a three-day weekend, Shichen had invited all of them to come with his family to Taroko National Park, and he rushed them toward the train station so they could meet up on time. "Let's go to the fountain," Gwen said. "I want a slow-mo train ride to carry me through the next few days."

"I don't think we have time," Shichen responded.

"We will," Gwen said in a singsong voice, but the others didn't laugh.

"It'll be good to get a break," Jill said, hooking her arm through Gwen's elbow, even though Gwen was a good six inches taller than Jill. "Just be in the moment for once."

And Gwen had thought about it for a bit. But there was an itch in her. It was as if without the fountain, she would lose all of this, she'd go back to just looking ahead, waiting for the future. To her, experiencing life with the water from the fountain was being in the moment.

"I'll catch up," she'd said, "I swear." She hadn't waited for them to complain or talk her out of it. She ran to the fountain and still made the train in the end.

From then on, if the others didn't follow her to the fountain, she knew not to push. Instead, she'd create situations that allowed her to sneak away or find little ways to bring it up throughout the day so that it would feel like someone else's idea to go back, not hers.

✦ ✦ ✦

The extra time granted by the fountain allowed Gwen to explore more of Taipei than any other city she'd lived in before, and it made her hungry for more.

Which was, of course, quickly ruined by her parents sitting her and Aiden down for the kind of conversation that had long ago stopped feeling momentous.

"New marching orders, kids," their mom announced.

"Already?" Gwen said, a little surprised at the whine in her voice.

Aiden right away asked where to next, but Gwen barely heard the answer. Now she only had a few days left in Taipei.

Up next: a few weeks back in the States, visiting cousins, visa appointments, and wardrobe adjustments for the new climate. But what was there to look forward to? The anticipation for the future that she was so familiar with was nowhere to be seen. It was stifled by the desire to stay, the desire for the past.

No matter how much time she'd managed to squeeze into a year, there was no going back. Taipei had piled on the firsts: her first real close-knit group of friends, her first hookup, her first time driving a motorbike. She knew her life wasn't over, far from it. But it felt like *this* life was coming to an end. And for the first time, she wasn't looking forward to the future.

So Gwen had decided to visit the fountain, and do as many of the Taipei things as she could one last time. She had already had her last day at school, and her last afternoon at her favorite coffee shop, with its three cats and the sweet baristas who gave her extra whipped cream every time and the occasional free cookie.

Gwen had even had her last night with her group of friends already, a calm and bittersweet day at Jill's place. They'd started at their favorite boba shop, avoiding talk of the fountain, avoiding talking about Gwen leaving, like it was just a normal day.

After an hour, Gwen couldn't help herself. "Do you guys mind . . . ?"

"Ha!" Raul said, picking up his glasses from the ground for the third time already. "I told you guys she could last this long."

"You thought I'd drag you straight to it?" Gwen asked, more amused than offended.

"Pretty much," Jill said, hooking her arm through Gwen's. It was a little sad to think that it might be the last time her friend did that.

At least they had the fountain to stretch the day out.

Once the effect kicked in, they played their games and acted like guardian angels one last time. "I guess we could do this in real time," Jill had said. "Find little ways to help people."

"That's just me," Gwen said. "You'll get to keep doing it on fountain time."

On their way to Jill's house, Gwen let her friends talk during the train ride while she tried to cherish the hours, the minutes, the seconds. Even the spaces between the seconds, as the fountain did its thing and gave them more time than they had any right to. Her friends harbored fantasies of meeting up again soon. Of taking gap years together before college or traveling over the summer to wherever was the midpoint between all of them. Shichen, the lone native Taiwanese person among them, had recommended all of them meet back up in Taipei every five years. They saved the date into their phones, so that the internet would never let them forget.

And though part of Gwen was excited by the idea, it still felt like some unknowable, unattainable future. Who knew what would happen between them, who they would be by the end of the summer, much less when they finished high school, or in five years? She couldn't even imagine being away from Taipei next week, away from the fountain and her friends, away from the stationery stores she loved perusing, the friendliness of the people who shouted, "Welcome to Taiwan!" when she biked past.

Gwen wished she could physically hold on to time. Just trying to imagine it, she could feel it slipping through the cracks between her knuckles. She used her phone to take videos of all of them on the train. Raul and Shichen were giggling about something. Shichen was wearing the shirt from his school uniform for some reason, a little splotch of sauce or tea, maybe, staining his collar. Raul's eyes often flitted to Jill, who made a face for the camera, unaware that Gwen was taking a video, not a picture. Maybe Gwen would appreciate this later on when she was missing them. But it didn't make her feel like she was savoring time at all. The opposite, actually.

She had felt like that the whole night, when they ate pizza, played video games, and watched funny videos online, up until the goodbye itself. She begged her brain to remember the hugs, remember Jill's eyelashes fluttering against her neck, the way Raul had paused while saying good night, as if he was trying not to cry.

It was gone already, that night. Now she just had this last day. Ten hours or so before she'd be at the airport waving goodbye to the first place that had really felt like home. She had told her parents she'd be out soaking in the city one last night, which they were okay with as long as she came back by midnight.

Her first stop was the fountain. She stood before it, remembering its accidental discovery. She'd always wondered how many other people knew about it, how many were keeping its secret. At school, they hadn't found anyone else outside the group who seemed aware that it was special in any way. They talked often about who to ask directly, or maybe even who to bring along with them, though in the end they never did. Gwen had the sense—and she was sure the others did too—that sharing the secret with the wrong person might make it all fall apart, kill the magic, one way or another.

She put a hand on the button as if it were a skittish cat that might at any moment flee from her touch. It felt silly to want to say bye to an inanimate object, to feel like she was breaking up with it. But she felt like she owed it so much more than just a goodbye kiss, to put it that way.

In the end, though, that was all she could offer. So she leaned down and drank from it, long and slow, as if she'd just made it through a days-long hike through a desert.

She went to the beef noodle spot, both thrilled to know about it and sad to say goodbye to it. When would she eat this dish again, the exact way they prepared it here? She got the spicy version and topped it with plenty of pickled mustard greens and grabbed a side of cucumber salad.

Her dad had learned to make it, and she would be able to carry the dish with her from Taiwan to Peru, as long as they could find the right ingredients, but it wouldn't be the same.

At least there were some things that could be carried away, in some form, from one place to another. Recipes, memories.

Leaving the restaurant, the fountain's effects began kicking in. She pulled up the app on her phone and called herself a scooter using Grab, a car service that had the option to ride on a motorbike. The first time she'd done it, with Shichen driving and her gripping on tightly to the handles, she'd been terrified. Her leg muscles had been tense the whole time, and she'd been sore the next day as if she'd worked out.

But when time was slowed down, the fear gave way to wonder. She loved crossing the city on motorbike. Chasing that feeling, she climbed onto the Grab. From her precarious position on the back, she saw the drivers in their cars, singing along to music, looking stressed, listening intently to the news, knuckles gripped at ten and two, or one wrist resting loosely on top of the steering wheel. She loved passing by all the neighborhoods, seeing them change from storefronts to homes to parks and back again. It made her feel impossibly small, in the best way. Like she was among so much life that even fathoming it all was overwhelming.

At Taipei 101 she paid the excessive fee for the observation decks. She put in earphones so that she could play her favorite sweeping music as she looked out at the city, but the music came through in slow motion, so she had to settle for the noise of the crowd. She had tried to time it with the sunset for maximum sentimentality, but timing was always hard when the fountain was involved.

There were too many people around, and she had already been to the observation deck twice before (once when they'd first arrived, once more when her parents' friends had come to visit with their kids), so the catharsis she was expecting was a little muted. She tried to get lost in the views, but her heart wasn't along for the ride, instead mired in the kind of sadness she had been hoping to avoid until she was on the plane. She thought about the times that Jill and the others had tried to convince her not to go to the fountain before doing anything else. For this particular instance, she kind of wished they'd been around to talk her out of it.

Maybe there was another fountain somewhere in Taipei that could reverse time, let her live this past year over again. It wasn't fair that it was over, that she was getting uprooted again so soon. She'd be happy if she could just do it one more time, that's it. Just this year.

That first party, that first time she brought them all to the fountain, when they thought she was kidding, or out of her mind. She would love to relive the moment Raul first felt the effects, the smile on his face, the awe. The basketball game she'd played in slow motion, dropping forty points so easily she'd felt like she could go pro (she'd only done it that one time; her guilt at cheating and her worry of getting caught too great to overcome). The many nights exploring the stalls of the night markets, on her own, with her family, with her friends. She wanted to taste stinky tofu again for the first time and see if it had been as jarring as it was in her memory.

That first kiss, too. Not because it was any good or the boy, Minh, held a special place in her heart or anything, but because it had been unexpected and pleasant, and the makeouts that had come after were heavy with anticipation and performance of feelings they did not have for each other. And it would have been nice to have that little pure thrill again. Even if there were greater loves, greater makeouts to come, that one experience felt lost, never to be replicated.

As she went back down the tower and called another Grab, she wondered how many experiences she'd let pass unappreciated all those years as she was looking forward to the next place. How many first experiences had she ignored, not given the proper attention? Could she remember her first time snorkeling? The first time she stayed up all night? The last time her dad picked her up in his arms? Or her mom, for that matter? When was the last time she'd picked up Aiden in her arms? How was she sixteen and life was passing by this quickly?

The Grab motorbike let her off right in front of the fountain, and she could barely resist running to it and drinking hungrily, big desperate gulps that she couldn't get enough of. She wanted it to last the night, wanted to rip the fountain from its base and bring it with her. But just picturing the effort to take the fountain with her made her want to cry, so she wiped her mouth and looked at her phone's map and her favorite food stands that she'd saved as a list over the past year. It had only been a couple of real-time hours since her last meal, but she was famished again. She and her friends were hungry all the time anyway, the boys especially, but the fountain made them bottomless pits of food. Taipei was a pretty good city for that.

At the first night market, Shida, she had some fried sweet potato balls, and then grilled corn, all smoky and spiced in a way that made American corn on the cob feel like cardboard by comparison. Then she took the MRT to Shilin Market, where they had an almond milk drink with black sesame, and she couldn't believe this might be the last time she would drink it. She'd only had it a handful of times, really, but it was better than any coffee she'd ever had, any tea, boba or otherwise. And now she had to say goodbye to it? Because time had to march forward?

It made her want to cry, the way time only moved this one way, this one direction, faster and faster the more she thought about it. She ordered a squid skewer just for the chance to sit down and catch her breath (but also for the five-spice barbecue sauce this particular stand served with the skewer).

She thought back to all the countries she'd lived in, the people she'd met, the food she'd had. What a waste it had been to think just of the future and miss what was in front of her. Who knows how long she sat there racking her brains, sifting through memories like she was searching for clues to some crime she'd committed against herself.

"Gwen?"

When she looked up, she saw her family standing in front of her, holding red bean cakes. "What are you guys doing here?"

"Planning a heist, obviously," Aiden said, taking a bite of his cake. The effects of the fountain were gone again, quicker than they usually dissipated. It was as if the universe was telling her that she couldn't take it with her, no matter how much she wanted to.

Her parents rolled their eyes. Aiden, twelve, was deep into an obsessive heist phase, and he tried to make almost every conversation about them. "Just getting our favorites one last time," her mom said. "What about you? Are you okay? You looked out of it."

"Yeah," Gwen said. "Just thinking."

"We were gonna go get some snow ice. Wanna join us?"

Gwen had originally wanted her last day in Taipei to be her own, to not have to spend time with her family, who she would spend almost every waking moment with for the next three months. But the last few hours had changed that mood, and there was a nearby spot that served her favorite snow ice, maybe her favorite dessert of all time.

"As long as it's YiHa."

"You know it," her dad said.

"Can I get an XL chicken on the way?" Aiden asked.

Their dad laughed, then looked at their mom. "It's here, honey. The age of teen hunger is upon us."

"Is that a yes?" Aiden asked.

"You okay with that, Gwen?" their mom asked.

She nodded and stood up, accepting the second half of her mom's red bean cake.

"So, what exactly would you heist at a night market?" her dad asked Aiden.

"Sticky rice sausages," Aiden said, not missing a beat. "Enough to build a sausage empire."

Gwen laughed despite herself. She was walking alongside her mom, behind her dad and Aiden. She took a bite of the cake, but it didn't taste particularly good, so she handed it back to her mom, who took it quietly. Someone bumped her as they sped around her, and then she almost ran into a man speaking loudly on his phone.

Suddenly, Gwen no longer wanted to be at the market, didn't want to cross any more Taipei things off her list, didn't want to be around people. She wanted to go to bed and then just be back in the US to go through her usual stupid summer-in-between homes.

"You're gonna miss it here, huh?" her mom said.

Gwen nodded, even though that didn't seem to adequately cover everything she was feeling. It wasn't that she was going to miss it. It was that she had missed it. She'd missed so much already. How had she sat around for years waiting for the future, when time kept marching on ahead?

Without making the conscious choice to do it, she found herself unloading on her mom, telling her about everything except for the fountain itself. How she had wasted all that time looking ahead, and how she was afraid of what she might have missed. How for the last few hours her brain had kept returning to the past, combing for experiences she did not wholly appreciate. All the time she'd already lived suddenly felt like a heavy bag strapped to her back.

They'd slowed down, staying out of earshot of Aiden and her dad, not that the two were paying attention.

"How can I make that stop? I want it to stop," Gwen said, on the verge of tears, and feeling ridiculous for it.

Now her mom pulled her into a hug. Gwen was initially embarrassed and wanted to say it was no big deal, but the hug felt exactly like what she needed, and she let herself be swallowed up by it.

"Honey, if I had an answer to that, therapists the world over would be out of business. Or calling me a fraud. Because there's no way to do that." Her mom pulled away, but kept her hands on Gwen's shoulders. A group of white tourists maneuvered around them to get in line at a nearby oyster omelet stand. "Time marches on. It's human nature to look forward and to look back. There's absolutely nothing wrong with doing that. It can even be pretty healthy, at times.

"But there's only one thing I've found that helps. It's not easy to do, and just because we constantly fail doesn't mean we should stop."

"What's that?" Gwen asked, a hint of desperation creeping into her voice, a hint of hope, too, maybe. Aiden and her dad were getting too far ahead, so they started walking to catch up.

"Look around at the now," her mom said simply, with a little shrug. "You pay attention to the day as you're living it, and you forgive yourself when you fail."

Gwen let the words sink in. She wanted them to make it all okay right away, to cancel away the day's realizations about how much time she'd wasted on the future. Instead, they made her realize she'd just been doing the exact same thing in reverse. Spending her last day in her so-far favorite city in the world thinking about the past instead of actually saying goodbye. Even with the extra time the fountain had provided, she'd thrown the time away.

Gwen walked in a daze for the next few minutes, completely in her head, a cycle of regretful thoughts.

Little by little, though, something almost magical happened. Maybe it was because a crack had formed in her metaphorical pot. Her roots, once comfortably wrapped around her, now sought the outside. They wanted more.

She was pulled back to the world. By her mom's hand on her shoulder. By the sounds of vendors calling out for customers, the sound of people walking around her, talking, eating, laughing. There were the smells of so many things being roasted, grilled, wok-flamed, boiled.

They were at the snow ice place, sitting on the floor at their favorite spot by the window, where they could look out at the quiet street. Aiden was still going on about heisting the night market for sausages, and the whole family was being shockingly funny, one of those times that everyone is somehow on the same page.

Then the snow ice came, the restaurant's special, which had some fermented rice pudding that was sweet and tart, and little green tea flavored glutinous rice balls, all covered with condensed milk and honey. And with something like that in front of her, it was impossible to think about time, lost or otherwise.

Maybe tomorrow she would miss the fountain again. She would miss her friends, and Taipei, and the beef noodle soup that she ate at least once a week. Maybe the missing would start in a few hours, while she was in bed. Or when they were on the way to the airport. She would look out at the fading city and her heart would wrench at time's relentless march forward.

But that would come later, if it came at all. She did not have to worry about that now. Now, it was only possible to focus on the sensations in her mouth, the explosion of flavor, the company of her family.

The (Hopefully) Last Demon Summoning

BY KIKA HATZOPOULOU

The night is a dud from the very beginning.

It starts drizzling as I'm putting my makeup on (using my new setting spray spell, courtesy of my alchemist friend Calla), and by the time I throw open the door, it's downright *pouring*. It takes less than ten seconds for my phone to start pinging with new messages in the group chat, announcing that the music festival we were supposed to go to is canceled and that we're hanging out at Cesar's place instead.

I groan so loudly that my mom calls, "What's wrong, baby?" from upstairs.

What's wrong is that tonight was supposed to be the highlight of our summer before college, the culmination of the six-week-long series of perfect hangouts in perfecter places with the perfectest people. It was supposed to be the seven of us—me and my boyfriend, Gio; Cesar and his SO, Sébastien; Calla; Trev; and Iseul—arms around one another, sticky with sweat, cheeks hurting from grinning, singing along at the top of our lungs to our favorite bands.

It was supposed to be the Best Night.

The resulting pout on my face must be deforming, because the moment Cesar sees me fifteen minutes later, he gives me a very judgy look.

"Nina!" he chastises. "Don't be a Grumpy McGrump tonight, all right?"

Which is totally unfair and, fiiine, completely deserved.

Grumpy McGrump is a term coined by Cesar when we were in middle school and I didn't talk to any teacher for a week after they canceled our Bring Your Favorite Hedge Witch to Class Day. I swear, I have outgrown Grumpy McGrump. I just *might* have my moments, like we all do, when things *might* feel especially stupid and unfair, and I *might* stick my jaw out like a toddler and sit in the corner saying nothing for a whole hour.

"Storms happen. Concerts get canceled," Cesar says, leading me to the kitchen. His dark hair is slicked back in a tiny bun at his nape and he smells strongly of cologne, which is completely at odds with his worn sweatshirt and basketball shorts outfit. "It's not the end of the world."

Which is an infuriating argument, because how can you argue with someone who's absolutely right?

"I know that," I say. "It just, kind of, feels extremely unfair, you know? Iseul is flying to UNC tomorrow and—this was supposed to be the *perfect* last night together."

I know Cesar's place like the back of my hand, a natural phenomenon when you've been besties-forever with someone since you were eight. I head straight for the pantry, where Cesar and I pull out bowls and glasses, stack up chips under our armpits, and grab whatever sodas are left in the fridge.

"Well," Cesar says, pretending to toast me with the B+ blood soda he always keeps in the fridge for Sébastien. (Sébastien is a half-vampire, and Cesar's a were-jaguar—they met in gym class.) "We better put our big-kid pants on, Nina, because there are a lot of goodbyes ahead."

I can't help it: I sigh so deeply, like full-body sigh, that the Doritos bag under my arm opens with a *pop!*

The day after tomorrow, Trev is moving to Silver Spring, an hour away from Hexville, to start training for the Paris 2024 Summer Olympics. Tomorrow, Iseul is going to the University of North Carolina, and in three days, Cesar is moving to Nashville to pursue singing-songwriting. Sébastien is taking a gap year to visit their family in Europe, while Calla is off to New York at the end of the month, having scored the much-sought-after spell-writing internship at leading cosmetics line Majestique. I'll be commuting to the University of Maryland, Baltimore, only an hour away, while Gio is—Gio—

I can't even think about it without hyperventilating. *Gaaah.* I really need to get myself together.

Gio's driving off to UPenn in a week. Seven days. A hundred and sixty-eight hours.

Cesar sees me hyperventilating and bends down to touch my forehead with his, an incredible feat, considering how short I am and how tall he is. "Say it with me," he whispers. "We'll be all right."

"We'll be all right," I echo emptily.

I wish I were a witch, so that my wish could be magicked into a spell, or a faerie, so that my words were bound by truth.

But I'm a naiad. River spirit, sweet water nymph (on my mom's side), connected to all things water, but no things heartbreak.

"Come on, then," says Cesar. "Everyone else's in the patio."

It's a pretty place, the Martinezes' greenhouse patio. Cesar's dad is a practicing hedge witch, and the octagonal room is packed tight with plants of all kinds. Sage, rosemary, thyme, moonflower, wolfsbane, hemlock, nightshade, jimsonweed. I know each one by name. I've spent countless afternoons here after school, tending the garden with Cesar. My powers come in handy in jobs like these: I can feel the water coursing through stems and leaves and petals and can tell exactly how much watering they crave.

For maximum vibes, the greenhouse lights are off, and my friends have all discarded their phones around the room, screens facing down, flashlights beaming an ethereal crisscross of lights on the surrounding glass panes.

My arrival is met with a chorus of *heys*. They are all sprawled on the soft pillows and armchairs; knees are folded, and legs are pulled aside as I trek through them to deposit my loot on the wooden coffee table at the center.

"Ah, tesoro mio," Gio greets me in a soothing voice.

He looks particularly good tonight, with his floral shirt buttoned all the way to the top and his curls falling over his brow, all effortless and sexy. His knuckles are dusted with necromancer runes in various stages of fainting into his flesh, but his palms are warm and soft, his skin on mine as familiar a feeling as sunlight.

Gio loops an arm around my waist and pulls me into his lap; he's sitting in one of the many beanbags in the room. The plush cloth enfolds us, and as Gio sneaks his nose into my neck, I think, *This isn't so bad*. It isn't a Best Night by a long shot, but it's warm and cozy and smells of moonflowers and Gio's soft eucalyptus deodorant, which is all a girl can ask for in the end, isn't it?

And we all look so cute in our concert outfits, Iseul with her curving haetae horns, Calla with her blueberry tulle dress (yes, *the* blueberry tulle dress—she saved up and got it for herself as a graduation present), Trev with his soft-feathered seraphim wings draped over the back of the sofa. Even Sébastien's normally deathly pale skin looks rosy today.

(It sounds like the beginning of a joke, right? *A naiad, a necromancer, and a were-jaguar walk into a bar. There's a Korean haetae, an alchemist, a seraphim angel, and a half-vampire sitting in a booth.* But when you live in Hexville, thirty miles out of Silver Spring, Maryland, and there's only one high school with paranormal AP classes in your area, that's what happens. What can I say? Lump all the weird magical kids together, and the weird magical kids will become friends.)

"Are you okay?" Gio whispers against my skin, where he's pressing his cheek on my upper arm like a cat nuzzling catnip.

Gio is obsessed with my skin, and I'm not saying that to be obnoxious. He finds it super soft and warm and smooth, and says it feels euphoric when he's touching me. He tried to explain once—something to do with his life-sucking magic being attracted to my life-giving one—but I started teasing him ("That's just a cute way of saying you're a creep"), and his cheeks blushed the color of beetroot for a good half hour.

"I'm fine," I whisper back, and I do feel marginally better. (Cuddling will have that effect on the grumpiest of grumps.) I let myself inhale a deep breath of Gio, ink and leather books and eucalyptus. I peck little kisses on the top of his hair and close my eyes to the swaying rhythm of the rain pelting on the greenhouse walls.

Then the spell is broken.

Gio's phone pings—he all but tumbles me to the floor in his haste to grab it from where it sits on the side table behind us. His eyes are wide and eager for a moment, illuminated blue from the screen, then he scowls.

"Cerberus-net?" Trev asks excitedly from the settee next to our bean-bag, passing Gio the Sprite bottle.

Gio's back is to me, so I can't quite see his expression, but his shoulders look unmistakably tense when he replies, "Nope, just a discount email."

Wait. What's Cerberus-net? Why is Gio using his trying-to-not-make-it-a-big-deal voice?

Gio stretches his torso to slip his phone back on the table and, in the process, tips the Sprite bottle over with his foot. He picks it up fast, preventing the worst of the damage, and breathes a sigh of relief—at which point he glances down to find me half-sprawled on the ground, legs dangling up the beanbag, what must be a dumbstruck expression on my face.

"Oh, piccola!" he exclaims, immediately reaching for my hands. "Did I do that? I'm so sorry!"

I can feel my jaw inching out, my teeth gritting, my arms itching to cross over my chest. But I will *not* be the Grouch tonight. I refuse to ruin this night for the rest of them, even if I'm very close to fuming out of the ears myself.

I settle on the floor next to the beanbag and help Gio and Trev dab the spilled soda with the napkins Calla hands us, then pour myself a cup and pass the bottle along. When Gio's attention finally drifts back to the conversation in the room (something about Calla's big Majestique internship, but who cares right now? *My boyfriend is keeping secrets from me*), I discreetly take out my phone and google *Cerberus-net*.

It's an internship. A weekend internship for college students to work on what's promising to be the latest breakthrough in long-distance necro spell-work activation.

Weekend internship. Which means Gio has no plan to drive back home every other weekend like he promised.

I should be happy for him—and I am, I swear, I'm not *that* much of an asshole, this is exactly what he wants to do: necromancy mixed with coding, every nerd's dream—but I can't help thinking about myself, alone back here in Hexville (Trev doesn't count, he'll be training 24/7), while everyone gallivants around the country.

I know all the logical arguments: I'll make new friends at college, I'll have new and exciting experiences, I'll be studying something I've dreamed of since my family visited the mer-people terrarium in Crete, yada yada.

But it won't be *this*, will it? It won't be six people I've known my entire life, my first (and so far only) love among them, giggling about that time Sébastien had an allergic reaction to Cesar's Majestique lip gloss and passing around a fizzled-out bottle of Sprite and a bag of Doritos, dressed in our finest, smiling our brightest.

And the worst thing is I know *exactly* why Gio would hide this internship from me. And I can't even blame him, to be honest. Because Cesar is right. I'm Grumpy McGrump, and I can't handle the prospect of graduation and college and change without collapsing in a pit of dread—and they all must know it.

All my friends must think I'm a wimp, no matter how hard I try to hide my ever-rising panic from them. Like when I hurried to the bathroom during prom to hyperventilate in peace, and when I came out, they were all looking at me with worried eyes. Or when I lied and said my parents wanted to take me to dinner after the graduation ceremony, so I could skip out early on what were bound to be some *heart-wrenching* goodbyes.

My heart is thumping in my chest, ribs constricting, throat clenching.

I feel like I'm about to start sobbing, and I really, really don't want to be doing that, because, let me tell you, when a naiad cries, it's the equivalent of a wailing blue whale dueting with a volcanic eruption. It's not exactly pleasant to the people around her.

So instead, I lie back against the beanbag, where my crumbling face is hidden behind Gio's body. Above us, the domed ceiling of the greenhouse is speckled with a thousand tiny dots of rain, hued with the piercing white light of our phone flashlights. I can see my own reflection up there: my unruly bangs, my black-minidress-and-white-Converses outfit, my impeccable makeup.

We're like this greenhouse, I think. We grew up protected, warmed by the sun, watered by our parents, clinging to one another like plant supports. But take any one of these plants out of its pot and place it in a forest, where the rain pours hard and the bugs chew on its leaves and the rodents gnaw on its roots, and what do you think will happen to the little houseplant?

The world's such a big and hollow place.

I just wish—

I wish it didn't have to change so much. I wish we could all stay together and go through this together, too. College, work, traveling, or whatever it is that comes next. I wish things could stay the same.

I close my eyes, succumbing fully to my own pity party, when I feel my skin prickle all the way down my spine, as though an invisible claw is raking my flesh. It's an otherworldly feeling, terrifying—an involuntary yelp escapes my mouth.

Thunder cracks overhead, a deafening sound that rattles every window in the greenhouse. All the lights in the neighborhood go out.

I prop up on my elbows. We stare at one another, eyes goofily wide.

"On a scale of one to zombie apocalypse," Iseul whispers, "how menacing was *that*?"

"Samara crawling out of the TV?" Trev offers.

"Thanos snapping his fingers," Sébastien says.

"When Dakota Johnson went, 'Actually, no, that's not the truth, Ellen,'" Calla says.

Eyebrows rise, and we're all nodding. That's a good example: that teeth-gritting feeling of the hammer about to drop. We lapse back into silence, gazing at the dark world outside our little pocket of phone-flashlight, greenhouse-glass safety. I reach for Gio almost at the same time he reaches for me, and our fingers lace like a perfectly embroidered brocade.

Ping!

We all jump out of our skin. Trev's wings flick open, squashing Calla against the pillows of the settee they're sharing. Cups topple off the table, and a lone feather drifts in the air, tauntingly slow.

The culprit is Iseul's phone, which she picks up from the side table next to her armchair. "Oh," she says when she reads the notification. "My flight got canceled."

"Makes sense." Calla points to the sky above our heads, dark and heavy with roiling clouds. "When's the next flight to Raleigh?"

"The day after tomorrow," Iseul says. "But I'll miss the Asian Paranormal Student Union orientation tomorrow night. I was looking forward to finally getting to meet other East Asian paranormals."

"What if we start our road trip early and drop you off?" Cesar offers, bending across Sébastien's lap. "If we—"

He swats at his partner's face, whose fangs have elongated at the sight of Cesar's neck.

"Amor, control your fangs, por favor," Cesar goes on. "If we set off early tomorrow, we should be at Raleigh by one o'clock? Two? We can spend the night there and drive to Nashville the day after that. What do you think, Seb?"

Sébastien is blushing, hurriedly downing the last of their blood soda. We're all accustomed to their vampire shenanigans by now, but they can still get very self-conscious about it. Softly, they reply, "Sounds like a plan."

"Road trip!" hoots Cesar.

"Road trip!" coos Iseul, beaming at them.

I feel a pang of bitterness, just a teeny-tiny one. Problem solved, just like that. And they get to have fun while solving it. Why couldn't that happen to me? Why couldn't a fairy godmother just arrive on my doorstep and say, 'Hey, you know what? UPenn is opening up a terrific new magical creature biologist department, and you can actually follow your dreams *and* live in the same town as your boyfriend'? Perhaps with some financial aid sprinkled on top?

A gust of wind makes the wind chimes outside clang in a cacophonous frenzy. Rain spatters against the windows, like tiny hands pounding on the door, trying to get in.

Something buzzes in the silence.

Calla grabs her phone from the table and frowns at the caller. "Hello? Yeah, this is she," we hear her saying before she jumps up and disappears down the corridor.

"I was thinking." Gio bumps his shoulder against mine. "How about I cook you dinner on Wednesday? I made you a new talisman, like, um, a going-away present."

Oh, god. Don't cry, Nina. Do. NOT. Cry.

I make my lips stretch into a smile. Gio looks soft and cautious—he's probably expecting teasing from me, which means that's what I'd normally do, if I wasn't currently crumbling under the melancholy of *going-away present.*

"How necro are we talking about?" I try to add playfulness to my stiff voice.

Amazingly, it seems to work. "Just a little bit." He laughs. "No snake entrails or fossilized maggots this time, I promise."

The rhythmic buzzing of a phone interrupts him. He reaches out and grabs it from the side table, light washing the gentle features on his face. His eyebrows pull together in an uncharacteristically deep scowl. He says nothing, but as he clicks off his phone, his frown deepens. Bad news?

I have a fleeting moment of elation—maybe he will visit every other weekend, after all!—followed immediately by shameful, *shameful* guilt.

I nudge him with my elbow. "What's wrong?"

"Nothing, piccola. I was trying to do something for—anyway, it didn't work out." He brings our joined hands to his lips and kisses my knuckles.

"I'm sorry," I whisper.

And I do. Feel sorry, I mean. He is the best person I know. A ray of sunshine sandwiched in marshmallows and baked inside a cinnamon roll, all wrapped up in this cute necromancer form. I would choose his happiness over my own loneliness any day. *Every* day. No matter how much I might miss him.

Calla sulks into the room with shuffling footsteps. Everything about her looks miserable, like someone popped her fluffy dress and she's deflating like a balloon. She slumps back into the settee and announces, "Majestique dropped my internship."

We all react in a chorus, exclamations and questions and devastated apologies.

Calla shrinks further into her seat. This spell-writing internship at Majestique was a godsend. Her parents had been pressuring her to go to law school and abandon all notions of making a living through her wildly successful YouTube channel, which she spent three years cultivating into *the* tutorial channel to watch for makeup and hair spells.

"I can talk to my mother," I say immediately. It's been her backup plan: freelance spell-writing. My mother's water purification company wouldn't pay as much as Majestique, but maybe it's a step in the right direction?

"Yeah," she mumbles, "thanks."

Others are chiming in, Trev with his dads' bakery and Gio with his own charmed resin jewelry line. (Don't ask.)

"Thanks, guys," Calla repeats, but I can outline the disappointment in her face.

Then two more phones *ping*. Trev's and . . . mine.

The silence is stiff, expectant.

Trev is faster, already glowering down at his phone. "I don't understand. They're saying our flying team got disqualified from Nationals."

"Whoa, what?" Cesar mumbles.

"Nina?" Iseul prods. "What does yours say?"

I gingerly lift my phone from the coffee table, reading the email in a haze of trepidation.

But I can't process. The words don't compute.

My feelings are articulated by Gio, who's been reading over my shoulder. "Shit."

The screen reads: *We regret to inform you your merit scholarship has been withdrawn. Our funding has unexpectedly been pulled, and we are unable to offer you financial assistance at this time.*

"Nina?" someone else says softly—I'm not sure who.

"University of Maryland, Baltimore, is rescinding her scholarship," Gio whispers.

This can't be happening. I have worked *so hard*. For the past two years, I've sacrificed countless hours of sleep and making out with Gio and hanging out with the group in order to study for this scholarship. This isn't how it was supposed to go. I was supposed to get the scholarship and spend a lovely summer with my friends making up for all the things I missed out on, before we all start college in the fall—

Oh, god. I don't even think my parents can afford college now.

"WAIT—" Sébastien exclaims. It's a loud sound, foreign among our hushed, worried voices.

I lift my eyes to them, feeling like I have to drag myself through a murky swamp.

Sébastien has stood, in their pristine gray-and-pink checkered suit, face so shocked I can see the whites of their eyes. "First Iseul's flight. Then Calla's internship. Then whatever mysterious bad news Gio got, and Nina's scholarship, and Trev's flight Nationals."

"*WAIT.*" Calla bursts out of the settee, palms spread.

I have no idea what's going on, but Gio does, because he's rising from his seat like a resurrected mummy, eyes intent on Calla and Sébastien. "You're not saying . . . There's no way."

"It's gotta be it," says Sébastien.

"*How?*" crows Calla.

Cesar raises his voice. "Will you *please* tell the rest of us what your witchy sixth sense is picking up on?"

The three of them, Sébastien, Calla, and Gio, have a moment of silent eye-glaring before Gio finally takes it upon himself to deliver the bad news. "We've summoned something."

"Bah," Cesar comments with a flick of his wrist. "There are no candles."

The witchy paranormals all glance around, like hounds on a chase. It's Calla who points around the room and shrieks, "The phones! They were placed in a circle, and the flashlights were all on."

"There are no offerings," Cesar counters, but he's sitting on the edge of the sofa now, looking ready to squirm out of his skin.

We all look around the room again. Calla stabs her finger in the direction of the Sprite bottle. "Didn't we all pass that around? Didn't Gio spill some on the floor?"

"Oops," Gio whispers. "But there has to be intent," he goes on. "Someone must have wanted all our plans canceled, and who would wish *that*?"

Oh, no.

No, no, no, no, no, NOOO.

Shit.

"Well, *someone* did," says Sébastien, sounding harsher than I've ever heard them.

They all look to Calla, our resident dabbling-in-black-magic paranormal. "You guys think it was me?" she snaps. "Why the hell would I want my own once-in-a-lifetime internship to fall through? Do I look *that* diabolic?"

I am the diabolic one.

The diabolic one is me.

I know it instantly, deep in my water spirit bones and my black, selfish heart: *I did this.* I looked at the glass ceiling and watched the rain drip down the glass, and I had my pity party, and I was so scared and unhappy that *I. Summoned. Something. That is. Eating. My friends'. Dreams.*

How the hell do I tell them *that*?

I'm gritting my teeth so hard that my jaw hurts. My naiad powers are starting to run rampant—I can see the soda bubbling in our cups, droplets lifting off the surface.

"Doesn't matter," Gio says, his voice calm. "It was obviously an accident. I mean, who could imagine the phones would make for a candle circle and the Sprite would spill and work as an offering? What matters right now is figuring out what kind of demon we summoned, getting a binding circle together, and exorcising them. Before things get worse."

The moment he says *worse*, our phones collectively go off.

We squeal. Someone's foot jolts the coffee table, and Doritos go flying everywhere.

Cesar climbs over the sofa to get to his phone. "My gigs are all canceled. My agent dropped me."

The room dissolves into chaos, panicked voices toppling one over the other.

"UNC has gone bankrupt," Iseul is saying.

"My social media are all blocked." Calla looks on the verge of crying.

Things are escalating *fast*, which means the demon is extremely powerful, which means we need to bind it, pronto.

But my friends are all devolving into white-hot, my-world-is-ending panic, and I'm the only one still sitting cross-legged on the floor, keeping my wits about me, watching them all screech, like a *proper, fully blossomed fucking villain.*

I take a deep breath. All right. Pity partying is all well and good, but it needs to stop now.

First things first: identifying the demon. You need the demon's true name to cast them back into whatever abyss they've crawled out of.

I grab my phone. There's another email from UMB on the top of my notifications, but I don't click on it. I'm pretty sure it'll be something like "the entire profession of magical creature biologist no longer exists, our sincerest apologies." I pull up the Demonology app instead, and browse the "Summoning Symptoms" options, clicking all the ones that apply to our resident demon, like bad luck, rewriting reality, devouring teenagers' dreams. The app gives me a few demonic candidates, along with a list of options on confirming their identity. One of them is specific for water-casters like me: instructions on forcing a dream-sucking demon's name out of any liquid spilled on porcelain, because no demon can resist showing off their fancy tea-drinking tastes. (No time to process *that* information.)

I'm scanning the room for something made of porcelain, tuning out all the flailing and screaming in the room (the only thing I catch is Sébastien's panicked "Paris has *literally* disappeared into thin air!"), when my eyes fall on a small saucer Mr. Martinez is using as a holder for one of his tiny sage pots. I shoulder through my friends' stiff bodies, all bent over their screens, and grab the saucer. It's speckled with dirt, but I think that might actually help. I grab the notorious Sprite bottle from the table, tilting a spoonful onto the saucer.

For a moment, nothing happens.

But then, soaked by the sticky soda, the granules of dirt begin moving. Tiny maggots, crawling across the porcelain, forming a word in minuscule, earth-smelling font: *Acerba*.

That's the name of the demon—*demonette*, if I'm to take a guess.

"Acerba," I whisper, standing a little way off from my friends.

"Hello to you, too, darling," says a voice.

It's less a voice and more a *sensation*, like a bug scuttling across your legs or a hot breath brushing against your neck even though you're alone in the room.

We all freeze. Our eyes meet across the room, a ricochet of *what-the-hell*. Cesar pulls Sébastien behind him protectively. Iseul lets the haetae out, her irises blazing cobalt blue, her horns elongating, fur sprouting out of her smooth skin. And every rune on Gio's skin comes ablaze, necromancer spells pulled to attention like cocked guns.

Then we start scanning the room, trying to find where the demonette's hiding.

"You've found my name, have you?" says the demonette. *"Do you like the sound of it on your lips? Tastes sour, doesn't it? But you must like sour, if you could summon me."*

I shudder, from my heels right up to my nape.

"Who is she talking to?" Trev whispers.

Gio answers, "Her summoner."

The demonette sounds like a disembodied voice, but demons always have a manifestation of some kind, even if it's a lone, oddly shaped shadow in a web-filled corner of the ceiling. If I locate Acerba's corporeal manifestation, I can get my friends into a binding circle and perform the exorcism.

"What do you intend to do with my name, darling?" Acerba is susurrating around the greenhouse. *"Bind me? Didn't you want things to stay the same? Isn't change scary? Isn't this better?"*

Better?

"The world's a big and hollow place—you said that. I have made it smaller for you, haven't I? Why would you ever punish me for that? Eh, Nina, darling?"

I don't need to look to know everyone is twisting to gawk at me.

I'm standing a few steps behind them, among Mr. Martinez's pot-brimmed bookshelves, shoulders hunched, cheeks flushed.

"Nina." Cesar says. He's the closest to me, his eyes bulging with alarm. "Why is the demonette talking to you?"

"Honey," Calla is saying, on my other side, "it's okay. We won't be angry. Just tell us. Did you do this?"

I suck my cheek between my teeth, trying to stanch the tears gathering in my eyes. But they're all looking at me, and they all know what I wished and how terrified I am—and you know what?

It all comes out of me in a rush, and I don't get two words in before I start concurrently sobbing, and it's all a big mess, but I say it anyway. "I might look like the villain, and I have fucked up royally—I know that. But I'm also just terribly, ridiculously *afraid*, of what comes next, what comes next *without* you, and you don't get it. You're all so excited, so elated to be leaving, and I didn't want to spoil it with my own *stupid* fear, and so I pushed it down and down and never told anyone, and I guess *this* is what happens. I was so scared *that I summoned a demonette that's disappearing all our dreams!*"

Aaand now I'm crying.

Full-on ugly crying, sobs racking my shoulders, tears spilling down my cheeks, and I'm making the Noise. That damned naiad-wailing noise that could send a howler monkey running, covering its ears. I must look ridiculous, I *feel* ridiculous, so I bury my snotty face in my hands and make a blind beeline for the patio doors.

The rain welcomes me. Its cold touch slithers down my bare arms, dampens my hair. I drop my hands and turn my face up to it. The spattering ice on my skin is soothing, in a way. Raindrops cling to my skin. Slip through my curls. My naiad powers are called to life, basking in the energy of so much water around me.

"*Isn't it better this way?*" the demonette's voice whispers around me. "*Isn't it easier?*"

And I won't lie, it *is*.

It is easier here, in the city I've known all my life, in the house I've hung out in since I was eight. It's easier with the seven of us in our little greenhouse, friends for fucking *life*. But I want to be a magical creature biologist so bad. And Gio wants to nerdily combine necromancy with coding. And Trev wants to go to the Olympics and kick ass with his spectacular flight gymnastics. We all have such beautiful dreams.

And yes, achieving these dreams might not be easy, but maybe it doesn't matter?

"Piccola?"

A hand comes around my wrist and gently guides me to turning, and I know instantly that it's Gio. His touch is feather-light on my skin, and when I lift my eyes to his, he is my tenderhearted necromancer, who I fell in love with the first moment I saw him and lusted over for years before he finally, finally asked me out. Was he scared, I wonder, when he decided to ask me out? He must have been—I remember his voice shaking, his hands fidgeting. But he faced that fear, because . . .

Because it was worth it. Like *this* is worth it.

My friends are all standing behind Gio, Cesar closest, everyone else on the brim between the patio and the drenching rain.

"I have changed my flights four times," Iseul confesses into the sheltered silence.

"I've rescinded three apartment applications," Cesar huffs, "because I'm scared my roommates will turn out to be assholes."

"I tell my coach I'm quitting, like, every week," Trev says.

"I'm stressed," Sébastien says, "that Cesar will meet a cute drummer and break up with me."

("Drummer?" Cesar says. "Yuck. Maybe bassist.")

Silence falls, and Iseul elbows Calla in the ribs.

"What?" Calla says, rubbing her side. "I'm type A, honey. I have no second thoughts when I decide something. But, yeah, it's all very scary. Leaving Hexville. Moving to freaking New York. Not having you guys by my side."

"We're *all* scared," Cesar tells me. "We just don't talk about it. It's one of the unwritten rules of the summer before college, I guess? Pretending everything will be all right to manifest everything being all right?"

"Well, it's a stupid rule," I grump.

Gio reaches up to cup my cheek, his skin warm against mine. "I wanted it to be a surprise—or, I guess, not too much of a disappointment if I didn't get it, but . . . I applied to a weekend internship," he says, and my stomach turns with acid dread. "It's in Baltimore. It's five hours a day, and they pay a hefty stipend. And you know what's the best part? Their headquarters are five minutes from your dorm, so I'll get to see you—at least for a bit—even on the days we're busy."

Oh.

Well, I have been a much bigger ass than I thought I was being.

I don't know what to say. I'm on the verge of starting to sob again, so I let my body fall into Gio's, my chin tucking into his shoulder. When I stretch my arms out, my friends all come pouring in, arms folding over one another in a massive, soul-restoring hug.

I feel it in my heart: Magic blooms. Our hug is becoming a binding circle.

The demonette must sense it, too. She screeches around us, *"You need me, darling! I can make the fear go away!"*

But the fear doesn't need to go away, does it?

You can face fear, with the right people by your side.

The magic grows stronger, a bubbling of hope and courage and love, surrounding our little binding circle. The rain smacks harder on our skin—

That's where Acerba is hiding her corporeal manifestation, I realize. In the rain.

I let myself delve fully into my naiad powers. My consciousness runs over my body, Gio's body, everyone's body, Trev's wings included. I sense every droplet on us, every atom of water—and I *pull.*

The water rises, slurping off our skin and hair and clothes, and hovers inches above us, a cloud of wet, sour demonette. Magic works best for me when it's instinctual, so I don't think about any specific exorcising spell—I just say the first thing that comes to mind.

"Acerba, will you fuck off, please?"

The result is instantaneous: *POP* goes the bubble of water over our heads, *SCREECH* goes her voice, and the rain cuts off, like turning off the faucet. Back in the patio, everyone's phones start clanging, the world restoring itself to its right place. My friends begin to peel off our group hug one by one, trotting excitedly to the greenhouse to check if their dreams are intact once more.

I'm alone with Gio in the Martinezes' yard. His own phone is buzzing, I imagine, with the *good* internship news he was supposed to get tonight, but he doesn't even turn to look at it.

"Won't it be exhausting?" I say quickly, lest I run out of courage. "All this traveling, all this extra work? If you're only doing it for me, please don't. I don't want you burning out your freshman year because your girlfriend is a crybaby—"

"Stop," he says, his lips fighting a grin. "I'll get to code and spend time with you—it's the dream. And if it turns out not to be, we'll figure it out from there. Together."

"Okay," I whisper.

I want to tell him I'm more in love with him than I've ever been, if that could be possible. I want to tell him we'll graduate and get married and buy a beach house with an office equipped with a dozen computer screens for him and a double pool for me, one sweet water, one salt water. I want to tell him I'm terrified that won't happen and terrified it will—but I don't.

I think he knows. I think he feels the same way.

He tugs me back toward the Martinezes' greenhouse, where our friends are waiting.

"Come on," Gio says, with one of his soft, tender smiles that thaws all the sour, grumpy ice inside my terrified heart into a puddle of pure joy. "The world's a big and hollow place, isn't that what you said? It's up to us to fill it."

The Last Goodbye

BY LOAN LE

Faye watched her mother's reflection in the car window. Her tired image changed with the passing nighttime scenery. On their trip out of the Cam Ranh airport, her face was a long strip of potholed, dusty highways and silver traffic barriers. It revealed the rural side of Nha Trang: concrete houses with tin roofs, coconut trees, and scrappy motorcycles tucked into the tiniest driveways possible. And now, leaning in, her face joining her mother's, Faye could see small lights dangling outside a pocket of nightclubs and bars crowded with revelers.

Fairy lights. Like her. Vietnamese people always looked confused when she was introduced; *Faye* was rare even among English names. According to her mother, when she was born and bundled up in her arms, the world glimmered around them. Her mother saw the spirits of the hospital's patients over the last century, who gazed at Faye in envy, in happiness, in reverence, and because Faye was glowing, too, like fairy lights, her mother knew Faye would inherit her gift. Her mother couldn't really name her baby *fairy*, so she thought of *fae*, one of her favorite English words.

A hand covered hers. Her mother, still gazing out of the window, had reached out for comfort. Faye squeezed back. Over the last year or so, she'd felt a gap between them, intangible but disruptive, and with her touch, that gap was temporarily closed, like a poorly sewn patch on a piece of clothing. Her workaholic mother had launched her line at Target, Walmart, and just about any retailer. Busy yet fashion-conscious moms seemed to like Michelle "Mish" Trân's designs. Late nights alone became more frequent for Faye, which allowed her to work on her filmmaking, but also meant that whenever her mother *was* home, their apartment felt abnormally crowded. In just two months, Faye was going to start college; she feared that the gap would become irreparable.

Her childhood had been much louder; work was scarce for her mother back then. Faye's world *was* their apartment; their spirit friends were her family. During Christmas, visitors from all centuries came through, like Fernando, who entertained everyone with his surprisingly nice opera voice. Emily, who'd been part of the Century Association in the nineteenth century, argued that she could have written a better *A Christmas Carol*.

Tonight, her mother's touch was safe and familiar. Faye had never visited Vietnam before. As for her mother, it'd been more than two decades since she'd been back. She left as a teen, escaping the remnants of the war, when death was an uncertain, looming thing. And now a death was the reason for her mother's return.

The car slowly whined to a stop, after turning a corner into a village dirt road. Street vendors were closed for the night. Pastel blue and pink plastic chairs were stacked away under dusty tarps. The remaining road, leading to what Faye imagined were more houses and maybe a rice paddy field, was only half-lit.

The air was a humid, unwanted embrace. The alleyway leading to her mother's childhood home was narrow, and its cement walls were fractured by weather and weeds bursting through its cracks and along the ground, littered with Heineken caps, straws, and torn newspapers. Faye struggled with her blue Samsonite along the uneven ground.

It felt illegal to be here, like some lights would snap on and blind them, and an angry voice might tell them to leave. Or maybe Faye's reality was clouded by her mother's memories.

She'd heard her mother's story so many times that it became a bullet-point list in her head. Age thirteen: escaped under the cover of night in 1982 to America—Pennsylvania, where some cousins sponsored her. Age eighteen: a scholarship allowed her to go to college in New York City, where she majored in fashion design. Age twenty-two: a "serious detour," her mother jokingly called it. By detour, she meant OB-GYN appointments, birthing lessons, and then: hello, Faye burst into the scene. Single and preferring to never mingle—"like, ever again," her mother stressed—while caring for her, her mother worked her way up from the back rooms of fashion shows, needle-pricked fingers and sleepless nights, to the runways themselves.

Her mother examined their surroundings. "There aren't as many spirits as I remember."

Faye stopped and turned. "Me, not now." Her annoyance flared.

Her mother responded with her own look: *Okay, okay, I won't go there.*

Faye wasn't her mother; she never openly acknowledged or acted on their shared gift. She still remembered her second-grade teacher's shock and fear when Faye complained about Mrs. Green blocking the view of the Smartboard. How was she supposed to know that Mrs. Green had been *her* teacher's teacher thirty years ago? Her classmates had teased her throughout elementary school; she couldn't shake off the nickname Ghost Girl until junior high school. Faye's mother, though, had zero qualms about talking to strangers: While checking out groceries at Trader Joe's, she'd *casually* told the chatty cashier that his uncle said, "Don't pack the bags too tight." One time, at the Union Square Holiday Market, she bumped into an expectant mother, reached out for the stranger's wrist, and said, "Don't worry. Your mom will watch over her." As Faye practically yanked her mother away, the stranger called in confusion, "How did you know I was having a daughter?"

Her mother was a beacon. It would amuse many to know that Mish Trần's fans and colleagues extended beyond the mastheads of fashion magazines. They would be astounded to learn about the deceased fashionistas—perpetually around Mish and other designers—who loved to critique their mentees or bolster the discouraged up-and-comers. Not even Faye's mother knew why some in death were bound to earth and others could leave. She supposed spirits were those who needed something to be done, either to someone or for someone. A good number revealed themselves to her mother, Faye, and their circle of paranormalists—all in the arts industry, which was an interesting occurrence. Other spirits knew how to stay hidden. Some had ages, and others had forgotten not only their ages, but also everything about themselves.

Ghosts had bothered Faye as a child, but after the incidents at school, she'd taken to politely ignoring them. Pointing to her earphones if one on the subway sensed her sight. Looking over their shoulders if Faye passed them. Most accepted their invisibility. But there were centuries-old spirits in denial, who lived near demolished buildings, who would stray into more crowded streets, see Faye, and plead for her help. They reeked of despair, and being around them made Faye feel as if she were sinking. Helpless because she couldn't really do much to end their pain.

Faye couldn't deny what was in front of her now. A ghostyard. There were four spirits—always solid, not transparent as some movies make them out to be, but perhaps diminished in color, like clothing that had been tumbled in a washing machine far too many times. An elderly woman dressed in light green pajamas was sweeping the ground, humming along to her own bài hát. Maybe she was as senile as when she was living, because she didn't even look up at them. There was a pair of bed-headed, half-naked children, boy and girl—sinh đôi—which made Faye's heart throb, as it did whenever she saw young spirits. They smiled and giggled, before running through the house's walls, holding hands.

Her bleary-eyed mother watched them and said sadly, "Oh, I remember them."

Faye didn't have the right response. As she followed her mother into the house, suitcase squealing along, there was a fourth ghost, a girl her age or maybe younger, dressed in jeans, engulfed by a ratty oversize black T-shirt.

She waved hello. Faye tiredly waved back.

✧ ⬦ ✧

Bent-backed Bà Xuân was the great-aunt who took care of the house; she readied the house for Faye's mother's cousins who visited from Seattle every year. After pushing in their luggage, they were led to the bedroom that Faye and her mother would share. The hellos were quick, the house tour quicker. Kitchen, two small bedrooms, ancestral room, patio, bathroom. Soon enough Faye was crawling into a spindle bed covered with a plush mink blanket that all Vietnamese and Asians seemed to have, no matter what continent they were on. They were sharing a bed, which they hadn't done since she was eight or nine, Faye realized.

Her mother, dressed in a white slip that her company released last year, was putting on an overnight mask.

Faye sighed as she sank into the mattress—much better than the uncomfortable economy seats on their flight. "So, what's the plan for tomorrow?"

"Visitors in the morning. People I haven't seen since I left. We'll be forced to eat so much food, so get ready, babe. Another warning: Most of these people will probably be girls from my school, and they won't be so nice."

"Why?"

Her mother gestured to the two of them, and the answer clicked. Single mothers were mothers, yes, but kept in a separate box from all the other mothers. They were given a tight smile at the answer "No, it's just me and my daughter." Looks of sympathy or confusion were common. Vietnamese—Asian families—were all about that: families. And it seemed impossible that a family could consist of only a mother and a daughter.

"But I'm ready to fight any disapproving auntie. Don't worry. At this point . . . nothing can get worse." She paused. "The ceremony's not until next week; that's when the forty-nine days of mourning are really over." And there it was. The reason they were here.

When her mother learned about Uyên "Unnie" Le's death, Faye had been at her high school, editing a short film project. Low-budget horror at St. Mark's Church in-the-Bowery. "You only met her a handful of times, when you were still in diapers," she had explained at dinner later that night. "As teens, Unnie and I had left Vietnam together, along with my cousins and her older brother. Unnie was my closest friend, and we sort of navigated America together. We went through the same high school, worked part-time at the same factory. Watched K-dramas together, which was where she got that nickname. She knew how to have fun, definitely more fun than me. Then I got the FIT scholarship, and she . . . drifted." Her mother had sighed. "No, we drifted apart, but I was just so busy. And I had to learn how to live in the city. We only reconnected after she heard I had you. And that was when I learned she got mixed up in some bad things."

"Bad how?"

"Drugs," her mother had said simply. That was the thing about having one parent. The burden of explaining things fell on just one person, and telling the truth was the best way of lightening that load. "She was also in a bad relationship with someone who probably abused her, which was why she sought me out. Because she knew I'd shelter her. And she would have done the same."

Now, regarding her mom through one open eye, Faye asked, "Do you miss her?"

Her mother rolled over to face her, using her hands as a makeshift pillow. "I don't know. Sometimes? I've been thinking a lot about that last dinner we had together. The three of us. You sat in her lap the whole night. The next morning, she was gone. Along with some of the savings I kept under my mattress."

"I still can't believe she stole from you. I thought she was your friend."

"That was *why* she stole from me. *Stealing* is not the word, either." She reached over, brushing aside a strand of Faye's hair. "When we bunked together at the sanctuary, after landing here for the first time, the safest place to hide things from the other girls was under our mattresses. Food, snacks, soap—if we needed anything, we knew where to find it. If she really needed help, she really needed it. And I had hoped—all these years, that she got that help. But now . . ."

They fell into silence for a while until Faye commented, "Your foot's cold."

Her mother added the other foot, sandwiching hers in between. "Tough."

✦ ◻ ✦

Later at night, Faye woke up to a scraping sound. Muted, like it was in another room. The ancestral room. Her mother was gone. Faye parted the net that warded off mosquitoes and crossed the stone flooring, missing the soft carpet of their two-bedroom in the East Village.

Faye froze when she arrived at the room housing the family shrine. A spirit must have wandered in. A young woman. Facing away from Faye, she kneeled before the altar, where the portraits for Faye's grandparents and great-grandparents were kept. People she never had a chance to meet because they'd passed when her mother was too young. Their family line was full, but often unlinked.

The spirit's head was bent in prayer, shining black hair dangling. Her shoulders shook.

A weeping woman in white.

Something tugged at her, and so Faye stepped forward. Finally, the spirit got up from her knees, then turned and—

Faye hugged the wall behind her.

No, not a spirit.

This was how her mother cried. Alone, in secret.

✦ ◻ ✦

The morning began at six with her aunt flinging open the windows of the bedroom, allowing their faces to bake under the sun.

Once Faye was somewhat vertical, clean, and dressed, she headed into the kitchen. A rainbow pile of flip-flops covered the entrance, which was attached to a ramp that allowed Bà Xuân's motorcycle in and out of the home on rainy days. Today, the sun poured in. And there was so much screaming and laughter from visitors her mother's age.

A larger-bodied woman wearing thin pajama-like garments—who reminded Faye of someone who would probably bow to no one—swept her mother into a hug. "Look at you, all bones!" she teased in Vietnamese.

"Your hugs are just the same," her mom answered back, seamlessly switching to her native language, her voice clogged with emotion. Her eyes brimmed with tears.

"Is this—?"

After Faye was confirmed as the daughter, she too was hugged. Over and over again by the other women. This was the routine for three days straight. Guests, people from her mother's old life, frequently brought food: catfish, tươi, just caught from the Cái River; the greenest rau muống, begging to be tossed in hot oil and garlic; addictive homemade kẹo đậu phộng, its peanuts and sesame seeds bound together by caramelized sugar.

Faye was learning so much about her mother. After her grandparents' untimely deaths from illnesses, Mish Trần was unsurprisingly scrappy, mending clothes for herself and for their neighbors. But Faye also learned that she took in sick animals and nursed them back to health. That she was always the first to visit when someone was ill, with a basket overflowing with fruits. No matter what, Mish had been there for the village.

In a way, her mother was still the same, having worked so hard to build their village of two in New York. But that led to Faye's loneliness, especially this last year with her mother's fashion line expansion—when family dinners needed to be rescheduled—and the emptiness left by unfinished conversations.

Her mother clearly belonged here. But Faye was an outsider—in age and in culture. She ended up wandering into the courtyard, observing the dragon fruit vines, picking from trees overflowing with her favorite fruit, trái nhãn. She'd peel its brown skin, suck on the sweet white meat, and spit out its black seed. She used her iPhone to make some B-roll for future projects.

Like her mother said, there weren't too many ghosts here. The sweeping woman still didn't acknowledge her. She hadn't seen the twins again. And the other girl was nowhere to be found.

Yet Faye felt something occasionally, a prickle along her nape.

Whenever she turned around, she found nothing.

On the fourth day, the routine switched up. They went out to a coffee shop on Võ Trứ Street, this time to meet up with more friends, including Unnie's relatives. It was bustling with Vietnamese and expats. To get to their seats, diners had to step onto a trail of stones in water. Curious fish swam up to the rocks' edges before scattering. Faye absently wondered if anyone had ever fallen in.

"Practically begging someone to eat shit here," her mother muttered from behind her, watching her own feet. Faye grinned. Their minds always linked up like that, but her mother also used slang that Faye never used herself.

Then the rest of the guests arrived, including a Vietnamese family with a man, a woman, and a boy who looked to be Faye's age, around seventeen. "The guy might be the son of Unnie's older brother—oh, yes, it is! God, he looks so much different from the Facebook pictures! Someone found the right acne medication for him, finally," her mother whispered to Faye, right as the family passed behind them to take their seats at the end.

"Mẹ!" Faye hissed, even though it was unlikely that anyone heard her mother's careless insult. "You sound like the other Vietnamese aunties. Just gossiping and making judgments."

"Ouch."

As the boy sat down, Faye locked eyes with him. He grinned back unabashedly. Totally looked like a troublemaker. A flirt, with windswept hair and a thin forest green bomber jacket, white tee, relaxed jeans. Someone who'd fit in walking through Williamsburg. Faye forced her eyes away, cheeks burning.

Hearing so much Vietnamese flying around, Faye felt as if she was submerged in water, yet she still tried to pick up the crumbs of the language. Thankfully her mother's friends only asked her the basics—how old was she, where was she planning to go to school, what major she picked.

Several times, Faye found herself glancing over at the guy, and each moment, he was looking at her, a smile readily available. The servers descended on them with platters and bowls with their breakfast. Faye had ordered bò kho, and the beef stew before her, infused with lemongrass, tomato sauce, and anise, made her mouth water.

Before she knew it, the boy had sidled up to her, sitting between her and her mom. He introduced himself in English, which caught her mom's attention. Jackson, that was his nickname.

"You're all grown up!" she said in English. "Faye, he's taller than you."

"Um, thanks for pointing it out?"

Her mother smiled at her. "No, it's just you two played with each other when you were still in diapers. Jackson was born in the States like you, and before we . . . lost touch again, I visited his aunt at his dad's place. But I don't think you remember, Jackson."

Great, now Faye was imagining them in diapers—embarrassing!

"So *you're* Mish, my aunt's best friend? You're the one who can see ghosts, aren't you?"

"Yeah, that's me." Her mother gestured to Faye. "She has the gift, too."

She said this like it was a normal thing to say to a cute guy! Jackson's eyes widened, and Faye began to worry—*Isn't that Ghost Girl?* her classmates would snidely say—and now she just wanted to disappear into the walls like the spirits she'd seen throughout her life.

And yet, somehow, the conversation turned to sightseeing, and the boy volunteered to be their guide.

Her mother waved away Jackson's offer to call a taxi, saying that she'd drive herself and Faye, who hadn't known her mother knew how to operate Bà Xuân's motorcycle until this morning.

"Wrap your arms around my waist. Hold on tight."

Faye listened to her mother.

"Tighter."

"Okay," she yelled as their motorcycle came on.

"Tighter. C'mon you won't hurt—oh! Not that tight."

As her mother laughed, Faye smiled under her helmet.

Maybe it was because of her city living, but roaring down the streets of Nha Trang on a motorcycle, amid an army of other motorcycles, wasn't all that bad or scary. Just crowded. On her left was what appeared to be a couple out on a date. She hugged her mom tighter. On her right was a beat-up Toyota Vios, carrying bundles of sugarcane. The air was thick with a gasoline smell, and she was thankful for the helmet, which kept dust out of her eyes.

Eventually, the red-lettered sign for chợ Đầm appeared. Jackson slipped into a tiny parking spot, and they followed him. He nodded to a guy who looked like the attendant and gestured for Faye to follow.

The open-air market was the shape of a saucer. Inside was a maze of narrow aisles and rows, sectioned off by categories of need: fish, vegetable, clothing, luggage, and on and on. At the helm of these vendors were pajama-wearing aunties with fierce eyes, snoring grandpas, overworked women with children hanging off every limb while their lazy partners sat on stools, hunched over and scrolling through texts. Faye inhaled. There were spices that smelled anachronistic, evoking images of bustling open-air markets in the middle of a desert. These scents collided with the fishy pungency of cá lóc and catfish, waterfalling into plastic bags to be brought home by knowledgeable cooks.

Faye had been to Chinatown in the city so many times, but had never seen an open-air market of this size—in terms of items, people . . . and ghosts. Men, women, children slipped in between hanging fabrics that touched tourists' backs as they bent over to examine overpriced souvenirs. Spirits squatted down next to their hardworking descendants during lunch, savoring their own ghost meal from the store's compact shrine. Faye's mother pointed out an elder cursing out a descendant who wasn't tending to his own customers, and soon enough Mish had the idea to go and soothe the spirit's worries.

Her mother trusted Jackson to direct Faye, if needed. He brought her over to the dessert section. At one shop, a young man held a menu of chè and ice cream. He was turned down every time by both tourists and locals. His shoulders dropped as he retreated to his stool. But then his shadow—an elderly woman, perhaps the previous shopkeeper, touched him by the shoulder, leaned in close. Whether he heard the spirit or not, Faye couldn't be sure, but he stood back up.

Jackson stepped into her view. "You look like you disappeared somewhere."

"Wha—oh, no. I'm here."

"Your eyes, they were sort of out of focus. But, like, in a good way. Like you just saw the heavens." He was smiling, but there was a little touch of concern in his eyes.

"Sorry, it's just. It's everything all at once. The seen and unseen. I feel . . . a part of something." Faye colored once hearing her words out loud. To divert his attention, she pointed at the dessert shop. "Let's grab something?"

The tired but undeterred shop owner eagerly pushed menus toward them when he realized they were staying.

"Have you had the xôi since coming here?" Jackson asked. "This one's famous for it. My fave's pandan rice."

Jackson ordered from the shop owner: "Anh ơi, cho em hai chén xôi lá dứa." His Vietnamese was much better than hers. The owner hurriedly relayed the order to one of the aunties in the open kitchen, and before they knew it, two heaps of green sticky rice in bowls appeared before them. The elderly woman who had encouraged the shop owner before—likely a descendant—nodded approvingly at the presentation. She didn't seem to sense that she was being watched, and because of that, Faye grinned.

"You're doing it again. Seeing someone." He looked over at where the woman had been. "God, that's literally the coolest thing ever."

She thought of her grade-school classmates who had scoffed or just stared at her when they discovered her ability. Faye swallowed a perfect bite of rice and coconut. "How are you so casual about this, me seeing ghosts?"

"I like the idea of endless mysteries. It'd be so boring if we just *knew* everything. There'd be no discoveries. There are just *some* things we can't really explain. Those moments where the temperature's perfectly fine, then suddenly you're shivering. The moments where your thoughts are clear and present, then suddenly, they just go away somewhere."

Faye grinned. "My mom once told me that's because the spirits are stealing away your ideas."

"And that's what my aunt had told me, too."

"But it's not real," Faye explained. "Spirits can't touch our world, but they interact in other ways. A suggestion or something. My mom and I can see them, and there are millions and millions of sensitive people who can, at least, feel them. Like that shop owner. His ancestor just wants him to do well."

She scraped at her bowl, feeling Jackson's eyes on her. She hid this part of her from her high school friends, but he readily accepted her. Maybe there were more people like him in the world.

Faye's mother emerged from the crowd, carrying a plastic bag filled with colorful fabric. Her grin was so wide that Faye couldn't help return it.

"Look at all these colors! I was probably ripped off, but I don't care. They're gorgeous! I'm going to sew some shirts and pants when we get back to the States."

"Can't you get that kind of fabric back home? Why buy them here?"

"It's the smell." Faye tilted her head, so her mother thrust one fabric under her nose, prompting her to inhale. Spices. Medicinal herbs. Fried foods. She had to admit: For some reason, it felt like she was—

"Home," her mother sighed, unknowingly finishing her thought. Her eyes were soft as she gazed around the market. Free of burden. Content to be a part of the tourism crowd, instead of the New Yorker who walks around wandering herds of tourists. Was her mother seeing both real ghosts and ghosts from her own past? Faye easily envisioned her teenage mother weaving through the aisles, collecting anything that looked pretty or needed saving from a dusty fate.

"Okay," Faye admitted. "It does smell good. Can you make me something when we get back home?"

"Only if you pay me—ooh, I want what you're having. Looks wonderful." After being pointed in the right direction, her mother again left her and Jackson alone. But a presence pulled Faye's attention away.

The young girl, from that first night. She stood at the entrance, by a wall covered with advertisements and banners from local businesses and services. Faye confirmed the spirit was around her age and height. A teenager, wearing jeans and a worn T-shirt. It looked like a band's name: *The Everlasters.* Her long black hair fell just below her shoulders. Maybe she was recently dead, but Faye couldn't quite tell.

"You're seeing a ghost again, aren't you?"

"Yeah, I've seen her before . . ." Faye trailed off.

Faye turned back to the entrance again. This time, the spirit smiled with mischief at Faye, and pointed at the largest banner above her head.

"What does that banner say? That bright yellow one on top?"

Jackson squinted. "Oh, it's a famous club. Lots of expats go. Pretty fun at night."

"I think she wants us to go there." Why, though?

"Let's go, then. Follow her." Jackson had already stood up.

"Wait, seriously?" Even so, she stood too. His eagerness was contagious; excitement coursed through her. It wasn't like when she was on the motorcycle, but more like whenever she filmed a scene with perfect lighting, perfect movement, perfect acting. Or watched a classmate's film that blew everyone else's out of the water.

"What's this about a club?" Her mother had come back, carrying the same item that Faye and Jackson had devoured.

"Faye saw a—"

"I was just asking about that banner . . ."

Jackson understood her mom would bombard her with questions if a ghost was mentioned, and added, "And I thought it'd be fun to go! It's eighteen and up."

She smiled, her eyes distant. "A club! Wow, I haven't been in one since my younger days with—" *Unnie*.

"Um, it's no big deal," said Faye. She didn't mean to bring up any bad memories. "We don't have to."

"No, let's go." She pulled Faye close. "We came back for a somber reason, but that doesn't mean we should be sad the whole time." Her mother's laughter and smiles these past few days almost made her forget what she'd seen in their ancestral room. What other feelings could her mother be hiding?

For the second time today, Faye was pressed up against her mother's back on the motorcycle. Sunset crawled closer, so the sky was a brilliant yellow, orange, and pink, and she wished she'd brought her compact camera with her.

The spirit was a yard behind Faye, standing on the pillion of a total stranger's motorcycle, arms stretched out like she was welcoming the wind's hug. Noticing Faye, she smiled, but Faye couldn't. She remembered that the girl had died somehow and somewhere. She'd never be able to truly feel this wind, ever.

"This night's for you, then, whoever you are." She whispered this promise to the girl.

✧ ⊠ ✧

In front of the nightclub, waiting for entry, she watched the girl disappear through the walls. Faye glanced at her mother. Did she see the spirit too? No, she would have said something.

Once inside, she took in the dim room, set alight at intervals by alternating pink and purple strobe lights and lasers from the ceiling. The living and the dead mingled without knowing. Her eyes landed on the spirit who led them here. She, hopping around with raised arms, had made her way into the middle of a little circle, which people—Faye's age, her mother's age—had instinctively formed while dancing. It would have made more sense for the spirit to dance that way if the DJ was playing something upbeat. But the spirit didn't seem to care, and her smile was brilliant. She looked free.

Now she was beckoning Faye.

Jackson had disappeared, spotting a coworker from the café where he was a part-timer.

"Looks like I'm not the only old person here."

"Mẹ, you're not old!" Faye shouted over the music.

"I don't know—these hips don't work like they once did. But I can try. Come on, let's show them how the Trần girls move."

Music and dancing: languages that both realms easily shared. There was no room for hesitation; you had to just go for it. The DJ switched up the music, the beats mounting, frenzied and chaotic and pure fun. Faye didn't want it to end; she saw her mother as she was before Faye came into the world, before she came to know how drastically one night would change the trajectory of her life.

Jackson joined them to make a circle. They danced a few more songs until her mother went to get them all water. It was just the two of them, Faye and Jackson, until the girl who'd led her here took her mom's place. This time, her movement matched the music.

"You look just like her!" she said.

"Who? My mom?" Faye responded, surprised the ghost was actually talking to her.

A nod from the ghost. "It's cool that you and your mom are spending time together."

Jackson looked over his shoulder, but quickly realized what was happening. He moved closer, gesturing between him and Faye. *Pretend you're talking to me,* he was saying.

Faye smiled gratefully. "It is. It's been a while, actually. She works a lot; the fashion industry's hectic."

"And you? What do you do?"

Faye told her about being accepted to UCLA, and her future career in film. Being behind the camera had always felt right to her. The ghost's eyes widened, as if Faye had said she was going to the moon, and that spurred her on. She talked about her interest in horror, the challenges of being a woman in film, the hope that she could work her way up without much struggle.

"UCLA, though. Are you going to miss her?"

How did she know?

"It's always been the two of us," Faye answered. "But now it feels like time's fast-forwarding. And I can't really do anything to stop it."

"Tonight's a pause. A chance to slow things down. You look like you're having fun. The both of you. And you seem awesome!"

"Are you having fun? I want you to have fun, too!"

"Best night ever," the ghost answered.

Then Faye heard glass shattering. She whirled around. Her mother stood two bodies away. One hand still cupped the air where the cocktail glass had been before it spilled. She stared beyond Faye.

"Mẹ?"

The crowd shifted at the sound. Partygoers started pushing one another to avoid the mess. In a flash, Faye lost sight of her mom.

"Be careful, there's glass on the floor," someone yelled. As the club lights flashed overhead, another person elbowed Faye, but used to the crowded subways back in New York, she barely flinched, standing her ground. She squinted, trying to find her mother, but there were too many shifting shapes.

"You okay?" Jackson. He was still behind her.

"My mom—did you see where she went?"

An employee with a broom and dustpan pushed through. Either inebriated or plain annoyed, the partygoers pressed back as one harsh tide.

"I think I saw her go outside. Come on." Jackson led her toward the exit, opposite of the crowd, and they burst through a back door, which opened up to a sidewalk that hugged the Trần Phú Beach. "Did something happen back there? She left pretty quickly."

"I don't—" Though she was standing still, she felt like her body was still moving at a warp speed. They had been dancing. Faye and the girl were dancing. That was when her mother dropped her glass and it hit the floor, and her mother—

Excited screams caught her attention. Daredevil beachgoers jumped into the dark-as-night waves that played tag with the shoreline. Her eyes naturally slid over, and there, a couple of yards away, stood her mother—a lonely statue facing the sea.

It was silly, but Faye imagined, just now, the waves reaching for her mother's ankles and pulling her underwater. She hurried over with that feeling of dread, and sensed that Jackson would know not to follow.

"Mẹ? Are you okay? Why did you leave so quickly?"

No answer. Faye's worry grew, and she placed a hand on her mother's shoulder. Finally, there was movement as the other woman turned to face her.

"I almost named you Fate, did you know?"

Perplexed by her nonanswer, Faye shook her head.

"I saw fairy lights, yes, but I also thought of that word, *fate*. I was meant to have you. I was meant to be your mother. You were meant to be mine. *You* were my future. I didn't care to even *think* about the past because I had you, and what was the use of looking back at things we can never, ever change?" She exhaled loudly. "But being back here, seeing a snippet of a life I could have had if the war didn't happen, if I hadn't left, and maybe, if Unnie were still alive . . ." She trailed off as she chewed on her bottom lip. "Actually, that's the thought that's been with me this whole time. I can't help but miss her, mourn what she's lost, too."

Now her mother held Faye's arms. "I'm happy you have a different life. You get to *see* so much. And I'm not just talking about ghosts. It's the way you pick up your camera whenever there is something new in front of you. And apparently, you saw something I couldn't tonight. Someone."

"What are you talking about?"

"Can you describe the ghost you were dancing with?"

Faye looked uncomfortable before she started speaking. "She was around my age. Vietnamese, or Asian at least. She wore this shirt of some obscure band. The Everlasters, I think?"

"When we were your age, Unnie became obsessed with all sorts of music, but her top favorite . . . was the Everlasters."

The images flashed through her mind; the spirit waving silently to her that night they arrived, gesturing for her when her mother went to get food, ensuring that only Faye would see her; dancing wildly with her, and then that was when her mother—

"Oh my god. It was her; it was Unnie."

"Yes."

"But she's my age. How—"

"Ghosts appear as they want to be seen. *When* they want to be seen. Makes sense that she would bring me here, the beach. Us and some other kids in the village, we'd bike all the way here and swim under the rising sun. Then we'd lie in the sand like starfish until we were dry enough to go straight to school. I had the best time."

"Ghosts appear . . . When they want to be seen." Faye softly repeated her mother's earlier words. Her mother must have seen Unnie at the club, and that was when she dropped the glass in surprise.

"I think she wanted this night to be ours. Not just me and her, but me, you, *and* her. She missed out on so much." It came to Faye, then: the image of Unnie dancing and grinning close to her. They had existed in their own little bubble a few minutes ago.

"So you think she's going to appear soon?" Faye asked. Her mother nodded. "Do you want to talk to her?"

"Yes and no. Yes, because I miss her. No, because that might make me miss her even more, the Unnie when she was alive and well."

"I can go. Give you privacy."

"Thanks, I think we'll need that."

Faye began to walk away, but her mother called out then, her voice raised to fight the waves: "Somehow I think Unnie must have known how I've felt the past few months—like time is running out. Time with you. I haven't been around as much as I should have been." Faye nodded, having sensed the same thing. "But I just want to say: I'm so goddamn happy to have this trip and these moments with you, and I know they might stop for a bit, when you go off to school, but I hope we'll have more and more moments together."

Bursting with emotion, Faye ran forward and threw her arms around her mother. Mish had been "on" for the whole week, presenting the happy face of someone who'd finally returned home. But she was also that weeping woman in white who had cried their first night in Vietnam, who'd squeezed Faye's hand because she needed reassurance in the beginning. She was just as scared as Faye about the changes looming over them.

"Sorry, I'm sorry," her mother whispered to her, fighting back her tears. "God, I just love you, Faye. You're all I have and all I ever wanted."

✧ ⧖ ✧

When Faye returned to the motorcycles, Jackson had gotten them McDonald's, and they leaned against the vehicles, feasting on McSpicy Chicken Rice, completed with a side of tomato and cucumbers. It wasn't like anything in the States, and for that she was glad.

Her mother texted Faye to ask if Jackson would escort her home. She "needed more time with Unnie."

Back outside her ancestral home, Faye slipped into bed, and the singing old woman and the swish of her broom lulled her to sleep.

She dreamed this moment: her mother's side of the bed dipping sometime later in the night. Her mother embracing her from behind, as if she were a kindergartener taking a midafternoon nap. Unnie, sounding as if she was just a few steps away, saying, "She's cute."

"She's a teen; she'd *hate* to be called cute. Also, shhh," her mother whispered back.

"You were like that, too. Hated to be complimented. Like mother, like daughter, I guess."

A hand caressed the back of her cheek. Yet her mother's arms were still around her.

The touch was warm, like any parting gift should be—

Faye opened her eyes, gasping out of her dream.

No, that wasn't right. Ghosts couldn't touch the living like that.

She looked to her left, and there was her slumbering mother, her arms hugging the gap Faye had left behind. Parts of her feet and arms were flecked with sand.

Voices slipped into their room from the courtyard. The singing woman was now laughing, and Faye heard another laugh that was lighter, like a girl's. Faye scrambled to the window, hope pounding in her chest. But the only thing she saw was the woman's back as she waved to a wisp that flickered, then disappeared outside the courtyard's entrance.

The Last Concert

BY RACHEL LYNN SOLOMON

Eli does this thing when he tunes his bass that's impossible not to watch. His features pinch with concentration, one tiny corner of his tongue peeking out from between his lips.

Margot is used to teasing him, doing exactly the same thing and waiting until he notices. But tonight in the greenroom, where she sits on the threadbare couch idly tapping a drumstick on her knee, there's a strange, swoopy feeling in her stomach, one that's uncomfortable and unfamiliar and a little frightening. And frankly, if she opens her mouth, she's not sure what will come out.

She doesn't want it to end like this. Not the potential projectile vomiting, although that wouldn't be ideal either, but the band. The Starry Nights. That thought has been playing on a loop inside her head for the past month, a needle trapped in the groove of one of her dad's old records. She's barely let herself think about it—because when she does, she spirals. Fortunately, there's been plenty to keep her mind occupied: finals and AP tests and paying off that library fine from sophomore year, when she lost *Mrs. Dalloway* for five weeks before unearthing it beneath a stack of music theory books, because she heard a rumor once that you're not allowed to graduate if you don't.

Graduation. The ominous milestone of a word taking place two weeks from now, somehow both freeing them and tearing them apart.

And then maybe they'll never play music together or speak to each other or sit in Asha's basement listening to the latest Phoebe Bridgers while J.J. waxes poetic about the future of indie rock and Eli catches her eye, one side of his mouth lifting in a there-goes-J.J. kind of way—

She's doing it again. Spiraling.

So she focuses back on Eli crouched in the corner, tuning his sleek, deep-cherry Squier, a wave of light brown hair falling across his face. Eli, who always grounds her, without even knowing it. Right before they start playing, when her anxiety is at its worst, all she has to do is look at him. There's something in his stance, the relaxed bend of his shoulders as he thumbs out a bass line, the way he gently sways with the music while keeping his feet firmly planted on the floor. And she immediately feels herself steady. There could be a hurricane raging outside, uprooting trees and tossing cars along the highway, and Eli would need to finish a chorus before taking cover. In every situation, it seems, he's the coolest of cucumbers.

Margot is a really, really neurotic cucumber.

"Almost sold out." Asha slides onto the couch and drapes her arm over Margot's shoulder. Even when she's not onstage singing, her voice is warm and honeyed, the kind of voice that always sounds slicked with confidence. Her curly black hair is in two buns on top of her head, eyes rimmed with gold liner. "I think this is the biggest crowd we've ever had."

"Figures that they decide they love us right when they're about to lose us," J.J. says from where he's seated in an armchair, picking at a sticker on his guitar case.

Eli glances up, a softness in his dark eyes. "It's humbling," he says. "People want a chance to say goodbye."

It just made sense, Asha said when they made the decision last month. They're all seniors, headed to different colleges at the end of the summer, though circumstance will split them even sooner: J.J. has an early-start program at his East Coast music school, and Asha works as a camp counselor on Whidbey Island every year. This way, they could end the Starry Nights on their terms. And it also made sense for their final show to happen here, at the Station, where it all started two and a half years ago. An old firehouse turned teens-only music venue in a Seattle suburb. Rumor is that Death Cab played here too, once upon a time.

It doesn't matter if it's for the best. It still feels like she's losing something.

"Does anyone else feel like throwing up?" Margot asks, tap-tap-tapping her sticks on her jeans to the rhythm of Metric's "Black Sheep," the cover they always save for last because it has such a satisfying buildup. A perfect crescendo.

"I have some Pepto in my bag," Asha says without even flinching. "Or do you want a can of Sprite? I'll split it with you." She starts digging into her black hole of a purse, the one she takes everywhere, positioning it behind J.J.'s or Eli's amp onstage "just in case" she needs an Altoid or a bobby pin during a set.

"How can you even find anything in there?" J.J. asks. When he's not messing with the sticker, he's scraping a hand through his new buzz cut, a choice made after four years of sporting dark hair down to his waist. It looks about a million times better, but Margot can tell he's not used to it yet. "I'm not judging, I'm just impressed."

"It might be chaos, but it's *my* chaos." Asha removes a tube of gloss and slicks her lips with it, bright red against her dark skin, a perfect match to the minidress she's paired with fishnets and combat boots.

When Margot started high school, she hid herself in baggy clothes, unsure how much of her body she wanted to put on display. Asha took her shopping for jeans that finally fit her hips the way they were supposed to—or at least, the way Margot wanted them to—and now their thrift store dates are her favorite way to spend a Saturday. When she isn't drumming, of course.

In the fall, Asha will be studying math at Stanford, and Margot will be up in Bellingham at Western Washington. At least Eli won't be too far away at UW, but a ninety-minute drive seems like an eternity compared to the nine minutes it takes her to get to his house now.

"I think I just need some fresh air," Margot says, glancing toward the window.

J.J., having successfully removed the sticker, pinches it into a tiny ball, flicking it at Margot. He might be a music snob, but he's *her* music snob, and even his ego has a soft center. He's the one who's always told her to be proud of what she listens to, whether it's on a major or indie label, whether she's one of billions of fans or just a handful. And she is, confidently composing playlists filled with Ezra Furman and Lorde, First Aid Kit and Taylor Swift.

"We're on in ten," he says.

"I'll be back in five. Swear."

Suddenly, Eli gets to his feet. "I might join you," he says, giving his guitar a pat before tucking it back into its case.

✧ ⌗ ✧

"Do you remember the first time we played here?" Eli asks once he and Margot get outside. They're leaning against a fence that separates the

Station from a day-care center parking lot. Such is life as a teenage bad-ass in the suburbs. On their way out, they waved to a few friends chatting in groups, passing around bottles of mystery juice and hiding vape pens in their coat pockets.

In spite of everything, Margot smiles. "I don't think I could forget."

There had only been a dozen people in the audience, all of them friends of the band. Still, Margot had been ridiculously nervous—she must have peed five times in the twenty minutes before they went onstage.

"I'm not sure if I can do this," she had said, so quietly she wasn't sure if Eli would be able to hear her. Or if she wanted him to.

He was sitting next to her on the couch, and he nudged her knee with his. "You know these songs. You are a *beast* on these songs." Then, when she barely offered up a quarter smile between frenetic taps of her sticks against her jeans, he turned serious. "If you start feeling anxious," he said, "don't look out at the audience. Just look over at me, okay?"

Once they made it out there, Asha's vocals were too soft and J.J.'s guitar was too loud, but they played like their lives depended on it anyway. Margot probably spent more time looking at Eli than at her own hands, but she attacked her drums so viciously she cracked a stick. J.J. broke a string. And then Asha, dancing around the stage with her eyes closed, tripped over Eli's cord and plummeted face-first into Margot's bass drum. It was a small miracle that her resulting stitches didn't end the band right then and there, and to this day, she wears the jagged stripe above her left eyebrow like a battle scar.

They'd only been playing together for a few months at that point. Asha is best friends with J.J.'s twin sister, and J.J. and Margot are long-time neighbors, destined to be friends before they were born. As soon as Margot started playing drums, J.J. bugged her to jam with him, and once they overheard Asha singing while they were practicing, they thought they might really be able to create something. Eli was the wild card. They put up flyers for bassists around school, and Eli was the first and only person to reply. It was sheer luck that he happened to be good.

Margot swallows hard. "I don't know why I feel this close to losing my shit," she admits, reaching around to her back pocket, as though needing to remind herself that her sticks are still there. "How are you so chill?"

"I listened to a lot of Sigur Rós before I got here," Eli says with one of those half smiles, but then he shakes his head, hair shifting before sliding neatly back into place. Why is that so mesmerizing? There's no way his smile has always been that hypnotic, is there? "No, I probably just try way too hard to hide it." At that, he holds out his hand. It's trembling—not a lot, but enough.

She's never thought of Eli as being particularly anxious. Margot was an anxious kid, an anxious toddler, probably even an anxious infant. Baby Margot probably spent hours debating whether she wanted mashed blueberries or pureed peaches, weighing all the possible outcomes, and then she probably lay awake all night in her crib, wondering if she'd made the wrong choice.

Toward the end of middle school, when her therapist suggested a creative outlet, she chose the drums simply because she thought they'd be the biggest, loudest thing to distract her anxiety. A fuck-you to her brain. And once she started playing, her mind just . . . quieted down. For a little bit. It was nothing but her and the instrument, an all-consuming rhythm. The solid heartbeat of the kick-drum and the hiss of the hi-hat.

It didn't cure her, of course, because nothing could—and she'd accepted that. But it made everything else so much easier to handle.

"I wish I were a little better at hiding it," Margot says. "Everyone else must think I'm . . . not all there."

He frowns at her. A streetlamp catches the faint freckles across the bridge of his nose. "They don't think that," he says, and points to himself. The faded Beatles tee he's wearing, the one she's shocked he isn't shivering in. "*I* definitely don't."

"Thank you," she says quietly, because she believes him. And it makes her feel so *visible* in this moment that she isn't sure what to do with it. So naturally, she deflects. It's easier to talk about the Band as a unit than Margot, Individual Person. "It's not that I thought we'd be playing forever," she continues. "And logically, I know it doesn't make sense for us to stay together when we're in college. I guess I just . . . thought we had more time." She hugs her arms around her favorite black T-shirt. "I'm not good at change, if you can believe it."

Eli's quiet for a moment, triangling a foot against the fence and bouncing it a couple times. He almost never responds right away, and this is something else she likes about him. He considers what he wants to say, each word chosen carefully. "You're an incredible drummer. You'll find another band, if that's what you want."

It isn't, she almost says. "But will their bassist be as adamant about using a pick as you are?" she asks.

That earns her a soft elbow to the shoulder. A grin. "Paul McCartney plays with a pick," Eli says with all the bravado of someone who's said this a hundred times. And he has, because it's the only defense he ever needs.

You're an incredible drummer. It takes her mind a few extra seconds to process the compliment, and then it lingers there, though he's said similar things about her music countless times over the past couple years. She knows she's an incredible drummer—or at the very least, an above-average one—but there's something about hearing it from Eli that sets her on fire. She's no longer shivering, a spark in her belly warming her from the inside out.

Eli has always been kind, but either she's been paying more attention lately or he's on a good-deed kick, because now she's thinking about their show in Seattle last month, when Eli helped her take down her kit. Or two weeks ago, when she skipped band practice because of a stomach bug and he sent her a link to a "get well soon" Spotify playlist he'd made, with song titles that made her laugh in between trips to the bathroom. "Feel Good Inc." and "I Wanna Be Sedated" and "Recover."

She didn't know what it meant then, but maybe she's starting to.

The gestures, not the stomach bug.

"Do you remember the show we played in Olympia last summer?" she asks, because the nostalgia game is easier than facing the present or, worse, the future.

"Where we went on so late that the club was no longer for all ages, and we had to sneak out the back when we finished our set?"

"That audience was amazing, though."

"Drunk but amazing," Eli agrees. "And then you fell asleep in the back of the van on the way home."

"And you covered me up with your sweatshirt—" Margot breaks off. She'd been sleeping. Or at least, she'd been mostly sleeping. She'd woken up briefly when Eli turned in his seat to drape his sweatshirt over her, the sweat-and-soap scent of him cloaking her like the sweetest comfort. She'd been so worried he'd stop doing it if she stirred, so she kept deathly still, certain her thudding heart would give her away.

"You looked so cute," he says, half to her, half to the pick he's just dug out of his pocket. "I didn't want to disturb you."

There's that swoop of her stomach again. "You didn't," she says, her voice hoarse. Unfamiliar. Eli has never called Asha or J.J. cute.

He points to her hands, her fingers tapping out a rhythm on the fence. "You always do that before shows," he says. "Sometimes with your sticks, sometimes without. I always try to figure out what song it is."

Margot's face goes warm as she immediately stills her hands. "You . . . notice that?"

His mouth kicks up into a small smile. "I notice a lot of things about you."

This would be the perfect time to tell him that she notices him, too. All his preshow rituals and quiet kindness.

But their five minutes is up, and Margot isn't sure the words will make it past her throat.

"Shall we?" Eli says with a nod of his head toward the Station, and together, they tremble their way back inside.

✧ ⋈ ✧

The Starry Nights' music is raw and unapologetic, crunchy guitar and wild drums and angry vocals. If Margot is being completely honest with herself, it's also not very good. Separately, they're skilled at their instruments, but it took them forever to learn to keep time together, to work as a team instead of each person trying to be the loudest one onstage. They defy genre, J.J. always says, while Asha confidently calls them post-punk lo-fi dreampop. Margot and Eli usually just call them rock.

Tonight, though—tonight, they sound like seasoned veterans. Margot is Janet Weiss, Meg White, Karen Carpenter, dark blond hair flying around her head as she drums, keeping perfect time. Asha is

Debbie Harry and Nina Gordon and Courtney Barnett, J.J. is some guitarist none of them have ever heard of, because that's what he'd want. And Eli is . . .

Looking right at her.

When the Starry Nights took the stage, the crowd roared for them. Especially from her position behind the drums, it's rare for Margot to be able to pick out any faces. But maybe tonight's magic helped her quickly spot her younger sister and her friends, all packed in toward the front.

Right now, she can't focus on any of them. Only on the soft angles of Eli's shoulders, the way she's certain she could pick his bass line out of any song.

Asha throws back her head as she sings about broken hearts, the spotlight illuminating the scar above her eyebrow, while J.J.'s guitar crunches its way through a chorus. And Eli's bass, the deep, steady sound underneath everything. They've never been this in sync, this *on*. Margot's earplugs, the ones her parents make her wear, are basically useless at this point. There's an electric energy here, one that she wishes she could catch in a jar and keep forever.

Suddenly, she's overwhelmed with affection for these people. The friends who dutifully paid $5 on a Friday night to watch them, the family who let them use their garage and drove them to gigs and invested in noise-canceling headphones.

She has never loved the drums, loved her friends, more than she does in this moment.

Eli inches closer and closer, up through "Don't Move (I Dare You)" and "Windmill" and their cover of "Black Sheep." Teasing her metronome heart. He grins up at Margot from beneath his curtain of hair, and she meets his gaze. She knows she looks fierce when she's up here, and she hopes he sees that. His gaze arrowing into her makes her certain he does.

Their eyes remain locked when she smashes the cymbals for the final time, finally letting her own face split into a smile.

Margot's never been in love. Sure, she's had crushes, a few weeklong relationships that never ended with the kind of heartbreak Asha sings about. But this feels different.

She might be in love with Eli, and that she's realizing it now, the very last time they play together as the Starry Nights, is incredibly inconvenient.

She blinks a few times, the lights playing games with her vision, as the stage comes back into focus. That was their last song. The audience is cheering and whooping, the stage quaking, and Asha's makeup is starting to run.

"Thank you, thank you!" she yells into the mic. "We've been the Starry Nights. We love you all very much and we'll miss you dearly."

J.J. steps up to his mic, swipes a hand through his short hair. "Thanks for giving us the best send-off we could imagine. Good night, and don't get into too much trouble out there. Unless, of course, that trouble is extremely fun, in which case . . . enjoy." He throws out a wink.

Margot plays a rim shot.

"And thank you to the Station for having us," Eli adds. "We can't wait to be back here soon—in the audience, next time."

The three of them turn to Margot, giving her the chance to say something. The invisible drummer. So she takes a deep breath and bends the nearest mic stand toward her.

"Hi," she says into it, her ears still ringing. "Everyone else pretty much said it perfectly, but this band has been kind of the highlight of my life. And, well, hopefully that won't always be the case—hopefully I'm not peaking at seventeen"—this draws some laughs, and the response compels her to keep going—"but I can't imagine a better way to say goodbye. Thank you."

She never sang into a mic while onstage, never said anything, so maybe it's fitting that she's doing it for the first time at their last show.

And then the Starry Nights are just . . . done.

The lights flick back on. The audience starts to disperse, eyes snapping down to phone screens, people heading for the bathroom or to the parking lot. Amps are unplugged. It's all a hazy, wobbly blur.

Somehow Margot stumbles off the stage, her sticks limp in her hands. The adrenaline is still racing through her veins—she doesn't know what to do with it.

Once they're back in the greenroom, Asha beckons everyone in for a group hug.

"Is it weird to say I already miss you guys?" she asks when she releases them, digging into her purse for a makeup wipe.

"We'll see each other on Monday," Margot says.

J.J. shakes his head. "Nope. Senior skip day."

"Which I'm sure you've had circled in your calendar for months," Eli says.

"What can I say, I like traditions."

Margot doesn't want them to forget what just happened out there. "It was a good show," she says.

Eli meets her eyes again. "The best."

They have plans to meet up at a diner with some friends, but first they have to pack everything up. Milkshakes and greasy burgers can wait.

Back when they were starry-eyed baby musicians, they joked about pooling their money to get one of those Volkswagen hippie buses in bright orange or pastel blue. Something they could cover in stickers without their parents worrying about the adhesive they'd leave behind. They'd have rules about what kind of music could be played on its stereo, and when they made it big and headed out on their first tour, everyone would know it was them when they rolled into town.

It never happened, of course, so after every show, Margot stows her drum kit in the back of her parents' minivan. It always feels like a victory when J.J.'s and Eli's amps and guitar cases fit, too.

As they load the trunk, Margot realizes it's not just the Band as a unit that's kept her from unraveling during high school. It's Asha and J.J. and Eli, Individual People. Asha's last-minute tutoring before a math test that helped her understand inverse functions. J.J's ability to race down the street when Margot's home alone and make sure the weird noise she heard was just the groaning of her house.

Eli. Eli. *Eli.*

"I think I'm missing one of my bolts," Margot says, zipping and unzipping her Zildjian bags. "Be right back."

Eli digs his hands in his pockets. "Oh—and I'm missing my lucky pick. Might have dropped it onstage."

Asha rolls her eyes. "Fine, fine. But don't take too long, okay? I'm starving."

"And my ears are cold," J.J. adds. "Maybe I should grow my hair back out."

The Station isn't a place that's meant to be empty. It's eerie without anyone inside except for a couple volunteers still cleaning up. It must have taken longer than Margot thought for them to tetris their instruments into her van.

Eli is solid warmth behind her as they move through the dim hallway. They're not touching, and yet she's fully aware of his presence, even more so when the volunteers wrestle a mountain of trash bags into the alley, leaving them alone.

She spots her missing bolt right away, silver glinting from the back of the stage, and after she picks it up, she doesn't make a move to leave. Instead, she walks toward the front, a view she never gets as a drummer, and gazes out at the nothingness.

"Are you okay?" Eli asks softly. He places a hand on her arm for the briefest moment, a singe of contact that she wishes didn't end so soon.

For some reason, she lets out a small laugh at that. "I think—I think I'm just sad. About it ending, but also what it all represents. It wasn't easy for me to get onstage, and I guess I just wonder . . . if I ever will again."

Eli sits with this a moment, fiddling with something in his hand that Margot can't see in the dark. "Do you want to?"

"Yes," she says without hesitating. "I love performing. I know that might sound weird, because I'm such an anxious mess most of the time. But everything else just falls away when we're up there. Maybe this sounds corny, but it's like . . . it's like nothing else exists but us and the music."

"Not corny at all," he says. "I feel that, too. Maybe it won't happen right away, but if you love it this much—and I know you really fucking love it—then you'll find a way to get back up there. I have zero doubts."

Eli swears so infrequently that she can't help cracking a smile.

"Thank you," she says. And then she notices something in Eli's expression, too, something that wasn't there onstage, or outside, or in the greenroom. "Your turn. What's going through your head right now?"

"I think it might fall away for me too much," he says. "I've always worried that."

Margot's brow furrows. "What do you mean?"

A few seconds of silence, Eli taking his time as usual. "I wonder if I get too in my head, to the point where I've made the bass my whole personality. And that this is the only thing people know about me—that I play the bass. I'll be walking down the hall at school, and someone will say, 'Hey, you're that bass guy, right? In that band?' And without the band, I wonder . . . who am I? *What* am I?" Then he attempts to laugh this off. "Too philosophical?"

She shakes her head. "That's . . . actually one of my favorite things about you. You're so focused, so reliable. When we're in the middle of a set or a practice and things are getting chaotic or out of control, I still look at you, just like you told me to before our first show. And I immediately feel grounded."

Eli presses his lips together, his eyes filling with an emotion Margot can't name. "I had no idea," he says.

"You're not just this." Margot waves a hand at the stage. "And I think you know that. You're great at math, and you can bake a killer batch of brownies, and you collect stamps with your grandpa." It's another one of her favorite things about him, that he spends every other Sunday at his grandfather's retirement home, the two of them sorting through their stamp books. She's never been there, but he's told her enough about it that she can picture it perfectly.

"That's true," Eli says. "He'll be thrilled I can spend more time with the stamps."

"See? We're both going to be okay." There's more confidence in her voice now, a surer set to her posture. She might be starting to believe herself. Then: "Shouldn't you be looking for your pick?"

He opens up his palm, revealing a flash of neon pink and giving her a guilty look.

"Oh," she says quietly, the pieces falling into place. *He wanted to be alone with her.*

"Margot," he says, inching closer, and she wonders if he's ever said her name like this before. In a way that makes it sound beautiful. "What you said up there. The Starry Nights . . . This has been the highlight of my life, too. For a lot of reasons."

"I notice you, too," she says, aware she's responding to something he said earlier tonight, but suddenly finding the courage to answer. They might be the bravest four words she's ever uttered. "Before shows. It's like you can't tune your guitar if your tongue isn't sticking out. You always make these ridiculous faces."

He doesn't blush. Not like she did. But he bites back a smile, his eyes lighting up. "I do not," he says.

"You do!" she exclaims. "Every time. But that's okay, because it's—"

It's cute, she was about to say.

"It's what?" he teases. He *knows.* He fully knows what she was about to say, and he's going to make her work for it.

But maybe that's okay—because now they're both blushing, and the swoopy feeling in Margot's stomach is starting to feel almost . . . *pleasant.* This isn't post-show exertion on his face; it's something else entirely. Something she thinks might be painted on her own face, too.

"This doesn't have to be over." He steps closer, stage creaking. His scent, like when he wrapped her in his hoodie, is all she can focus on. "Not all of it."

Margot takes the last step, her chest so close to his that if they both inhaled at the same moment, they'd be touching.

So she lifts onto her toes and kisses him.

His mouth is warm, soft, and she moves apart a second after making contact—mostly to make sure she hasn't completely misread the situation.

Then he grins this lovely, magnificent grin and draws her in to him again, lips meeting with a new kind of hunger. This time, one of his hands cups her face and the other finds hers. She can feel the firm press of his bass pick against her skin. And then he's skimming it up her arm, plucking a rhythm in her hair while she settles her hands against the back of his neck. There's no music playing, but they can create their own soundtrack, breaths and sighs and the squeak of the stage when they shift even closer.

They kiss while their phones buzz with *where are you?* texts from Asha and J.J., onstage with an audience of no one.

Tonight isn't just an ending, Margot realizes as they thread their fingers together and head back to the parking lot.

It could be a beginning, too.

The Last Time I Saw Her Alive

BY DIANA URBAN

It was the last time I saw my best friend alive.

Not that I knew it then—it seemed as ordinary a moment as moments get. Emilia had tapped her red Solo cup against mine and flashed me a grin before heading out to the patio, where most of our junior class had congregated because it was the first warm night we'd had since fall.

Thinking back, a part of me noticed how her smile—that glimmering row of perfect pearls—hadn't quite reached her milky brown eyes. A bigger part of me ignored it.

But the corners of her eyes always crinkled when she meant it.

I should've known right then.

She'd been my best friend since the second grade; I knew her tells better than my own. And that fake smile, the way she'd just given me a necklace out of nowhere—one of her favorites, too, of two silver snakes intertwining to form a heart—the way she'd slinked off without a word, hiding her gaze under a curtain of red waves, the way she was drinking *at all* should've told me something was wrong. On their own, each was innocent, but in combination, they told a story. A story I chucked aside like the stack of books collecting dust on my nightstand.

Denial is a wicked beast.

If I'd have known that would be the last time I saw Emilia alive, I would've said something. Would've stopped her from leaving, would've pulled her into one of the bedrooms, away from the thrumming bass blasting from the speakers, and apologized for the terrible things I did. For the terrible friend I was. I would've told her she deserved better than me, that I'd understand if she didn't want to be my friend anymore, though it would've killed me just the same.

Instead I downed my drink, some fruity concoction masking the booze's strength, sulking over the fact that she was the one who'd get to kiss her boyfriend, Connor, out there in the shadows under the trees, under the stars, even though his lips had roved over mine just hours ago.

Yeah.

Like I said, I was a terrible friend.

But you can't help who you love, and I'd loved Connor ever since I laid eyes on him the first day of freshman year. She just happened to gush over him first, had the guts to ask him out first. I was never bold and brave like her. And I'd do anything to avoid a fight, even if it meant stabbing myself in the chest.

I knew once they'd started dating, I should've let it go. Let *him* go. But how could I when those wide blue eyes of his always lingered on mine a beat too long? How could I when every time he passed me his phone to show me a funny video, a chill shot up my arm like an electric current? How could I when a few weeks ago, he finally kissed me, his lips soft against mine, his hair like tousled silk under my fingers, and it felt like the world could be sapped of oxygen and we'd still be able to breathe?

How can you let someone go when every fiber of your being is screaming they were always meant to be yours?

So I chugged my drink as I stood at the window, watching as she found him on the balcony, tugged his hand, and pulled him down the stairs, out back toward the woods.

Maybe she knew what she was about to do.

Maybe she wanted me to see.

At the time, I had no idea it'd be my last chance to talk to my best friend. Instead, I turned and drained my cup, hoping to numb this agony for at least another day.

I had no clue what new, far worse agony would soon take its place.

✦ ⛢ ✦

"Jess . . . I *have* to end it," Connor had said to me earlier that day. I'd been pressed between him and the wall in that dimly lit hall by the school gym, the one leading to the janitor's closet.

I'd winced and rubbed my lips together—I could still feel him on them. They were probably extra pink and puffy from all that kissing. "What?"

"With *her*," he clarified. "I need to end things with Emilia."

"No!" My heart lodged in my throat. I knew this had to end one of two ways: losing Emilia or losing Connor. But I hadn't been prepared to have this conversation so soon.

His eyebrows shot up.

"I mean, not yet." Heat rushed up my neck at the mere prospect of telling Emilia the truth, to even briefly imagine the tortured look that'd cross her face. "Oh, God, she's going to *hate* me."

Emilia and I had shared everything growing up, ever since the first day of second grade when her parents forgot to pack her lunch. Despite my shyness, I'd offered her half my turkey sandwich, wanting to wipe that crushed look off her face. We became fast friends, and she practically lived at my house on weekends, especially after her big sister, Hannah, passed away. Hannah was the favored firstborn, so Emilia claimed, and she needed to escape her mother's grief-ridden benders. I glommed on to her right back; she was the bubbly, talkative, vivacious one who snagged all the invites. I'd always expressed myself better through dance than words. But with our forces combined, we had a happy home and sparkling social life. We did each other's homework, each other's makeup, shared our clothes and fears and dreams.

But Connor was one thing she'd never want to share. Not that she should have to.

Connor pressed his forehead to mine and cupped my cheek. "This is going to come out sooner or later."

"I can't . . ." I tugged down his arm and pressed my fingers to my lips, unsure what to say. The panic clawing up my throat at the prospect of losing either of them would only make me blurt out the wrong thing.

He took a step back, furrowing his brow in frustration. "Well, what do you want, then? We can't sneak around like this forever." He'd made that clear when he showed up at my dance recital last week, even though Emilia had other plans. Even though I'd told him not to. I'd spotted him in the audience, right in the first row, and he'd flashed me that encouraging grin. A comforting warmth had bloomed from my heart, quelling my nerves, and it felt like I was dancing just for him.

"Not forever, obviously . . ." My breath hitched, guilt crushing my chest like it did whenever I thought too hard about the inevitable pain we'd cause Emilia. I'd loved her like a sister for so many years.

But I was *in love* with Connor, my feelings for him stronger than I'd thought possible.

I never had feelings for boys in middle school, other than actors in certain TV shows, though Emilia circulated through crushes faster than a cyclone. Mom grinned when I'd confided in her about it. "Oh, don't worry," she said. "Someday, when you're in college, or later, maybe, someone will come along and sweep you off your feet." She hadn't had a boyfriend until she met Dad at NYU.

But then my whole feet-sweeping incident happened earlier than expected—when Connor showed up the first day of high school—and I couldn't stop thinking about him. The way his face was the last I imagined before falling asleep and the first when my alarm jolted me awake, the way my stomach lurched whenever anyone mentioned his name, the way the floor seemed to evaporate whenever he met my gaze . . . it was so all-consuming, it was almost maddening. I figured it was all one-sided, that I'd built it up in my head, that there was no way he could ever like me back.

Nor should he. He was Emilia's.

Or so I thought.

"I don't know," I said to him now. "We have to figure something out . . ."

"*When*, though?" His voice was low and husky. "I can't do this anymore. Every time she tries to kiss me . . . I can't pretend to *want* to anymore—"

Something clattered down the hall, like someone had careened into the janitor's cart around the corner. I gasped, and we broke apart and turned to look, but nobody appeared. Maybe they were further down the hall.

I shook my head, my heart thrashing against my rib cage. "I don't know what to do . . ."

"We've been through this. I have to at least break up with her. Even if I don't tell her it's for you."

My stomach plummeted. "No, don't."

His face hardened. "Why not?"

"She'll figure it out."

"So? She'll find out eventually. I . . . Dammit, I should've been with you this whole time."

I crossed my arms. "Well, no one *forced* you to date her."

He winced. But Emilia *was* a force of nature, and I could see how she'd be impossible to resist. Besides, it wasn't like I'd made my own feelings clear. A tear slipped down my cheek as I remembered that time freshman year our group of friends went to the movies, when Emilia first pulled Connor aside to tell him she liked him. I remembered how his eyes had drifted to mine, how I'd averted my gaze, my cheeks burning with shame for resenting her for this, even though she deserved happiness just as much as me. But I'd said nothing. And he'd said nothing. Until all that nothingness exploded like the Big Bang.

Still, I pressed on. "Did you love her?"

He groaned. "Don't do that—"

"No, I need to know." Before I destroyed my and Emilia's friendship for good. "If you really knew you liked me, why'd you ever hook up with her?" We never would've been in this impossible situation if he hadn't caved to her easy charm . . . or if I'd been braver.

A pained look crossed his face before his blue eyes turned icy. "Oh, so we're playing *that* game now?"

"It's not a game. It's a legit question."

He raked his hair back. "God, Jess, I put *everything* on the line for you." He shook his head and sighed. "I didn't know you felt the same way back then."

"Bullshit," I snapped. Emilia always said she could read me like a book; I always turned bright red at the slightest embarrassment or attention. My feelings for him must've shown on my face. Then again, even Emilia never seemed to notice. In fact, she'd convinced me to go to homecoming with this sophomore in her drama club, saying he had this huge crush on me. Or maybe she *did* notice and was hoping I'd fall for someone else.

"No. I don't know." Connor gently banged his fist against the cinder-block wall. "Dammit. I just . . ." He shook his head again, then reached out and tucked a strand of my blond hair behind my ear. "It just kills me that if she were out of the picture, we could just be—"

"Well, she's not," I snapped again, louder this time. "She's my *best* friend. I can't hurt her like this. I can't *lose* her."

He yanked his hand back and cursed. "So that's it, then?"

"*What?*" I breathed.

"You just said it yourself—" He pressed a fist to his lips. Was he holding back tears?

Fissures spread through my heart. "Wait, what're you saying?"

"We can't be together, because of *her*." He backed away further, wiping a hand down his face.

"*No.* Connor—" My own tears choked off my words. He couldn't have been saying what I thought he was. Had he misunderstood me? I wasn't choosing Emilia over him—I only needed more time to figure out how to pull the rug out from under her without her cracking her skull.

Oh, God. I couldn't lose him. Not when I finally almost had him.

But when I opened my mouth to clarify, a teacher rounded the corner and found us there alone, unsupervised, and ushered us off to class. I had to talk to him later. I had to explain what I really meant.

But later never came.

I knew I'd see him at the party that night after my dance practice and his track meet, but how could I talk to him then when Emilia was *right there*? And then at the party, she acted so strange, so distant, her smile not quite reaching her eyes.

She must have known. She must have found out. And I never got to explain.

And then.

The police ruled it a suicide.

The toxicology report came back showing high amounts of fentanyl. An overdose. The suicide note—saved right to the desktop so it'd be easy to locate—corroborated this finding. Everyone was so willing, so eager to accept that a teenage girl had ended her life over a broken heart.

They had no idea.

✧ ☒ ✧

Everything had been hazy since the funeral, like I was seeing the world through a clouded glass prism. I'd only been to one funeral before—the one for Emilia's sister, Hannah, a couple years back, after she died by suicide. Her mother had sobbed so hard her legs buckled beneath her, likely never imagining she'd have to endure this again.

It rained during the funeral, because of course it did. Families and kids from school clustered around the open grave, huddled under umbrellas, the priest's droning interrupted by the occasional sob and boots squelching over soggy grass.

Connor had stood a few feet from his family, hands stuffed in his pockets, barely seeming to notice the raindrops dripping from his drenched hair and nose as the coffin jostled into the earth, those blue eyes boring into me, making me feel like I was drowning. We hadn't spoken since before the party, since before our world imploded.

We both knew what we'd caused. And we both knew what we'd lost. No words could fix this.

The very next day at school, Connor was already in English lit when I arrived—it was the only class he, Emilia, and I had together this year, and we'd always sat in a cluster near the window. He was hunched over with his eyes downcast, like he was fascinated by a scratch on the desk's surface. But I knew he just couldn't bear to look at the empty seat nobody else would dare take.

Our classmates spoke in hushed whispers, waiting for the bell to ring. I took my usual seat in front of Connor, but he didn't look at me— just kept trailing the pad of his finger over the scratch, his brow furrowed and jaw taut.

"Connor," I whispered.

A flicker of a grimace, maybe. He wasn't going to say anything, was he?

My gaze slid to Emilia's deserted desk next to his, and my very essence seemed to clench from the wrongness of it.

I covered his hand.

He winced back with a shudder and rubbed his neck, shaking his head. And his eyes—God, those eyes of his—were filled with pain and this terrible yearning that tore my soul to shreds. We could never be together now. Not after *this*.

But there was something else about his expression—something I couldn't quite read. Was it guilt? Anger?

Did he know as well as I did that the police were wrong?

I was terrified to ask, like merely saying it out loud would make it real. I wished he'd say something. I needed to know what he was thinking. What he *knew*. I steeled myself, about to prod him, but right then he bent over to dig a pen from his backpack. He took so long to find it, it almost felt like he was searching just to avoid speaking to me. And he had this permanent grimace etched on his face—

Oh. That's what it was.

Shame.

He was ashamed over something—something that had shrouded him like a storm cloud ever since the funeral. Maybe before. Was it shame over cheating on Emilia? Or was it something more?

I remembered that pained look that crossed his face when he thought I was choosing Emilia over him, when he thought he might lose us both.

How far would he go to make sure he got to stay with one of us?

✧ ⌧ ✧

I didn't know what I expected to find in Connor's room, but he had a track meet after school, so I made a beeline for his house right after the last-period bell rang to search it.

It was easier to get in Connor's house than I'd expected. His mother was heading to the car to get the rest of her groceries, so I snuck in before she could close the door.

I might've had better luck searching his gym locker at school, though—there wasn't exactly much to sift through here. He once complained how his mother had no concept of privacy; she tidied up in here every morning before her nursing shift, so his bed was always made, his dresser always stuffed with neatly folded clothes, his hamper always empty. Apparently, picking out his own decorations had been a hard-fought battle, and even then she'd insisted on framing the *Star*

Wars and *Mass Effect* posters lining the walls. His desk didn't have any drawers, and his gaming laptop was shut—not that I'd have any idea what passwords to try.

Last time I was here, he'd sat at that desk, calm and collected, notebook splayed open, scrawling a list of possible ways to deal with this messy situation. To deal with Emilia.

1. *Tell Emilia the whole truth.* ✶ *Emilia hates us.*

2. *Connor to dump Emilia. We "start" dating a few weeks later. Emilia hates us.*

3. *Connor to do something horrid to make Emilia dump him. We "start" dating a few weeks later. Emilia hates us.*

4. *Jess to tell Emilia how she feels about Connor. Connor feigns ignorance.* ~~*Emilia steps aside?*~~ *Emilia hates us.*

But no matter how many scenarios we volleyed back and forth, the outcome would always be the same. Emilia would hate us. Hence Connor scribbling a star next to option one. If I'd lose her anyway, we might as well be honest. On a Best Friend Betrayal Scale of one to ten, I was already at least a seventeen. Maybe I didn't deserve her. Maybe I didn't deserve to fix this.

And now it was too late to fix anything. Now the worst outcome had happened, one I never even imagined—

Connor burst into his room, jarring me back to reality, wearing his running shorts and a loose T-shirt . . . He must've gone to his track meet and sensed he was about to lose control, then sprinted home so he wouldn't crumble in front of everyone.

"Jess," he said, his voice cracking as he collapsed onto his bed. Within moments, the decorative pillow under his cheek was dark with splotches. I'd never seen him cry before. Seeing him like this made me feel like I was shattering into a million pieces. I wanted to climb into the bed to hold him, comfort him, assure him that everything would be okay. But nothing would ever be okay again.

"I'm here." I reached out to stroke his hair, to push aside the dark strands that had fallen across his forehead.

"How could you do this?"

I jolted back. Heat surged through me as his words echoed in my mind. He thought *I* did this? How could he think that?

Yes, I'd suspected him.

Yes, I'd come here to snoop around.

But how could he think *I'd* do such a thing?

"I loved you," Connor went on. "I loved you so much. I'm so . . . I'm so fucking *mad* at you."

Loved. Past tense.

Panic tore through me. "Connor." I knelt next to him, desperation bringing me to my knees. "I swear I didn't do this. I *swear* it."

But he only shook his head and buried it deeper into his pillow.

Oh, God. I couldn't let him think I did this. Because it *wasn't* me.

And if it wasn't him, either . . . there was only one other person it could be.

✧ ⌧ ✧

Emilia always left the window of her first-floor bedroom open at night. She slept hot and liked the cool breeze to lull her to sleep, to hell with the risks of mosquitoes or serial killers.

"Aren't you afraid some axe murderer will climb in?" I'd asked one of the rare times I slept over.

She'd scoffed. "Chill out. This podunk town's not cool enough for axe murderers." She'd chucked a pillow at me.

I'd swatted it away and shivered. "I'm chilled, all right."

Now I stood in her dark bedroom just after dusk, her window unlocked as always. I'd waited until her parents' car disappeared from the driveway, just in case. Now I had the house to myself to search.

There had to be some clue as to what *really* happened.

I shuffled into Emilia's cramped bedroom, aglow from the bright floodlights illuminating the driveway. Hannah's spacious room down the hall had remained an untouched mausoleum her mom refused to clear out after she died.

Emilia's purple comforter was a rumpled mess on the bed, exactly how she'd left it; her shelves were crammed with books and makeup and knickknacks. Anxiety pulsed through me as I eyed her school-provided Chromebook on the cluttered desk. I could probably search it if I needed to—we'd set our passwords as each other's birthdays the first day of freshman year when we couldn't think of anything else. I bet she never bothered changing hers.

Invading her privacy would usually make me cringe, but I needed answers. With nobody home, I didn't have to worry about making noise, but still was too afraid to touch anything. Despite my desperation for the truth, I was terrified of what I might find. Of what it might mean.

An engine rumbled close by.

Wheels crunched over gravel.

Someone just pulled into the driveway.

I froze. Were Emilia's parents back already? I inched to the window and peeked outside.

Connor. It was his black SUV in the driveway. I ducked fast, and a shiver coasted through me.

But I'd barely even started looking around.

Willing myself to stay calm, I scanned the top of Emilia's dresser where her jewelry box was splayed open, earrings and necklaces in jumbled clumps of chains and fake gemstones. I still wore her necklace, her last birthday present to me. When I'd first put it on, it sizzled my skin like a brand, guilt searing every nerve in my body. Now I was numb with loss.

But it reminded me of a birthday gift I once gave her—a book with a cavity in the middle where I'd hidden her real present. She wasn't much of a reader, and when she first unwrapped it, I could tell she was masking her disappointment, a skill she'd mastered ages ago, when she mostly got her sister's hand-me-downs as presents. But when she riffled through the pages and a charm bracelet slithered from the secret compartment, she squealed in delight.

A faint click.

A slamming door.

But I had to finish my search. I had to *know*.

I scanned her shelves for the book—*Pride and Prejudice* by Jane Austen—and found it right in the middle of the row of classics her parents had foisted on her. Sliding it out felt like a dream in slow motion, where I could barely move my legs as some creature chased me.

Footsteps on the stairs, growing louder by the second.

I panicked, and the fake tome fell to the floor. Something rattled inside. She'd hidden something in the secret compartment. But it might be nothing of substance—more jewelry, maybe, since the box on the dresser was overflowing. Still, fear rooted me to the spot, and I couldn't move, couldn't think, couldn't stand to occupy this space, and yet here I was, immobile as the door flew open.

It wasn't Connor.

It was Emilia. Her red hair fell in loose, shiny waves around her shoulders, her angled cheeks flushed from rushing upstairs. She bounded to the bed without casting her bright brown eyes my way and plucked a sweatshirt from the foot of it.

"Where'd you go?" Connor's voice called from downstairs.

"Sorry, just grabbing a sweater—" But then her gaze slid toward me in front of the bookshelf.

Toward my feet.

To the fake book that had tumbled open, facedown.

All the blood seemed to drain from her face, and the sweater slinked from her grip. "What the hell?" she muttered, stooping to pick up the book. As she did, an unmistakable orange prescription bottle rolled out onto the hardwood.

I was close enough to read the label before she picked up the bottle. *Fentanyl.* The drug that showed up on my toxicology report. My cause of death.

So it *was* Emilia.

As she felt around behind her to shut her bedroom door, her eyes settled on the mirror over her dresser. She gasped, nearly dropping the book, then snapped her head to face me. A mix of fear and frustration twisted her features.

She'd spotted me.

She'd once said of her dead sister, "I see her every time I look in the mirror. That spoiled brat is totally haunting me now." I never imagined she meant it literally. I'd assumed she meant she could see the similarities in their features, and was fraught with anguish and anger over losing her the way she did. The way I *thought* she did.

Drugs. A suicide note. A *fake* suicide note?

Had Emilia killed Hannah, too?

Emilia always hated to see her dreams come true for someone else. I'd almost taken the boy she loved. And she knew. She *knew*.

I remembered that clattering sound down the hall as Connor and I argued, when he said he couldn't pretend to want to kiss her anymore.

I remembered her handing me that red Solo cup at the party, that tangy sweet mix of pineapple and rum and God knew what else—well, now I knew what else.

I remembered the room going hazy, the buzzing in my ears growing louder, my eyelids growing heavy, and then nothing. Nothing.

I remembered how she'd stared straight ahead at the funeral, her face dry under her umbrella as Connor stood across from her over my grave, staring down at my coffin as it jostled into the ground, the weight of the world pressing on his shoulders as the earth buried me.

"Emilia?" Connor called again, his voice muffled through the door. I'd brought my backpack to the party, my laptop still inside. Emilia knew the password. She'd typed up that fake suicide note.

But if Connor thought I'd died by suicide over a broken heart, he'd blame himself forever. The shame, the guilt . . . it'd torture him. And I couldn't let my parents think I did this, either. My poor parents, who blamed themselves for not spotting the signs. I needed them to know none of this was their fault. They needed to know the truth.

So did Emilia's parents. They should know what their daughter was capable of . . . and what their other daughter wasn't. Maybe then Hannah would find peace, too.

"Just a minute," Emilia shouted back, her voice unsteady. I half expected her to stuff the bottle back in the book's hidden compartment, but as Connor's footsteps pounded the stairs, Emilia surged past me—*through* me—to her en suite bathroom, where she dumped the pills into the toilet.

And there was nothing I could do about it. I'd barely been able to move the book enough for it to fall to the floor. It wasn't like I could pick up a phone and call the police. "How could you do this?" I asked.

But Emilia ignored me, if she could hear me at all.

It reminded me of that time after homecoming freshman year, after that guy from her drama club only danced with me once, then got busted hooking up with some sophomore in an empty classroom. "I thought you said he had this huge crush on me," I'd said, but Emilia only replied, "Ugh, what a jerk, I'm so sorry," ignoring my accusation. At the time, I thought she'd been mortified to disappoint me. But he never liked me at all. She'd convinced him to ask me out like she'd convinced me to agree, all to make Connor think I was interested in someone else.

How else had she manipulated me over the years?

She rushed from the bathroom, eyes ping-ponging around the room as she searched for another place to hide the bottle.

A knock at the door.

"You okay?" said Connor.

In a sheer panic, she threw it in the trash bin next to her desk, then grabbed the sweater and pulled it over her head, darting another glance at the mirror. "Come in, sorry, I was changing real quick."

The door creaked open. Connor barely shuffled in before Emilia folded herself into his arms, resting her head on his shoulder.

"She did it, Connor," I said. "She killed me. She must've found out about us." But it was like the words evaporated as soon as they hit the air, just like in class. Just like in Connor's bedroom. I knew then, too, that I couldn't reach him. No matter how softly I whispered or how loudly I screamed, it didn't matter—he could never hear my voice. *I couldn't even hear it.*

"You're shaking," Connor told Emilia, his brow furrowed.

Was she really? Had it killed her to kill me like it destroyed me to betray her, or was she trembling for fear of my presence, for fear of almost getting caught? "I just . . ." Emilia hesitated, but her eyes glinted with a hint of a smirk. "I still can't believe she's gone."

Connor's eyes fluttered shut, like he couldn't bear the thought of me being gone for good.

"Everyone's always leaving me," she went on. "First Hannah, now Jess."

Bullshit, bullshit, bullshit.

She was only pretending to be crushed. That was probably why she stayed home from school the last two days, too.

I had done a terrible thing. But I didn't deserve *this*. I never wanted to hurt her. I'd wanted to fix this . . . to fix us. But I never had a chance to own up to it. Never had a chance to make things right.

And now it would be the last mistake I'd ever make.

Anger ripped through me. I tried to channel that fury, tried swiping things off Emilia's desk behind Connor, tried yanking open the desk drawers, anything to get his attention. But even after all those years of dancing, of learning to sync my limbs in perfect harmony with music, now I couldn't control anything at all. Maybe toppling the fake book had sapped any strength I'd had to break through to their plane of existence.

Emilia pulled back to look at Connor's face, her eyes glistening with crocodile tears. "Promise me you'll never leave me like that."

His eyebrows shot up. "I'd never—"

"*Promise* me."

But before he could so much as whisper a promise, her lips were on his.

No. I never spoke up for myself, letting her steamroll me for years, ignorant of how low she'd stooped to get whatever she wanted.

She'd taken everything from me. From her sister. I couldn't let her take everything from Connor, too. I loved him too much to let him live with the pain of thinking my death was his fault. And God knew who'd be next—I couldn't risk letting her ever tear him from this world, too. That love steeled my resolve, and with all the focus and strength I could muster, I lashed out and knocked over the trash bin.

They both gasped.

The orange bottle rolled out, empty, coming to a stop at Connor's sneaker. He frowned down at the letters faceup, bold and glaring. And nothing was louder than the lack of rattling pills inside, nothing clearer than Emilia's embittered expression.

They told him more than I'd ever have to.

About the Authors

Julian Winters is the author of the IBPA Benjamin Franklin Gold Award–winning *Running with Lions*, the Junior Library Guild Selections *How to Be Remy Cameron* and *The Summer of Everything*, and the multi-star-reviewed *Right Where I Left You*. A self-proclaimed comic book geek, Julian currently lives outside of Atlanta. He can usually be found swooning over rom-coms or watching the only two sports he can follow—volleyball and soccer.

Monica Gomez-Hira is the daughter of Colombian immigrants, the wife of an Indian immigrant, the mother of a half-Latina/half-Indian daughter, and the quintessential Jersey girl who loves her salsa as much as her Springsteen. Her first novel, *Once Upon a Quinceañera*, was a Junior Library Guild Gold Standard Selection. Since getting her BA in English at Wellesley College, Monica has spent most of her professional life surrounded by books and the people who love them. She began her career working for literary agencies, moved to publicity and editorial at Simon & Schuster and Random House, and most recently was a children's lead bookseller at Barnes & Noble. She lives with her family in Minneapolis, Minnesota.

Nina Moreno was born and raised in Miami until a hurricane sent her family toward the pines of Georgia, where she picked up an accent. She's a proud University of Florida Gator who once had her dream job of shelving books at the library. Inspired by the folklore and stories passed down to her from her Cuban and Colombian family, she now writes about Latinx teens and tweens chasing their dreams, falling in love, and navigating life in the hyphen. Her first novel, *Don't Date Rosa Santos*, was a Junior Library Guild Selection, Indie Next Pick for teen readers, and SIBA Okra Pick. The companion YA novel featuring the same beloved town of Port Coral, *Our Way Back to Always*, is out now with Little, Brown Books for Young Readers. Her middle-grade debut, *Join the Club, Maggie Diaz*, is available from Scholastic.

Tess Sharpe was born in a mountain cabin to a punk-rocker mother and grew up in rural California. She lives deep in the backwoods with a pack of dogs and a growing colony of formerly feral cats. She is an author and anthology editor, and has written several award-winning and critically acclaimed books for children, teens, and adults.

Anna Meriano is a writer, teacher, and former band nerd from Houston, Texas. She attended Rice University (where she always dressed for the party theme) and earned her MFA in creative writing from the New School in New York. She lives in Houston with her dog, Cisco, and her husband, Ariel. She is also the author of *This Is How We Fly*, and writes about magical pan dulce in the Love Sugar Magic series. You can visit Anna online at annameriano.com.

Shaun David Hutchinson is the author of numerous books for young adults, including *The Past and Other Things That Should Stay Buried*, *The Apocalypse of Elena Mendoza*, *At the Edge of the Universe*, and *We Are the Ants*. He also edited the anthologies *Violent Ends* and *Feral Youth* and wrote the memoir *Brave Face*, which chronicles his struggles with depression and coming out during his teenage years. He lives in Seattle, where he enjoys drinking coffee, yelling at the TV, and eating cake. Visit him at shaundavidhutchinson.com.

Keah Brown is a journalist, author, studying actress, and screenwriter. She is the creator of #DisabledAndCute. Her work has appeared in *Teen Vogue*, *Elle*, *Harper's Bazaar*, *Marie Claire UK*, and the *New York Times*, among other publications. She is currently cowriting a musical and jumping into the film and TV space. Her debut essay collection, *The Pretty One*, her debut picture book, *Sam's Super Seats*, and a YA novel, *The Secret Summer Promise*, are out now. Connect with her at keahbrown.com.

Yamile Saied Méndez is the author of many books for young readers and adults, including *Furia*, a Reese's YA Book Club selection and the 2021 inaugural Pura Belpré Young Adult Gold Medalist. Her books have received many accolades, such as the Junior Library Guild Gold Standard, Whitney Award, Cybils Award, and Américas Award, among others. She was born and raised in Rosario, Argentina, but has lived most of her life in a lovely valley surrounded by mountains in Utah. An inaugural Walter Dean Myers Grant recipient, she's also a graduate of Voices of Our Nations (VONA) and the Vermont College of Fine Arts MFA in Writing for Children and Young Adults program. Connect with her at yamilesmendez.com.

Laura Silverman is the author of *Girl Out of Water*, *You Asked for Perfect*, *Recommended for You*, and *Those Summer Nights*. She is also the editor of and contributor to *It's a Whole Spiel*, *Up All Night*, and *Game On*. *Girl Out of Water* was a Junior Library Guild selection, and *You Asked for Perfect* was named to best teen fiction lists by YALSA, the Chicago Public Library, and the Georgia Center for the Book. Laura has also been a freelance editor for several years and currently lives in Brooklyn, New York. You can contact Laura through her website, laurasilvermanwrites.com.

Joy McCullough's debut young adult novel, *Blood Water Paint*, won the Washington State and Pacific Northwest book awards, as well as honors such as the National Book Award longlist, finalist for the ALA Morris Award, a *Publishers Weekly* Flying Start, and four starred reviews. She has since written picture books and middle-grade and young adult novels that have been Junior Library Guild Selections, Indie Next Selections, finalists for the Washington State Book Award, and a *New York Times* best seller. You can find her online at joymccullough.com.

Amanda Joy is the author of the River of Royal Blood duology. She has received starred reviews from *School Library Journal*, *Kirkus Reviews*, and *Booklist*. Her debut, *A River of Royal Blood*, was a Junior Library Guild Selection, and *A Queen of Gilded Horns* was named to a best teen fiction list by *Kirkus Reviews*. Her work has also appeared in the anthologies *Up All Night* and *Game On*. Amanda earned her MFA in writing for children from the New School. She currently writes and teaches in Chicago, with her dog, Luna.

Adi Alsaid was born and raised in Mexico City and is the author of several young adult novels including *Let's Get Lost*; *We Didn't Ask for This*; *Before Takeoff*, an Amazon Editor's Pick; and *North of Happy*, a Kirkus Best Book nominee. He currently lives in Chicago with his wife, son, and two cats, where he occasionally spills hot sauce on things (and cats).

Kika Hatzopoulou is the author of *Threads That Bind*, a Junior Library Guild Selection released in summer 2023 by Razorbill. She holds an MFA in writing for children from the New School and works in foreign publishing. She currently splits her time between London and her native Greece, where she enjoys urban quests and gastronomical adventures while narrating entire book and movie plots with her partner. You can find her on Twitter, Instagram, and TikTok @kikahatzopoulou and on her website, kikahatzopoulou.com.

Loan Le is the author of *A Phở Love Story*, a YA rom-com that earned praise from NPR, POPSUGAR, Bustle, *Bon Appetit*, *USA Today*, and BuzzFeed. *Solving for the Unknown*, her next YA contemporary novel and a companion to *A Phở Love Story*, is slated for Spring 2024. She lives in Manhattan and is a senior editor at Simon and Schuster. Visit her website at writerloanle.com and find her on Twitter @loanloan and Instagram @loanloanle.

Rachel Lynn Solomon is the *New York Times* best-selling author of *The Ex Talk*, *Today Tonight Tomorrow*, and other romantic comedies for teens and adults. Originally from Seattle, she's currently navigating expat life in Amsterdam, where she can be found exploring the city, collecting stationery, and working up the courage to knit her first sweater. Connect with her on Instagram @rlynn_solomon or online at rachelsolomonbooks.com.

Diana Urban is an internationally published author of dark, twisty thrillers, including *All Your Twisted Secrets* (HarperTeen), *These Deadly Games* (Wednesday Books), and *Lying in the Deep* (Razorbill). When she's not torturing fictional characters, she freelances in video game narrative writing. She lives with her husband and cat in Boston and enjoys reading, playing video games, fawning over cute animals, and looking at the beach from a safe distance. Visit her online at dianaurban.com, on Twitter or Instagram @dianaurban, or on TikTok @dianaurban_author.

Acknowledgments

Mom and Dad, I love you and am so grateful to have you both in my life.

Contributors, thank you for all of your brilliance. This anthology contains humor, depth, warmth, and so much more. I'm truly honored to have worked with all of you. Thank you for your time and your words.

My friends and family, we've shared countless first and last memories together. Thank you for being in my life. Thank you to Papa Bobby, Bubbie, Kayla Burson, Kiki Chatzopoulou, Katie King, Alex Kuntz, Elise LaPlante, Katherine Menezes, Anna Meriano, Lauren Sandler Rose, Melissa Sandler, Amanda Saulsberry, Lauren Vassallo, and Kayla Whaley.

Jim McCarthy, thank you for being an exceptional agent and partner in this business. Anu Ohioma, thank you for your insights, creativity, and passion. Rudi de Wet, thank you for this stunning cover art. Mary Claire Cruz, thank you for the wonderful cover design. And thank you to everyone on the Penguin Workshop team who had a hand in bringing this anthology to life. I appreciate you all so much.

Readers, teachers, librarians, and booksellers, thank you for everything you do to share stories. Your passion and drive impact countless lives for the better.

Thank you all,

Laura Silverman